CONFESSIONS
OF SUMMER

Books By
PHILLIP LOPATE

Confessions of Summer (Fiction)
Being with Children (Non-Fiction)
Journal of a Living Experiment (Non-Fiction)
The Eyes Don't Always Want to Stay Open (Poetry)
The Daily Round (Poetry)

CONFESSIONS
OF SUMMER

———————⊰◦⊱———————

A Novel By Phillip Lopate

DOUBLEDAY & COMPANY, INC.   GARDEN CITY, NEW YORK   1979

ISBN: 0-385-12619-0
Library of Congress Catalog Card Number 78–19715
Copyright © 1979 by Phillip Lopate
All Rights Reserved
Printed in the United States of America
First Edition

To Peter Minichiello and Diane Kaye Stevenson
for their loving support on this book.

PART ONE

Gamine

I

It was a period of my life I am not particularly proud of. It happened before the era of accomplishment. I had not yet become the hero of my life, nor was I even its villain. I was twenty-six, a graduate of a prestige college, believing that I was meant to lead and not take orders—a belief which in no way was shared by those who employed me. Powerlessness gave life a peculiarly iodized taste, like mercurochrome: it seemed to me that before I could enjoy to the full a sunset, a love affair, drunken nights, the so-called pleasures of youth, I would have to get this taste of powerlessness out of my mouth.

I remember it was the first of July when I returned to New York, to the city where I had grown up, after two years of trying to leave it.

I remember it being July, because it was a time when everyone with any sense was leaving. The air was close and listless and white. A hot wind blew into my mouth. Sweat-soaked travelers waiting by the taxi stand at the airline terminal gulped for oxygen.

I relaxed in the backseat of the cab, with my bags beside me. I had adjusted already. One look at the gunmetal bridges and the warehouses and factories brought me back; I knew I was returning to myself. It was a landscape as convincing and stoically familiar as sadness itself. Who would choose, consciously, to live outside his arena of known sadness? Running away from New York had been a blunder, I thought now, a relapse into the *pursuit of happiness*. That American mistake.

Yet, even as I was evolving this program of resignation, I still had an instant of wishing we could avoid the West Side gutters (especially coming as I did from Santa Cruz, where it had been so clean), and told the driver to take the road through Central Park. The cabbie misunderstood, and headed uptown along Broadway, past Verdi Square with its winos and overdosed transvestites in tank-tops leaning over cars. The gasoline smell and the garish residence hotel marquees and fast-food chicken signs sizzled and fried together in the early evening. Zabar's delicatessen with its large bread loaves and dangling salamis caught my eye, and staring through Zabar's window, the little hatted man with the dog and heavy Sunday *Times*. Nothing had changed. Eternal City, battered but faithful to its codes.

The cab pulled up in front of Charlie Kroegel's large West End Avenue apartment house.

As I finished paying, the elderly cabdriver began to grumble that my tip was not big enough. I told him it was 15 per cent.

"I could have charged you for the bags," he said.

"Go on, charge me," I replied. And the next moment, before he could respond, I was already out of the car into the lobby, thinking with a laugh that he deserved it, he should have taken the park route.

Charlie Kroegel threw his arms around me at the door. His wife Edie offer her cheek to be kissed, and warned me not to sit on the couch with my dark jacket because it would get all full of cat hairs.

Charlie looked shockingly older, with his premature bald spot and potbelly. I saw Bruno and Michael and Lee and Ted O'Neill standing vaguely up. Bruno gave me a Russian bear hug and a kiss. That's right: Bruno thought American men should kiss, like the Europeans. Michael, on the other hand, put out his fingers gravely, as much to keep me from embracing him as to welcome me. He was a small man, with small guitarist's hands, and great reserve. He disliked being ruffled affectionately by larger men. It was all coming back to me, how I always had the urge to slap Michael on the back or mess his hair. It was a wonder we ever became friends, since I am six feet two and awfully proud of the fact.

It had been Charlie's idea to have over a few of my friends for an impromptu welcome-home party. We had gone to Columbia together, and been part of the literary circle. Stars of the college poetry magazine, we had been accustomed to thinking of ourselves as the future Kafkas, Shelleys, Edmund Wilsons and Fitzgeralds, and what a shock it was when our fame evaporated on receiving cap and gown! From being at the top, we had sunk to the bottom, faded like laundry marks, which explains why, in addition to friendship, we clung to each other. Within this tiny émigré world, I was looked up to. They still made much of a chapbook of poems published when I was nineteen, and of some little stupid articles and reviews. The only way I'd found to tell them that their opinion of me was exaggerated (and potentially as dangerous to me as contempt) was to run away to California, where I had no trouble indulging my appetite for anonymity and failure. Once back, however, I was afraid of letting myself be seduced into playing the part of the much-traveled, successful man of letters.

The Kroegels had a gloomy faculty apartment sagging with books which they were able to get because he was an instructor at Columbia, and the university owned the building.

Charlie offered me a bloody mary. He seemed positively lit up with cheerful hospitality.

"You look different," Charlie said.

They all studied me carefully.

"It's probably that my hair is short. I'm no longer a hippie."

"Maybe . . . Your glasses are different."

"I've had them for five years."

"It's his mustache," declared Edie.

"No. You look thinner. You've lost some weight," Charlie observed with concern.

I smiled at this, knowing that I had been the same one hundred seventy ever since high school, and it was only in the imaginatively piercing scrutinies of friends that I ever gained or took off pounds.

"He looks mature, that's all. He's a man of the world now," Bruno said smoothly. I thanked him for coming to my aid.

"How was your flight?" Charlie asked. "Tell us about it!"

"It was uneventful. I wish I could think of something racy to tell."

"No stewardess action, eh?"

"Come on, Charles," Edie groaned.

"I'm just asking. What did you fly, Pan Am?"

"TWA."

Charlie nodded several times, as if this were significant information. "TWA is supposed to be among the best."

"They've got to serve better food than American—that's the bottom as far as I'm concerned," exclaimed Edie, who could get quite worked up over bad culinary experiences.

I didn't feel like having a discussion about airline food. "This was a jumbo jet. Gigantic rows, packed. The one funny moment was when they handed out napkins soaked in alcohol to refresh your face—you know, the kind they give out in Japanese restaurants? I looked around, up and down the aisles, and all at the same moment, the passengers were mopping their brows with these towels. It was like a political demonstration, with hundreds of people waving little white flags."

I had everyone's attention. I wanted the description to go on and on but there was nothing more to tell.

"What happened to the washcloths?" asked Charlie.

"Most people left them on their trays, to be picked up when the stewardess came by. I kept smelling mine. A few people blew their noses into them! I saw someone, the woman next to me, with her washcloth in her fist. She had obviously forgotten about it, and was holding it up against her blouse, like a flower, like a corsage someone had given her at a dance."

Bruno grinned at my description: he always liked it when I got carried away with the whimsical. I felt a pressure to be entertaining, not so much because they expected it of me, as because I did. It was crazy to be around all these people after the flight. My ears were clogged and my body jet-lagged.

The doorbell rang. Several people whom I didn't even know came in, upstairs neighbors of Charlie's he thought I might like to meet. Charlie and Edith were pillars of their building, and seemed to collect mousy neighbors. I didn't know what to make of these nice, bland, friendly strangers. I excused myself, to telephone Jack Bogardes. *He* was the one I wanted to see.

I was so pleased when Jack picked up the phone; I had expected him to be out of town, like everyone else who had the means.

Hello, he said in that formal, tired, morose telephone voice of his, almost like someone else's answering service. Then he heard my voice. "Eric! Where are you calling from?"—New York, I told him. I was back for good.—"Eric, let me pick it up in the other room. Hold on, okay?" He got very excited, like a little boy hearing from his father.

We talked for five giddy minutes; the sounds from the party forced me to cover my ear.

"Why don't you come over here," I said impatiently, "instead of spilling everything over the phone."

"You sure its all right for me to drop by?"

"I just invited you, didn't I?"

"Well, I don't know when I can get away . . ." he said with a darkness in his voice, which I was quick to pick up.

"What's the matter?"

"No, I just don't know whether I'll be able to break away politely. My mother has some people over and it's this—" he lowered to a whisper—"dumb dinner party, one guest is unbelievably racist. I'd better get out of here, I've already opened my mouth more than I should have."

"So come on over. Kroegel tried to reach you before to invite you—"

"He lives somewhere uptown—I mean, it's the other end of town, isn't it?"

"The other side of town," I said sardonically.

"Okay, okay." He was quick to pick up my innuendoes, this one being a dig at Jack's Park Avenue address. "I just meant it would take me longer because that's two buses."

"What's that?" I heard some shouting in back.

"I'm getting off in a minute! Will you stop it?" he yelled at someone else. "—My mother. She thinks I'm twelve years old. Eric, this isn't a good time to talk. I'm really sorry to expose you to her rudeness. And I apologize for sounding so scattered."

"Don't apologize. Maybe we should make it another night."

"Listen, is it all right if I bring someone else? It's Marie Curtin and she'd like to meet you," he said.

"Of course. I'd love to meet your new girl friend."

"Only I don't know. She's in pain because she's had a tooth extracted, she might not be able to make it," he hedged immediately. "I might have to drop her off at her house first. Will that be all right? It might delay me another forty-five minutes."

I laughed. "Of course it's all right."

"But will you still be up? After that long plane ride . . ."

"I'll be up for a while, don't worry. Get here whenever you can. I'll even pay your cab fare."

"Don't be silly. I figured because of your flight you'd be tired —I just didn't want to hang you up by getting there late. I shouldn't be using horrible expressions like 'hang you up.' I know how you hate that sloppy California slang."

"You're not 'hanging me up.' Why are you so nervous?"

"No, I was just thinking you won't want to talk to me: I'm not so bright any more. I didn't want to disappoint you."

"Don't worry about it!" I snorted. "You're getting pathologically unable to promise anything you might not be able to deliver."

"Don't start on me, Eric," he rejoined. "I've been in a depressed mood lately and I've got bronchitis."

"Sorry. I didn't mean that as picking on you, I was just, I don't know, being psychologically glib."

"Okay, well I thought you were. For*get* it. I'm very jumpy lately. I wanted to warn you, I'll probably misinterpret half of what you say. I've been reading Karen Horney, *The Neurotic Personality of Our Time,* and it's affecting me. You know the book, don't you? It's pretty perceptive. Actually it's probably simpleminded stuff and nothing you don't know already, but her analysis seems on-target to me! It's the first time I've heard it. Anyway, I'll see you in an hour-and-a-half to two hours. Glad you're back, Eric. I mean it."

"I know. Just hearing your voice," I said, "makes me accept being back."

I put down the receiver, shaking my head and smiling at our defensive misunderstandings, but also enjoying the harmlessness of them, and how rapidly we were able to bounce back to affection. It was funny, and typical, in a way, that he should think I had read a book I'd never even heard of, and that I was already superior to it. I made mental note to read some Karen Horney.

Jack and I had been friends for almost ten years now; but since graduation, one of us was always in Europe, or California, while the other was based in New York, so that we saw each other at most three weeks out of the year. These visits, which usually coincided with the holidays, were compressed, romantic times for me. We would walk all over the city and talk all night—one Christmas Eve, I remember, we stopped to lean on a car outside his apartment house, not wanting to separate just yet, and discussed love and feelings for an hour while the snowflakes fell on us. Jack was the only friend I could say anything to, and always count on an intelligent, sympathetic, truthful response. It was something in our voices: a tuning, like viola and violin.

It took less than forty-five minutes for Jack to arrive; and nevertheless he apologized, saying that they'd had to wait for an uptown bus. . . . It was glorious to see him. He smelled of light summer rain, briar, a million cigarettes. Neat and rumpled at the same time, with his hair all askew, he stood in the doorway, smiling bashfully, looking down, then suddenly up at me.

"Long time," he said, putting his arm around me. "Too long. Good to see you, Eric. This is Miss Marie Curtin—Marie, Eric Eisner." Jack hopped out of our way like a rabbit and passed into the main room.

Jack's girl had an astonished smile on, as if to say, Did you catch the way he left me standing here like a fool? *Your* friend!

Edie came out of the kitchen with an apron in her hands, and I quickly introduced the two: "Edith, this is Marie—what was your last name again?"

"Curtin. Last names don't matter."

Edie took her around. I went over to Jack. There was something in my manner of approaching him which singled him out as the chosen one, the *best friend*. I don't know if I consciously intended to give the others pain by it, or even if they felt any. The ludicrous part was that I found myself promoting Jack at the same time as he made it clear in his insistently chameleonlike way that he wanted nothing more than to disappear into a corner and become one among many, someone to swell the crowd. I caught a glance of Jack's girl, Marie, smiling at this, half-winking at me: she seemed to share the comedy of our friend's nervous, compulsive modesty.

I kept stealing looks at her, to see if I thought she was good enough for Jack. First impressions are fascinating, but only if you know the prejudices of the viewer. I tend to be afraid of very pretty women, and yet to be well defended against less striking ones by an overdemanding standard of physical beauty and an eye for flaws. Marie was pretty enough to attract attention, but not in an immediately threatening way. She looked about twenty, twenty-one, with something of the tomboy or teen-ager clinging to her still. Gamine is I think the word. She had a waif's large brown eyes, exquisite cheekbones with a touch of coral makeup which gave her a virginal blush, a merry red mouth that seemed to contradict that impression, with a bottom lip that plumped a little forward. There was a freshness she brought in the door with her, like a tulip opening up. Yet alongside that sparkling quality was an unsureness. She sat in a sling-back chair, which swallowed her up, except for her slender, articulate legs, the largest part of her, dangling over the sides.

Her backless evening dress was of a dark blue clingy elegance, with thin shoulder straps which left her arms and neck bare: an outfit so chic, in fact, that it may have scared off this crew of educated paupers—Michael proctoring undergraduate exams, Ted fixing air conditioners—because when she looked around the room at strangers with a hopeful smile that said she would be happy to talk to any of them, no one took her up on it; and she gave a little shrug, sighing, as if she knew what that was about, receded patiently into herself, calling on inner resources to entertain her.

I was touched by that sigh. I looked over to Jack to get him to rescue her, but he had a habit when he brought a woman to a social gathering of releasing her as soon as he got in the door. He was already deep in conversation with Charlie Kroegel, "interviewing" Charlie about his thesis and listening with flattering seriousness, as if that other man were the sage of the hour, the next Buckminster Fuller. Jack probably thought it was his duty to make fifteen minutes' worth of conversation with the host.

So Jack was trapped in dialogue with Charlie, and Bruno was trying to open Michael's reserve a crack, the neighbors were about to leave, Ted was drinking with concentration, and I, the welcome-home kid, the alleged center, suddenly found myself outside every group. I contemplated joining Charlie and that learned conversation, and even took a step in their direction, but then I felt pulled to Marie, sitting alone, with an empty chair beside her. I went over towards her, checking first with Jack to see if it was all right; and he nodded, but whether to my silent question or to Charlie's point I never found out.

"Hi. Mind if I sit here?" I said.

"HIE!" She said it with the most rapturous, buoyant surprise I had ever heard given to that mundane word. She was ready to play: not a trace of the sadness of a moment ago.

"Jack's talked a lot about you," I began.

"Nothing compared to you. He's told me all about his friend Eric so often, and it's always those three words, My-friend-Eric, never just Eric, plain old Eric," she laughed.

"Well, we've been friends for so long."

"You're very special to him. You probably know that. What are you doing with yourself?" she asked.

"I just got here. I'm looking for a job and an apartment. Starting from scratch again. Know of any leads?"

"No. But I'm sure you won't have any trouble finding either."
She said it with such conviction that for a moment I believed her,
and considered both problems settled.

"And you?"

"Finishing up college and writing papers," she said apolo-
getically. Suddenly I remembered what Jack had written me about
her: in the midst of praising her loveliness and quick mind, he
wondered if she might be too young—part of that next generation
after ours, the Woodstock generation, which it seemed to him
had missed out on some of the old formal culture. "Ow!" she
cried. "Excuse me, I just had a tooth pulled out and my jaw is
throbbing. I must look gruesome."

"No, you certainly don't," I said honestly.

"Oh good. It feels like my cheek must be big as a house! It's
such an incredible experience to have your tooth pulled?" Marie
said. She looked at me wide-eyed like an eight-year-old girl who
has just gone to the dentist for the first time and is telling her
classmate. "And my dentist is very good: Dr. Danzig. He's my favorite specialist! But I was in such pain afterwards that my face
felt like it was lifting off the bones and flying!"

"Like that Redon painting, the face in the sky."

"Exactly. I couldn't believe the pain, but at the same time I
loved it. I'm always happy when I have something *really* wrong
with me physically."

"Why?"

She was disappointed; she had assumed I would understand.

I tried again: "Because then you've got confirmation, eh?"

"Sure. It's terrific knowing where you stand. Especially for
someone who's a hypochondriac. But I'm not—I take that back.
I'm not a hypochondriac." She looked at me so sincerely: I didn't
say she was.

To get out of it I brought up Proust. "It reminds me of the nar-
rator in *Remembrance of Things Past,*" I said self-consciously,
making my second cultural reference in a minute (was I testing
Jack's suspicion?), "who was so sure that everything wrong with

him was psychosomatic because of his asthma, that even when he had a *bona fide* fever he treated it as a self-indulgence."

"It's amazing you just said that. I've had a terrible case of asthma for years." Marie stared at me.

"Really?"

"Uh-huh,' she said breathlessly, and flopped her head forward like a rag doll. One wave of brown-red hair fell over her sparkling eyes.

"What's it like, having asthma?"

"Asthma's *too much!* You can't get the oxygen in and you don't even care and your heart stops and you think you're going to die and this goes on for hours."

I was disturbed. "That sounds frightening."

"It is, it's so frightening!"

"There's nothing they can do about it?"

"Oh I take very good medicine," she said. "Stops it right away."

I smiled, I don't know why—from relief, or from enjoyment at her up-and-down dramatic style. "So it's not so bad after all."

"It's bad, all right."

For some reason we both cracked up at this.

"It must be the laughing gas," Marie said playfully.

"Did your dentist use laughing gas?

"No." She stopped and thought. "But I knew you'd understand."

"Why are you sure I'll understand?" I asked, out of curiosity.

"One can tell," said Marie mysteriously.

"Sometimes one can be fooled that way. It looks as if someone understands, but he doesn't, it's just an air of empathy."

"I know that. But it's still worth taking the risk."

I was stopped by this.

"But it really is terrifying, you know," she insisted. "Have you ever seen anyone having an asthma attack?"

"No. I've seen people having epileptic attacks, though."

"That must be worse."

"Yes, but probably not as bad as leprosy," I added, and laughed in spite of myself, marveling at my own bad taste.

"Come on now," she chided me. Her eyes were pained at my lack of compassion.

"Did you hear the story about the leper who went to Miami?" Charlie Kroegel called over (I was surprised he had been listening in on us).

"Oy Gott." Michael rolled his eyes disapprovingly.

"No I never heard that one."

"Please, do we have to go through that again when we're having dessert?" Edie objected.

"All right I won't tell it," Charlie clammed up sulkily.

I felt sorry for him; after all, my leper remark had gotten him into this. "Did you hear the story about the leper who was drinking coffee?" I called to him, simply because I was drinking coffee: in fact I had no story, and would have to think fast.

"Another Eisnerian Saga, eh? Go ahead, tell us."

"I don't think the lady would like to hear it," I said.

"No, tell it, by all means," Marie said, fortified for anything now, however crude.

"I'll tell you in private," I stalled.

Then she said, decisively, "Terrific!"

She lit another cigarette. "Care for one?"

"No thanks, I don't smoke."

"Wise decision."

"Isn't it—uhm—bad for you to smoke if you're asthmatic?"

"Of course it is, silly," she said, laughing. We talked for a few minutes more, then I went over to Bruno and Michael. I feared she was getting a bad impression of me, and I didn't want to make it any worse.

I, on the other hand, came away admiring her. She no longer seemed so immature either: underneath the youthful effervescence —a charm bordering on feverishness—there was something principled and refined about her. It wasn't so much anything she said, as a gracefully sympathetic manner, which let people off the hook, even as her expression showed she understood what they were doing.

I saw Jack glancing briefly at his watch, and Marie nodding her head. What a good-looking couple they made! Marie was certainly attractive enough. And Jack had that face full of restless character and sensibility that somehow wears well in every situation. It didn't much matter if he was in fancy dress or a moth-eaten army coat, if he was feeling happy or sad, sick or well: it was an attractiveness that, in a sense, he could do nothing about. Tonight he looked almost like a war correspondent in his functional corduroy jacket with black elbow patches, ready to move out any second.

"How have you been? I didn't even get a chance to talk to you," I said.

"I know. It's pointless to try to have a real conversation at a party."

"So how have you been?"

"Not so bad. Not so good either. I've got a bronchial condition again." His fingers held a lit cigarette. That was another way he and Marie were well matched.

"That's too bad. You should take care of your health. How's your television job?"

"It's idiotic. Easy, but that's about it."

"What kind of assignments have you been getting?"

"I just finished writing a treatment on computer art. Moronic! I've got to go out to California now for a few weeks. To research the oil-spill scare."

"Since when did you become an expert on ecology?"

"I don't know beans about it. That's the way they work now—they want non-experts, generalists. They send out a poetic ignoramus like me to record his first impressions: 'On the rainbow-sleek Pacific the petroleum-choked pelicans are gasping, on the beaches of Babylon . . .'—you get the idea. I'm sure you could do it with your eyes closed."

I accepted the flattery provisionally. "But do you have to do a hack job?"

"That's all they want. It's bunk!" He wrinkled up his nose.

"So how soon do you leave?" I asked.

"Friday. It may be sooner, or not at all. They keep changing their minds."

"It's a shame you'll be going so soon. I wanted to spend more time with you."

"I know. But I'll be gone only for two weeks, and after that I'll be here permanently, more or less."

"Do you realize this will be the first time we're living in the same city since we graduated?"

"Is it? I guess you're right!"

"I'm looking forward to seeing you on a natural, day-to-day basis. We can have a real feast of seeing each other."

"That should be something. Maybe you'll grow tired of me."

"Maybe you'll grow tired of *me*."

"I think it will be the other way around," Jack said with moody conviction.

"Why assume it will ever happen? It's always been good to see you."

"It's great, Eric." We patted each other on the shoulders. Jack went over to collect Marie. He lifted her up out of the sling-back chair.

"Bye, Marie."

"Good-bye," she said. "Enjoyed talking to you."

As they were about to go, Jack added, wincing, "I'm really sorry about this trip taking me away. If I had known earlier that you were returning . . ." He stopped himself, realizing that this was not true, that there was nothing he could have done in either event.

"Forget it. We'll see each other one more time before you go."

II

Jack and I met in our first year at college. Within a few months, we were walking each other from the classroom to the snack bar to the student lounge, talking about literature, personal philosophies and music and films. In those days everything made sense to me. Nietzsche, Coltrane, Dostoyevsky and Godard were all part of a grand synthesis I was forging in my mind, and which I gave up as nonsense several years later, realizing that I had mistaken the arbitrary growth of my personal taste for a consistent world-view. Nevertheless, for a long time I tried to make everything connect. I actually believed that my tastes constituted a defendable system which, once traced to the common root, would function for everyone, like atomic theory. The teachers kept throwing longer reading lists at us, more and more culture, and the only way I could make any order of it was to wield my divining rod: Whitman was the real thing, Hemingway was not. Carl Dreyer yes, Ingmar Bergman, no. God alone remembers how I justified every contradictory affinity. All I know is that, in those days, taste was a very important matter for us: we would jeer at someone who made the "wrong" choice.

Jack was interested in all the same subjects I was, but ecumenically, without my need to reject half of everything. And Jack knew more. Ah, he was incredible in those days! Already as a freshman he knew more about twelve-tone rows and early Gnostic sects and Freudian theory and the *nouveau roman,* Arabic philosophy, and Icelandic sagas, Simone Weil's books, and the importance of Chomsky, Schwitters and Vico, than it seemed fair for anyone under twenty to know. I used to tell myself he was so far ahead because he had gone to a fancy private school. But then I met other graduates from the same private school and they were rather ill-informed. Jack alone had taken on himself, as if it were a normal burden, the responsibility to know all of world culture.

Jack Bogardes was, from the first day, it seemed, one of the stars of our class. There were the athletes; there was the smooth kid from Florida who was already plotting his gubernatorial strategy; and for the intellectuals, there was Jack Bogardes. His first book reviews for the campus newspaper had caused him immediately to be singled out by the upperclassmen literati and taken under their wing.

I remember so well my first introduction to him (unless I'm making this up, but I don't think I am): a compact nervous young man of medium height and thin, muscled physique, trying to joke around and be one of the boys, yet isolated by the others' respect. They were a bit cautious of his brain, like an endangered glass figurine about to burst.

He was wearing a sports jacket negligently in the cold while the rest of us were bundled in toggle coats and parkas; I remember his hacking cough and his blue packs of French cigarettes. His handsome long fingers, covered with yellow nicotine stains, and his chewed fingernails, made me thing of Albert Camus in the dustjacket photographs. Stared at wherever he went, because his eyes were so expressive and his bold-nosed profile so arresting, so (to use a word one hardly hears any more) *noble,* his talk so interesting, he tried to draw attention away from himself, towards the other person. His good manners and reluctance to dominate only made him more conspicuous. That was the final curiosity—his meekness. He was the most meek, diffident superior person I had ever come across.

Up until then, I had known only two kinds of people: those who tried unavailingly to convince the world they counted, and suffered from invisibility; and those who, managing to make people look at them, gloated and lorded it over everyone. Jack was neither. For the moment, I was an "invisible": no one paid attention to me in my freshman year. What a surprise then, when the first time we talked, Jack was receptive and even avid to listen to me. He actually excused himself for taking up my time. What a strange guy, I thought. Why should a thoroughbred like Jack Bogardes even care about my opinions? I don't want to seem falsely modest, I was intelligent and I knew it. But it was an intelligence with a vulgar edge: I used it as a stick to hit people with. I had managed to survive in the dogfight among the precocious poor, sponsored by a meritocracy that respected only test scores. Some of that fight was still steaming off me when I got to the university, secretly afraid of the gentility that might be expected of me. I was angry at being poor—at the upper classes for not being poor and for having social ease, manners, even advantages of vocabulary, a certain "linguistic capital," because their parents had been doctors and French professors and not factory workers like mine. At the same time, I was proud of having grown up in the slums. Of course the first good friend I made was a rich boy—Jack. In point of fact, Jack was not so rich: he and his mother were living on alimony checks, and their Park Avenue apartment was the last vestige of a plumper time. But his fancy address was all that I needed to fantasize him into the role I wanted him to play.

I remember the first time Jack took me home with him, I pretended we were in *The Prince and the Pauper*. Going up in the elevator: that elevator itself was a museum piece! It was my first ride ever in such an elegant lift, with mahogany paneling and full-length mirrors and a little bench like a throne, with a plush red cushion. I just loved sitting on that pillow while the lift rose slowly. The Irish doorman who was running it, an old guy with a face full of broken veins, cracked a joke and made me smile, though he seemed to have the opposite effect on Jack, whose spirits sank the closer he got to home.

Jack and his mother lived in one of those palatial, twilight apartments that have no smell at all and go on for room after carpeted room. It was the kind of household where you instinctively took off your shoes. My memories are all in stocking feet: the heavy Spanish tables with lace doilies, and deep walk-in closets with stacks of old phonograph records, and candy dishes and dozens of weak lamps, and high bookcases with almost nothing but hard-cover volumes, and orange paintings on the wall, and a Steinway piano.

After the first shock of luxury, it seemed to me an oddly impoverished environment, the decor all in that strange, mirthless style of a fancy hotel, impersonally well-to-do.

"What makes you think it's so great growing up on Park Avenue?" Jack said to me one time. "There's no place to play on the street, no kids outside, no feeling of community, nothing but doormen and big apartment houses. I don't know that I wouldn't prefer growing up the way you did, Eric."

"I think I'd still take the anomie of Park Avenue to the *esprit* of Bedford-Stuyvesant," I laughed, not letting him get off so easily on that one. Still, I had to admit that there was something to what he said.

There was no place to unwind. The only neutral, innocent places were Jack's room and the kitchen. I had the feeling that we were continually running from each of these oases to the other. Jack's bedroom was retrieved by student mess and a nice flat-top desk with a banker's green ink blotter, on top of which sat a massive ham radio. Jack used it to pick up classical music stations from Europe. We would close the door of his room and talk, one of us taking the chair, the other sitting on the bed. It didn't matter much what we were discussing, just so that we could get it going, finding agreement, disagreeing while trying to understand the other's point in terms of the peculiarities of his character. Was John Updike any good? What about Charlie Mingus, was he mainly a synthesizer or an innovative composer? Sometimes it switched to our family problems. We would talk until we were overheated; then we would sneak into the kitchen to help ourselves to a snack. If the Negro cleaning woman was home, she would bring us tea and sandwiches on a tray (all this was magical to me), but Jack did not like asking her. I thought it was because of his embarrassment and discomfit at being servanted, which in part it was. Later he told me another reason: the maid carried bits of information about him to his mother.

Even when we were alone in the apartment, I got the feeling that someone was spying on us, and would, like a ghost behind the designer wallpaper, reproach me for sitting on the wrong couch, or touching something I shouldn't. But, for all its formality, I loved being in that house.

When Jack's mother came home, merely hearing her key turn in the lock set Jack on edge. I was expecting Mrs. Bogardes to be a monster. Instead she was quite animated and warm, and as soon as we had been introduced, she invited me to dinner. She was in her late forties, and rather coquettish: the way she moved and made gestures, the fashionable suit she wore, the fast and slightly scatterbrained flitting from subject to subject reminded me of an afternoon television talk-show hostess. She asked me many questions, but didn't always wait for answers. Underneath her curiosity, I sensed her worrying if I would make a good friend for "Jacques" (how he winced at the name!).

Around the dinner table, conversation took wing. Mrs. Bogardes was the belle of the ball, and I was showing off for her. As the maid served us, I became so expansive that I told them about a scheme I had devised to cheat the university out of some fees. I was afraid I might get a look of disapproving scorn from Jack's mother; but instead, Mrs. Bogardes was all for it.

"Now you see that, Jackie? Why can't you come up with something clever like that and save your mother some money?"

"Oh, sure! Because it's crooked, Mother."

"Well you have to be crooked in this world," she said, with that combination of common sense advice and Billie Burke other-worldliness that made Jack and me exchange a private smile.

"Would you like me to go to jail when they found out I'd swindled the Bursar out of three hundred dollars?" Jack asked.

"Of course I wouldn't want you to go to jail," said his mother heatedly, warming to the subject. "Don't be silly, how can you even talk that way to your mother? Insinuating that I'd want you in jail!"

"All right, all right," he waved her on.

"I'm simply saying that you need to be clever. Resourceful. Not like your mother—don't be like me or you'll lose in the end. Besides, I don't think Eric's going to go to jail, do you?" she said, with a pampering smile in my direction, as if the very idea that anyone taking a second helping of creamed broccoli and pot roast at her table could ever land behind bars was unimaginable.

I accepted her protection. She and I hit it off famously. Jack pretended to be chagrined, though later on he said he had predicted it. We were two of a kind, he thought—enthusiasts.

Jack was in many respects a better thinker than I was, his intelligence more subtle. Yet he also had more doubts, which caused him from the first to defer to me. That is to say, he had knowledge, but on the conclusions to be drawn from this knowledge he usually allowed me to have the last word. I don't think I actually convinced him to change his mind about anything, but he never failed to admire openly in me something which he thought he lacked. He seemed to see me as a down-to-earth tough-minded sort who cut through the complexities tormenting him.

A typical example is the time we were sitting on the plaza of the Seagram Building during intersession and enjoying a few leisure hours, leaning our arms on the stone ledge, watching people go by, and talking, when Jack started asking me my feelings about the alienation of modern man from nature, the destruction of wilderness and dehumanized environment of big cities. I had a hard time understanding him. I was perfectly content with the city as it was. He realized he was not getting through to me, and so he cited images from Antonioni's films, which were then all the rage and which we both worshiped, I, however, thought the mirage-like purity of these images was proof that life in modern cities couldn't be all bad—or how else could you wrest beauty from it? Jack started from a new perspective, now referring to a tradition of environmental criticism, from Lewis Mumford to Paul Goodman on down, which I had simply not come across yet in my reading. The more he presented their views, the more confident I became in my position: I had the advantage in that I was working directly from experience (my love of my city), whereas he was trying to translate from someone else's texts, and highly abstract texts at that.

It was only when he spoke of his own loss of nature—and, *loss,* loss, loss, he kept using that word—that I understood he was referring to something personal to which I ought to pay attention. Jack described a summer cabin he had gone to as a little boy, when his parents were still together. The cabin had an open sun porch, with mosquito netting, where he knew the slow viscous sweetness of being, of growing up without noticing; a childhood smell was part of it or something or other which I took him at his word to have been really powerful, and—gone.

What I chiefly retain from that conversation is his introducing me to the idea of Loss as a great melodic theme in life: a musical refrain to which I have now become addicted, but which in college I had not yet any inkling of. Childhood had been a most humiliating time for me; I much preferred being an adult. But it was possible, I conceded, that *some*one could miss his childhood.

Later on, as I traveled, it became perfectly obvious to me that the wilderness was being ruined. What Jack had tried to tell me had become common knowledge. Whether it was a question of the erosion of the family structure, the significance of youth culture or anti-psychiatry, or women's liberation, he had simply gotten the news before me. Yet he never made me feel the lag as my ignorance—often he let me have the last, more traditionalist, word. It seemed he always had his finger on the pulse of the next global problem, but he distrusted his own anxious analyses enough to wish they could be overturned.

Jack practiced a funny method of dialogue with me I can only characterize as "Inverse-Socratic." He started with a fairly rational question, or concern, and provoked my innate contrariness to produce a counter-argument: but instead of correcting my error, he became fascinated with it, he made it legitimate. He would rephrase it fully and sometimes more than fully, so that what I had said was presented back to me in shined-up, respectable form. I don't think Jack was himself aware how much his creative listening had a role in transforming me. The more I looked at myself in the mirror of his responses, the more I regarded myself as a thinker. Since he expected me to have an answer for everything, I did! I manufactured myself on demand, as it were, to please him. And the pleasure in his eyes when I had pulled off a neat formulation! With Jack I loved to play the Big Bad Wolf to conventional morality. But there were times I said things that were perfectly ridiculous.

I remember once when I was arguing a little *too* vociferously for euthanasia. Our discussion had been prompted by the scandal of babies born with birth defects caused by the drug thalidomide. I was arguing the costliness to the state and the hardships of keeping such pitiful children alive. It was doubtful that my advocacy was purely humanitarian, however. Adolescents can be quite bloodthirsty; and at the time, it seemed important to keep alive at least the possibility of cruelty as a precondition for mental freedom.

Jack knew this, and was trying to lead me away by argument.

"Where would you draw the line?" he asked. "What if a child didn't have an earlobe?"

"No; only in cases where he'd have a horrible life, and he'd make his parents miserable, like a pinhead or a retarded cerebral palsy case."

"What if he had no penis?"

"I'd want him killed."

"What about the *castrati?*" Jack asked.

"I'm opposed to the *castrati.*"

"According to your view, you would be able to run into the street and kill 15,000 people right away."

"No, because they're not related to me. They're not my kids."

"But you're putting too much emphasis on the body," said Jack. "A Catholic mystic would tell you that the flesh isn't that important."

What did I care about Catholic mystics? As far as I was concerned, they were targets for euthanasia too. "It's obvious," I said instead, "that if a kid is badly deformed he'll live a horrible life and make his parents miserable."

"But some people who are completely healthy make their parents miserable, or are miserable themselves . . ." he said, with an undercurrent of referring to himself.

"But at least they're given better odds, and you don't know from the start that their chances are doomed."

"What if the kid is schizophrenic? Would you kill him?"

"No. I think you can do things with a person's mental problems, but you can't put a torso on a half-man or give a mongoloid idiot a brain."

"Would you want to kill the child yourself? You're just talking theoretically, but if it happened to *you*, Eric . . ."

"I'd want the legal option. I would want a law that said that, if the baby is badly deformed, you can look at it in the hospital and say, I don't want it. Get rid of it."

"What if the hospital says it won't, and tells you that you have to kill it yourself?"

"Then I'd walk out of the hospital and dump it in the incinerator."

"Please, I'm squeamish!"

"Well you asked me what I would do," I shrugged. Then we dropped the subject.

I kept going to Jack's house. Mrs. Bogardes was always happy to see me, as I was her. Their apartment was not so formidable any more: I regarded it more like my second home, the home I should have had. Even when they started quarreling with each other, I felt at home. And they certainly did argue. I never could tell how much of Jack's irritation around his mother was feigned, only a game they liked to play. Clearly she did pick on him at times, and show her petulance or jealousy when he went out on "too many dates." But it also seemed to me, as an outsider, that Jack would flare up at rather innocuous motherly statements. He was increasingly quick to feel her pressure on him. This pressure seemed to come not necessarily from anything she said or did, but from mere co-existence in the same apartment with him. Yet it was obvious Jack cared deeply for his mother. In fact, he was almost too receptive to her moods. When she started to feel sorry for herself, he would get nervous, and try to badger her out of a depression, and finally become despondent himself. He had no distance from his mother, except that which was won at consid-erable cost of temper. His yelling seemed a thrashing desperation to put more space between them. But as passionate displays often do, they had the opposite effect, of chaining them closer together.

Jack told me that his parents had divorced when he was eight. His father married a much younger, prettier woman shortly after-wards. Jack's mother naturally felt jilted and enraged. She refused to marry again and retreated to a narrower world, centering on her son, her music (she gave piano lessons) and her apartment. For a lively woman, Mrs. Bogardes was subject to frequent fits of melancholy. Jack had tried unavailingly, as a boy, to coax her out of them. As he grew into manhood he seemed to be struggling with the meaning of his tie to her; sometimes he would be upset about her future, he would brood about an argument they had had, and I would suggest that it was time he moved away from home. He answered that he couldn't yet. The strain on his face made me drop the matter.

Part of the problem was that the responsibility which he under-took towards his mother, and which would have been applauded in another age, had to be practiced by Jack almost covertly, because it subjected him to the psychologizing of his peers. We all spoke about his Oedipal Complex openly, as if it were a proven thing, alive in the room, like a big white dog; and Jack developed a de-fensive sense of humor with Kafkaesque overtones about his ina-bility to move out of his mother's house.

We graduated from college in 1964: Jack won all the fellow-ships, and went to a good graduate school, while I entered "the world of work." Somehow, Jack made me feel as though I had been the brave one by going into what is euphemistically called the real world, while he had been a coward in accepting scholarly advancement. In fact he simply had a much better mental temperament for academic life; it was another example of his turning his virtues into a source for apology.

I often wondered at the real reason for Jack's self-disparagement. He was a person with superior endowments of every sort—intelligence, good looks, social grace, tact, a high moral sense—and yet he lacked self-esteem. How he could dismiss the evidence of his worth so easily, and treat all his achievements as meaningless, was a trick of legerdemain I had trouble following.

I came to the conclusion that two factors in his family life—his early failure to hold his parents' marriage together (which he admitted had left him with guilt feelings), and his inability to make his mother content with her life—accounted for his sense of powerlessness, weariness and self-distrust. No doubt this is a gross simplification of much tangled history. But the point is not what the real reasons were, but that I was satisfied I knew them. The conviction that one can explain a friend's behavior is all that one needs, and the truth may have very little to do with this particular satisfaction.

In one area Jack was not lacking in confidence at all: with women. I never knew anyone who had better success snaring lovely women. Whenever I turned around he was dating someone who seemed to have stepped off a magazine cover. First they were the pick of the Eastern girls' colleges. Then, as he grew older, they were the beautiful graduate students everyone else wanted, the young intelligent models, the famous folk music queen, the fashion designer . . . every one of them with gorgeous figures, subtle faces, bewitching hair: unbelievable creatures! I used to ask him what his technique of seduction was. He said he didn't do anything; they made all the moves and he just went along. That sounded too good to be true, even for Jack. He may not have leaped on them—I can well imagine him being courtly and gentlemanly and holding back until they lost their cool and made the first move—but he did spend an awful lot of time around them. At first I had no idea how much time, because he hid that side of his life. But as I began to get a feel for his daily routines, I saw that he would spend hours with women, going from place to place with them on shopping errands, sympathizing with their panics of vanity and dress. He was a womanizer. Leaving aside the sexual chase, he preferred their company to men's, I think.

I could barely contain my envy at Jack's success. I thought at first it was a matter of luck: access to the right parties, the right circles, to which Jack had a foot in the door because of his social background. I kept asking him to tell me about parties. He never did. Perhaps he knew that I was oversimplifying; or perhaps he did not want me to see him operating in that milieu.

I often thought, if only he would throw me a few of his left-overs: he wouldn't mind—he'd never miss them. Whereas Jack, who was swimming in beauties, still seemed miserable, I would know how to be happy with one. I who was so frugal when it came to sexuality, who could live off a dime's worth of eros for a month—could warm myself on so little: a memory here, a kiss there—just give me *one* of those silky creatures. It seemed so unfair!

Envy is always ugly. But we lived with it, as friends do. Perhaps it was a fair trade: I was jealous of his magnetism with women, and his connections; he envied me a practical ability which enabled me to work hard, and believe in my work, whatever it happened to be at the moment. Jack was usually discontented with his professional labors. Still, it came as a surprise when, at twenty-four he threw over his academic post to become a free-lance journalist. He worked for news magazines and the TV networks, which valued his cultural contacts, and used him, I thought, as a kind of pilot fish to steer them toward the latest in intellectual fashions. The mass media are so hungry for daily copy that even the avant-garde gets covered as a beat. Some of what Jack wrote seemed to me not far above the level of fan magazines, not worthy of his intelligence—but then, who was I to judge another person's accommodations with power to make a living? He was still young, he had plenty of time to do original work and fulfill his earlier promise.

Meantime, as a journalist, his social access became wider than it had ever been. He was now at the exact center of things. If an important man came to town, it would only be a matter of time before I could hear Jack's report of meeting him at a reception, or interviewing him in his hotel room. I enjoyed these reports of the great and the inflated. It didn't surprise me at all that Jack should be accepted readily into these heights: after all, he had the alertness, the sensitivity. In our own world, he had always been something of a figure. And, now—how shall I put it? Jack had a *following*. He seemed to travel all the time, making his brief appearances rare and desirable. A week before he was to come into town, people would start talking about it, calling his mother for the dates, arranging parties, trading phone numbers to make it easier to track him down. Before he had even set foot in New York, his first few days would be completely booked-up.

I admit, I liked having a friend who was so popular. And it pleased me to think that I was closer to him than anyone except his family. However, it was getting harder even for *me* to make appointments with my best friend. On an ordinary night he might have several dates or semi-business engagements: a drink with Mr. X, a concert with Miss Y, a party he felt obliged to drop in on for a few moments because he didn't want to hurt the hostess' feelings. That was his *problem,* I told him; he didn't want to disappoint anyone. So we consulted our schedules. Jack was cast into the role of the adored one, fickle and torn, and I was—who? the man in the stuffy blue overcoat, trying not to lose patience. How quickly we fell into those parts! His popularity was a simple fact, a reality which I should have accepted long ago. Instead I wanted him to pay a price for it by making him act apologetic and feminized—a role, strangely, which he was quite willing to play.

As soon as I had become conscious of this pattern, I tried to go around it. But it took all my self-restraint to resist his own itch to make apologies. I finally understood the resentment and hostility underneath these meek forms. I could see now that his modesty was a choked-down grandiosity, and even his politeness was a form of declawed aggression. It amused me now to hear other friends of his get together and tell Jack Bogardes stories, about his quirky insistence on not putting people to any trouble, not wishing to impose, and so on—without their understanding what lay beneath it. Yes, it made him popular, this winning combination of being both highly gifted and self-effacing and complimentary to others. It allowed people who might otherwise have feared him to feel expansive around Jack, even fond of him in a patronizing way.

Sometimes it seemed I was the only one who could see through his humble tics. I felt more valuable to Jack as a friend. He came to equate me, though, with being tough on himself. Sometimes he would begin to flinch defensively before I had even said anything. Obviously the level of criticism he directed at himself was quite deep. I was merely poking around in a clumsy shallow way; but occasionally I would touch something, and then he got frightened for a few moments that I would reveal the whole sunken ship of catastrophe. Really, I had no idea what it was. He need not have worried so much; I probably never would have understood. His fears were so different from mine.

Jack talked a great deal about terror. He was becoming a sort of specialist on fright in the modern consciousness. Whether the subject was Isaac Babel or Gaudi's architecture, he always brought in a similar vocabulary having to do with "terror." He seemed to be on intimate, first-name terms with the emotion. I was never certain whether he meant 1) terror of the void, or 2) the bloody record of the twentieth century, or simply 3) this harsh business of living. I tried to get him to explain it to me. He spoke about panic in airplanes, beaches in Europe, crowded movie halls, the birthday parties of children and being alone before certain sublime works of art, like the Gothic cathedrals. Angels and terror: and he quoted that passage from Rilke's *Duino Elegies:*

> For beauty is nothing
> but the beginning of Terror we're still just able to bear,
> and why we adore it so is because it serenely
> disdains to destroy us. Every single angel brings terror.

The truth is, I could never feel the world as particularly terrifying. Sad, yes; funny, miserable, broken, degraded, poor; but not—this other thing. I suspected that I must not have a good imagination. If terror and beauty did go hand in hand so often in this world, then I, in refusing one, was suddenly worried about finding myself locked outside the gates of the other. They must be right, Rilke and Jack, I thought. The risk that beauty insists on our taking probably does bring us closer to terror, as it does to happiness. I was thinking at the moment not of Gothic cathedrals, but of the pretty women, those Blue Angels whom I wished would rip my heart out of my chest and dash it on the ground and trample on it while laughing saucily at me. For this was my happiest fantasy: to be caught in the destructive power of a love stronger than myself, and to throw my life away on a beautiful woman.

I was too prudent, that was my trouble. Or so I kept reproaching myself in those days. Yet prudence is a funny thing: you can't get rid of it so easily, you can't leave it on the bench like a newspaper.

III

In my first days back in New York, I found myself going through a resistance amounting to physical revulsion. Along Broadway, on the upper West Side, the summer wastebaskets were overflowing with crushed soda cans; torn garbage bags lay leaking with coffee grounds and flies. The sidewalk smelled like a rank cantaloupe. There were still the sights that I loved, the men unpacking meat trucks, or loading cartons along a ball-bearinged chute into the basement of a supermarket; I wanted to feel part of all this fecundity, and it was frustrating not to. I had forgotten how to stand the ugliness on its head, and convert the squalor into beauty.

To live in New York, you need to have that perceptual knack of being able to look at a cross section of intersecting streets and find, instead of blare and danger, an order, history and the solace of neighborhood. You might stare down at a pile of rubble and see it as art, or be surprised by an orange moon at the end of Houston Street, over an avenue of burned-out cars. The lover of cities can cut a swatch from the facades of movie marquees angling into hotel cornices and frame it into a Japanese print every time. An urban aesthetic relies on a taste for poignancy, and on the ironies of overlap, where extremes of elegance and dinginess exchange qualities, like costumes; but you have to be at the right vantage point. Maybe you have to have a job. If I had forgotten the trick of disappearing into the bosom of the people, it was probably because I was too close to "the people" at that moment, being unemployed and terrified of the drag down to poverty.

At night the pathetic efforts that people made to keep off the heat, draping their pale legs over fire escapes, sponging themselves on their stoops, the kids unleashing fire hydrant gushes under the singed disapproving eyes of neon signs, brought back the old childhood memory of a time when everything seemed hopeless. I remembered how poverty was like living at the bottom of a brown rusty metal barrel, with no way to climb out.

The Kroegels had gone to Martha's Vineyard for six weeks, leaving me to sublet their apartment. I locked myself in their dark living room over the Fourth of July and played Bessie Smith, Bill Evans, John Coltrane, Charlie Parker records, to find again the rhythm of New York. I wanted to recover the mood in which I used to go to St. Mark's Place when it was filled with jazz clubs: even then it was a seedy street, but with limousines and ladies in fox furs pulling up in front of the Jazz Gallery and the Five Spot; and up at the head of the block, past the Ukrainian baths, was Iggy's Pizzeria with corn on the cob and that sickeningly tempting melted butter smell. I would be there sometimes in the early morning, having just heard a final set by Coltrane or Ornette Coleman (whom everyone was talking about that year), and in the dark I would catch a few bars of something familiar from a tenement window: Billie Holiday maybe, herself dead, her old phonograph record still playing "I Must Have That Man." It was like a hand reaching right into my heart and squeezing. Massaging it: first the right ventricle, then the left, easing it open to receive the night's sadness. I stood listening. And then I realized that the music was that hot-buttered smell, and the concrete under my feet, the footsteps, and Astor Place, dirty like a human face: that they were all part of an underground code, and the key to it all was—jazz, which had been created solely to explain how the life of this city connected. At two in the morning, when everything seemed Negro, I thought I understood: it was that wry connivance with the environment (whatever environment had been dealt you), the realization of ache, and on top of everything, weariness, serenity, indifference. In her voice, I could hear the wobble between the top of the note and its infinite drop, between the hope and its refusal, like the distance between the rush and laying a heroin'd head on a pillow and closing her eyes halfway and say-ing, "What man must I have? I can't even remember what it was all about any more . . ."

Then I inched away from this world. I wanted to learn some-thing other than impaling my heart on the blues, which I knew already—suspected would always be there if I wanted to come back to it. I told myself I wasn't betraying my background, I was only trying to fight off the provincial smugness that could come from reveling in the artistry of urban despair. Years passed, I traveled around; now I was back, the pastorale of other, quieter landscapes had estranged me temporarily from my home town. I needed an insider's fix. So I listened to the music, without under-standing at first. My mind was racing too much. I had to go out-side and see what the night looked like.

Everything was silent. White fog blew in from the Hudson River. I passed a convent on West 113th Street, and three nuns in gray habits were emptying the garbage. I don't know why this struck me as funny. I went up to Broadway to buy the next morn-ing's newspaper. At the luncheonette counter, glad for the silent company of other nightbirds on revolving stools, I looked over the employment ads and the apartment ads until the agate type made my eyes smart. I ordered a chocolate milk and grilled American cheese sandwich. This child's meal had a soothing effect on me.

On Thursday, I spent the morning calling for jobs, to people who all seemed to be on vacation. In the afternoon I typed my résumé, and with a pounding headache stepped outside into the day. It was already almost five. I got sucked into a bookstore, read a few pages of ten different books, and started walking down-town with no destination in mind. Broadway looked beaten up. I tried to knit an urban romance out of it, couldn't.

What do you want? I asked myself sharply. To see Jack before he leaves, came the answer. Calling from a pay phone in the street, with the trucks rolling by, I reached his mother, who said I might try another number (obviously his girlfriend's, though Mrs. Bogardes would never say that).

Jack was there. "When are you leaving?" I asked.

"Tomorrow, unfortunately."

"That's too bad. I wanted to see you."

"We were just on our way out to eat. But why don't you come over," he offered.

"Okay. Wait for me, will you?"

It was within walking distance. I ran. Marie lived on a nice block in the West Eighties, in a floor-through brownstone flat right off Central Park. They were both so pleased to see me: I had the feeling they'd been lounging around all afternoon listening to records. Marie brought in cherry sodas. The Sunday *Times* lay on the coffee table, though it was already Thursday. A lazy life.

The big air-conditioned living room had cool parquet floors, high ceilings, potted trees by the window, a deep white circular rug and a fireplace which looked operative. New York wasn't such an oppressive place after all. My headache fled. I was in a good mood. Sometimes what you need is so minimal, I thought: a bit of the comfortable life.

Jack and I talked about people we knew, California versus New York, authors, this and that; the conversation meandered wherever it wanted to go. In the kitchen, Marie was singing to herself, a rock tune, I think, which she made sound like an old English folk song with her sweet, aimlessly lyrical voice that kept dropping away.

She looked different somehow. Maybe it was that her shoulder-length brown hair was in a pony tail. She also seemed taller in her own house. And more *zippy,* or jaunty, I guess is the word. She wore white sailor pants and a midnight blue top, and high-heeled sandals which made her totter forward like a colt trying its legs, but that was also appealing. I was glad that Jack had finally gotten such a nice bouncy vital girl friend, after all those self-contained model types.

She flopped down next to us, and looked with a radiant face from one to the other. "Am I interrupting something?"

"It's a beautiful place," I said.

"I've fixed it up!"

"Can I ask you something? What—what is the rent here?"

"It's four hundred fifty dollars."

"Oof." I rolled my eyes.

"I know it sounds like a lot, but I share it with a roommate. And it's worth it to my parents to pay two hundred twenty-five a month, which isn't that much in New York, for a place where they can feel I'm safe."

"Come off it, Eric, you've made dough in the last few years, that slum boy act is an anachronism."

"You're right," I said.

"Let's go before the supermarket closes," Marie suggested.

We went out to Food City for provisions. The plan was now to have dinner at home. I didn't want to get in their way on their last night together but I felt so comfortable with them, and they seemed to be at ease with me. We were like a family together, tossing items into our shopping cart. Jack and I got talking on French structuralism, I asked him to explain Foucalt to me, and we almost banged into an old man. Marie took over the cart handle, laughing at us. Her teasing didn't hurt, it felt good.

At the wine counter I had the inspiration of buying them a good bottle of wine.

Jack made a big thing out of it: "No don't be silly—you're crazy, Eric—Are you sure?—no, come on—it's too much, at least let me pay half—No?—all right, well thanks then, thanks very much, Eric, that's really generous of you." Marie gave me a bubbly smile, and for $7.50 I was made to feel like Maecenas donating a silver wedding chest to the happiness of the young lovers.

The sun was setting when we left Food City. It was close to eight-thirty. The sky still looked deep blue, though it no longer held any daylight. A keen copper light was rising up the wall of the bleached apartment complex on Columbus Avenue. We all stopped to watch it with relish, as though it had been arranged only for us.

Marie cooked a delicious dinner of veal Marsala and aubergines, rice pilaf, salad and a fruit soup. As we sat around the table, we began telling stories about the anti-war demonstrations we had been in. Though the war was far from over (it was 1970), we already had a nostalgic distance towards activism. It seemed Marie had gone in for SDS as a sophomore and had a few years ago been quite a firebrand. She even spoke to crowds. Jack's anecdotes were more self-mocking, of the which-way-to-the-front variety. I told stories of my battles as a caseworker with the Welfare Department in California. Everyone tends to tell a certain type of anecdote, which reveals his or her character as much as a fingerprint. My anecdotes usually gravitate toward the point where everyone comes to depend on me for my judgment, and I become indispensable. I described how I began organizing the clients, how fools in the bureaucracy tried to get me fired; with Jack's and Marie's enthusiastic promptings, I let my self-love take flight. In their supportive presence, the defensive part of my egotism dropped away, and I was left with an astounded affection for this bright, amusing, resourceful, plucky fellow who just happened to be me.

I was so relieved at being allowed to express freely this feeling for myself. Their appreciation showed that they knew how to value me: I had finally come home.

After dinner, we sat down on the capacious white couch. Jack had gotten that dark hooded look. I saw him withdrawing suddenly, turning into himself under his brow. Marie was in the kitchen washing dishes, considerately leaving us alone so that Jack and I could have a talk. I asked him if something was the matter.

"No, it's just this bronchial thing—my chest."

"Oh." I debated whether to let it pass. "I thought maybe you were feeling bad because you were dissatisfied with your work and here I've been boasting about my work."

"That's part of it. It's true I'd like to be occupied with something useful. But I don't think I'm capable of doing what you do, Eric."

"Nonsense."

"No, I mean it. I don't have the guts you have to walk into a roomful of strangers and organize them. I'd probably say, 'Er—

agh—mind if I trouble you for a smoke? Excuse me, I've got to go to the bathroom—' *You* know."

"You do journalism, that's talking to strangers."

"That's different. I'm invisible half the time. I go away in my head, and they don't even notice it. Not everyone's as sharp as you are at keeping me honest."

He was romanticizing me but I brushed it aside.

"If you're not fulfilled, you've got to find another profession."

"I know. But what?" Jack made a face.

"I'm sure there are lots of places willing to train a brilliant young apprentice."

"Not so young. Not so brilliant any more, either. I haven't used my brain in years."

"Don't be so overly modest! You can't imagine how shoddy the competition is out there."

"I'm not so sure." Jack clawed at his cheek. He stood up, he sat down the next pillow over, he crossed his legs. Even his doldrums were animated, which is why I loved being around him. He had the kind of suffering eyes that, even when I couldn't read them, I knew feeling was there. Jack's eyes were like black inkwells of vulnerability you could draw into at any time.

After all, what are friends for if not to thrill at the dark feeling-tone in one another?

"What do you want to do?"

"I don't know. . . ." he said impatiently.

"What are you looking for?" I asked it differently.

"That's just it, I don't know. I mean I do know, but it's got nothing to do with this business of career or East Coast-West Coast."

"What is it then?"

"You'll think it's nonsense."

"Try me."

He made a wry, self-skeptical face. "I once told it to an analyst I was seeing in London. I told her I wanted something self-consuming, like to be in a continuous state of orgasm. I wanted the orgasm to keep going. I wanted to walk around with that floating feeling all day. You know the way women can have one orgasm after another? I envy them, it must be nice to hold onto that. It's all about capacity for surrender and giving up controls. It's *adolescent!*" he declared. That was the worst name you could call something in our vocabulary. "It's probably got to do with adolescent fantasies about spirituality, the Godhead, reaching the Godhead, and all that stuff about needing a Father because my father walked out. It's stupid!"

I waited until I was sure he had stopped. He was looking at me for a response of some kind; and I didn't want to come down too hard on the idea because I knew that was what he expected. So I asked: "What did your analyst say about it?"

"She said it sounded great. To her it was a pleasant healthy fantasy—she said she'd like to keep it as a fantasy for herself. I was surprised, usually they think that mystical stuff's goofy. Maybe because she was a woman she felt closer to it."

"What kind of therapist was she?"

"Eclectic. Freudian, basically. Down-to-earth, like all the shrinks I've known. I find most of them to be very pragmatic common sense types. She was the only one who gave me support for what you call my foggy cosmic tendencies."

"You should have stayed with her."

"I couldn't. Both of us moved away from the area. Besides, that wouldn't have solved anything."

"Maybe she would have helped you with a few orgasms "

"Very funny. She was about—twenty years older than I am— actually she wasn't bad-looking. I used to have sex fantasies about her, and she said she did about me too."

"Wonderful."

"You don't have much sympathy for this business, do you?"

"I'm trying to think what I think. . . . I don't understand it. How could you get any work done if you had continuous orgasm?"

"I'm not sure that's the point!"

"It sounds suicidal to me. How could you maintain a self, in the face of that feeling?"

"That's just it, you probably couldn't."

"Then there would be no Jack Bogardes as we know him."

"There would be no ego; the ego would have to surrender or disappear."

"Why do you want to get rid of your ego? It's probably the best part of you."

"Most holy men wouldn't agree with you there," said Jack.

"I know, I know," I batted that aside. "Look I don't want to play dumb, but I just can't imagine it. It sounds so—hippie self-indulgent to me."

"You can put any kind of derogatory labels you want on it, Eric —I admit it does sound pretty vapid when I describe it. I'm not trying to rationalize, but it's not *that* silly. It's more about transcendence than self-indulgence."

"Well," I said, trying to keep an open mind, "what would it feel like?"

"Don't ask me! One prolonged release, I imagine. Something like the oceanic state Freud talks about. Maternal rocking in the womb of the universe—I don't know. Maybe it is just a masochistic fantasy."

"No, don't say that. It's a legitimate wish . . . if—if an impractical one. . . . It reminds me of something you once told me in college, about *Don Giovanni*. Remember?"

"No, I don't remember," he said, as if expecting the worst.

"We were standing in front of the barbershop on 115th Street, and you said that you wished people could go around singing Mozart duets to each other like in *Don Giovanni,* communicating in arias instead of speech. You felt that everyday conversation was too flat and it should be more inspired."

"I said a lot of dopey things then," Jack shrugged. "What's the point?"

"The point is that then you wanted everyone to go around singing all the time, and now you want them to have continuous orgasms."

This came out a little harsher than I had meant it to be when I first began the sentence.

Jack winced. "You're being a bit intolerant."

"I can't help it. It sounds totalitarian to me."

"Why totalitarian? I wasn't prescribing it for anybody but myself. And it was meant more as an ideal, a metaphor for experience—"

"But why can't you accept the nature of life as it is, instead of wishing for impossible states of being?"

"Can you accept the world as it is? Don't you want big changes? You get upset about political and social injustices. Don't you think this society is sick in some pretty basic ways?" Jack demanded.

"Yes," I admitted, slowed down a bit. "But it's biologically impossible to have orgasms all the time."

"I know that! All that I'm saying is that you want big changes too, Eric, so you should be more tolerant of other people's yearnings for liberation. And don't bring *Don Giovanni* into it. It's my favorite piece of music. Even if what I did say back there was dopey."

"All right, no *Don Giovanni*. But I think you're missing my point."

"Explain it to me," said Jack, with a sudden receptivity which I knew was sincere. He had that ability to put aside his own feelings in pursuit of another person's truth.

"Where can I start? Okay, I'll tell you my philosophy of life," I said half-jokingly. "I have certain—progressive ideals which you might say I inherited from my father and my mother. I want there to be a more equitable distribution of property, I'm a good little anti-imperialist, I'm also for the preservation of civil liberties, freedom of speech and art, minority rights and so on—in short, left libertarian. If a revolution ever broke out in this country, I know which side I would have to fight on. And if they ever started rounding up Marxist sympathizers and came knocking at my door, I would want to be included. But I think I would rather be a victim in a losing cause, than have to believe all the lies of the left. Because basically I don't trust them either: I don't believe in the inevitable victory of the proletariat, I can't swallow the aesthetics of 'the people's culture' and there have been too many massacres in the name of socialism. Okay. I think there is vast suffering in the world today. And I don't expect that suffering to be rolled back in my lifetime, or ever. I will work as hard as I *personally* can to relieve it and to support my ideals, but I am skeptical about their chances of succeeding. I don't believe in setting up a paradise here. You might even say I dislike the whole idea of liberation. I can't imagine it—liberation from *what?* As long as we're bounded by mortality it will be the same. To me the world is the World: the 'given,' as they say in geometry. I can't imagine what real sexual liberation would be like, orgasms forever, or utopias, or transcendance, or anything which 'releases' me from this life as it is. And even if I could imagine, I can't see liking that liberation better than what I have now. I like this world."

"Well, fine, Eric; but not everyone's as satisfied and cheerful as you are. Some of us are in more pain."

"I don't think it's a question of pain. I don't think pain is what makes one person turn toward liberation and another person not."

"What is it, then?"

"I think it's fashions," I said, blushing.

"Oh come on now. Is it fashions that make the people in Angola join a National Liberation Army?"

"That's not the kind of liberation I was talking about."

"How is it different? Liberation is a continuum: my liberation, women's liberation, homosexual liberation, the freedom fighters in Angola, they're all part of the same connected struggle. It's a continuum," Jack reiterated.

"You're dignifying your rather immature hedonistic wish by linking it to national wars of independence in Africa. I can't see that," I shrugged. "Besides, when did you get so political? I'm surprised to hear you talking this radical line."

"Maybe I'm changing," said Jack.

"You sound the way I used to."

"Well I'm just coming to it. I'm a late bloomer."

I had to laugh: Jack was anything but that.

Marie came in. "Politics?"

"Sort of."

"Continuous orgasms," Jack mocked himself.

"Oh. Sexual politics," Marie winked.

"That's it."

"Why don't you join us?" I said.

"I will. In a minute. Would anyone like some coffee?" she asked, passing her hand comfortingly over Jack's shoulder.

"I'd like some. But why don't you join us first?" I said.

"In a minute. Besides, I love it when men talk. I think there's nothing more romantic than heart-to-heart talks between men friends. I'm a sucker for that," Marie smiled. She started to walk off, but added as she was going, "A woman would only spoil it."

"Not very enlightened-sounding, is she?" Jack quipped.

"Since when did I pretend to be an enlightened woman?" Marie called from the other room. Then she began humming to herself.

I turned to Jack. "I used the wrong word before. Forget what I said about fashions."

"No, you're probably right about the totalitarian side of transcendence."

"I don't know the first thing about it. I was just sounding off—I was responding to the fact you seemed to be in pain."

"Forget about that," he said, shrugging it off now. "It's nothing to worry about."

I gave his arm a squeeze. Physical contact. "You'll find what you want. You've already got Marie."

"Did I hear someone call my name?" Marie bounced in.

"I was just starting to say that I'm jealous, seeing the two of you in love."

"You really think we're in love? Hear that, Jack? That's wonderful. Tell us why you think so."

"He can't tell. He's not inside us," Jack said.

"Listen, you, shut up—" said Marie in a good-humored way. "Go on, I want to hear this." She turned to me.

"Maybe it's painful for Eric to talk about this. He just said he was jealous. He may feel left out around us."

"Not at all," I said, surprised. "It's nice of you to be so considerate, but I wasn't feeling left out. I used the word 'jealous' lightly."

"Okay. Skip it."

"Go on—I want to hear Eric. How can you see we're in love?" asked Marie.

"Well it's obvious," I blushed. "I feel a little silly explaining. There's so much warmth between you. From the way you talk to each other, from the way you touch her leg or she touches your shoulder as she goes by. . . ."

"See?" she said.

"That could all be superficial," Jack replied. "You more than anyone should know not to be fooled by the appearance of couples arm in arm."

"I know. But come on, Jack," I insisted, "weren't you telling me last week how good this relationship has been for you?"

"It's true, these last few weeks—near the park, with the weather so nice . . ."

"You see? You just won't admit that things are going well. You're becoming a professional malcontent."

"It's true, it's absolutely true!" Marie leaped up, taking my part. "He's a hopeless, discontented old *grump*."

"Hey, quit it, you two."

"An old stick-in-the-mud sourpuss. No matter what I do, I could stand on my head, you're never satisfied."

Jack tossed a scatter pillow at her.

"Ouch! You missed!" she laughed, having it both ways. She ran back behind the couch and threw it in his lap, and he pelted her on the back with all the pillows, one after another. She was shielding herself with one arm and grabbing them and hurling them back with the other hand. It looked like fun. I wanted to join in.

Soon she collapsed exhausted, with her head on his arm.

It was getting late. I knew I should leave, give him a chance to pack, give them time to make love. But it was hard to pull myself apart from them: I felt so much better around them than I had for the last several days. They seemed in no hurry to be rid of me either. I had the feeling they had come together more during my visit; perhaps they were afraid of what mood they would fall into as soon as I left.

At eleven-thirty I collected myself to go.

"How long will you be away?" I asked Jack.

"Three weeks at most. Can I deliver any messages for you?"

"No. Just tell everyone I'm well."

"What about that girl you were seeing in San Francisco?" Jack asked.

"We broke up before I left. I don't know. . . . For me it's probably: Lucky at work, unlucky at love."

"I'm not sure I want to accept that distribution," Jack said moodily.

"No, you're right, I was, that just slipped out."

"That's all right."

"Anyway, have a really great trip."

"Thanks. You too, Eric, I hope being back in the city doesn't get you down. As usual, it was great seeing you and you did cheer me up."

"I'm glad. Good-bye, Marie—thanks for a great dinner."

"Give me a call when Jack's gone. I'll need cheering up too."

"Okay, if I get a chance . . ." I said hesitantly.

"I won't bite. Call me."

"Okay, I'll call you," I laughed at her insistence.

I looked at Jack. He was facing Marie.

"Well, good night everyone," I said. As the door swung gradually behind me, I was still holding on to their profiles through the narrowing closure.

IV

My friend Bruno Fisher was working as a vocational counselor in an anti-poverty agency called Project Turnaround, a job-training operation, and he told me there might be a job for me as a teacher in the remedial education wing. The agency ran a small street academy for high school dropouts. So I made an appointment for an interview; I went crosstown by bus to the central agency, which was smack in the middle of East Harlem.

As I sat in the waiting room, I heard a telephone operator inside one of the offices say in a curiously uninflected voice, "Project Turnaround. . . ." The main floor was subdivided into frosted glass cubicles, like the examination booths in a shabby optometrist's office. Everything was slow and sleepy and the walls were absolutely filthy. The speckled linoleum floor had been mopped recently, at least in the front part, but there was still underneath and over and in the very lighting fixtures a grime that wouldn't let up: part-circumstantial, part-bravado, like a shiny joker's grin that gleams under cheap building materials.

When I was taken up to the second floor to the "school," I noticed the stairs had a suspicious-smelling glutinous black shine.

There were only five students around, on that humid afternoon. I was told that most of the absentees would be back when the weather turned cold; for the moment, it was slow season. A few teen-agers in cotton T-shirts were bent over multiple-question examinations with glazed looks, as though hypnotized. Most of the staff and all the clients were black or Hispanic, which I had expected, but it still made me a little tense. What made me even more nervous was that I had never taught before, and would have to bluff experience from pieces of my résumé.

A Mr. Rafael Diaz took me around to show me the various departments. He was a tight little rooster of a man, with a very bad skin problem, a thin black tie and a frayed pink shirt embossed with satin discs. He had the habit of talking very quickly with frown lines on his brow and never looking directly at his listener. He introduced me to several people and they shook my hand and we chatted. To my surprise, this was the interview. There was no formal interrogation about my experience, which both relieved and disappointed me. They explained the various parts of the program with shamefaced, half-forgotten rhetoric, as though I were a state inspector who could see right through them, rather than a job applicant myself. At the end of the day I got the dim impression I was hired. In fact they never said I was in so many words; all that happened was that the director, a man named Chipper, played with his pipe and smiled, while a huge black man who was second in command made a joke about the agency probably needing a white "communicator" who could speak the language of the Establishment.

The pay wasn't great, but I was ready to take anything.

Bruno and I went out for a beer afterwards, to a dark cocktail lounge on the corner.

"Gave you the Cook's Tour, eh?"

"Yes. Rafael did."

"He's the husband of Sylvia, the woman who works upstairs. That's how he got the job. What a dodo that man is!" Bruno scoffed with relish. ". . . You meet the dude in the front cubicle next to mine?"

"Walter? He seems nice."

"Oh, he's very nice—especially if he likes you. Takes some of the Rican lads home. Buys them clothes. Wants to adopt one of them! Yeah, one of the clients just moved in with him—Chino. He really believes in home visits." He shook his round, good-humored face tolerantly; Bruno himself was a person of strong appetites—for food, sex, alcohol—who tended to characterize other people by the appetite or vice he took to be their dominant one.

"How do you feel about that? Do you think it's unprofessional?"

"Doesn't phase me. But Hinton's a Puritan. The big black guy. They're talking about axing Walter, claim he's bad for the agency's image."

"What is the agency's image in these parts?"

"Crud. People know it's a jive outfit. But the kids go here because some of our competitors pay even less of a stipend. You should hear the kids talking about the Neighborhood Youth Corp gigs, all the way up in the Bronx, in Brooklyn—comparing rates. Half the clientele would walk out of here in a second if an outfit like Save the People down near 103rd Street raised its stipend fifty cents *per diem*."

"That would be a disaster for the intake staff."

"They wouldn't care. The administrators would run it for themselves, just to keep pulling down a salary. That happened once. The city grant didn't come through for a full program, but there was still a little money left over in the kitty, so we kicked the clients out and kept the agency running on a purely bureaucratic level: answering phones, doing paperwork, filing reports."

"It sounds pretty neo-colonialist, the way you describe it."

"Forget the neo—" said Bruno, and a big slow grin spread over his chubby face. "It is nothing if not colonialist."

"Well, I still need a job. I can't feel bad because I'm not black. I mean, I grew up in black neighborhoods. I have as much right to work here as anyone. And I think I can do as good a job. I've seen programs run completely by ethnics from the community and sometimes they can be more callous to their population, and give poorer services. Local control isn't everything." I could hear my voice getting more and more defensive, uncovering emotion that I hadn't meant to be there. Bruno didn't say anything—he didn't have to. I knew he was watching me twist and scrape against a tightening harness that he had struggled and lived with for years.

In the first few days there was no pressure, it was understood that I was to move around and feel my way into the job, sit in on the staff meeting and make up a schedule. This freedom was the best part of the job; I was even able to go home early. But attending the meeting was the worst—the staff was in a state of demoralized disorder; there were ghosts of old feuds and rumors of attempted takeovers; some staffers seemed to belong to one Democratic party club, while others owed allegiance to its rival in the upcoming primary fight; one man angrily wanted to fly the Black Liberation Flag from the roof of the agency, and this was, to my surprise, approved. The fighting bothered me less than that there was no shared conviction of purpose, no real program. Everything just drifted.

The head of the agency, Chipper, was white, an ex-Unitarian minister who quietly sat back, smoked a pipe and wore a Mexican sarape around his shoulders. He had the dynamism of a turtle.

His lieutenant was a towering black man, as round as he was high, named Horace Hinton. This man Hinton fulminated a great deal in the style of a Baptist preacher, chastising the youths for their deviation from program rules, and occasionally reinforced his point by touching a gun he wore at his side—a gesture which always made me begin agreeing instantly. The revolver, he explained to me, was there because he moonlighted as a bank guard in the evenings, which I still thought was a rather insufficient explanation. During the meeting Hinton made a fierce, fuzzy oration, à propos of nothing, about the dignity of the community, and touched his gun handle twice.

After the meeting, I caught up to Bruno. "What was that all about?"

"Nothing. *Nada.* You see the dude who was making all the fuss about the flag? That sharp-dressed smooth guy, Akhmed, the Black Separatist? Used to be a big pimp on 125th Street. Now he wants Chipper's job. They're going to invite him further in and further in, keep making concessions, let him think that he's taking over. Then he's going to find he's way over his head. Suddenly— no more Akhmed. I've seen them work it before."

"Sounds like a pretty pointless exercise," I said.

"Sure it's pointless. It just goes round in circles. Project Turnaround, right? They should call it *Project Runaround!*" Bruno laughed insouciantly.

I laughed too, though I wasn't sure how much of Bruno's cynicism was actually justified, or how much was a worldly pose he liked to take. I knew he had a reputation around the agency for being a good, conscientious worker, which seemed to belie, at least in my mind, some of his pessimism. "You think they'll really let him fly a revolutionary flag over a city agency?" I asked.

"I don't mind. Fat lot of good it'll do him. This isn't even a black neighborhood, it's Hispanic, and the Ricans aren't gonna dig it too tough when they see that Black Liberation flag flapping." Bruno smiled, in anticipation of the furor.

On Friday the agency was asked to participate in painting a street mural and I went outside to watch. Enthusiasm ran high, our kids were having a good time painting the side wall of a gray tenement, facing a bottle-strewn empty lot. It became something like a fiesta for the whole neighborhood. Too bad the mural was so horrible. As the large, symbolic figures started taking over the space—first a man with Afro and gun, then a brown-skinned mother holding a child, then massive-muscled workers with bulging arms, the Puerto Rican Independence flag, the Black Liberation tricolor, the peace sign, the clenched fist, the panther, each icon a new assertion of pride and strength—I felt traitorous to be thinking how boring all this Power-to-the-People art was, as humdrum as the worst socialist realism from which it derived.

Everyone was saying how beautiful it was. I shared in the mouthing of compliments, a perfect imposter, yet secretly swearing fidelity to the rigorous logic of my art education. Was it really so awful, or was I only being a snob? Never mind: I was feeling an unaccountable energy; it was good to be working again, good to be outside. That beautiful, hard New York light, that blue between the buildings—I was starting to see it again.

All New Yorkers are looking for at least one of three things: a job, an apartment, or a lover. This is what unifies them as a people. If by chance they happen to have all three, they begin to graduate to the next search: a nicer job, a bigger apartment, a better lover.

I had found the job, I was on the hunt for the other two, so I was beginning to feel right in step. Two weeks after the Fourth of July, I realized I was enjoying the city. Being there in the heart of a heat wave had its moments. The city had thinned out. Galleries and caviar shops were closed; the therapists were all refreshing and recharging themselves in places like Bar Harbor, Maine. An invisible hand came down from the sky and removed certain types, leaving only those who were stuck at jobs, too lazy to get away, or too poor. It made for a solidarity among those crazy enough to be out in the street at noon. "Man it's hot!" people would mutter at me. "It's impossible to be this hot!" I heard myself repeating, to no one in particular. There was no way to have an original thought in this weather: it reduced one's mental powers to those of a burro. You had to pause every half-block to mop away sweat and catch your breath, as though merely walking ahead were a steep mountain climb.

In the late afternoon, around six, the air calmed down a bit. People's faces were sapped into relaxation by the heat, the cheeky flesh under their eyes slackened and swelled, with cork-smeared shadows of sweat, like the aftermath of a black eye. The armor of city living was dropping off, melting into resignation, tolerance, mañana. . . .

The crowds came out after dark in Greenwich Village, it was carnival every night, the tanned girls in pairs in pink tank-tops and shorts strolling past tables on Avenue of the Americas with garish paintings on velvet of flowers or tigers; ambling, stopping to look at homemade earrings. Religious fanatics were out in force, accosting everyone, starting debates on Free Will and God's Will. Gospel missionaries addressed crowds, smiling Scientologists approached loners, Hare Krishna chanters hopped like pogo sticks and danced, Jews for Jesus clashed with Orthodox Jews. Pedestrians who would ordinarily have rushed by were moving so slowly that they could hear each speech, standing on the fringes of crowds, nodding or arguing, as if it were their planned evening's entertainment to do nothing else but make the circuit from one end of the zealot-glutted street to the other.

Musicians were also playing to the crowds. There would be a steel-drum band of black Trinidadians on Eighth Street, usually one brash boy to warm the audience, and two older, sober-looking young men staring impassively at their mallets. It was free, of course, but it seemed unfair to stay longer than a song (or at least that was my rule) without giving some money. But wherever one looked, on every street corner, there were musicians, mimes, jugglers, even fire-eaters. Half of New York was playing to the other half.

On Fifth Avenue, up around Fifty-seventh Street, I came across a classical quintet of Juilliard students, performing Handel in front of the Hallmark Greeting Card doorway. A respectful crowd had gathered around. "Look!"—a woman yanked her husband toward them—"street music!" The wind quintet was playing *passacaglias,* sedately and so sweetly and harmoniously one forgot to hear the traffic, except when a Fifth Avenue bus ground alongside and several bars were lost. In between scores, the players, two men and three women, all young, in jeans, wearing glasses, took swallows from quart beer bottles at their sides, while bystanders gingerly leaned forward and tossed dollars into the bassoon case, green bills on a blue felt backing.

Over a week had gone by since I had seen Jack and Marie. I found myself thinking of the promise I had made about getting in touch with her. It seemed a stupid thing to have done. I barely knew her, and it would have been awkward to see her without Jack present.

I let a few more days go by, and then one evening after work, sitting in the Kroegels' dark apartment, with too much energy in my veins, I called her. As I dialed her number I told myself that I was getting over an obligation, like phoning a second cousin whose name had been given to look up in a foreign city.

She sounded very subdued when she first picked up.

"Oh, hi, Eric. I'm so glad you called."

"Have you heard anything from Jack?"

"He phoned today. He seems to be having a good time. He may be a little longer out there than he thought."

"What have you been doing with yourself?"

"Oh . . . I've been feeling a little low lately—moping around."

"What about?"

"Just little things. I hate to bore people with complaints. It should be enough just to be alive. Usually it is—usually I feel that way."

"Want some company?"

"Sure? When can you come over?"

"Right now?"

"Right now? That sounds great!" she laughed. "Terrific!" We both laughed at the leap of optimism her voice had taken.

"I'll be over in ten, twenty minutes."

I should have known something funny was going on from the way I hurried to her house. I rang the downstairs bell of the brownstone, under the antique gas jet. When Marie opened the door for me, I got an unexpected stir of happiness just from seeing her.

We sat down at the same table and began talking where we had left off talking ten nights before. But she looked different again somehow: each time I saw her she surprised me. This time she was wearing a wine-red sweater with half sleeves, and she seemed older, with a bittersweet-wise quality. I saw her for a moment as one of those twinkling observant octogenarians compassionate toward the troubles of youth.

Maybe because I was thinking it, I said that trite line. "I feel that I've known you for a long time already."

"Yes. It's always that way when intelligent, strong people meet. There's a family resemblance. We're like brothers and sisters."

"Maybe that's . . . it, you remind me of one of my sisters. She has dark eyes like yours."

"And I have a brother who's like you. I mean he's nothing like you in body type, he's more stocky like a football player and he's in business with my father. But in deeper essentials, you and he could be twins."

"In what way?"

"He's solid as a rock. In fact he just had a baby. I'm an aunt now," Marie said proudly.

"Congratulations!"

"The *bris* was just last weekend—the circumcision—"

"I know what a *bris* is. I'm Jewish myself."

"Okay, well don't get so huffy about it," she said kiddingly.

"I wasn't. Do you believe that theory that with everyone we feel an immediate rapport for, we're really just projecting feelings onto them we have toward a member of our family?"

"That sounds terrible," she replied, and her long brownish-red hair shook from side to side. "It could be. And you?"

"I do believe we project a lot. But go on, what was the *bris* like?"

"Oh it was so funny," Marie perked up. "There was a big dumpy lady there who wanted me to marry her son. She kept saying to me, 'You're so adorable, how old are you, dear, and what do you do?' I said, 'Thank you I'm twenty-one years old and I go to college. I'm a student.'—'Oh that's wonderful, honey, and what are you studying?'—'Right now I'm taking Melville and Chinese history.' She said, 'Oh you would really get along with my son, he loves Chinese food.'" We laughed till tears came to our eyes. "Then she showed me a picture of this wonder boy—Bernie? a thirty-eight-year-old accountant? No wonder his mother was getting worried. I don't believe in putting people down for their looks, but this guy was *really homely*. I said, 'Excuse me, I have to help with the hors d'oeuvres.' But she wouldn't leave me alone. Everyone was trying to grab me—you know how sparks fly off you, sometimes you can even be in a bad mood and feel ugly and not trying, but everyone stays glued to you?"

"I know what you mean," I said warmly.

"I know you know. So suddenly I was an aunt. I felt so ancient. My father was making wonderful toasts, predicting the baby's future like the wizard in fairy tales. And suddenly took my arm and said: 'To our own fairy godmother, Marie; may she bless us soon with children.'—It was much more clever than that but I can't remember the words. . . . Then I took the baby and held it in its blanket. I was so happy it was like splashing under a waterfall. I was never so happy—it's difficult to explain. Then the baby's mother, my sister-in-law Jan, who's terrific, stepped forward to reclaim her kid. I must have looked as though an arrow had shot into me. Dr. Groman said, 'Oh Marie, you're so transparent.'—'What do you mean?' I said—feistily; but really pleased to be called transparent."

"Well, it's a compliment," I interjected.

"I think so too. Who wants to be a mystery all the time? That gets to be so boring. So he said, 'It's clear you want that baby.' I said, 'That's right!' I knew he'd see through me because he knows everything. Dr. Groman is my brother's psychoanalyst. Then he put his arm around me and guided me into the next room where all the fur coats and jackets had been piled high on the bed . . . in July! 'I want to have a talk with you,' Dr. Groman said. 'What *about?*' I asked, really excited that he wanted to talk with me. All the while I had been thinking, Dr. Groman is terrific. He's highly respected in his field in psychoanalytic circles, and I can't tell you what it is about him that's so special, but *you* would see in a second. He said, 'You seem to be having a wonderful time.'

" 'I'm having a wonderful time,' I repeated as if he were hypnotizing me. 'Everything is just so funny. How about you?'

" 'I'm having a reasonably good time,' he said.

" 'You're always reasonable,' I said. 'That's what makes you so great.'

" 'But when I'm around you, Marie, I lose every ounce of reason.' Then he pulled me against him and I shivered like a leaf. Dr. Groman—my brother's psychiatrist! The most respected doctor in his field, kissing me on the neck! I didn't know whether to cry out or punch him or step on his foot or kiss him too. But I felt protected by my white crocheted dress, which is a dress I've had for years and nothing bad has happened to me in it. And besides I knew that the kiss was just gallantry of the Old School, because he's very European, has an accent. . . . It felt nice, too, his beard scratching my neck, not exactly white—you know, salt and pepper! Then he said, 'In all my years of clinical practice, you're the most delectable aunt I ever saw.'—'Did you just get back from vacation?' I asked, changing the subject.—'Only three days ago. As soon as I came in your brother called.'

" 'Where did you go?'

" 'The Swiss Alps. I spent the month on a mountain-climbing expedition.'

"I said, 'I knew it would be something challenging like that.' Dr. Groman is the most manly man I've ever met. And his wife is incredible too. She's the kind of woman who makes everyone happy by raising children and taking care of the household—I know it's unpopular for a woman to say that but it's wonderful when it's done well, and I really respect women like that, I think they're saints."

"So what happened then?" I asked.

"Doc Groman said to me, 'I'm worried about your brother.'

" 'Don't be,' I said.

" 'Are you sure Barry knows what he's getting into? What fatherhood means?'

" 'I'm sure he'll make a tremendous father. Today I'm full-sail with optimism. Don't you worry about Barry. He's *okay*. He's grown up a lot since he started therapy with you.' Then there was a rush, like pushing outside the door? They had finished the ceremony, and I could hear Rabbi Glazer's nasal voice accepting compliments, and people clinking glasses. I think the whole custom is barbaric. Imagine, having all those people around watching your penis clipped! That's the Jewish religion for you. 'Come on,' Dr. Groman said, 'we'd better get out of this bedroom before people start getting the wrong ideas.'

" 'You mean the right ideas!' I told him."

Marie finished her story with a sly tilt of her head. She was a superb mimic and had acted out all the parts. Even if I thought this Dr. Groman a creep, I had been carried along by the sheer bubbling entertainment of her talk. It was easy to listen to—to give myself up to it like music. She had a lovely smile. Her teeth were rather yellow, which should have been a drawback for someone who smiled as often as she did, but it wasn't.

I cleared my throat. "Why was the doctor so worried about your brother?"

"Oh—" she paused, considering whether to tell me. "Everyone was worried about my brother for a long time. I told my mother, 'Don't worry about Barry, he's going to be the Rock of Gibraltar in the family.' But when he was younger—he had a nervous breakdown? Everyone does in adolescence. But they were afraid he was going to be catatonic or go into a coma. When he was seventeen, and I was fourteen, I remember this so well, we were watching the Ed Sullivan show. My brother was in the upstairs bedroom and he had made a cut on his arm with a razor, from the biceps all the way to the elbow. We heard a noise. I went to the foot of the stairs to investigate and I saw him up there. My mother came right behind me and they looked at each other. They didn't even see me. He was covered with blood. He smiled at her from the head of the stairs and mother smiled back. In some strange way he had pleased her."

"Wow."

"It sounds sensational but—I don't think these stories mean anything. Things have happened to me that are so horrifying, I used to tell them to people, when I was younger, to get attention. Now they're just stories to me. And they may not be the things that really count in life."

"I agree. It seems to me daily life outweighs the meaning of the traumas." Still, I thought of my four nightmare experiences that I carried around with me always, like pouches in a money belt, fingering them. "But they can be a great comfort," I added.

"Oh, of course. I wouldn't give up a single one of my really horrible experiences for anything. But it's more fun to save them for a rainy day."

"Funny, I tried to kill myself also, when I was seventeen," I confessed with an apologetic smile.

"It figures," she put in: "just like my brother. See?" and we laughed benignly. "How did you do it?"

"Sleeping pills. They had to have my stomach pumped."

It was wonderful to know that we had both gone through some hellish times, and we didn't need to dwell on them, but could pass over them in this light, generic way.

"What was your childhood like?" I asked.

"It was normal—happy. Decent. Except that I was sick a lot. I almost died when I was born."

"What was the matter with you?"

"I had a heart murmur. And I have holes in my lungs."

"Actual holes?"

"Big ones! My parents took me to the best specialists. They spent a fortune on me. And I got to know the inner workings of hospitals and surgery rooms. I know a lot about medicine. I had *terrific* doctors, my favorite was Dr. Maazel? He took me aside when I was eight and told me, 'Marie, don't ever marry, a treasure like you shouldn't go to one man.'—'I won't, Dr. Maazel' I said in a high squeaky voice. 'Call me Burt!' he said.—But at school I didn't have any friends until I was fourteen. My mother used to get sent reports that no one would talk to me. They used to punch me in the chest. Which was dangerous, because of my lungs! And they called me Pretzel because I had long skinny legs and was taller than everyone else."

"That's hard to believe. I would think you'd be popular. You're so—pretty and charming."

"Thanks. But it isn't the kind of charm that schoolchildren appreciate, I don't think. And really, I wasn't as pretty as I am now —didn't have breasts," she said merrily. "After I got them the boys started to take notice, and then I had lots of girl friends as well. I can remember, when I was fourteen, asking my father if they were coming and he said: 'Don't worry, you'll get them.

Look at your mother.' My mother has enormous breasts! Enormous. I waited and waited. Then one day they were there! I waltzed in front of my dad and said, 'How about it, Dad? Can you see them? Well?' He said, 'Babe, you got a gorgeous pair of knockers.' I always loved it that he said it in just those words. Looking me in the eye: 'Babe . . .'" As she spoke, I could see the gawky growing-pains youngster still inside the woman Marie. Her hips and buttocks were rather tentatively filled in, girlish. Her weighty round breasts were almost like an afterthought that God had taped on to make life more interesting. When she slumped over, her breasts became deceptively small. But then when she sat up they confronted you with their sauciness: like Marie herself, they gave the appearance of winking.

"Tell me about your father. What does he do?"

"My father is perfect. I mean he's not by any means, but he's just exactly who he is and that's what I mean by perfect. At the party last weekend a funny little man I've never met came up to me and said, 'Your dad is the most beloved man in the industry. I want you to know I'm proud to be associated with Murray Curtin. I'd give my right arm for that man!'—'So would I!' I told him. 'But hold on to it for the time being.' I was named after him: Murray—Marie?"

"But what does he do? What's his business exactly?"

"He owns a transistor parts factory in Queens. He developed things they used in the space program—actually invented them when he was young. And my mother's very intelligent too. She has a lot of energy. She's a dynamo! She reads a lot and she wanted to be a poet once. She still writes, novels she won't show anyone. And locks them in the cupboard. My mother is an hysteric? I guess I resented her a lot in my childhood because she had so many temper tantrums and I had to be the reasonable grown-up one, but I'm beginning to appreciate her more now. We're very close. I was always close to my father. He's quite a guy. Jack told me once I was too wrapped up with my family, that it kept me from developing."

"Look who's talking."

"That's just what I said! He goes on living year after year in his mother's apartment, and he's twenty-seven. And I moved out long ago. I don't think it's such a terrible idea to love your family—I don't want to talk about it. It's unfair, he's not here to defend himself."

"Okay," I said mildly.

The phone rang. "Excuse me for a moment, Eric."

She picked up the phone. "Hello-o?" Her voice rose to an infinity of expectation, like the first bounce of a trampoline, until she was stopped in midair by the caller's recognizable voice: "Hi, Barry," she swooped down again, still breathless. She started walking the white phone with its long extension cord out of the living room, cradling it in one ear. "I've been meaning to call you. How's the kid. . . . Oh, baby's sick? That's terrible. That's awful, I'm not kidding. . . . But it's not so serious? Good. . . . And Jan, how's she taking it . . . ?" Circling round to the kitchen with the slow absorbed tread of a mother pushing a pram down the street, she opened the refrigerator and took out a can of cherry soda and opened it. I peeked over her shoulder and saw that the refrigerator was stacked with rows of cherry soda cans! "You sound sort of blue. . . . No, no, I can listen. . . . Tonight? Well I'm with a friend right now—with Eric. He's very smart, a very special person, you would really like meeting him. Not now? Okay. . . . So what's this bluesy feeling? . . ." She listened for five minutes, signaling to me that she would be off the phone soon. "I understand. I do understand. . . . Have you talked to Dr. Groman yet? . . . Good! Just what I knew he'd say. . . . I have to get off now . . . I'll be home tomorrow. Sweet dreams."

She sat down next to me with a sigh.

"What was that?"

"That was my brother Barry. He's undergoing a crisis. He wants to leave his wife and baby and start a new life in Europe."

Evidently this brother was not yet as solid as Gibraltar. I wasn't sure how much I liked being compared to him.

"Do you think he'll do it?" I asked.

"No, he's just panicking about being a father. But he has Dr.

Groman, so I think it'll work out. But let's not talk about it any more. Suddenly I'm so tired," she yawned.

"Do you want me to go home now?"

"In a little while, not yet."

Marie asked me to tell her about my childhood, and I did. She listened eagerly. I found her as good a listener as a talker, and it was only with some will power that I finally dragged myself away, a quarter-hour past midnight.

I went home excited and disturbed by the strong tug I felt toward Marie. I still had plenty of detachment toward her, and as I thought over things she had said, several remarks made me leery, or pointed to veins of neurosis, like shiny mica streaks of confusion and self-deception. And yet I was entranced, even with the pathological family, it was all new to me—this particular middleclass, suburban way of being crazy, and the way she made Gods of people. And underneath whatever she said was that excited enthusiasm of hers. I had come armored that night against Marie's physical appeal, and had managed to convince myself that she was not my type: I preferred a more voluptuous, mature-bodied woman. But by sealing myself off from the sexual, I had not realized I had left myself open to another direction. Call it the psychic, if you like. We seemed to be drinking each other's souls through straws with each renewal of conversation. Since we were both listening so hard, I found myself looking into her face, and it was inevitable that I would notice at some point how exceptional it was, in the way that beauty breaks as a wave over you so powerfully when it comes from that other source: not the lustful, but the thrill of rapport. Her eyes had the poignant, sympathetic sparkle of a Gene Tierney in *Whirlpool,* or the young Jean Simmons in *Angel Face,* or Audrey Hepburn, or any of those achingly high-strung brunette actresses of the late 1940s and early '50s, with aristocratic cheekbones, dark lips and wide dark pupils that photographed as moist points of pain or hope in black and white.

Marie's face had seemed, at first glance, ordinary-pretty, not breathtaking. Then as you looked at her, she kept getting more and more beautiful, like a ruby turning darker, until you realized that she was the real thing. Let us assume that all faces are variations of five basic types: she was one of the five original faces that the others grew out of. I later learned that she had been a teen-age *Seventeen* cover girl, so my discovery was validated by popular taste; but under the conventional prettiness, which was of limited if habitual interest to me, there was a depth, a beautiful hurt in her expression, a quicksilver animation which bit into my mind. Such changeableness of expression always brings with it, for me, a promise of connection. Of course that means that I also thought of myself as a person of extreme vitality and animation. To have found another one like me was an immediate challenge, a throwing down of the gauntlet. I felt competitive with her surge; I had the urge to test my power of life against Marie's, and see if I went under or held my own.

And since I am trying to be honest, I have to add one more detail. We had kept each other at arm's length throughout the evening. Marie was behaving quite properly, as an "engaged" young woman should, and I followed her decorous lead. We were in some ways, for all our barrier-destroying talk, shy as mice. But right before I left I kissed her on the cheek, as she stood at the door. That was probably a mistake. Not that the kiss was anything romantic: it was meant more as a courtesy. But one kiss can lead to another kiss; and though it hadn't, it left me wide awake with a memory of her soft cheek and the scent of her.

V

I had insomnia. The bedroom of Kroegels' apartment was cut off from the street, no ventilation, nothing but bookshelves. This subletting was not really living; it was holding my breath underwater. I knew Michael Probst often stayed up late watching television. At one in the morning I telephoned him, and in the course of our talking about insomnia he said, "Drink a glass of milk before you go to bed. If you warm it in a pan first it will probably work better." This sweet advice, which seemed to come from an old *baba* or nanny speaking through him, immediately pacified me. I believed in the glass of milk, translucent and gentle. The idea of calcium, a piece of religion from childhood, had as great an effect as the drink in putting me to sleep.

The following night, I went over to Michael's house after work to pick him up, so that we could both have a pizza at the V&T, an Italian restaurant near Columbia University. Michael lived in a renovated building on West 106th Street that had been carved into cubed studios for graduate students. He had let his white cube degenerate into a rather grim, knicked die. A mattress on the floor, topped by an exhausted sheet, books piled crookedly on a kitchen chair, a television set. And a few coleus plants on the windowsill. Poverty alone could not have accounted for the bareness: it was more a conscious stylistic statement.

"I'll turn on the fan," he said when I came in. He switched on his electric fan, two blades in a circular peach-colored frame, which whirred and whanged to a higher note after some seconds. The warm air got more billowy, but not cooler.

We sat on his mattress, and Michael showed me a picture book of chimpanzees and orangutans he had just been looking through.

It was written by a woman who had studied chimpanzee behavior by living among them as an equal. Michael approved highly of this. He told episodes from the book for ten minutes.

"Why does this fascinate you so much?" I asked finally.

"I envy the ape life," he said.

"I don't understand this jealousy of animals. I've never envied dogs or cats myself. I prefer bright lights, Broadway, artifice, glittery gowns."

"That's where we differ," Michael said gravely. I stole a glance at his eyes, which were clear and tired, like a Jeremiah who had been in the wilderness a month too long. His close-cropped beard added to the impression of righteous and compacted energy. He found me a color photograph in the book that was his favorite, of two monkeys grooming each other. Michael had a way of reaching for the simple: it was one of the things I admired most about him, and also dreaded most. He loved to talk appreciately about children, lambs, mental patients, people who worked with their hands.

I listen in wonder to people's ideas of the natural. Maybe because I have such a pallid conception of it myself, when someone speaks lovingly about green growing things I get frightened. And yet I forced myself to listen when Michael spoke. He would tell about his cousin Sam in Montreal, who had once been in a concentration camp, and now raised astonishingly large tomatoes that baffled the scientists. He would describe sheep in the mountains he had once seen, in a way that would make me queasy. Not that Michael got into the country much. But he read about it: this book on chimpanzee behavior, Fabre's *The Life of the Spider,* the poets who spoke with a deep longing for an animal nature that was lost to man.

"How is it you like the streets?" he said, after a long pause.

"Why not?"

"As soon as I leave my house and go onto the street, I feel I'm starting to lose my mind. On Broadway it's especially bad. The houses crush me and people look dead—that happened to me yesterday. All the people had a tricky, unreal look to them."

"What do you mean, they look unreal?"

"You don't ever experience that, do you?" Michael said, gazing at me curiously. I wasn't sure that he didn't feel pitying or contemptuous of me for not knowing what a real anxiety attack was, the kind he suffered frequently, and for which his therapist gave him Librium.

"Well I'm sure I must have—felt something like that from time to time . . ."

"I don't think you have," said Michael. "You're quite comfortable in the city. Do you ever lose hold of reality just by walking down the street?"

I thought for a minute. "No, I have to admit I don't. I guess the place where I feel safest is the streets."

Michael shook his head. "A friend of mine was mugged six months ago. He's a big strapping fellow, a sculptor, and he was so angry that he got himself an enormous cudgel, and now he walks around with it brandishing it like Friar Tuck every time he goes into the street."

"You have some strange friends." I set aside the chimp book. "What have you been doing with yourself lately?"

"As little as possible," said Michael, with an inner amusement. "I'm trying to lower my pulse rate. The less I do or think, the better it will be for me. I went to the laundromat yesterday. There was a man in the laundromat . . . but forget about that. I'm trying to lead a life like a minimal painting, with two green stripes in the top corner. I've been watching television a lot. Unfortunately television is also too complex. But I like the Johnny Carson show. Do you ever watch it?"

I shook my head. "I never got into the habit of watching television."

"It's a very good habit. I was too tired to study; so I turned on the Johnny Carson show. He had Zsa Zsa Gabor on. And Shelley Winters. Their use of language was astonishing. I wish I could remember some of the things they said. Carson is, you know, pathologically afraid of showing any feeling. And Shelley Winters was talking about her analysis in very straightforward, frank terms that were terrifying him."

"What was Zsa Zsa Gabor doing?"

"She was—she was mostly on in another segment. But I think she was trying to put down Shelley Winters, who was holding her own."

"Sounds interesting."

"You should come over sometime, we'll watch television. But not tonight or the rest of the week," he added; "this week is bad for me."

I didn't inquire why it was bad for him. We went to the restaurant, a student hangout that made me both nostalgic and disturbed that I hadn't gotten farther away yet from his university milieu. Around us were seated undergraduates with long dirty-blond hair, boys: maybe I was still a boy like them. In the red vinyl booth we made ourselves at home, ordered pizza with sausage and beer. We were happily tearing apart, along with the pizza, our mutual acquaintances, when I made the blunder of saying that Jack Bogardes and he were similar in some ways.

"I don't think so. I think we're completely different," said Michael; he obviously found the suggestion insulting.

"Of course you're very different," I started to qualify, "but all I meant was that you both have this idea about wanting the world to be more natural, you both like to plunge to the bottom of things in conversation, you both like Hölderlin and the German Romantic poets, and you both have anxiety attacks." I wasn't making things any better, I gathered, from the expression on Michael's face. "Well what do you think of Jack? You saw him the other evening."

"What I always think," said Michael.

"Which is . . . ?"

"You know, the baboon, when he meets a stronger baboon, presents his ass to the stronger as a sign of surrender. It doesn't bother you because you think it's your due. But if I were you I would stay away from that," Michael declared. He was really warming up now. "The impression I get of Jack is of someone flying away from his center. I spent a day or two with him once. He was tied up in knots. His anger underneath is frightening. I have no idea what it's about, and I don't want to know. As long as he keeps converting it into neurotic symptoms, he'll be all right. But I don't want to be around when it goes off."

I was enjoying this. What is it about one friend attacking another that spreads such a balm over one's soul? I knew I should defend Jack, but my impulse was to do it ineffectually, so as to draw out Michael's full critique.

"Don't you think he might have been nervous around you because he knew you were also a friend I thought highly of; and there may have been an element of jealousy involved?"

"No. Not at all. I think his affect is seriously damaged. It's an aggression problem. I know, because I have the opposite problem."

"Look, I agree with some of what you said, that the apologetic stuff is a sham. But, once you understand what it really means, and take it for what it is, then you're free to like him as another sort of person. Many people I know have a chronic tic of some kind which means the opposite of what it's given out to be. That doesn't mean one can't be friends with them. Jack is nervous and has emotional problems—who doesn't? Besides, Jack is very loyal, generous, gifted and brilliant."

"I don't share your sense of him as being brilliant," said Michael.

"He's absolutely brilliant, believe me. I've read things by him— and listened to him, his conversation can be dazzlingly learned."

"He has a collector's mind. He reads all the right books, he drops the right names. He has a highly developed taste, that's all, but no originality."

"I don't agree," I said, unsure momentarily. "His perspective is very broad. He's more intelligent than I am."

"That's not true. You're much smarter than he is," Michael said impatiently.

"If intelligence means application of one's brains to practical problems," I said, secretly pleased, "I may be smarter than he is. But if intelligence is the potential to grasp new thought, or suppleness and range of mind—even if it's not put to use—then he has to be considered brighter."

"Ordinarily I would agree with you. But why is it I can't remember one interesting remark he's ever made?" asked Michael, leaning back in the red booth.

"Maybe he clams up around you."

"You're giving him too much credit. You're reading more into him than is actually there. It's a habit of yours."

"I don't want to argue about that," I said. "I'm not the only one who thinks he's got a rare intelligence, there are hundreds of people around the world who do. Anyway, what did you think of his girl friend?" I asked, trying to sound casual.

"She's beautiful," Michael said simply.

"You really think so?" I pretended skepticism.

"Absolutely. And clever. Her speech interested me much more than Jack's. The only part I can't figure out is what she's doing with him."

"Jack's always gotten very attractive women."

"How does he do it? I'm as good-looking at he is," asserted Michael.

I smiled. "I don't know. If I knew I would be doing it myself." We ordered coffee. "I wonder if having affairs with beautiful women is a discipline," I said. "It probably takes up a lot of time. You would need to be obsessed, I imagine—to believe in their beauty so much that you reflect it back to them and make them believe it. I think if one set one's mind to it, and were really determined, someone like you or me could make love to lots of beautiful women . . ."

Michael was not listening to me. "The idea that there are creatures out there like her"—he suddenly pinched his forehead, over the bare pizza crusts—"that that kind of loveliness exists in the world, and I can't reach it! It's enough to drive me insane!"

"I saw her again."

This brought him up short, as I knew it would.

"She invited me to visit her while Jack was away, and I did."

Michael looked at me rather peculiarly. "What . . . what happened?"

"I had a very nice time. We talked. She's a good talker."

"Be careful," Michael said. "Watch that you don't get in too deep."

"I know. Don't worry!" I laughed. "Nothing will happen."

I called for the check and we divided up.

VI

W hat a wonderful wheelchair!" It was antique, made entirely of carved blond wood, with a cane wicker seat. It must have been in another room of the apartment, because I had never noticed it before. It was so irresistible. I had to try sitting in it and wheeling about. "Where did you get it?"

"My friend Richard gave it to me. Didn't I tell you about him?"

"No," I said, testing the back wheels with my hands. Marie seemed to have no end of masculine admirers; I was getting used to the parade of ex-beaux' names in her account of her life, and besides, I like these stories. "Who is Richard?"

"Richard is someone I went out with in high school who went to live in Venezuela with the International Red Cross to help out in the slums?" she said, ending almost breathlessly in a question, as she always did when she tried to rush through a long sentence. It had something to do with her asthma, I thought. "Anyway, Richard is a wonderfully gentle person. He kept wanting to sleep with me, and I didn't want to sleep with him? Not because he wasn't attractive, he's very attractive, but just because—you know how sometimes someone thinks so highly of you and puts you on a pedestal, that you don't want to spoil it? So one night he had stopped the car in a grove, it was raining, and I really had to go pee. While he was trying to talk me into sex, all I could think of was that I had to go quick. I would have even made love to him, that was no big deal, but I didn't have the nerve to confess to such a mundane need."

I burst our laughing. "Did you finally get to pee?"

"I said, 'Take me home immediately!' As though he hadn't acted like a gentleman. Girls can do that. But really I just wanted to get home and run to the bathroom because I didn't dare jump out of the car in the storm. . . . Hurricane warnings! And now he lives in Venezuela, and once a year Richard comes back home and visits me and says he has not been in love with anyone since," she added, with a romantic sigh.

"At least that's what he tells you."

"And I believe him. If you knew Richard, you'd know it was possible."

"Were you a virgin then?"

"No, I had just lost my virginity a few months before. To some stuffed shirt named Morton Lewis. He was at Yale, and for some unfathomable reason I was in love with him, and he deigned to go out with me while I was in high school though he felt himself so intellectually above me and so much older and worldlier. Actually he was the unworldly one. I was already a woman in love."

"What was it like?"

"Well, when it finally happened—that's not so interesting, it's like everyone's stories of how they lost their virginity. I get so tired of telling whole stories. It's more fun when you don't."

"The beauty of fragments," I surmised. "That's such a modern idea. An unfinished sketch by Turner is considered more satisfying than the final painting."

"You sound as if you disapprove."

"No, I think fragments can be lovely," I said. "But I'm just one of those people who prefers the whole arch of the story. I'd rather hear too many details than too few. That hide-and-seek game of understatement gets wearing after a while."

"That's what I love about Melville. He wants the whole arch, too."

"Well go on," I said. "I didn't mean to interrupt."

"You weren't. There's nothing more to tell. Morton Lewis threw me over, for an older girl from *Bryn Mawr!*" She laughed. "My heart was broken. I was seventeen and in my senior year in high school. So for a graduation present my parents let me go to Sweden. I was traveling with my friend Carolee—you'll meet her, she's terrific. She's the one I'm taking this apartment with."

"I was wondering what happened to your roommate."

"She's upstate. So she and I were in a restaurant the first night in Stockholm with my Swedish cousin Karl? And we were having a heated argument about love; I was taking the side that true love was worth the energy and the risks, and Karl was being the cynic. And after a while he kept muttering something under his breath like 'Spaghetti! Spaghetti!' I couldn't understand what he meant, since this wasn't an Italian restaurant and besides we'd already ordered. It turned out he was saying, 'Sweden's-greatest-stage-actor-has been staring at you for two hours!' I looked over at the next table, where there was a beautiful young man who smiled and nodded formally at me. And the next thing I knew the beautiful young man came over to our table and touched my shoulder and signaled me to go with him and I followed him out of the restaurant. It was uncanny. Do you believe in magic?"

"Sometimes," I said doubtfully.

"Good, I was hoping you'd say that. Most of time I don't either. But this particular night there was magic in the air. Funny things kept happening. As soon as we left the restaurant we came across an American Negro who was drunk and had a cut over his left eye and was crying to himself. Sven asked him what was the matter. The black guy said he wanted to go home to Chicago. This place was all right but it was 'dead, man, cold.' Oh, the ladies had been nice to him, but it wasn't the same as his home, and he had no money to get back. Sven said something sage and cryptic—like, 'You are wise to have a home.' He took out his wallet, removed the credit cards and I.D., and gave his wallet with all his money to the Negro."

"The black guy probably spent it on something else and is still there balling Swedish ladies."

"That's what I said to Sven! But he wouldn't hear of it. At about this time it clicked in my head that a group of people had been following us a few steps behind. We would turn down the street and they would follow, standing behind arches like spies. 'Who are those odd people?' I kept thinking to myself. They turned out to be Sven's drama students from the Royal Academy, who followed him everywhere. Stayed out of his way, just wanted to observe him as much as possible? What a pretentious bunch. Oh, one thing you should know: Sven had a weak heart and he dramatized the situation by forgetting to carry his medicine around with him. So naturally the followers all kept vials of yellow pills to fling out in an emergency. I moved in with him that first night. It was nice. I was enjoying the comforts of the land and meeting all his friends, who were very sweet to me, except some of the women, which is to be expected. But I never opened up to him. I thought he struck too many poses to be taken seriously. He called me his 'little bird.' He told me once: 'My little bird, I szee a picture of my parents in it and my friends, but there is a special picture, just of *you* and *me*.' " Marie did a wonderful imitation of the man's soulful intoning accent and sleepy bedroom eyes.

"Pretty corny."

"You think it's corny? I've fallen for bigger lines. But I was so young and scared of being in a strange country; I was just trying to hang in there. I pretended to be cool and stern. I kept my mouth shut most of the time, not wanting him or his friends to find out that I was just little old Marie from Oceanside, Long Island. He would ask me, 'What did I do to make you stop loving me?'—'Nothing,' I'd say. 'I'm all right.' He couldn't understand that someone might not be purely happy after he had chosen her. And he couldn't figure it out when I just wanted to be by myself. Ordinarily I get very jealous, but I didn't really mind when he and one of his women students disappeared behind the bedroom door. They would come out later and be very sweet to me and put their arms around me. Children of Sex. It was something like a religion with them, they were so innocently sincere about spreading the faith. That was nice, I didn't mind: as long as I had my corner in the living room to do the crossword puzzles from the Sunday *Times* that my father sent me, I was all right. Sven couldn't see that that's what I cared about—my five feet of turf on the living room floor and the crossword puzzle."

"I understand."

"I know *you* do. But Sven was a different story. He always

thought, whenever I was feeling blue, that it was because of something he had done. He loved to make scenes. He was such a ham. But one night at a party he went too far. He was very drunk and he jumped on a table declaiming Russian names like *'Mayakovsky! . . . Dostoyevsky!'* 'I am not as great as Dostoyevsky,' he shouted, 'but tonight I want to make an announcement.' Pointing to me, he said, 'I realize I have been weak with you at times. I have not always been the man. But tonight I will prove to you that I am your man. I will take you to the church and marry you.' My first thought was, What's this church business? At least a *shul,* or a courthouse—how little he knows me! And what egotism to think that no one could resist marrying him! I was so humiliated I blurted out, 'You think everything is goddamn—theatre!' And I left the party. As I was leaving he stood there stunned, and I remember seeing little yellow pills flying from all corners of the room, like jujubes."

"Like jujubes!" I laughed.

"I know you like details, so I put that one in for you," Marie said offhandedly. "Afterwards I collected Carolee, who was out delivering milk with her Swedish boyfriend. And I said, 'I've had enough, I'm homesick, let's go home.' And she said, 'Good, I was getting tired of waiting for you to say that.' We went and packed and we were ready for the early morning flight at the airport. In the customs gift shop, I don't know how he found out I was leaving, but there was Sven. Dressed in a white suit, white hat, all in white, because that's what the good guys wear. 'You little fool,' he said tenderly. 'What are you doing?'

" 'I'm taking the flight to New York in an hour, that's what I'm doing, and nobody's going to stop me.' I was really tough.

" 'You little fool,' he said. 'My little bird. What are you doing?'

" 'I just told you, didn't I? I'm taking the plane, and in the meantime I want to buy some gifts for friends back home. Now you're welcome to stay with me and help pick out things if you like.'

" 'You little fool. Why do you do that? I looove you.' He was standing behind the display of whiskey bottles and looking tragically at me. I figured his heart wasn't completely broken if he could play the scene so well. But I was flattered and touched that he'd come down to the airport so early in the morning just to see me off. Carolee was trying to keep in the distance, but she was *really* impressed. Then he took off his ring and said, 'Here. You take this.'

" 'I don't think I should have your ring. I'd be taking it under false pretenses.'

" 'Why? We are engaged, no?'

" 'No! That's exactly why I don't want to take it.'

" 'Take it. You little fool, my pretty little fool. . . .' He kept holding it out to me. It was a wonderful ring too.

" 'I really don't think I should.'

" 'Let it mean whatever you want it to mean. If we never see each other, then remember, I am always thinking of you—and longing for you.'

" 'Well, in that case.' I was still undecided, and I saw Carolee motioning behind him, like, 'Go on! Take it, you idiot!' So I took it and said, 'Thank you very much, it's really pretty.' Then I kissed him good-bye and I got on the plane and went back to New York City."

"He's consistent, at least," I said. "He gives you the ring off his hand and the wallet and all his money to the Negro."

"Well, I hardly think they were the same!"

"Do you still have the ring?"

"Yah, I've got it in my drawer somewhere. I'll show it to you. Some other time, not now," Marie lit a cigarette and offered me one.

"No thanks."

"Oh, you don't smoke, that's right. I keep forgetting."

"I liked him from your description. He had a gallant style."

"Oh, Sven is a wonderful man."

"And yet, you talked about him with so much distance—shows how condescending you feel toward men."

"I don't think so. I was telling a story and so I had to tell it with distance. Especially since I was trying to make it funny," Marie stared at her cigarette, and poked it forward. "Besides, aren't men contemptuous and condescending when they tell stories about women?"

"Oh, certainly. I was only remarking that it worked the other way. Still, women have such—peculiar ideas about men."

"For instance?"

"Well, sometimes when women talk about men . . . I get the feeling they think we're so fragile, such little boys that need to be humored because our egos are paper-thin sensitive."

"I don't think all of them are—but I do think many men are that way," Marie cheerfully admitted. "And you? What's your view of women?"

"Oh . . . that would get me into too much trouble."

"Come on now."

"I don't know—I used to think there was really no difference between the two, that our minds worked the same and often women wanted the exact same things, and it would be better and safer in the long run to proceed from that assumption. Then I changed my views—I had a few experiences that changed my mind, and I went through a period of thinking that they were utterly different from men. Now I'm vacillating between the two."

"How did you think women were different?"

"Oh—more indirect, I suppose. They go at things around and around, they come at things in a more circular path. And I think they lie more than men," I admitted uncomfortably.

"You may be right. But some of that's the men's fault, because men expect women to be a certain way. It forces them to lie."

"Like how?"

"Oh, like the business of women faking orgasms," said Marie, taking me by surprise.

"I don't understand why women simply don't tell the truth about that," I answered. "They're hurting men more in the long run by deluding them and coddling their egos."

"Oh, sure. But it's such a touchy area, and in bed one can be hurt so easily."

"I guess. Still, it seems to me it would be better not to lie. I was in a situation once . . . where a woman was lying to me—about something else, because she thought the truth would shatter me. When I found out finally, I was insulted that she thought I was so breakable! We'd been living together—her name was Natalie— and even before I found out, we used to have abstract arguments about telling the truth. Natalie took the point of view that you have to lie to people you love sometimes for their own good. I could see how in the very marginal cases of borderline psychosis, it might be necessary to protect someone by withholding information, but they're so rare."

"That's why I don't like lying to children."

"I think people should treat each other as a lot stronger than they usually do, and just assume that they can take the truth," I declared.

Marie tilted her head, and said with a sudden sigh, "That's what I think too."

"Good." We shook hands. We were partners in a heady pledge; so it felt.

"But sometimes you don't know what the truth is," she objected.

"Then you just have to wait till there's a clearing."

"What about when there are two truths? Opposite ones."

"Say them both."

"You make it sound so easy," said Marie. "Men lie. They just have a different way of lying. They lie about their feelings."

"I don't."

"Maybe *you* don't, but most men do. You may be exceptional; most men I've come across—"

"I don't think I'm that exceptional. I just think it's a stereotype to say that men block off their feelings. Supposedly when men get together, we only talk about sports and the stock market! It's ridiculous. Whenever I meet a man friend, we spend nine tenths of the time talking about relationships and things like that."

Marie smiled. "But are you as honest about your feelings when you're with the woman?"

"I don't know. You'd have to ask them! You may be right." So we talked . . . It was a luxury to compare notes and impressions across sexual lines. Most of Marie's anecdotes were about men throwing themselves at her feet, yet she reserved a sardonically mistrustful view of their love; and I, for my part, was willing to cite chapter and verse from my experiences of the duplicitous unreliability of women. We were fast becoming what we had set out to be, platonic friends. I was happy that we could be so frank with each other; and I was delighted that I did not have to fall in love with her into the bargain. Oddly enough, by letting me in on all these tales of past lovers, she gave me a way of seeing her in a backstage, nonidealized manner, which inhibited the development of any romantic feelings on my part.

At least this is what I told myself. Though it had some reality to it, the greater truth was that I was falling for Marie.

When I called her a few nights later, she sounded so much sadder. She told me she had just heard from Jack. He said he would have to stay another two weeks in California; and he had been rather snappish with her on the phone. He had also implied that he was seeing another woman on the Coast. "All in all, a winning phone call. I think I'll get good and depressed. You sound terrific, though."

"I am terrific," I blurted out.

When I came over, I found Marie in a strangely lighter mood. She said she was ashamed of feeling cheerful when the phone call from Jack should have upset her more. I reassured her that it was senseless to be yanked up and down by Jack's manic-depressive string.

Now I wondered if she were starting to feel something for me. We talked, but not as fluently as the other night. My chest swelled with uncomfortable tides, and I kept following her with my eyes and forgetting to speak. Marie also seemed restless. She would break off in the middle of a comment, let out a sigh for no reason. We both apologized for being less than eloquent. I claimed it was thoughts of work that were distracting me; she said she had been feeling tired all day.

"I'm going to go out and get some cigarettes," said Marie. "Do you want to take a walk?"

"I'd love to." A walk—that was just what I'd been thinking. She locked the door; we went downstairs, headed over to Broadway, and for no reason at all began walking uptown, towards my house, instead of the usual downtown direction. This too had the effect of unnerving me. What made me most tense was that I was beginning to experience certain sensations in my body, from proximity with Marie, that made me want to press myself against something—mash my chest against hers. I had put my arm around her, pretending to do it as a friendly guiding gesture; it was a kind of brake on my urge to touch her, but I could feel there was so much more where that came from. I felt her ribs through the light cotton dress, and waves of self-restraint shook me. We went by a Japanese curio shop, and to break the silence I started talking about a Japanese film I was looking forward to seeing the next day at the Museum of Modern Art, a rare Mizoguchi. She expressed an interest in seeing it as well, so we made a tentative date to meet in the auditorium at five-thirty the next day.

Now my heart was really beating. We had made the arrangement so casually, but I knew when I brought up the subject of the film that I was hoping it would turn out that way. I could not have invited her; she needed to do that part, and she had. It was all working out like a dream, or like—magic. The night air, to add to my paranoia, was lovely. A pleasant breeze, a gentle coolness, uncrowded streets. The buildings seemed to have been pushed back to allow a valley for us to walk between. I suggested, with a lump in my throat, that we stop somewhere for a drink. We passed a neighborhood bar which I rarely ventured into—only once, in my student days, and had quickly left, finding only old men there. It had an Irish name and was darkly lit. Coonan's deteriorated facade seemed just the thing to undercut my fear of being pushed too fast by romantic conspiracy.

We sat down at a table near the door. I went up to the bar and ordered our drinks. I had gone silent. Marie was nodding her head to the music. There was a fat kid dancing to the jukebox in back, and the few other patrons were urging him on and applauding. It seemed strange for a kid who could not have been more than fourteen or fifteen to be in a bar so late at night, but his mother was alongside him, and her neighbors seemed to be regular customers. The boy had fatty deposits like breasts hanging from his chest. He moved quite well, he had an amazingly graceful balance in that heavy body; he knew all the popular steps, he wasn't shy about performing, I couldn't get enough of looking at him.

Marie gripped my hand as if to pull me back. The shock of her touch made me ask, "Why did you do that?"

"Because I wanted to. I thought about it, and then I did it."

I spoke very deliberately: "I'm scared. I feel Jack is watching us."

"Jack isn't watching us." Then she added, "It's funny—I decided that whatever you said when you finally spoke, I wouldn't believe you."

I had to smile. "You too? I was also getting paranoid."

"Why?" she said softly.

"Because . . . I opened up to you. I feel wide open now." It seemed literally true, as though from across the table her dark lips and cheekbones could walk into me on high heels. She permitted herself a smile; or was it a deep, shy blush? "Marie," I forced myself to go further, "I'm nervous about making a mistake."

"What kind of mistake?"

"Trying to make love to you."

"That's the mistake I figured you meant," Marie said, her dimples creasing.

"I don't want to do anything that will—make me—be ashamed when I see Jack again, when he comes back from the Coast."

"Things may change anyway when Jack comes back," she said cryptically.

"What do you mean? We should forget about Jack?"

"No, but Jack's not here. You're the one who brought up his name. If you're afraid of what's happening right now, it's not because of him."

"You don't feel he's watching us?" I asked. But this time I

didn't feel it either; I was just saying that because I didn't feel him, to test that the ghost was gone. We were alone in the bar, with the dancing fat kid and the others. We had melted in with the saloon regulars.

Marie shook her head, as if to say, I won't reassure you any more, nor can I understand why you're playing this game.

I was still thinking of her statement that she wouldn't believe the next thing I said, no matter what it was. That thrilled me. I asked: "Do you trust me now?"

"Should I?"

Impossible to know what to answer. Distrust was the proper due paid subtle souls. For a long indecisive moment I found myself debating between encouraging her trust or mistrust. I wanted to say aloud, Trust me! But at a certain point, like the juncture where parallel lines appear to converge, the statements "You can trust me" and "Don't trust me" had exactly the same meaning. If I honestly believed I should be trusted, I would not have to deliver the assurance, I could leave it to time. By saying it aloud I would show not only my doubt of her ever trusting me, but also an impatience with time itself, my tendency to want to control everything, to force issues, out of a fear of life unfolding. So I said nothing. I squeezed her hand.

What did it mean to be trusted in this situation?

My ears perked up. It was Charlie Parker on the jukebox. The cheeky, inexorable Parker, and he was playing *"Embraceable You."*

"Listen to this solo," I said. I knew every note by heart—I had gotten the music back. I began humming along with improvisation —she probably thought that I was being self-indulgent, or a pedant—but it was such an omen to me, connecting the past and present. This bar was in a time capsule. I put a quarter in to play the flip side, *"Out of Nowhere."* It was slower and dreamier.

Magic: the fat kid, Marie's hand grabbing mine, that that song should come on at just that moment, with its mellow reassurance, hints of danger and languor. . . . The line of Bird's solo, cutting sinuous syntaxes into my ear, gave me the confidence that there was no problem with my feelings for Marie, that everything would work out, with the same sophisticated logic of variations as in *"Out of Nowhere."* I didn't feel frightened any more; we had gone as far as we could in one night.

Marie had finished her drink. "Do you want another one?" I asked.

"No."

"Do you want to talk some more?"

"No, it's getting late."

"You want to go?"

"Sure!" she said spunkily. We both rose at the same moment.

We were out on the street. "How are you getting home?" I asked.

"A taxi."

"Good idea. Do you think you'll come to the museum tomorrow?"

"I'll try to. If I can get through a few errands I have to do first, I'll be there. If not," she said, touching my hand, "don't be disappointed."

"I won't—here's one!" I said excitedly, pointing my finger at the speeding yellow medallion and yelling, "Taxi!"

Marie kissed me: "Thanks. It was a wonderful, special evening."

"For me too." I put Marie inside the cab, kissed her good-bye again, and watched her in her summer shawl take off down Broadway, past 106th Street, the closed pet shop. I had again the sensation that the avenue had been widened, and all the city buildings spread far back, at my convenience, as I stood in the middle of the intersection, watching Marie's cab disappear, and, for a second or two immortal, daring any cars to hit me.

VII

In the morning I decided it was a terrible idea to go through with the museum date. It could only mean pulling me closer to the edge with Marie, which, given my love for Jack, would be a betrayal. It must never happen. Secondly, even if I wanted it to happen (and now thinking from the opposite viewpoint), seeing her right after last evening would be too soon, would spoil the resonance of that memory. Finally, I didn't like the way that the date was left up in the air, with her having the power to show up or not at the last minute. For all these reasons I would have to call it off. With that resolution carrying me through the morning, I came into the afternoon veering toward the decision that calling it off would only make things between us too self-conscious and melodramatic. The compromise I hit upon was a testimony to the wonderful flexibility of rationalizations: I told myself I would hide in the middle of the auditorium crowd, and we would simply miss each other. That way I wouldn't have to tell her not to come, and I wouldn't have to give up the movie.

At five I stationed myself in the prominent back row of the theatre with my eyes fixed on the incoming audience. Having put in a rough day at the agency school, I was in a cranky mood. I wanted her to come now, but I was determined that this time I would shut myself off to her attractiveness. I was building up an anger at her for getting me into this state of precarious expectations. I kept wanting to put the blame on Marie for making me infatuated with her. Like many a young man when he falls in love, my response toward the inspiration of this churning stress was not gratitude but resentment. At five twenty-seven I decided she wasn't coming. Good—she had acted to save us both.

This made me relieved; also furious at having been stood up.

Suddenly there was a noise in the aisle, someone trying to get someone's attention. Marie. People stood up to let her by.

"Am I late? I rushed as much as I could. Look!" She patted her head to show me her new hairdo.

I was so dazed I hadn't noticed. She had gotten a radically new haircut: it was very short, curving underneath in a well-cut bob, and it made her look even more stylish.

"It's very attractive."

"Feel it." Marie put my hand on her head. The hair was soft and airy. It gave me a jolt; I was frightened.

"You look like Joan of Arc," I said facetiously.

"Joan of Arc, she's my favorite saint! I was worried that you wouldn't like it . . . ?"

"No, it's lovely. I like it very much."

"I had gone with my friend Beth, and we kept wondering how different people would react. I was especially nervous how you— what Eric would think of it."

This statement shocked me. I was suspicious of her for implying that my opinion was so important to her, or that she already did things with me in mind. If she didn't mean it, it was an awfully misleading tease. I began to decide that she was nothing but an accomplished flirt.

"What's wrong? You look kind of upset," Marie stared at me.

"No I was just—feeling tired."

"Oh. You're not angry at me for being late?"

"No. In fact you aren't late."

"Oh good." She tossed her hair back and forth. "I feel like a young boy in this hairdo," she said friskily.

I thought of how delicious it would be to sleep with a woman with such a boyish scalp, and felt almost homosexually attracted to Marie.

The movie started. It was a black-and-white Mizoguchi made in the late 1930s, *The Story of the Last Chrysanthemums*. It began with a long Kabuki scene onstage; then it took us backstage where the story proper unfolded: the son of a great Kabuki actor is being given choice parts and groomed to take over the family troupe. The son is flattered and pampered on all sides, but the fact is he is not very good. Other actors gossip behind his back about his lack of talent. Only one young woman, a nurse in his family, will tell him the truth. A long tracking shot across marshy lots keeps pace alongside their first, painful conversation, in which he is both stunned and grateful to her for telling him what he knows deep down is the case.

The air-conditioning in the auditorium was on too strong. I caught Marie gazing searchingly at me, and she shivered. I put my arm around her. I convinced myself that the purpose of this was medicinal. While grazing her warm bare arm I was close to moving my hand down onto her breasts, endangering a friendship of ten years. But I didn't. I held my feelings in traction. Marie's head flopped onto my shoulder. Tender and scared, she seemed, wanting protection—anything she did could be interpreted in a number of ways. It was a relief to sink back into the movie and get away from my confusion over what to do about Marie. I loved the way Mizoguchi usually kept his camera far back, so that not only were we given the entire bodies of characters, but theatre architecture, rich shadows, Japanese lamps, streets, landscapes, passersby, a world indifferent to their hardships. I realized I had not been paying attention to the plot for several minutes. With Mizoguchi you could do that: there seemed so much calm and fluid camera movement that put your mind at rest, even as the story grew more and more inflexibly tragic. Now the hero and the nurse had run away together against the wishes of his powerful family, who disapproved of their union; the young actor began to sharpen his technique in the provinces, while the woman went to work to support him and make ends meet. After years of poverty and being buffeted around in shabby provincial theatres—the owners kicking out the drama company to make way for a troupe of lady wrestlers—the actor has finally learned his craft. But he is eaten away by bitterness, because he has no chance to join a major troupe without the patronage of a powerful Kabuki family, all of whom are boycotting him on his father's command. The woman contacts the actor's family, and agrees to their demands that she drop out of sight, in exchange for their accepting him back in the troupe. All this is done without the knowledge of the young man, who, self-involved, only discovers at the last moment on the train that his companion has run away. He searches the train, rushing from car to car in a scene of unbearable realization of loss, one of those great Mizoguchi forced partings.

The film was affecting me deeply; it made me feel sorry for myself. I was the young man without talent. But it was doubtful that I would ever find a woman willing to make such a life-giving sacrifice for me—especially in these days of feminist consciousness. Not that I didn't understand the justice of the women's movement: but still it seemed a shame that such gentle service and self-sacrifice should pass from the world. It seemed a beautiful idea that at least someone's role should have been to be better and more giving. If indeed that sort of nobility ever existed, except in the minds of artists like Mizoguchi.

Rejoining the family troupe, the actor scores an immense success. In the last scene the woman, who has fallen very ill, listens with satisfaction to the news of his triumph, in the impoverished quarters where she was hidden herself away. The film cuts between his triumphal floral parade, his boat advancing toward the camera as he accepts the tossed chrysanthemums of his followers, with tears in his eyes, understanding now how meaningless it is, and the woman dying in her bedroom.

Then the lights went on, people stirred, and I was back in the situation with Marie. I rubbed my bloodshot eyes; I decided I must look ugly. And I was annoyed at Marie, irrationally enough, because she was not like the woman in the movie.

As we left the museum, Marie asked if we could sit in Paley Park for a few minutes. "If you have a few minutes," she added imploringly, which surprised me again. It was just down the block, and she led me to it.

Paley Park was one of the first of the vest-pocket parks donated to the city by corporate largesse. There was an artificial sculptured waterfall in the background, and the sound of rushing water, a re-

freshment bar, and some white plastic chairs and tables with people sitting like posed figures in an architectural model. No doubt I
was feeling churlish, but this chichi park struck me as utterly
phony. Why did she like this place so much? To me it was nothing
but a millionaire's tax write-off; I felt I didn't belong there, but
she did.

Marie was still going on about her haircut, and about meeting
her parents in town for dinner. She told me some more of her
day. It was small talk and I kept tripping her up in a not too
kindly manner, to which she didn't know how to react. She was
trying to sparkle—and I would not let her. She's playing Daddy's
Girl, I thought cynically. Soon I'll be getting bored with her, I
convinced myself, having done for that day a successful job of
novocaining. At Fifth Avenue and Fifty-fifth Street I waved and
turned away, saying something offhand like "See you soon," but
she ran up and gave me a sudden kiss, not willing to let me go
away like that. That was beautiful of Marie. Then she skipped off.

Once, on that very same corner, some years before, I had seen
a fashion model unboarding a bus in a bright red slicker holding
a portfolio. She had looked so carefree and pretty and dainty that
I always remembered her fire-engine red as a perfect dot of
happiness. The figures of the two women now fused; I would
never be able to think of the first woman without giving her
Marie's hopeful face. I walked home, wondering if I had been
wrong about Marie. I had accused her of being a flirt, because
I couldn't quite believe that anyone of her quality could actually
care about me, feel romantic about me. Yet today seemed to have
been an important rendezvous for her. She had shown her
partiality to me all afternoon, and I kept—pushing her away,
making it into something ugly. She seemed to be sure of her affection for me, and willing to take responsibility for it. I was the one
who was the flirt.

VIII

There was only one thing to do. Speak to Jack. I decided to call him long distance. I was hungry to talk to him anyway.

We spoke for a long while about friendlier matters. I described my new job with Project Turnaround, making it sound more picaresque than it was. He spoke about the people at whose house he was staying, their characters, and the general San Francisco-Berkeley scene. I told him I had just finished reading a beautiful story by Robert Musil called *The Perfection of a Love.* This was my first, circuitous broaching of the subject on my mind: the story was about a woman who is unfaithful to her husband with a gross stranger, because of some uncanny pull toward promiscuity, or because, Musil suggests also, the adultery is necessary to "perfect" the married couple's love. Jack knew the story already, in fact it was one of his favorites; and we were amazed again at the similarities of our tastes. Unfortunately, this took us into a discussion of Musil's cleanly mystical prose style in *Five Women,* and of the problem in modern fiction of balancing the subjective and the objective in narration.

I had almost patiently resigned myself to the converstation going around and around in the realms of art, when Jack said something like: "But how are you, Eric?" It was a code-sentence that the conversation was about to plunge down another level. I liked his habit of saying my name, inserting it into the conversation like a reassuring pat on the shoulder.

"I'm all right."

"How is it going with you? Have you made the adjustment to the city yet?" he asked sympathetically, "or is it still unsettling?"

"Well—I'm feeling lonely a lot. New York's fine, I don't mind it but . . . to be honest, I'm too much by myself."

"Sometimes that can be enjoyable."

"The enjoyment has its limits."

"If it's a certain kind of loneliness, I don't want to sound trite, but—" Jack paused, "my best moments out here have been when I get up at dawn and walk around alone with the fog coming in by University Avenue. At that hour it's deserted except for a coffee shop for truckers and people who go to work early. Those are the times I'm most at peace with myself. But I have to be alone to contact it."

"I understand what you mean, and I've experienced that too, plenty of times. But there's a difference between solitude, which you're describing, and loneliness," I said.

"How would you describe that difference?"

"Solitude is self-affirming. You feel powerful and cosmic, above the world. Loneliness is dependency on others. Like a child who's afraid when his mother leaves him. It's degrading."

"But sometimes when I'm in that walking mood," answered Jack, "I start to get a very strong yearning for other people. And it doesn't always make me feel powerful. I think my own distinction is between what you call, 'lonely'; and 'lonesome.' 'Lonesome' is kind of a nice warm longing and being imaginative about sadness, which can be very likeable, don't you agree? I hope you're feeling lone*some,* Eric."

I laughed mildly. "I do too." I was laughing partly because he wished it on me so earnestly that he almost convinced me I was content. The coercive good wishes of close friends do have their restraining effects. "And how are you doing?" I asked.

"I'm all right. My cough is getting cleared up."

"I should imagine so, with all that California sunshine. Have you been seeing anyone out there?" I asked delicately.

"You mean for the cough?"

"No, not for the cough! Have you been 'dating' anyone?"

"I have been seeing one woman, as a matter of fact. Why?" he said suspiciously.

"Just curious. It's the kind of thing one friend likes to know about another."

"We met a week ago. Her name is Bernadette. There's a strong spiritual pull between us."

"Does that mean you're not sleeping together?"

"No. We sleep together. But the relationship is fundamentally spiritual. She has a strong understanding of inner life, and I feel I need to be around that at this moment." His voice was getting edgy.

"Won't Marie mind?"

"I'm sure she will mind," Jack retorted testily. "But Marie and I have a peculiar relationship anyway."

"In what way?" I asked.

"Well, I don't know that I can go into that without betraying confidences; but we're still new to each other, and there's a lot that hasn't been worked out yet. I'm not exactly sure it will ever be worked out."

"I've seen Marie."

"I know. She told me."

His voice had become quite formal now. I took a deep breath: "I've seen her a couple of times. I just wanted you to know."

"What about it?"

"She's . . . I'm awfully attracted to her."

"She's a pretty woman. That's not surprising. Most men who meet her are," Jack said.

"But what I mean is—she's also attracted to me a bit. So it's difficult. I think you ought to get home soon." I was choosing my words so carefully that the sound was coming out very thinly.

"I'm sorry, I didn't hear what you just said," injected Jack.

"I said, maybe you should come home soon."

"I'll come home when it's feasible for me to come home. I don't know what you're trying to say, Eric. Is this a threat?"

"I'm not threatening you, I'm trying to be a good friend. I'm just trying to be honest."

"And I appreciate that. But there's nothing I can do from here. Marie's a free person, she can do what she wants. I'm not going to keep strings on her and try to control her actions from three thousand miles away."

That wasn't what I had wanted to hear. I wanted to be told *No, you can't do this:* to be forbidden like a child. All this modern talk about freedom was getting us nowhere. "Well," I said, "supposing that something like our getting together did happen . . ."

"I'm not going to predict how I would react! Do you want assurances? All I can say is that she would have to accept the consequences for her actions. And you would too. All of us would."

"I know that, Jack," I said impatiently. "That isn't what I was asking."

"Well you shouldn't try to put me in a position where I have to predict how I would react."

I couldn't figure him out, this wasn't even an issue with me, but it was so important to him—this jazz about making him predict how he would react. I must have touched a sore spot in his therapy. You never could tell what was going to be the one thing to upset people. I let out a frustrated sigh. In any case he was right and I was wrong, I reflected, so it didn't matter what part he chose to get angry at. My job was to give him my word simply that I would keep my hands off Marie.

"I'm sorry for putting you in that position," I stated. "Look, the whole thing is academic. I would never allow myself to do anything like that anyway—make love to my best friend's girl behind his back. I don't go around betraying friends. You know that. I'm just talking about it to get it off my chest."

"I know. I understand—you're tempted."

"Well I *was* tempted. I admit. But putting this out in the open is helping to clear away the temptation for me. Sometimes I have to speak the possibility out loud to realize it's wrong. I'm sorry that I gave you a bad moment back there."

"Don't be sorry, Eric. You were being honest. I wish I could be that direct. It takes guts. Half the time I do things without any premeditation; I fall into stupid situations from sheer shortsightedness."

"No, you're pretty self-aware."

"Well, thanks for saying that, but I don't deserve it. Lately I've been trying to keep my eyes open—to be more like you, tough-minded, clear about what I want—instead of going around myopic-wishful-moony like a dimestore Werther."

"You're getting there all right."

"I don't know." We spoke for a few minutes longer, until finally Jack said, "Listen, I've got to get off." We had said all we had to say anyway. We both felt kind again toward each other.

"Listen, take care of yourself, okay?" he said urgently. "Try not to be so lonely—that can really sap you."

"I'll be less lonely when you get back from the Coast."

"I should be back in two weeks at most."

"Give my best to everyone out there."

"I will. Be good to yourself, Eric."

"I will. You too—you be good to yourself too, Jack."

IX

Ifelt mature about giving up Marie. Renunciation always left me strong and clarified: it made for a bitterness around the edges, like a flame that leaves a black charred halo on a matchbook, but my center was purer. Sydney Carton's speech on the scaffold, "It is a far, far better thing that I do, than I have ever done," came into my mind, and its floweriness did not embarrass me a bit. One should be allowed a certain amount of posturing in compensation for relinquishing a desire, it seemed to me.

Another compensation was that, now that we were not going to become lovers, we could relax more easily into friendship. I had never said I was going to give up Marie's acquaintance. In fact we had already fallen into the habit of talking on the telephone every day, making stories out of our daily rounds: a rainstorm, a run-in at the dry cleaners. We seemed to know a lot already about each other's routines and circles of friends, so that the need to supply background explanation kept growing less.

Now that the taboo had been set in place, we were also able to speak more freely about her relationship with Jack. It was the major problem on Marie's mind, and so it was bound to come up, and only a matter of time before Marie turned me into her confidant. I was prepared for the role: I knew how to give staunch brotherly support. Still, it was painful to learn how very much Marie was in love with Jack, and to listen to her casting about for any crumbs of evidence to reassure her that his feelings were equally engaged.

One day I asked her on the telephone, out of curiosity, how she and Jack first met. I wanted to hear it as a romantic story, and she obliged.

A year before, Marie was living in London, and she came down with pneumonia. At the time she had been going with "a very funny Englishman," named Teddy, who was also a friend of Jack Bogardes'. One day Teddy brought Jack around when he was visiting her; Teddy often came by to see if she needed any food or company. Marie was propped up in her sick bed, and (according to her), "looking as unappealing as you can possibly imagine," but she was happy to have visitors. That first day Jack was so shy he could barely bring himself to look at her. After a while she had to go to sleep. Jack went away, leaving her with Teddy. "And somewhere around then Teddy said a very peculiar thing to me, which I never forgot: he said, 'Now you've met Jack Bogardes. By the end of the year you'll probably be with him.' "

The next time Teddy came to call he arrived with Jack again, and Jack was even more nervous than the first time. He had brought her flowers, and he had a ridiculous tie on and he never looked at her once, except for offering the flowers, then giving his whole attention to Teddy. At the end of the visit Jack said he was leaving for Germany and he had wanted to wish her a get-well before he left.

Marie thought: that's the end of that. But in the next month, letters and postcards kept arriving for Teddy from places like Frankfurt and Berlin and Rome, with cautious little P.S.'s at the bottom asking after "Miss Curtin's health." It was always Miss: he never took the liberty of calling her by her first name.

A few months later, Marie was back in New York City, having pretty much recuperated from the pneumonia. One day Jack called on her at her apartment. He was circumspect at the beginning; but having ascertained finally that there was nothing going on any more between Teddy and herself, which she had had to keep reassuring him was the case, he asked her out on a "date." She was really happy, she said, because she'd liked him right away, and thought him very intelligent. Their first evening together they got along so naturally that—they went to bed. "I just trusted him: there was something about the way his hand felt in my hand, the temperature of his hand, and his curly hair, something adorable about him. Endearing—I can't explain."

He was very attentive also, and they had a wonderful time. He called her his "hoyden," a name she loved, and they had days of fooling around like kids in a nursery.

Then he began to brood. She thought she had done something wrong, or maybe he wanted to be left alone; she could understand that. One time she asked him: "Do you want me to go?" and he said: "It makes no difference." So she gathered up her shoes and things, and said "Good-bye," sweetly at the door. "No, stay!" he cried. "I didn't mean that; I really do want you to stay." So she stayed. But it kept happening: he would start to get that grieving look, and she would be patient and try to make him talk about what was bothering him. Finally she got him to open up: he was missing his old girl friends. That was all right. Whenever she had gone out with a man, there were always ghosts around: they'd either just been jilted or broken up with someone, or were coming out of a marriage, which prevented them from taking her quite seriously. When she visited the man's apartment for the first time, there would be photographs of this one and that one on the walls. "So I would nurse him back to life with my optimistic spirits and good cheer and my youth. And after a while, the pictures started to come down."

But with Jack it was different. She had had to wade through armies of ghosts. There was first of all Vicky, the great love of his life, the only one who truly loved him. . . .

"I know: he thinks it was the biggest mistake of his life not to have married her," I said.

"Especially now that *she's* married. She didn't wait long, either. Then there's Jeanne, the one in London. He tell you about her?"

"A little."

"She keeps writing him letters. Every time he gets a letter from Jeanne, it sends him into confusion for a week. Then his old flame Phoebe, and Anna, and Claire, and maybe a few others I don't know about. It's endless. But this little California wood nymph is the limit. Not that I care about his sleeping with someone else. But I do mind hearing that she's more 'spiritual' than I am."

"Did he actually compare you?"

"He told me that she had a very developed spiritual side. And he told me once that I didn't. Oh, it infuriates me, this piousness of Jack's!"

"I don't understand what 'spirituality' means to Jack," I interrupted. "He keeps harping on it. What did he tell you exactly?"

"What he told me, the first time, is one of my most hurting memories. We were in bed—where most homicides are committed —and he got that dark, little boy's look in his eye as if he wanted to go away? And I forced him to tell me in what way he thought I wasn't good enough for him. He told me: he said I wasn't spiritual enough. I could have strangled him. I asked him what he meant by that, and he just sat up and said—it was some definition from the Sufis, something about intense and invisible communication— I don't even remember, I was so furious."

Jack's criticism surprised me. To me, Marie was almost all Spirit, too airborne, if anything, not enough methodical prose. "I don't think he's right," I said. "But go on."

"Of course he's not right. I have more spirituality in my pinky than he has all over. But it's not really about who's more spiritual, I think that's just a cover-up."

"For what?"

"I don't know. It's endless."

"Is it worth it?" I asked.

"It's never worth it, or it's always worth it. But—you know what I was saying before about when the pictures start coming down from the walls, and the names of old girl friends stop popping up as if by accident? That should be victory time for me. But it usually makes me sad. There's a vacuum. Maybe it's loyalty to those other women; or a suspicion that, boy, how believable can this man's love be if he's already forgotten them? Men are *so* fickle."

"Or maybe you're sad because you no longer have any resistance from the past to fight against, and it's not as much fun any more. Now you're faced with this man's love and it's frightening. It's like facing the heat of an oven."

"I've thought of that. It would be awful if it were true. . . . But I don't think it is."

"Why not?"

"It would mean that I couldn't love, and I don't want to believe that about myself."

"Yes, right. It's an impractical idea," I said with grim irony.

"I *like* to think that I can love—don't you? I do think I'm able to receive a person's love, no matter how hot it gets and I think what frightens me is not warmth but hostility, deadness. I'm not frightened by tenderness. Really I'm not; it's what I love most in the world."

"No I know you're not. I just meant that perhaps you—thrive more on that early stage of removing barriers, because it's a challenge. And the vacuum you speak of is where the mistrust had been. And with Jack, of course, you can go a long way without ever getting to that vacuum; so you're safe, in a sense, with him."

"You think I'm safe with him?" she repeated in a sleepwalker's voice, as if she had only heard the last part of my statement.

"Yes. I do."

"Oh. . . . Good," she sighed. She seemed suddenly reassured. In another minute we hung up.

X

That weekend Carolee, Marie's roommate, had come down to the city, to pick up a few things she needed for her summer camp job. Marie threw together a party for her Saturday night, and invited me to come. I was not sure I wanted to come, because I was still feeling fragilely romantic toward Marie, and to go to a party on Saturday night with her seemed a mockery of my feelings. But in the end I went. Several of her friends introduced themselves: nice young people, preppy, well groomed, none as sparkling as Marie; they all seemed to have heard about me. I discovered I was a kind of star guest—as well as the oldest one there.

We had had a lot to eat and drink, and were sitting on Marie's fluffy white rug, thinking of how nice it would be to get out of the city and go up to the country for a day. Carolee had to return upstate the next day, and was dreading having to lug her boxes on the Greyhound bus and then hike into camp with them. "If only we could get hold of a car, we could drive you up," said Marie. Both her parents' cars were locked up in the garage, and they had gone to Israel for a vacation. No one else seemed to know where a stray car could be borrowed.

"My mother has a car," I spoke up finally. "She lives in Brooklyn, we could go over there in the morning and pick it up."

"Do you think she would let us borrow it?" They turned to me with interest.

"She could probably be convinced," I said, though it struck me as ridiculous that I, the poorest one in the room, should be offering my parents' beat-up car for this Sunday excursion. But everyone else seemed to think it was very sensible, and the best opportunity available. In the company's presence, I found myself dialing my mother's number and asking her if we could borrow her car for a few hours tomorrow. The request was so unprecedented— she knew I couldn't drive—that she must have figured it was important, and said yes as soon as I assured her that there were several licensed drivers in our party. My good-hearted mother must have gotten the idea that I couldn't let down "the gang." Visions of collegians in football sweaters and Rudy Vallee megaphones floated into mind: in truth, it was a pretty wholesome bunch. How did I get mixed up with them?

"My mother says it's all right. We can pick up the car anytime tomorrow morning."

"Great!" Marie sat next to me and gave me an impulsive kiss. Then she smiled demurely, as if to show me she knew I might take it the other way. I found myself extracting an additional reward, a close hug. She left her arm around my waist as we continued with the party. Everyone seemed to assume we were lovers, and we were certainly acting like it that night.

The next morning, at seven-thirty as planned, Marie came to my house to pick me up. The others were waiting downstairs. She walked into the Kroegels' clumsy apartment and lent it her grace. I was barely awake, and parts of my body, my cheeks, my legs, brow, were still asleep, so that it was all I could do to watch her taking in the room and—studying me. She kept looking at me as if for a sign. Since I didn't know what she was expecting, only that she was acting very strange, I let her look around as much as she wanted, and then suggested that we join the others downstairs.

(Later on, several days later, she told me what was going through her mind. She had almost decided to offer herself to me right then, to get it over with. I had no idea she was in the same state of nerves as I was.)

Only Carolee, with her bags, and Beth, another friend of Marie's, had shown. Beth would do the driving. She was a taciturn, bulky girl with one ear mashed against her cheek, whom

Marie informed me was "very intelligent," though it was hard to tell how *very* because she spoke so little.

We were about to descend into the subway when I said to Marie, "Let's take a taxi there."

"Good idea!"

"You're crazy, you can't take a taxi all the way to Brooklyn," Carolee said.

"It's cheap, split four ways. Right?" said Marie, looking excitedly at each of us with her let's-live-a-little expression.

"I'm for it," I said, sticking my index finger out.

"I'd rather take the subway," said Carolee moralistically.

"Oh, don't be like that."

A yellow cab was already slowing down on Broadway.

"Oh good, a checker," said Marie. She and Beth took the jump seats. Marie started talking to the driver, then swerved around and faced us; she was a girl going to a picnic. Carolee and I sat in the backseat, a bit wearier, the grownups. I had the intuition that Carolee disapproved of me: not so much because of anything she had said, but because of her set, tight mouth and her refusal to smile when I told a joke. It was too bad because I liked Carolee. She was nice to look at, a tall leggy girl with dirty blond hair and an honest, principled expression. It finally occurred to me that she was being loyal to Jack. Of course! It was natural for the roommate, who was used to seeing Jack in the role of Marie's male companion, to disapprove of me as a sneak.

Eventually we got to my parents' house. It was a depressing project building, one in a row of Mitchell-Lama towers built for lower-income families. We took the elevator to the eleventh floor. I was a little ashamed of the graffiti scratched into the elevator walls, although Marie smiled and hummed. It was all part of the adventure for her: she was an absolute chameleon, she could fit in anywhere. She charmed my mother, who was explaining to her the functions of the different keys, while my father watched sleepily from the sofa. We shared a masculine grin. Marie had to stop my mother to explain that she wasn't the driver, Beth was. She pushed her quiet friend forward, everybody laughed, and my mother started her speech all over again about the different keys.

"The brake slides, kinda. You have to go down all the way hard with your foot. You'll feel it, you'll see what I mean. It needs to be tightened. I really should have brought it down to Gus's shop. Damn!" my mother swore.

"Don't worry. We'll bring it back all right," I said.

"I'm not worried. Why should I worry?"

"Thank you so much, Mrs. Eisner, you're really being great," exclaimed Marie, hugging her, to my mother's surprise.

"Why should I worry," said my mother, "with a couple of experienced drivers in the car?" winking at Beth and Carolee.

"So long. Have fun," said my father, clearing his throat.

"We will!" We were off to the country.

Everyone was talking so much in the car that we barely noticed leaving the city and driving through industrial Yonkers, which led onto the landscaped parkway, where the country part proper seemed to begin. We got into a conversation about scientific curiosities, and Marie was telling us about eyelid worms—organisms that lived on people's eyelids, but were too small to see without a microscope. We made lots of puns about these worms, all hilarious at the time, none which would survive transplantation.

Tree branches hit against the window sides as we took a narrower road off the highway. Conversation became subdued after two hours of driving. I leaned my head against Marie, she put her arm around my shoulder and we rode the rest of the way in silence.

Camp Mohunkus was on an old estate whose buildings had been reconverted into bunkhouses and mess halls. As we got out of the car, uncramping our legs, we were impressed by the lushness of the grounds.

Carolee took us into the Art Barn, where she was a special counselor. It was busy and vast. In every corner of the sun-invaded A-shaped frame were looms, casts, easels, kite constructions, lathes, jewelry-making machines, kilns, vises, pegboards crammed with tools, tri-wall furniture, dollhouses, a marionette stage, puppets, movie cameras, tripods, darkrooms, poster paints, macrame —everything that a progressive enriched environment for privileged kids could offer. It was *too* enriched: if I were a child it would give me a headache. Not a square of the barn wall wasn't hung proudly with some child's painting or handicraft. Carolee took us around, and soberly explained each activity corner and the purpose of every machine. She knew her stuff; there was no shaking her. I asked Carolee about the philosophy of the camp; and the two of us engaged in a discussion of educational theories, Summerhill, open classrooms. She was intelligent, informed, and —she still disapproved of me.

"What's that?" asked Marie, going over to an intriguing device.

"That's our bookbinding machine."

"God, the equipment!" I groaned. "I wish I could bring one-hundredth of it back for my students in East Harlem."

"It's taken years for the staff to put together all this equipment," Carolee said defensively. "Do you want me to show you how it works, Marie?"

"No thanks. . . . Some other time."

"Well, I have to be getting to work. The head counselor saw me come in, and he'll be expecting me to take a group. I'll leave you here. Why don't you enjoy the grounds? Walk around. You can stay for dinner, can't you?"

"I really wish we could but we have to get the car back. But I think we will take a walk around—is that all right?" Marie asked me.

"Sure." I didn't understand why she was giving me the power to decide.

"I think you'll find it's a lovely place. *I* love it here. Anyway. You may not agree," Carolee said.

"It's so peaceful. I feel like taking a nap . . ." Marie yawned.

"Well I'll leave you here, if you don't mind. Good-bye, Marie. Thanks for everything." They embraced with roommates' warmth. "Good-bye, Beth; good-bye, Eric, it was nice talking to you."

So Carolee left us.

We stepped outside; the country overwhelmed us. It was so honeyed, so green and various; yet as we strolled around, I forgot to keep noticing it. I rounded it off in my mind into a basic countryside, content to catch the nuances through my pores. Joy is better when you don't have to pay close attention, and can let it lap at you like the tongue of a distracted dog. The countryside was for me that day a Great Dane who keeps putting his rough, wet, handsome paws on you and then goes trotting off.

We lay down on the sloping pasture in front of the mess hall. Marie was next to me, vibrant, like a bee hanging in the air. Beth sat away from us, the perfect third party, looking straight ahead over the fields. Kids passed by on their way into lunch; I didn't think about them much. Then they started passing closer, spying on us, as if expecting Marie and me to neck.

"What are you thinking?" I asked, looking down at her light blue linen skirt.

"I was just thinking how different this was from the camp I went to. It's nice here, isn't it?"

"Wasn't the camp you went to nice?"

"It could have been, but I had an awful time. Some mean older girls grabbed me and painted me red. My mother had to come up and get me and bring me back. What are you laughing at?"

"I remember, when I was at camp," I said, "I was crossing a large bare field and some big boys grabbed me and—took my pants off and ran away with them. That was the most humiliating thing that could happen to you."

"I'll bet!" Marie said suspensefully. "So what did you do?"

"I ran after them. I started crying. No, I didn't cry. If I remember correctly, it wasn't as terrible as I imagined. There was even something pleasurable about being held down and having my pants pulled off. I started walking to the bunk, completely naked from my waist down, and then I turned around again, hoping that they might have ditched them somewhere. Sure enough, my pants had been thrown down in the field. The horrible part was asking myself what I would do if I ran into those same boys again. I stayed away from that back field as much as possible."

"And did you run into them?"

"Not that I know of."

"That's a relief! Let's ask Beth if she wants to join us. I feel bad about leaving her out." Marie started to get up, and saw that some boys had been eavesdropping on us. She gave them a bug-eyed, mock-stern look, and they laughed twice as hard. "Let's *go*. These bushes have ears."

As we walked over to Beth, I noticed that Marie's long, milky legs had been crisscrossed with grass marks.

We collected Beth (she had no extraordinary camp traumas to tell), and went back to the car. It was decided that we would go swimming at a nearby lake, which Carolee had told us how to reach, and eat later. "Mustn't swim on a full stomach," said Marie.

It was a family lake. From above, near the parking lot, we could see the tan pebbled beach packed with children and life-guards; sedentary elders on blankets; town boys hurling frisbees; dogs chasing each other, pre-teen-age girls taking three steps into the water and then screaming and running back with their hands up. Turquoise cushions roped off a square of safety, and at the outer edge of it was a floating dock for stronger swimmers to have something to head for. It was all rather tame, urban and crowded, not at all what we'd had in mind when we pictured a country lake. Naturally we city folk had imagined they would hold the water and the landscape empty for us until we arrived. Once I had gotten over this disappointment, though, it was amusing in the way that unwinding families and cranky children usually are, if you don't have to be a member of the family. Beth spread her beach towel out on the soil, and turned her back to us to do some serious sunning.

"I'm going in," said Marie.

"I think I will too."

"Beth, we're going for a swim. Want to come?"

"No, I think I'll stay here and mind the stuff."

"Are you sure? We can take turns, you know. I'll watch the stuff first if you and Eric want to swim."

"No, I think I feel like staying here," said Beth mildly. I was grateful to her, whether she knew it or not, for letting me be alone with Marie. She turned her head toward the sand and shut her eyes.

Marie ran intrepidly into the lake with a belly whop. I was more cowardly about the cold water, but when I finally did immerse myself, I followed her lead, copying whatever she did. She knew how to play in the water, it was her medium.

Marie had on a leopard two-piece bathing suit, with yellow and black spots. I would lose her for a moment, and then be drawn to that insanely enticing leopard skin. She smiled at me. Somehow it seemed as if we were truly alone with each other for the first time. Just there for ourselves, without any inhibitions. The water was crowded with young bathers, of course, but they didn't count. I looked at the sky, the trees, and her, and felt—utterly healthy, in a way I had even forgotten I could feel.

"It's lovely here," I said. "Contented, Marie?"

"I'm not Marie," she answered wickedly. "You have me confused with someone else."

"I'm sorry, you looked exactly like a woman I know."

"A likely story!"

"Who are you, then?"

"That's for you to guess."

"You're—Moby Dick!"

"Wrong!"

"You're a dolphin."

"Not even close . . ."

"I could have sworn you were a dolphin from your smile: one of those smart ones with a high I.Q. Who could you be? I know: you're the White Rock girl."

"How insulting!"

"Are you—a mermaid?"

"I'm a mermaid, yes," she said primly.

"Do you come here often?"

"I live here!"

"My God, but you're pretty."

"That's what they all say—all you sailors."

"But I'm not a sailor."

"They all say that at first. And then they want to marry me. But they can't marry me, no one can. Because I'm all scales below the waist."

"What a shame. What a great pity! . . . But I could marry you, because I'm a merman."

"Don't come closer."

"Why not?"

"You're a *monster!*" she said.

"I am a monster. How did you know?"

"I know a thing or two," she replied mysteriously.

"Oh, yeah? What kind of monster you think I am?"

"A sea monster, of course. You come from the deep, with your hair all matted. Neptune. You're so strong, you move the waves."

That sounded nice. "And you? what about you?"

"I'm a porpoise," she said with absolute conviction, metamorphosing. She looked so voluptuous then, something like a porpoise. The cut of her bathing suit showed her rounded breasts, the line between them, and suddenly I wanted to fondle the cups.

I caught her in my arms and kissed her.

"Why did you do that?"

"I did it on porpoise."

She laughed, then looked at me scoldingly. It was a look such as women give you in dreams, one moment signifying "How dare you?" and the next moment liquidly assenting to anything. Moving toward her as though in a dream, I put my arms on her shoulders, my legs loosely around her thighs, and kissed her on the lips. My tongue reached into her mouth, our tongues glided around each other slowly, like goldfish. It seemed so private to be concentrating on our tongues' chase, this inner, silvery swimming, surrounded by people who could never see it. The sun warmed my shoulders. Still kissing her, I put my hands over her breasts for the first time. It was a wonderful feeling. She sighed, and drew me closer to her so that she could have my chest hard against hers. She pulled back her face for a moment—I thought, perhaps, she would push me away; but it was only to catch her breath a second, and bring her mouth forward and dreamily search out my tongue again. I felt my penis bulge against her.

"You mustn't do that."

"What am I doing?"

She didn't answer, but dropped underwater, and reappeared several yards away with a flash of teeth. I stood there, wondering what to do next. My heart was already swimming out to her; it had tried to leave my chest and was pushing towards her with such an ache. I suddenly understood those songs about your heart bursting. It was painful to feel so much swelling. I waited until it lessened a bit; I wanted to come behind Marie and trick her. Ducking underwater, I rammed her from behind.

She pretended to be shocked. I splashed her. She kicked water at me and swam away laughing; and I followed after her, panting because she was a better swimmer than I. "Stay still!" I called.

She turned around and faced me. "What?"

"Stay still for a moment," I said. "You're like a guppy, you never stay still." I caught up to her.

"No more kissing," she warned.

"All right, no more.—Just *one* more."

She smiled dubiously. I felt the whole sunshine of the day come down on me when she smiled so.

"I know you, you'll say just one more and then you'll change your mind and add a few more, and a few more, and we'll never get out of the water."

"No I won't. I'm reformed."

"Reformed, ha! You want to kidnap me—you're a *monstruo.*"

"No I'm not. Not any more. I just want one kiss and then I'll go in."

"Promise?"

"I promise."

Marie came up to me and closed her eyes. The sun was sparkling on her freckles through my wet eyelashes as I closed my eyes to kiss her. I had an insatiable hunger to kiss Marie, and to feel her warm flesh tingling against me. And I was doing it! What a rare coming together of need and satisfaction! I was at the right place at the right time, doing exactly the right thing. Life is so incongruous most of the time, it is worth remembering that there are those moments of absolute appropriateness.

"That was pretty," said Marie, when we stopped.

"I wish it could go on and on."

"You said only one now," she warned, and started wading toward the shore.

"But you know," I called over, "I wasn't the only one who made those kisses before. I didn't steal them from you; you gave them to me."

"I know. But a gentleman wouldn't say that."

"I guess I'm not a gentleman!" I snorted, hurt in spite of myself.

"You don't have to tell *me* that," Marie laughed. Then, seeing me pout, she came back and said: "I like you better for not being a gentleman. I've known too many gentlemen." She tugged at my arm; I smiled reluctantly. "I mean that sincerely. You're very manly and I like it." Marie looked down with shyness. I felt bashful myself. "Come on, don't fret," she said.

"I won't."

The beach population had changed since we'd been gone. We studied the newcomers, watched the overhead clouds. Then, all at once it was enough—we changed out of our wet suits with the aid of towels, and headed for the car, glad to be going home.

On the way back, we praised the Plymouth, which was over twelve years old and made ominous engine knocks but still got us down the highway. We praised Beth, for driving so well. And we praised my mother, for being such a good sport to trust us with her car (which I knew was very dear to her). The horses we passed, the fields we rode over, the mellow air we breathed—all of these came in for our salutes and praises. Maybe we overdid it. Presently there began to be a singed smell near the dashboard. The odor of burning rubber was too close to be coming from New

Jersey; it was definitely inside the car, and while it was too early to panic, everyone decided for prudence's sake it would be a good idea to pull over. As it happened, we were coming right into Hawthorne Circle, that gruesome traffic-sorter where five main roads converge. Just as we were pulling onto the gravel there was a pop, a whiff of smoke, panic; we all jumped onto the soft shoulder and ran, expecting the car to blow sky-high with orange flames. It didn't; it just sat there. We crept back to it, cautiously. Beth tried the motor again, but it wouldn't engage. Knowing nothing about fixing cars, all I could think was that the engine had overheated. I found a rusty paint can in the backseat and ran down the road to get water, trying to function "manly" in the emergency. There was a water fountain nearby, and I filled the can and came back to the car, pouring it in what Beth assured me was the right spout. She slid behind the wheel again and turned the key. The motor refused to engage. I decided that the best thing to do was to leave it alone for a few minutes. "Sometimes if you walk away from machinery, it gets better on its own." I had nothing on which to base this reasoning except wishfulness. Yet the idea appealed to everyone: so we stood away from the car with our arms folded, talking about other things, in the hope that the problem would gradually get bored and disappear. When at last, after ten minutes of ignoring it, Beth got set to try the engine again, and it failed with a dull consistency that was every moment adding verisimilitude to a situation we had hoped would prove unreal, I knew that this was going to be one of those horrible messes. God had several of these horrible messes waiting for me, ready to sprinkle like carpet tacks in my path (and I never believed in God more fervently than at these moments). The only question was whether such a catastrophe as this was completely random, or whether I was being punished for feeling so ecstatic and carefree in the water. It was petty of God to pull me back on so tight a leash, since He knew I didn't believe in permanent happiness. Why did I have to be taught such obvious lessons?

Marie caught me arguing with unseen forces and gave me a cheerful nudge. She had the ability to see this too as part of the adventure. A green-uniformed policeman came toward us, a member of the highway patrol with a broad-brimmed hat. We told him the problem. He scratched his nose; he had no idea what to do either. "I'm not a mechanic. The only thing I can suggest," he said slowly, savoring our eagerness, "is to call the tow truck. There's a place in town, Napolitano Brothers, they'll do it for you. But it'll cost you. Thirty-five dollars at least, maybe fifty, maybe more. They may charge more because it's Sunday."

"Well can we call them and find out?" I asked briskly. He gave me an odd look.

"You don't see any telephone booths around here, do you?" he said.

"No I don't, but there must be *some* place to call from—"

"Is there somewhere we could call from around here?" Marie repeated the question, only more liltingly.

"I could call from my car," the officer answered Marie, preferring to address her and ignore me—to treat this intervention as a personal favor to her.

"That would be terrific!" she said.

"I don't even know if they're open on Sunday. They might be closed. You can't leave it here overnight, that's for sure: it's illegal. I'm doing you a favor by letting you park here now, but this isn't a legal parking place."

"We appreciate it, officer," I interjected. The policeman shot me a whimsical look, full of held-in power, as if to say, "When will this guy ever learn?" Then he looked at the gravel and smoothed it out with his foot: he was giving me a lesson in protocol.

I was wondering why he kept standing around: why didn't he just go to his patrol car already and make the call? Was he expecting a bribe? More likely, he wanted a long, close look at Marie. He took his highway patrol hat off and creased the brim. Well, it was beyond me, this macho code of the provinces. I would keep my mouth shut from now on.

The officer waggled over to his patrol car, and sat in the front seat making calls for twenty, thirty minutes. Then he told us that a tow truck would be coming by somewhere between an hour or two hours, after they had finished a few other jobs. "It seems a lot of cars stalled on the highway today, and these people had phoned in first."

How were we going to get through the next hour? We had already been at Hawthorne Circle for ninety minutes, and I was growing nauseous looking at the bottleneck of automobiles sending their gasoline fumes into the quiet, unprotesting sky: that same clump of lemon sky with the barren field in the distance; the red brake lights flashed on in car after car as they approached the traffic signal, automobiles braking from six directions, edging into the circle and crawling along, until they had found their lead-out road. Dusk had fallen, it was to be a foggy nightfall, with a chill, more than we were dressed for in our summer clothes, and I wondered why it was so chilly for the end of July: maybe because we were exposed and the wind had that big open field to cross.

A tremor ran through me. I put my arm around Marie.

"Are you starting to get cold?" I asked.

"I'm okay. How about you?"

"I'm shivering."

"I'm sorry," she said. "Want my shawl?"

"No thanks. Just stay that way, and I'll rob some of your body heat."

"Okay." Marie let me cuddle closer to her. "What are you thinking about?"

"I was thinking . . . about us."

"And what conclusions did you come to?"

"I don't know. . . . We've been seeing so much of each other. Don't you think it's dangerous?"

"Yes?" She said it softly. I felt our hips press against each other, like Siamese twins joined at the hip: that constant pressure, that was all I could think of, that was all I wanted to know. Nevertheless, I forced myself to keep talking. "We both see that it's risky. I really don't know whether I should simply—stop seeing you," I said lugubriously, though the pressure of our hips proclaimed the opposite, and gave me hope. "A week ago I made up my mind that we would only be friends. I spoke to Jack on the phone and promised him that. But since then I've found myself getting more and more attracted to you."

"Well don't look so down in the mouth about it!"

"I'm sorry," I laughed.

"You make me sound like the Asiatic flu."

"No no no, you're fantastic, it's not your fault you're so desirable. But I'm worried that I'll spoil things with Jack. And I'm worried because I'm falling in love with you. I mean, I *have* fallen in love with you. And it bothers me to be so far out on a limb because I may be the only one who feels this way."

"You're not."

"No?" I could hardly believe my good fortune; yet I couldn't have heard wrong. "Well then," I said hastily, "I don't understand, I'm confused. Do you love Jack?"

"Yes."

I wanted to ask outright, "Do you love me as much?" but I didn't have the courage. So I said instead (hating myself): "Don't you think there's a conflict?"

"Before I answer that question, tell me what you meant by spoiling your relationship with Jack."

"That's very simple. I mean"—we were both leaning against the car, and I brought myself to look at her—"I want to make love to you."

"What makes you think you haven't been making love to me?"

"I don't mean 'making love' in the Victorian sense, I mean sex, fucking."

"I know that's what you mean, that's what I'm driving at!" cried Marie. "It infuriates me how men are so sacrosanct about the sex act. It's the end of the world, it's the only part of love that counts. If you stick your thing into me, that will be the only part that matters," she said contemptuously. "And until then, you're still a good friend to Jack. It's so legalistic! What about before? When you kissed me?"

"I agree. I may have already gone too far."

"What about simply having the feelings. Doesn't that count?"

"Yes. It does," I said slowly, trying to think hard. "Maybe it's the most important part, the feelings. But still, I think there's something irreversible about the sex act, like crossing the Rubicon. There's no turning back afterwards to simply being friends."

"Oh I don't agree."

"Well, let's say it's hard to bring things back to a simple friendship footing."

"It depends on the man. With some men it can be a natural extension of a friendship feeling. A nice friendly fuck—that can be the best kind," she said.

"But I'm not a nice friendly fucker. I'm a monster. I get too intense to be able to pull off that kind of controlled affection—desirable as it may be."

"By the way, I'm not inviting you to sleep with me, don't get me wrong," said Marie.

"No, I know, and I'm not jumping to that conclusion," I sighed.

"It's too bad there isn't more room for affection in this society. I love to hug, for instance. Sometimes it leads to misunderstandings, because men think you're promising to go to bed with them. Can't they *see* that it's just nice to touch? I feel the same way about kissing. I love to kiss. I just like the way it feels: so what?" challenged Marie.

"Who doesn't?"

"That's right, everyone does. Kissing's wonderful. Why should I deny myself that feeling because you or Jack or any other people might get the wrong ideas. As long as I know how to handle it and know what it means, is it my problem if other people jump to the wrong conclusions?"

"It shouldn't be," I said gloomily.

"But men call you a flirt. Or a 'prick-tease.' That's such a cheap way of controlling women's behavior. I think it's horrible, not being allowed to touch other people. There's a school for autistic kids in Canada where all the teachers hug the children. That's where I'm going to go: I'm going to enroll and say, 'I'm here to get my hugs.' You'll see. I'm going to hitchhike up to Canada right now. I'll bet this is a pretty good place to hitch from, too," Marie said buoyantly, pretending to start across the road.

The discussion was over: not that anything had been resolved, but we had banged our heads long enough on that particular rock. There is nothing quite so futile as two people discussing the pros and cons of whether to go to bed, stuck in Hawthorne Traffic Circle Sunday night at rush hour.

Marie came back with her hand visored over her eyes. "No takers."

"How long do you think we'll have to wait?"

"They'll be here," said Marie.

"I keep feeling like sticking my hand out and yelling 'Taxi!' and leaving the car where it is."

Eventually the tow truck came and hooked up our busted Plymouth. There were two Napolitanos, father and son: the older man unshaven, wiry and bent like a monkey, with a Sherwin Williams paint cap on his head; the younger man straight-backed, taller than his father, less willing to get grease on his clothes or exert himself, finding time to eye both Beth and Marie.

Jammed in the front seat of the truck with the father, listening none too clearly to Junior Napolitano's rap to the girls in back about his ambitions to go to forestry school on the G.I. Bill, I was thinking of how I would have to break the news to my mother from the garage.

I decided I would wait to phone her until after they had examined the motor.

At the garage, Marie and I paced around the black cement floor of the repair shop for the sake of moving our legs, while Beth watched over the shoulder of the older Napolitano, who was jiggling with the motor. A man came into the repair garage wearing a hunter's cap with the flaps down, and started ribbing the owner about racetracks. It seemed Napolitano Senior had bet on a horse that lost. Napolitano kept lifting his head from the hood and stopping his work to argue: "I didn't see you do any better. What about last week?" More local color. I had had my fill of country living.

Listen, can you carry on this conversation some other time? The remark was perfectly phrased on my tongue, and I had to bite back the words. It was taking so long; I tried to make myself patient by imagining that this dark body shop had been assigned to me for the rest of my life.

Napolitano wiped off his hands with a rag.

"What seems to be the trouble?" I asked Beth, when he had finished his examination.

"He says it looks bad," she whispered.

I went back to Marie and brought her this crumb of news.

"It's no good," Napolitano declared suddenly, smiling through his bent pushed-together gray teeth.

"What's no good?"

"Crankshaft's busted completely. You never be able to drive it this way."

"Well, can't I get a new—crankshaft?" I asked.

"A new one'll cost you more than this jalopy's worth."

"Still, I'd like to know if it can be done and how much it would cost."

"Cost you plenty. I don't even have one here. I'd have to order it from the factory, and that would take two weeks, maybe more. Better off just having it totaled."

"I don't understand what you mean, totaled."

"Scrapped, bingo," he said amiably. "It's not worth it to fix, my friend. Your best deal is to sell it for scrap."

The truth was taking a long while to register. "That's impossible," I stammered. "It's my mother's car."

Napolitano shrugged, grinned even more.

I took Marie aside and asked her if she thought they were just trying to cheat us. She didn't know. Neither did I: I decided I would have my mother talk to the garage mechanic.

Dialing my parents' number in Brooklyn, I came up with the best approach to take.

"Ma. Look. There's been an accident," I said in a flat, "Dragnet" police-blotter voice, all the more melodramatic for being so understated.

"Oh my God! Is anyone hurt?"

"No: every...e's in one piece, fortunately. But the car's in bad shape."

"Don't worry about the car. Are you sure everyone's all right?"

"No one's hurt. We're in a garage in a town near Hawthorne Circle." Pause. "We won't be able to get the car fixed by tonight."

"All right."

"The man says car's in pretty bad shape."

"How did the accident happen? Was it yours or the other person's fault?"

"Well it wasn't really an accident, it was more like the whole car conked out at once. We pulled off by the side of the road."

"I see. . . . Anything else?"

"Ma, I think you better talk to the garageman. He'll be able to explain it to you better than I can."

"All right. I'm here, put him on."

"Mr. Napolitano, could you speak to my mother for a moment? . . . He told me the car may have to be totaled," I added.

Silence. "Oh?" my mother said witheringly.

"He'll explain it to you. Thanks for being so understanding about this. It wasn't our fault, actually. Beth did a wonderful job driving. It was just one of those things that was bound to happen."

"Well if it's just one of those things, it's just one of those things I guess. It's only a car. A car can be replaced. As long as none of you is hurt, that's the important thing. Just get home safely."

"Don't worry, we will. Thanks, Ma." I handed the receiver to Napolitano.

Marie and Beth came over to me. I must have looked pale, because they asked sympathetically, "How was it?"

"She took it very well. Much better than I would have expected. In fact, much better than I did. It was a little like telling someone about a death in the family. I know how much she loved that car."

"I'll bet," murmured Beth.

"I think we should pay the bill," offered Marie.

"It's nice of you to say that. Let's see what the whole thing comes to first."

"I think we should pay for all of it," Marie insisted.

Napolitano got off the phone, and told us my mother had arranged to come by the next week and sign for the car to be totaled. He would settle the bill with her. Meanwhile, his son would drive us over to the train station, where we could catch the local back to New York City.

The next city-bound train would not get in for another three quarters of an hour. By now we were starving. There were no restaurants in sight near the ramshackle station. Inside, though, I found a candy-bar machine and bought six packages of peanut butter-and-cracker snacks. "Dinner," I said, handing them out; we laughed and ate. The worst was over (for me it had been that phone call to my mother). Our mouths stuffed with dry peanut butter, we looked down the tracks for something in the distance.

It wasn't clear which direction the train would be coming from. We stared down both ends, and at the railbeds, graveled with sharp gray rocks, and at the fog that was settling over the night. It was a lovely, moody fog that brought out the reds in the signal lights with a peculiar acuteness, but too sad to look at for very long.

We sat down on a bench. To pass the time, we started talking about favorite old films.

The train pulled in; we were still in the world of old movies when we climbed aboard. It was the sort of train that belonged in an old movie, with the wicker seats facing one way. Marie and I looked at each other with delight: perfect—we couldn't have ordered a better one from Wardrobe if we'd tried. Beth took a seat several rows in front of us, and Marie and I shared two adjoining seats, Marie by the window, I on the aisle. The train jostled into a start; Marie fell against me, and I put a steadying arm around her, with that masculine and protective reassurance she had a way of bringing out in me.

Ah, she looked so edible in her tight, busty blouse and delicate shawl! I kept feasting my eyes on her, and she returned the stares, her eyes full of daring. It was all starting to break loose, the love we had talked about and pushed down. We held each other's hands with fondness, squeezed more tightly together into a hug, then pulled away to see if it was true: if the same truth was in the other's eyes. I kissed Marie on the neck. She looked so contented I thought she would swoon. The train rolled into a local station. Slowly as it moved, it could not possibly be too slow for us. Without so much as a word of corroboration, we knew this train had come along to crystallize our love. I was too happy: I encouraged her to fall asleep against me.

I began to think of another romantic train ride, when I was a junior in college. I was riding home from Boston with Natalie, and we were passionate for each other, and kept petting and kissing, not caring what the other passengers thought. That evening, after the train ride, we made love for the first time. I wondered if that would happen with Marie. In comparing the two train rides, both seemed milestones in my life, but this one, I felt, was coming out even better, because there wasn't such frantic urgency. We were more relaxed, at ease, I was more confident; or maybe it was just that I'd grown older and appreciative of what I knew now was rare.

I slid my arm under Marie's blouse onto her breast (there was nothing she would forbid me now). She turned toward me and kissed me, tenderly, sleepily, holding my cheek.

"Tired?"

"Uh-huh."

"Were you sleeping?"

"A little."

"Go back to sleep."

She sat up and looked around uncertainly. "Where's Beth?"

"Went to the bathroom a little while ago."

"She's really special, isn't she?"

"I like her a lot," I said.

"She likes you a whole lot too."

"How do you know?"

"She told me last night!"

"Your friend Carolee doesn't like me though."

"Oh, yes."

"Oh, no." I lifted her fingers playfully.

"You're being too sensitive; you're imagining things. She likes you. What makes you think she doesn't?"

"I can tell. She disapproves.—Because she's used to seeing you with Jack."

"No, I think she likes you a lot. It's me she disapproves of. You know what she told me?" Marie said naughtily.

"What?"

"That she was worried about my *reputation!*"

"See, I told you she disapproved. What else did she say?"

"You should have heard it. She gave me a lecture the other night about going out with two men at the same time. It was terrific! She got all beady-eyed and said, 'Well all right. If you make your bed, you're going to have to lie in it.'"

"I love that expression," I smiled.

"I *hate* that expression. What's it *mean,* anyway?"

"It means, If you don't make your bed in the morning you'll have messy sheets, so you might as well make your bed up before you lie in it."

"No!" Marie socked me on the arm. "Some moralist you turned out to be."

"Ouch!"

"The night is so pretty," she said, looking out.

"Are you comfortable that way?"

"I'm all right. Huuh. . . . Only I can't stop yawning."

"Why don't you go back to sleep? You're probably tired," I said. "You want to put your legs over my lap? That way you'll have more room to stretch out."

She gave me a mischievously skeptical look.

"I won't take advantage of you. Just lean back and relax, and put your legs on me."

"All right." Marie rested her face against the window, and slung her legs over my lap toward the aisle. She didn't close her eyes, though; she looked steadily out the window at the passing country. From where I was sitting it was all violet-black, except for a phosphorescent gray shed or a tree dabbed with white.

I stared at Marie's legs as they uncoiled from her light blue linen skirt. She had long, articulated, eloquent legs, and when I lay my hand down gently on her calf I felt that miraculous skin of hers, smooth and creamy, with the slightest bristles delicately brushing against my palm.

My hand remained unmoving, devotional, for another quarter-hour; and then I had to change because my legs were stiff. We switched positions. I placed my head on her lap, and she ran her fingers through my hair. Ordinarily I don't like to have my hair pushed back; but when Marie did it, I kept staring up at her mysterious kind eyes as though I were her cat lying on her lap.

We stayed like this until the train pulled into Grand Central Station.

What would happen now? Neither of us had said a word about what we would do when the train arrived. I was steeling myself for Marie's good-bye in the taxi, prepared to take what she had already given me and let that be enough. The day had been so full, that one part of me wanted nothing more than to go off alone and squirrel it. But when the taxi stopped at my house, it seemed difficult to unglue ourselves. Or at least not in that way, with a casual leaning-over kiss in a taxi and friendly good-byes all around. Something more was demanded of us. I wish I could remember who said what, how we got over that particular bump. I seem to recall Marie asking if she could use my bathroom upstairs for a moment. But maybe I invented that later, to shift the blame to her. . . . Well, what's the difference? We were both active, both passive. Beth went on home alone in the taxi, and in less than two minutes Marie and I were sliding our hands over each other on my couch.

XI

The kissing had gotten more violent. Our mouths were dripping with each other's saliva. We were "making out," tugging at private parts like blind dates who barely know each other and hope that a brave pawing will take them past the strangeness. It was, in an odd way, a trampling on the intimacy we had reached earlier, as though we were trying to ignore that understanding and tenderness because it might get in the way of sex. We were fighting to turn each other into anonymous lusty bodies, animals responsive only to touch, without thoughts, without consciences.

Something was wrong. It wasn't happening.

Marie caught her breath, and in the moment's pause I said, "Let's not do this."

She nodded. "I'm going to go home."

"I think that's a good idea," I said, exhaling in despair, yet with relief.

"Could we stay here and talk a minute longer?" she asked.

"Sure."

She lit a cigarette. "Want one?"

"No thanks."

Marie took a deep puff. "What do you think's happening?"

"It doesn't feel right," I said. "It felt like we were doing something dirty. I don't mean that sex is dirty—but this feels sordid, in a way."

"I know. I felt the same. Only I thought I should ignore that and go ahead because you were so intent on it."

"Hardly. Anyway, why pretend you're feeling something you're not, just on my account?"

"I thought—*you* know, I thought I would get into it eventually," she said. "That doesn't usually happen, does it?"

"Mostly not . . . I was feeling very outside the experience. Looking at it from above. I wasn't very turned-on, to be honest. Maybe we're not so attracted to each other after all," I said disparagingly.

"No. I don't think that's it." She swept away this objection with a generosity that both absolved me and refused to allow me to deny the amorousness that had built up between us.

"What, then?"

"I just think we were trying too hard."

I let her have this interpretation. I wasn't so sure about it myself, though. I knew I could experience lust for Marie, but it was a yearning that seemed to need the right backlighting. As long as we were playful, like in the water, or the setting was magical, like on the train, I could feel sexy. But as soon as it became serious, with the bed a foot away, making love with her felt grim and workmanlike and—pathetic.

"Maybe we need more fantasy," I said obliquely.

"How?"

"I think we're trying too hard because we have doubts, and we want to get past the doubts and do it already. But the doubts have validity. We should listen to them."

"You mean, because of Jack?"

"Because of Jack, partly." I was beginning to detest that name. "And because of—whatever other uncertainties we're feeling. We should respect our hesitations. I really don't think we should sleep with each other," I forced myself to say. "At least not while things are as mixed-up as they are."

Marie hung her head. "I guess. Let's not, then!" she said with sudden determination.

"All right," I replied, not completely happy that she had agreed so fast. "I'm content to leave it that way, as long as we can still be friends."

"I hope we can be, and maybe even better this way.—I've got to go." Marie stood up. "Don't be blue. It was a great day all around, I mean it, one of my favorite days ever. The train and the camp and the beach and the garage—" Her eyes watered. "Good-bye, Eric." She walked over to me with deliberation and put her arms around my neck. "I think you're a wonderful man."

"I love you," I answered.

"I love you," she murmured back.

I kissed her, on the earlobe, pressing her tight, not so sure any more that it was right to let her go—suddenly changing my mind and wanting to make love! Marie accepted my kisses weakly, then slipped towards the door. She turned around once more to say good-bye, with a sweet sad wave, and was gone.

XII

That night I had a dream. When I awoke I wrote it in my journal, not sure what it meant but convinced somehow that it had to do with Marie and the trip upstate, by which it seemed inspired:

I was driving my mother on an excursion. As we approached a large city park like Golden Gate Park or Prospect Park, I remember her arguing with me, and I began following one of the car routes through the park, when suddenly I no longer wanted to control the car. It was not that the car had gotten out of hand, but that I was curious to see what it would do without me. We rambled onto a field of grass. "Hit the brake!" my mother yelled disgustedly. Then she swore to herself that she would never let me drive her car again.

I had trouble remembering where the brake was. I couldn't find it at first, and when I located it my leg dangled hopelessly above, like a paraplegic's without any feeling, or a Raggedy Ann doll's.

I was able to graze the surface just barely but not to put any pressure down—which suited me, since I didn't really want to be in control. We rolled to within an inch of several people on a bench who jumped away just as we knocked it over. The people who had been on the bench looked disconcerted, and came around us.

"Now see what you've done," said my mother.

We would have to lift the car onto the automobile path before any policemen came. Several onlookers gave us a hand: one in particular whose face I got a look at had generous Czech eyes and thinning hair—a family man, perhaps an engineer with a foreign company. I would have liked him for a father, I thought. We lifted the car up like a toy. Then the front wheel fell off the car onto a girl who was helping. She lay on the ground with a bloody gash over her eye. With her shiny wavy hair and pretty black eyes she had the look of a Mexican peasant girl who was used to being a victim.

I knelt beside her to inspect her wound. A great darkness came over me—perhaps the car was falling on me too; and then I heard voices indicating that they were putting me on a stretcher. I was too tired to move, and was glad that they had found a way to transport me horizontally.

At the admitting clinic a doctor came up to greet my mother and me. (I could stand now and felt in perfect health.) I recognized him as an old French professor of mine, Professor Morse. As a doctor he was just as dignified as I remembered him, but his eyes had become shrewder, his thin hair cropped Swedish-style close to his scalp, and his shoulders bulged out of the soiled white coat.

Knowing that my mother would take care of the formalities, I allowed my interest in the new surroundings to wane, putting to myself instead the question: What was I doing by driving so irresponsibly? Why this foolishness? My inner voice responded immediately: *You were trying to kill your mother.* I asked, Are you sure? Usually in these cases it's wanting to fuck your mother.

No, the voice answered; *this time it's very definitely wanting to kill her.*

I was relieved in a way, but I felt impelled to tell the doctor my discovery. "Could we speak in private?" I asked him.

"In a minute," he said. Meanwhile his assistant threw me into a hammock, turned me to the side and the next thing I knew my left thigh was throbbing. "We'll let him sleep seventy-two hours."

The doctor placed a metal cap on my head.

25 24 23 22 21 20

I began to feel weightless.

"Did you see that?" cried the assistant. "He didn't relax enough to make use of the hammock."

"How could I relax?" I protested, jumping up off the hammock.

"You put me that way and then you caused a great pain in my leg!"

"But any other person would have found time to roll around and play in it. *I* would have," the assistant sneered. He demonstrated by climbing into the hammock and rocking loosely from side to side.

"That's so unfair!" I cried. In any case, the assistant was of no importance. It was the doctor that I had to impress.

"Can't we go outside for a moment?" I asked him more urgently.

The doctor told my mother to wait there, and led me through several hospital doors. In the corridor, I began to explain when I noticed a creepy spy, a friend of Michael's whom I didn't like, eavesdropping on us.

"Get out of here, Lawrence, you sneak!"

He sidled away, but not far enough to be out of hearing, unless we spoke very low.

The doctor removed my metal sleeping cap so that we could talk.

"I have something important to tell you, Doctor. I figured out why I let the car go out of control. I was trying to kill my mother!" I confessed.

He looked skeptical and unimpressed. He rubbed his eyes.

"Is it really necessary that you put me to sleep for seventy-two hours? Can't you make it shorter? I feel perfectly all right— especially now that I know what was behind it."

"Do you expect me to release you just like that, after what you told me?"

"Look, Doctor, I respect your being a competent clinician. I'm sure you know all there is to know about treating people. But in this particular case I don't need a doctor. I've got to work it out in my own head, by myself."

He shrugged. Since he had the power, he didn't have to argue with me.

Just then, a mass of mental patients poured out of the elevator in flannel hospital gowns. Their faces I vaguely knew: one a troubled girl named Mousey from the agency, and some I remembered from the time I had been under observation at a locked psychiatric ward, when I was seventeen, after I had tried to kill myself. Everyone was pawing at me, happy to have me back: "Welcome back, welcome back!" like a scene in *Freaks*. It gave me a fatalistic feeling. Wherever I turned, I saw women whose suffering eyes immediately sought mine. I found I was able to cure their suffering by the numinous sympathy which came from my eyes. I placed my arm comfortingly around them, hoping all the while that the doctor would notice my attraction to and for women, and would consider me a normal.

It was no use: he was paying no attention. I broke away from the crowd of patients encircling me, to importune him again. "At the very least, I *can't* stay beyond Sunday. I've got to get to work at the agency by Monday. You're not going to keep me that long —promise?"

"We'll see," said the doctor. "Meanwhile go upstairs and practice on the barbells. Let's get rid of some of that flab!" And he pinched a wad of flesh from my arm, which hung down shapelessly like baker's dough.

"But . . . but aren't I supposed to fall asleep first?"

"No, you can go to sleep anytime," he replied, turning to attend another patient.

XIII

I went off to work and tried to immerse myself in students. By the afternoon I knew I was depressed. After spending all weekend with Marie, after so much mooning and romancing, I was back to Square One.

In the evening Marie phoned to thank me for being so "perfect" Sunday. I didn't ask for specifics: in fact I thought I had been idiotic a good deal of the time, but I accepted her enthusiasm, because you never can tell what people are seeing in you; and besides, she was probably imagining something she needed to imagine. Meanwhile she had badgered Jack into promising to return soon—he had been considering staying a few more weeks but she got firm.

I put down the phone, feeling used. Well, what had I expected? That was the agreement: we would be friends, and she would continue with Jack. By what crazy logic had I expected that by giving up all, I would get all? The trouble with selfless acts by immature people is that we expect to be recompensed right away. And if our lives continue as blandly or barrenly as before, we come to regard the sacrifice as a further self-betrayal.

Rather than thinking that I had done the right thing in saying we should not sleep together, I now suspected that I had sold short my chances: not because of virtue, but timidity. I was all too prone to give up the pretty girl. Why couldn't it be me who had her love? Why had I always thought happiness was for others? With Marie to go through life with, *I* could be happy: we were well suited for each other, by the iron law of fun, whereas Jack would only make her morose and miserable. . . . Ah, it was a waste! Jack would never make her happy . . . one day treating her like a good fairy rejuvenating the crippled king, and the next day sleeping with other girls and fantasizing about his long-lost this one or that one. I was fed up with him! My anger at Jack puzzled me: I could not put my finger on why I felt suddenly so disenchanted and betrayed by him; all I knew was that he had disappointed me. Leading everyone to think he was going to become a bright light in the intellectual world, and then settling for life as —what? a media hack. For years I had been making excuses for him, but I had to admit, he was turning into a mediocrity.

Still, deciding your best friend is mediocre is no reason to steal his girl. But even this temptation seemed to me his fault. Why had he stayed away longer than he had promised? Didn't he see that it was an unfair test that was torturing Marie and me the longer he kept it up? In a way, it seemed a plot of Jack's: if we *had* slept together it probably would have suited him; he could have dumped best friend and girl in one move and told his next lover the sad tale. I was pretty sure he would have stepped out of the way if she and I did become lovers, since he had a neurotic uneasiness about male competition. But who cared about Jack? I was tired of his routines. Either way I acted I felt controlled by him: to be gallant or to be the heel, both merely confirmed his limited mythologies of the universe. That was the worst of it—I no longer felt like a free man.

If I had thought that giving up Marie had been truly altruistic, I could have lived with it. But what bothered me was a doubt I am almost too embarrassed to admit: perhaps I had only stepped aside because I didn't feel aroused at that moment. Why had I made the statement so sweeping, then? It seemed not brave at all, but cowardly: as if I hadn't been able to stand the tension any longer of waiting for a decisive sign of sexuality, and so put an end to everything.

Was it Jack's taboo that had inhibited me, or something about Marie herself: my uncertainty that she was "my type," even if Jack had never existed? But how could I ever separate the two in my mind? That was what frustrated me so—I would never know what my true feelings for Marie were, independent of Jack.

I wanted to do the manly thing, but not be a sucker. To be manly was—what? Stoicism: to give up Marie because of my loyalty to Jack. That was one possibility. *Or,* to treat it as one of the turning points in my life, which called for huge effort of will and a disregard of conventional morals because the life-force dictated it. A biological imperative: what Freud called approvingly "the flight to the Woman." I had heard that there were times in one's life that called for extraordinary measures.

Some little bald man kept running alongside me, arguing with me, poking me in the ribs, and getting the final word in. *"No* situation gives you the right to step outside of morality. There is only one thing to do, the right thing, and you know what that is . . . so do it and keep your mouth shut. You've already done it; now be a man and accept it."

Oh, but the paleness of the course disheartened me! To renounce with a grand gesture was one thing; to renounce silently, day by day, every minute, with no one seeing you renounce, was another. Sydney Carton could stand on the platform, say his speech and be decapitated. He had it easy. I had to chew over the same speech every time I thought of Marie's face, every time I felt like picking up the phone and talking to her. A day passed; another; I kept fantasizing that she would telephone me, and I would bravely insist that we not see each other. I needed more opportunities to exercise my resolution. I began to wish minute by minute that Marie would call.

It was already August 2. Jack had been gone—three and a half weeks. It seemed longer than that: so much had happened in that small amount of time. I had lost my balance, fallen in love, gone distraught.

Wednesday night I got drunk, and wrote a long poem to Marie, in which the taste of dark beer got mixed in with my sweat. I sat curled in a woolen armchair under a hot lampshade with yellow fringes, and went on for pages, confessing. It wasn't a very good poem and I realized that, but somehow when I had finished it was as though I had broken through. I had acted at last.

Now if I could only keep sublimating through writing. I would get her out of my system. But even as I told myself this, I knew in the back of my mind that the poem was a bait meant to catch Marie.

The next evening, discipline shot to pieces, I called her. She was in tears. I got her to explain what was the matter. Marie had talked on the phone to Jack before, and he had told her that he might not be able to come back just yet. He had contracted a slight venereal infection, and had to stick around Berkeley for a doctor's appointment. That was the last straw. She told Jack she didn't care whether he came back or not. They had had a big fight on the phone, and she had been crying ever since.

That was it. He had forfeited all credibility and sympathy by this venereal thing. That was the break I had been waiting for. I asked her if she'd like to get together. "Sure," she said bitterly, "I'd love to see you." We would meet for dinner at an Indian restaurant near her house. I told her I had written her a poem. "Bring it along," she said. "I could use a poem."

I waited in front of the Maharajah. I was fifteen minutes early. I had made up my mind to take Marie that night.

She came up alongside me and must have read my mind because she blushed at once. We went into the draped Indian restaurant and, finding ourselves virtually the only customers, sat on low hassocks across from each other. The night air was alive with decision. We opened our large menus. "What's good here?" "The curries." The bearded waiter took our order, and left. I was dying to give her the poem. Instead I waited, to see what she might have to say.

"Well, you look very dashing tonight. I like your shirt—what is that, purple, green and—?"

"Green and brown, I think."

"You always have such nice shirts," she said encouragingly.

"Thank you. I love your dress as well." We smiled. "Well, here we are."

"Did you bring your poem?" Marie asked excitedly.

"Yes."

"Oh good! I'm dying to read it."

"It's not very good but I didn't get a chance to perfect it—"
"Never mind that, hand it over!"

I passed it to her over the red-glassed candle. She held the pages close to the flame, which roseated both the poem and her slender fingers.

The waiter came over with our salads and condiments. She was chuckling to herself, turning the page quickly, frowning; he went away; I bit my fingers until she laughed again.

THE EYELID WORMS

to Marie

Marie, it was fated that every man should love a woman
with a silent ee at the end of her name
because this silence is as beautiful as your absence
and is your absence
my hand taking your fingers in loneliness

I am in love
with your insides
the light from that mango pulp
is the light around your yellow teeth
how can a beauty have such yellow teeth?
how you always laugh

Three reasons for not sleeping with me
1) you believe in friendship
2) you went off the pill a month ago
3) you just met me
4) our mutual friend

You are for me, Marie
even if
I'm not even sure who you are
and besides I'm drunk on Wurzberger beer

But I do know this:
I believe in long grasshopper legs
painted red in camp by vicious bullies
I believe in twin cousins

with identical confessions
and a bathing skin
which leaps at you like a leopard!
I believe in silicone breasts

You remind me of "Leave It
To Beaver," when he got that fuming look in his eye
concentration of self
or wincing
or flying off
like Peter Pan on wires

you remind me of peanut butter restlessly pitching
on a slice of bread, refusing to lie flat
you remind me of fibers of jellyfish
under a microscope
the strands doing a Charleston,
lapping up the compliments
yet feeling unaccountably soiled

you remind me of the breath of cigarettes
buried deep in violets
in a dream of running through manly hugs

I am saying good-bye to you now like an African steamer
you remind me of a very fine Matisse
I am saying good-bye to you
all aboard

You remind me of white houses stacked against a hill
in the port of Tangier, under an uncertain sky
Last chance to board
You jump up like a sleepy Moiseyev dancer
I am saying good-bye to you
you remind me of someone I could love forever—
even for ten minutes
I'm as full of departures as a smokestack
you remind me of innocence   an angel
what a cute kid!

I'm always saying good-bye to you, giving you up
I want to turn around and hug you now

Go to sleep on my shoulder
the train is leaving the boat's already left
Wake up Marie

"It's fantastic! Can I keep it?"

"It's for you."

"But you'll need a copy also, won't you?"

"I made a copy of it before I came here."

"I thought so!" she said. "It's beautiful! I love the part about the sleepy Moiseyev dancer. There are so many funny bits."

"I thought of someone leaping energetically, and then going to sleep in midair."

"I know. And the part about 'Leave It to Beaver'! That's my favorite, that used to be my favorite show on television. But I also love it at the beginning, the way it starts out slow. And the silent 'e' is so beautiful. Oh, and the peanut butter—"

"I got that from the line before; Peter Pan made me think of peanut butter—"

"I know, dummy, will you let me explain it? I'm supposed to do the complimenting! What else?" Marie glanced it over. "It's all good, Eric; the ending, Tangier, everything. Thanks, I'll really treasure this. I can't wait to get home and read it over and over."

She folded it up and put it in her shoulder bag. Then she took my hand across the table and crossed fingers with it, as though sensing I needed more reassurance.

We ate our dinner and got around to talking about Jack's phone call. Marie was by now in better control of herself. She even managed to laugh about it: "Some spiritual nature! In my day they used to call it something else."

"But Bernadette is such a lofty name—you know, *The Song of Bernadette.*"

"I'll thank her to keep her singing to herself."

We had coffee and custard for dessert, then left.

"What do you want to do now?" I asked, outside the restaurant.

"I don't know. What time is it?"

"Quarter to nine. The night is still young. We could go to a movie. . . . There's a nice Renoir film showing tonight."

"I don't feel like sitting in a theatre tonight," said Marie. "You know what I mean?"

"Sure. We could go dancing."

"That's a great idea! But not tonight. Let's do it some other night, okay?"

"All right. We could go bowling; we could take a walk—by the marina."

"Everything you propose sounds so energetic!"

"Are you not feeling well?" I asked solicitously.

"I'm a little shaky," she admitted.

"We could take a short walk."

"Let's do that. That sounds the best."

The boat dock at Seventy-ninth Street was a guarantee for some romantic feeling, on a nice evening; and it was a nice evening, with a breeze blowing across the river from New Jersey and the yacht lanterns lighting up the night. In the bushes behind the cool grass where we chose to sit, away from the footpath, there were even fireflies. I had not seen fireflies in Manhattan before, but Riverside Park was full of them.

I sat up on my elbows behind her, with my hand on the small of her back. "Storm clouds. Do you think it's going to rain?"

"I don't know. 'Mm-mm-mm, do you think it's gonna rain?'" she sang.

"'Mm-mm-mm, don't you think it's kinda nice?'" I joined in.

"'Mm-mm-mm, would you like some sarsaparilla?'"

"'Gee, the moon is yeller—'"

"'Something's gotta come from that!'" we sang together.

"How about . . . 'Marie, the dawn is breaking, Marie, you'll soon be waking . . .'"

"My father used to sing that all the time," she interrupted.

"I don't know the words so well. You know 'The way you hold your hat'?"

"My father used to sing that to me too!"

"Okay, you sing it with me," I said.

"No, you sing. I'd rather hear you."

"Oh, come on!—" I coaxed.

"I'll join in if I feel like it. You go first," she said.

"Okay:

> 'The way you hold your hat
> The way you sing off-key
> The memory of all that
> No, no, they can't take that away from me
>
> The way you—I don't know the words
> The way you—I don't know that line either
> The memory of all that
> No, no, they can't take that away from me'

"What goes next?" I asked.

Marie sang in her shaky voice:

> " 'We may never never meet again
> On the bumpy road to love
> Still I'll always, always keep the memory of' "

and we went back to the first stanza.

"That was good," she said. "What else do you know?"

"Oh I know 'My Funny Valentine' and 'Ten Cents a Dance' and 'Mean to Me' and 'Stormy Weather.' I know lots of them."

"You know all the sad songs, it seems like."

"All the torch songs, yes. My mother used to sing them to herself, so I picked them up."

"Sing one."

". . . All right, I'll sing 'My Funny Valentine.' "

"Oh good, my father used to sing that all the time."

"Your father used to sing everything all the time," I joked.

"My father knows every show tune. He's incredible.—Just like your mother."

"That's what we have in common: both our parents of the opposite sex sang to us."

"Sing it." She closed her eyes and prepared to listen.

"Okay, as soon as this man walks by . . ." I waited and she kept her eyes closed: then I started singing 'My Funny Valentine' to the boats and the water. It must have carried a good distance across the river, it was a very still night. I sang it straight through, gaining force—at the end I hit the high note. Then it was finished; Marie opened her eyes.

"Ooo," she shivered.

"Now I want a kiss."

I lay full-length on her and we kissed. They were beautiful, slow kisses like the kind at the lake; they made me forget everything but the business of tongues. I put my hand under her dress. My hand felt beneath her underpants with slowly circling excitement. My hips moved on top of hers and we were rubbing lushly against each other. I thought of having her then and there.

She began shuddering underneath me.

"Is something the matter?" I asked calmly.

She sat up, frightened. "I'm okay."

"Are you cold? What is it? You're trembling."

"I kept imagining different pictures. They were bright and they kept changing. Like merry-go-rounds . . ." Her teeth chattered; she felt feverish. I waited for her to catch her breath.

"What else did you see?"

"I thought you were a tiger in the jungle. Then I thought you were a doctor. There was something white and medical about you."

"Sounds unflattering."

"Oh it's a compliment. To me it means you're in control and yet compassionate. Sometimes you seem so strong and certain of yourself—I don't understand how you can be so certain of yourself."

I wanted to tell her, You're imagining it. But I was too flattered. Besides, it might be something in my favor. She was identifying me with the doctors of her childhood, who terrified her but to whom she had to make herself surrender, for her own good.

"I'm not that sure of myself," I forced myself to say finally.

"You are. You're a man! Maybe I'm ready for a man after being with so many boys. I was thinking, before, that you made me feel some things I had almost given up on."

"Like what?"

"Like hope."

I squeezed her and rubbed her shoulder to make it warm. "Is that better?"

"Just keep your arm there," she said softly, distractedly.

"Are you all right?" I asked, noticing her tremble.

"I'm okay. It's just that the grass was cold and making me shiver."

"Maybe we should get out of the park."

"That's a good idea."

I helped her up. We left the marina, taking one more look backwards, and headed east, towards her house. She seemed happy to be moving again, and began skipping, so sudden and unpredictable was her joy—skipping up the hill.

"Do you know this one? 'It's very clear, our love is here to stay . . .'"

"I love that song," said Marie. "That's my favorite song. 'The radio . . . and the telephone . . . and the movies that we know . . .'" she sang breathlessly. "'Are just passing fancies.'"

"'And in time may gooooo . . .'"

We skipped along, past the delicatessens, feeling light as air. I made believe I was Gene Kelly, doing a tap dance on the sidewalk, and Marie pointed her leg in a lovely ballet figure, Cyd Charise or Leslie Caron. It only lasted for a moment, the dance, to show that we *could* if we wanted to. Nobody seemed to pay attention anyway. Then we went back to swinging our arms and singing. We were approaching her house now, and I was trying to keep the carefree mood, to hold on to the magic as long as we could. In a short while I would have to make clear my desire to spend the night with her: and then either be rejected, or succeed. "'In time the Rockies may crumble, Gibraltar may tumble, they're only made of clay; but—our love is here to stay!'" I wanted her to realize I was singing those words to *her*. She kept laughing and not taking the sentiments particularly seriously. We came up to her brownstone steps.

"Let's sit out here for a minute, okay?" I said.

"I was going to suggest the same thing. I can go upstairs and get my sweater and bring us some cherry sodas. Would you like that?" Marie nodded to make me nod.

"That sounds good." She went upstairs. I looked up at the sky, trying to decide if it was better to prepare what I was going to say, or to let it spill from the heart. As usual, I concluded it was better to do a little of both.

I looked around as soon as I heard her returning, and thanked her for the cherry soda as she smoothed down her skirt and joined me on the stoop.

"This is like when I was younger, sitting on a girl's step and talking," I said.

"What did you talk about?"

"Oh, everything. We talked so long because the girl's parents were home and I couldn't come up."

"You can come up."

"If I come up I won't want to go down. . . . I'd like to spend the night with you."

"I know."

"Well?"

"Is it all my decision?" she asked.

"At this point, yes. My mind's made up."

"Oh gee. This is the part that's . . ." Marie sighed. "I don't know what to say."

"Just say, yes."

She said it in a timid voice, "Yes?" almost questioningly.

I kissed her gratefully on the cheek. "Good. Now that that's settled."

"Let's stay here a little while longer," she begged me.

"Fine."

She searched the sky. "Not too many stars."

"Not too many."

I put my hand over her hand.

"Oooh, Ooo. I feel like an owl. . . . Did you know that an owl's eyes don't move?" she said.

"No I didn't."

"That's—" she coughed. "Excuse me."

"Go on."

"It's probably—" Marie coughed again. She fanned the air in front of her. "Wait a minute . . ." She was coughing pretty badly now.

"Take your time. Do you want me to pound your back?"

"No, don't!" she gasped.

"All right, I won't."

Marie was still trying to catch her breath. I didn't understand what was taking place. She was wheezing out air and searching in her shoulder bag.

"What's wrong, Marie?"

"Asthma. I'm looking for my pills."

"What do they look like?" I asked, feeling so useless. I started rooting around inside the leather bag, but it was large and full of junk. "Let's just dump everything on the steps!" I cried, starting to overturn the tote bag.

"I think I found 'em," she coughed. She was choking, and turning blue. I was alarmed at the chance she'd stop breathing before the pill bottle could be opened. She kept shaking her head, and her short hair swam around her. Her eyes were wet and filmed-over with tears. She swallowed two brown-and-white capsules with a swig of cherry soda. The moment she gulped them down she looked panicked, as if she was afraid she couldn't control the muscles in her esophagus long enough to get them down. It was horrifying. I had never seen a full asthma attack; I had never known they could be so serious. After she had swallowed the capsules, she continued to pant and gulp for air.

"Do you need anything?"

She shook her head no.

"How long do you usually have to wait before the medicine takes effect?" I asked.

"Not long. Fifteen minutes. . . . There's another pill I take.—It's upstairs."

"Well let's go up and get it! What are we waiting for?"

"I'll be all right. That was the stronger pill—of the two." Everything she said came out as a rush, or a gulped sigh. "I was afraid of this," she said on the stairs, as I tried to get her to lean on me. "In the park—I felt it coming on. . . . I always know when it's coming."

"What does it feel like?"

"It's too complicated—explain. You just know after a while. Every asthmatic knows. Here, I have the keys." She opened her door: it seemed very important to her to show me she could handle the keys, even if she couldn't breathe well.

"Please don't worry about me!" she said emphatically as we entered her flat. "It's happened a million times before. It's something I know how to take care of. I can't stand it when people worry over me when I'm sick."

"All right I won't worry. Just go in and take your other pill and I won't worry!" I gestured so forcibly toward the medicine cabinet that she started laughing.

"I'll be back."

While Marie went into the bathroom, I sat on her plump couch with throw pillows, squeezing one. I had time to think about the connection between her attack and the imminent sexual scene between us. People said asthma was often "psychosomatic" (whatever that meant—a stigma word that attached itself to certain diseases and seemingly entitled you not to sympathize with the sufferer). I was still too recently under the shock of seeing her breathing-scare to "blame" her for it; yet I did suspect it was linked to our having sex, and was a roundabout way of evading me. I wanted to sleep with her, but not if it meant her turning blue and practically suffocating. What should I do? I could offer to leave. That was the noble thing to do: to release her from her promise without humiliating her.

"Here I am again!"

"Oh, good."

"What's the matter?" she stopped short.

"Marie, I've been thinking. Maybe it's better if I go."

She hung her head guiltily.

I stood up. "You'd like me to leave?"

"I didn't say that. Would *you* like to leave? Is that it?"

"No. But I thought that . . . I don't know how to put it. . . . I thought you were having an asthma attack to avoid having to go to bed with me."

"That's silly."

"I'm sorry."

"I have lots of attacks. All the time. I'm an asthmatic." She crossed the room with dignity, her arms over her chest. "I thought I told you that."

"You did, but . . . I had always heard that, to the degree that asthma was a psychosomatic ailment—" I had let the bruising word out.

She looked amused: "Yes? To the degree it's a psychosomatic ailment—?"

"I don't know, I just figured—there was a connection. I really don't know."

"There probably is a connection," she said, crossing over to me, and gracefully, pityingly, touching my shoulder. I turned around.

"I don't want to go, Marie. I want to stay with you tonight."

"I said it was all right," she smiled sadly.

"That's the truth. I just want to stay with you. I don't care if we make love, if we don't make love, I just want to be with you this whole night and watch over you and take care of you." I kissed her on the forehead. We embraced almost chastely.

She yawned. "Let's go into the other room." We went inside to her bedroom. "I want to get into my nightgown and get under the covers. You can still stay dressed," she added. I took this to mean: Please stay dressed. I sat at the edge of the double bed. Marie passed into her walk-in closet and came out in a green nightgown, and slipped under the covers with a naughty grin, part-Little Red Riding Hood, part-Wolf. I was unable to resist hugging her in her soft frilly jade nightgown through the bedcovers. Her breathing was growing more regular now, and I noticed her eyes were very wide, as from drops of belladonna. It must have been the medication.

"How are you feeling?"

"I'm still a tiny bit shaky. Talk to me. Tell me a story—that always calms me down."

"Tell you a story, eh?" I said teasingly. Then I realized that she was in fact still trembling. Her skin was filled with goose bumps.

"Don't you think you'd be better with more covers?"

"No, I'm all right," she shook her head. "Just *talk* to me."

"Okay. . . . What kind of story do you want me to tell?"

"Any kind. Something from your life. Tell me about Natalie, the girl you went out with for so long."

"Why do you want to hear about Natalie?"

"If you don't feel like telling me, that's okay."

"No, I will." It was a challenge, and I rarely turned down a challenge.

Why did I tell that particular part, though? All I knew was that I had to speak from my deepest self; she would see through any insincerity in a second. I had to tell whatever came to mind, and for some reason *that* swam into mind. First I described how Natalie and I had fallen in love, how we had lived together for several years. Then I told about my best friend from high school, Curt, who became close to both of us. One year I went away by myself for two weeks, and when I came back Natalie acted differently toward me. Always so warm and partial to me in the past, now she was cold and distant; she said that our relationship would have to change; I would have to go into therapy; she kept finding fault with my every action, calling me unbearably selfish and so on. Then, all at once she became strangely seductive, but still cold, as though she preferred being my whore to my life-companion. After that came a period when she was oddly contrite, walking around with her head bowed and begging me not to pay attention to her. I could make no sense of it. When I pressed her to tell me what was in back of all of it she refused. All I understood was that something had gone wrong between us and, in the dark, groped for a way out of the falseness and suffocation which had become our life together. Finally, I made myself leave her. I was still working up in my tale to the discovery of their treachery, that climactic wound of enlightenment that had not left off hurting me and energizing me for the year or so I had spent digesting it. And all the while I was edging toward telling this part to Marie, it was not lost on me that she must be seeing the symmetry: I had been cuckolded by one male friend, I was preparing to turn around and do the same to another; to pass on the universal thump, as it were.

Not that I put these thoughts against myself into words: no, I kept telling my story as I had rehearsed it hundreds of times since it happened, right up to the point where I came across the diary.

"To make a long story short, I came back to New York last year for a few weeks' visit around Christmas. And I saw Natalie. She had never given up, I think, on the idea that we would get together again, and she had invited me to our old place. Oddly enough, Jack stopped by that night also, to see me and Natalie for a few minutes. I went into the bedroom to make a call, and there on her night table was her diary. I have a very bad habit: I read anything that's lying around. As I was getting ready to dial the number, I was reading through the diary, and I opened up accidentally to a page in which she was describing the difficulty of being lovers with two men at once. She wrote something about her old confusion of having to choose between me and Curt. . . . I put the phone down and the book down and the room began to turn. I couldn't stand up. It was like an earthquake had hit, and I'd been thrown to one side of the crack. I swear to you, my knees were like jelly, and there were pins and needles in my feet. I tried to move foward—I staggered into the living room. Jack asked, 'Did you make your call?' But Natalie just looked at me. She knew.

"We walked Jack to the bus. Even though he didn't know what had happened, and was too tactful to ask, he did everything right. He lent me support, told me he was sorry to see me so upset, that he knew what that felt like . . . and he made it clear that he was at my disposal later on, if I needed to talk. I know I probably shouldn't say this, but—he was everything a loyal friend should be."

Marie nodded, unsurprised, eyes wide.

"It was snowing. We had to walk up a steep hill in the snow; and we said good-bye to Jack at the corner, and snow was pouring round the streetlamps. I remember that I started crying, and suddenly I thought . . . 'How beautiful it looks.' The snow coming down with the tears on my face, and the old apartment buildings on West End Avenue with their wrought-iron balconies, and the tire tracks left on that tan slush. We were standing on the corner, and the streetlamp was holding all these things together, like an orchestra conductor. 'How beautiful it is!' I thought. Suddenly I felt free, as though I had stepped away from something hard and leaden around my ankles, and I remembered, 'Ye shall know the truth, and the truth shall make ye free!' I was so moved by everything I saw, and at the same time I was shivering. Natalie stood waiting—already cowering, waiting for my anger to explode against her. I felt no anger toward her. I was entranced with this new way of looking. She seemed to be calling me back to a duty on the human plane that I still had to perform: to unleash my pain, or my forgiveness, or whatever, to—to express something enormous toward her. On the one hand, the saintly snow; on the other hand, this person's appeal calling me back to vulnerability. I felt torn, with such agony, between the two responsibilities, the unearthly and the worldly. And then I—got angry and blurted out names and punched her. I didn't punch her very hard because my hand was too cold. But I kept punching her on the arm; it was what I thought she wanted. There was something so light-headed and dreamy about socking her without any anger any more, more from a sense of obligation, as cars passed slowly through the slush. People watched. Everything took place in slow motion. Natalie was crying and her nose was red and mucus was bubbling out of it.

"We moved to a restaurant to get warm. Natalie was still sobbing, she went through a whole packet of tissues. But she also was relieved that the secret was out. I got her to tell me exactly what had happened; how their affair started, how often they had done it behind my back—not that many times, she said. It had started while I was away. Now everything made sense: her coldness and refusal to make love that first night, her harping on my deep flaws, which she never adequately explained. They had been afraid to tell me, afraid that the truth would shatter me. Strangely enough, that was the part that really bothered me: not so much that they had had sex—I think I could have forgiven that—but that they had lied about it. They kept it from me for so long, pretending other emotions between them! *That* seemed monstrous. I was betrayed by the two people in the world I thought loved me the most. I'm ready for anything, after surviving a blow like that!

"Natalie was hopeful. She thought, now that I knew everything, we could try again to make a go of our relationship. She said she must have left her diary out unconsciously, for me to find out at last. To me it was still accidental: it horrified me that I might have gone on for twenty years without knowing, and both of them lying to my face.

"The more I thought about it, the more full of rage I became. I went crazy that week. I waited outside Curt's print shop and when he came out, although he was bigger than me, I started punching him like a wild man. He fell to the ground. He offered no resistance, so it wasn't as much of a catharsis as I expected. These things never are. He kept apologizing. He said he had been envious of me, of my greater success, ever since we were younger. As if the word 'envy' could excuse every act. Then he had the audacity to pretend that he was leaving the country to sort of 'repent'— as if I didn't know that he had planned to go to Europe as a pleasure vacation! I was disgusted by his whining. I had nothing more to say to him.

"That's all I have to tell," I concluded. Suddenly I lost all my self-righteousness. I had the sense that she could see right through me, to my ugly unconscious side. Oh, who knew what she was thinking, behind those big brown eyes!

Marie *was* breathing quietly and evenly again. At least I had accomplished that.

"Are you—disillusioned with me?"

"Of course not." She smiled; she had forgiven me the catastrophe of my personality. "No, I feel sad for you. You were hurt a lot. And I feel sorry for Natalie too."

"So do I," I said.

"Were you ever able to become friends again?"

"Yes. But not with Curt."

"I can understand that," she said. "But I'm glad you made up with Natalie."

I sat solemnly at the edge of her bed, not knowing what to do next. The story had pulled me into another mental state. I was sunk in feelings of the power of betrayal—dark thoughts of being stabbed in the back, and vengeance: it was a harsh, rocky terrain that I recognized well, like a Spanish stone field, and it seemed to have an ancient exclusive claim on me. How would I find my way out of it to make love?

I prayed Marie would know what to do. She took my hand, and yawned.

"Do you want me to get into bed with you?" I asked.

"First I want to take a shower. Is that all right? I promise—I'm not stalling. But I really do want to take a shower, I'm so *sticky*."

"It's fine. But we are making love, right?"

"M hm," she said, sliding out of bed in her airy sleeping gown.

I followed her out of the room. "This is an awkward question but—what are you doing for contraception?"

"I'm at the end of my period. It's all right," she said. I wasn't sure, but I let it drop.

In the bathroom I got out of my clothing. I looked up, and Marie was completely naked.

There was something very shocking about our having no clothes on. We smiled, secretly pleased that we could still be so shy. I stared at Marie's springy, young, incredibly girlish body, with her long thighs, and a reddish pubic region that conveyed a sense of modesty. Her posture seemed to say: "Here I am! Am I all right?" She was more than all right.

It was a good idea to take a shower: Water was our lucky medium. We soaped each other and jostled our bodies. But I couldn't help noticing for the first time, at the base of Marie's chest where her breasts ended, a concave hole like an indented stone. The hole was no bigger than a pebble, but it kept drawing my eyes to its shadow. I knew it must have had something to do with her lungs; and I felt such pity for her I had to turn away.

In the wet, I maneuvered behind her and put my hands over her breasts, as if to protect them from illness. I kissed her ear; she tilted her head back to meet me, and I rubbed myself against her ass, slowly, absentmindedly. Her flesh was slippery and lathered up. I felt myself going hard. Why wait to dry off and get into bed, where I might have a return of that despair? As we stepped out of the shower I said:

"Let's do it here!"

"On the tiles?" she asked, surprised, but ready to be a good sport.

"Why not? Use the mat!" I pushed her shoulder downward to show I meant business, and she folded concisely onto the floor with the bath mat shoved underneath her buttocks. There was no going back now. There, on the bathroom floor, we did it.

It was a fuck of pure terror. As I slid into Marie I thought that I wanted it to last for a long time, to be good for her, for me; but I was conscious most of a flooded motor in my chest, a fluttering, an emptiness somewhere, like a horror, and the sense of having gone through too much already: my nerves were used up, I had handled too much suffering in one night. To the degree that I could register pleasure (and it was there, too, along with everything else), it came mostly from looking down at Marie. Marie was an angel. A faint whiff of her traveled up from her legs, drugging me with its sweetness. When I came, I continued to move for as long as she rose underneath me, or until she crossed her arms on my back and drew me close and still to signify that it was over, that I could stop.

As I collapsed onto her, I felt inexpressibly relieved. Thank God we had got through that part. The first night with someone new often didn't count for me as sexual release: it was a kind of groundwork to establish the conditions for sexuality the next time. I knew Marie would understand, in any case. I had such total confidence in her, and gratitude towards her, I couldn't have been fonder of her as I helped her up from the floor, noticing her skin was so rosy and soft now. Now we could be tender to each other in an unsuspenseful way, without everything having to lead up to sex. We could lie in each other's arms and sleep like children.

We climbed into the bed together. I luxuriated in the feel of her expensive sheets.

Marie said, "I want to have a cigarette, first, all right?"

"Sure."

"It's great to have a cigarette sometimes after you make love." She lit up.

"What's it like?"

"I can't explain. Like dessert."

"Let me have one." I reached for her pack.

"Don't! I don't want you to get started on that awful habit."

"I won't make it a habit; I just want to smoke one cigarette, to share what you're going through."

"Here," Marie shook her head, and gave me her own cigarette to light the other's end.

I took in a puff. She smiled, trying hard to control her laughter. "What's the matter?" I said, blushing.

"You look so funny when you smoke!—I'm sorry, I didn't mean to laugh."

"I told you I couldn't smoke . . ."

"No, don't be embarrassed. I like the way you smoke. You look really cute."

"It's something I just never"—I inhaled—"learned how to do."

Marie kissed me impetuously. I was happy to amuse her.

"Tell me how to do it."

"Can I tell you one thing? You're smoking it like a joint. Just take in a little at a time and puff it out. If you swallow the smoke, it will give you a headache."

"Okay," I said good-naturedly. "Thanks for the tip."

We finished our cigarettes in silence. I set the alarm clock for seven-thirty, so that I could get to work by nine; then I reached over to turn off the bed lamp.

"Eric?" Marie said, in a little voice.

"What?"

"Can you make love to me again? I feel so shaky suddenly. I need you to come into me one more time."

"I—I don't think I can. Ordinarily . . . usually I like to make love more than once. But tonight I just feel, everything's been drained out of me. I feel gutted. For some reason this—took a lot out of me, everything that went before. . . ." My throat went dry. "I could try."

"No that's okay; I understand." Marie leaned over and smoothed my hair, seeming much older than I.

"I could touch you."

"No, I don't mean that. If you want to go to sleep, go to sleep. . . ."

"I would, rather." I didn't dare admit that I was under the influence of a kind of horror, which made me draw away from her, as from a fellow-murderer. We had crossed the forbidden line. A part of me wanted to be *very* far from her: it was this that Marie sensed, I think, and that led her to ask that we make love again. She felt lonely: I could see that in her eyes. After the risk she had taken for me, with Jack, I could understand completely how she felt; and I was a heel for not being able to give her what she wanted; but something else was pulling me, a desire for oblivion and withdrawal, that could not be denied either. "Can't we just hug? You always say you like cuddling the best," I added, putting my arms around her belly and nuzzling her with my mustache.

"I do like to cuddle, yes," said Marie.

"Let's cuddle, then."

We kissed each other good night a last time, and went to sleep that way.

XIV

The next morning the clock radio woke us up. A Top 40 rock station. . . . Marie put on a pink quilted robe and made breakfast, some coffee, toast and corn flakes—I remember she had those little six-packs of dry cereal, and I chose sugar-frosted flakes and she took a raisin bran. At the kitchen table she watched me sleepily in her robe. She seemed to come awake much more slowly than I, who had the tendency to be ready for work the moment I opened my eyelids. I was anxious to get to the agency that day to meet with a new group. I was thinking over what I would do with them, how I would approach the first class. I told Marie the idea I had for an opening, more or less thinking aloud. She said it sounded like a good plan.

"When will you be through?" asked Marie.

"I should be finished about four-thirty today. Then I'll rush back here and we can do something that's fun. Maybe go to a show, have dinner at a fancy restaurant. Anything you want. It's Friday, I get paid today! Does that sound nice?"

"Very nice. . . . 'Scuse me, I can't stop yawning!"

"Why don't you go back to sleep after I leave?"

"Maybe I will," she said.

"You're like the wife who has to get up at six o'clock to make her husband breakfast."

"Except I usually get up at this hour. I don't know why I'm so sluggish today. . . ."

"It's the humidity." I was enjoying the picture of us as an old settled couple. Marie looked so domesticated in her puffy padded robe; her attention seemed attached to me with that lingering look women are supposed to have for their menfolk rushing off. One would think we had lived together for years. I felt loved, secure. How easy it was to adjust to good fortune! Yesterday I had been a lonely isolate; today, a good provider going off to work. Even Marie's logy-bodied dependency added to my sense of well-being. When she kissed me good-bye, she clung on me at the door. Then she leaned out the window to wish me a good day.

I know she leaned out the window because when I had reached the street, outside her brownstone, I turned to look up and there she was, following me with her smiling eyes. That put the cap on my happiness.

At the agency, I worked with a calm concentration that had been absent from my teaching for weeks. Details were met, absorbed and gotten through cleanly. When problems developed— the usual disorders, misplaced materials, hurt feelings, sullen disputes—I was able to deal with them tactfully and economically. I seemed to have a sharp appetite for work. One beneficial side effect of sex was that it quieted the part of my psyche that had been worrying about not getting any, and freed me to address myself to other people's problems, claims and tasks, with an interest that was generous and, at the same time, dispassionate. I don't know which I valued more: the submersion into passion and surprise that came with sex, or the surge of discipline and clarity that followed the next day.

At lunchtime I met Bruno and we went across the street to the Boricua, a greasy-spoon café which served rice and beans, plus. The daily "plus" ingredients were listed above the counter in incompletely spelled Spanish words of white and pink letters pinned onto a black menu board; but no one paid attention to that. You had to ask, and wait to see if they came up with what you wanted. Most of the clients from the agency hung out there too, playing the jukebox at lunch: they were still kids, sixteen to twenty-four, most of them ex-addicts with very complicated "life problems," as the social workers said.

Bruno palled around with several of them at the door before sitting down. They called him Gordo and Porky Pig because of his corpulent belly, and he countered with traditional insults about their masculinity. He had more of a taste for "the dozens" than I did. All that playful hostility bored me, when it didn't disturb me. Maybe it was partly that Bruno took it and dished it out so much better than I could. He was actually well bred, with polished manners when he wanted to show them, and scholarly interests in literature; but he loved affecting a loutish style. Lately he had taken to speaking a combination of mispronounced Spanish, bureaucratese, encounter talk and old bopster slang, with ironic emphases to show how swinishly vulgar he knew he sounded—but after all, he implied, we were living in a swinish age where the language was debased.

" 'Ey, *cerveza, por favor!*" Bruno called gruffly. "And a *café con leche por mein amigo* here, *andalé!*"

"I'm serving this man at the counter first," the owner retorted. "How you like your coffee, cream or black?" he asked the counter customer, Calvin, one of our agency youths.

"Cream," mumbled Calvin.

"He don't want nothin' blacker than hisself!" roared Debbie, a bigmouthed Amazon who was shaking her can at the jukebox.

"Oh snap!" echoed Flossie, her friend.

"Debbie—she's fierce!" Bruno shook his head, adding a private smile for me, at once appreciating the scene and shutting it out. "You look happy, Bro. What gives?"

"I'm feeling good today."

"As my old man used to say, you must've scored last night."

"I did."

Bruno wolf-whistled. "Who's the lucky woman?"

"It's not gentlemanly to tell," I smiled.

"That's why I asked *you,* Bro."

"What difference does it make?"

"If you're going to take umb*rage* about it—" He burped loudly. "Excuse me. It's not like you to be so concealing."

I thought for a few moments. "Her name's Marie. You met her once."

"Jack's piece?"

"That's the one."

"Good-looking filly!"

"She is that."

"How did it go?"

"Well. I like her very much. Be careful what you say."

"Sounds like serious shit. Are you willing to fight Jack for her?" asked Bruno, in that man-of-the-world tone of his I admired, even if I could never take it completely seriously.

"I am."

"*Bueno*. You're going to need to fight."

"How do you suggest?"

"I have one word of advice." He paused, slapping his chest. "If you're going to go into this, go all the way. Don't stop in the middle."

"What does that mean?"

"All the way, Bro! You more than anyone should know what that means. All the way means all the way. Give it your best shot. No *fonfering* around. No halfway, *comprende?*"

"Yeah."

"No you don't, you haven't a clue! Poor *amigo,* wake up, man! You have to be ruthless. Somebody's got to get hurt. Either you take him to the cleaners or they both take you to the cleaners. Are you ready for shit like that?"

"Be more precise. I'm having a hard time following you."

"Be ready to cut him loose. What else? You *shtupped* his girl. He ain't gonna go for that! This dude's sensitive—I met him."

I laughed; he made it sound like a gangsters' quarrel. "All right, I'll be ruthless."

"Then you have to get ready to say good-by to Jack. A clean break. *Feshtashte? Comprende?*"

"I think so."

"That's the ticket." Bruno looked at me worriedly, penetratingly. "Do you love her?"

"I really think I do. I think this could last, for a long long time, for a lifetime. I'm in love with her, and we get along very well," I stammered.

"This sounds serious," he scratched his head. "I'll have to give it some thought. But—good, congratulations! About time you fell in love. It's been too long since the last. And if all your cards fall right, you've got it. In like Flynn. But don't forget: Express train. Ruthless—all the way."

"I'll try my best." At the moment I was so proud to have Marie's love, that I could almost feel her lively self next to me, listening in keenly and enjoying this discussion. Drinking my second *café con leche,* I could still smell Marie on my fingers. The sea brine traces made me hungry for her in the middle of the day.

I worked steadily through the afternoon. At cleanup time I could no longer resist picking up the phone to call her and tell her I would be over soon.

"You can't come over," she said, immediately harried.

"Why not?" I had already seen the flash of lightning; in a few seconds would follow the thunderclap. "What's the matter?" I demanded.

"Jack came back. I met him at the airport, he was very very angry."

"So what?" I couldn't make real what I was hearing. I was going into a state of shock. Marie started talking quickly, one word after the other.

"I'm leaving for Boston for the weekend with him. I have to pack now. The train's going in forty minutes. I'm sorry, I don't know what to say. Everything I say would be inadequate. You must realize how much I hate myself. I blame myself for everything, I feel responsible for the whole sickening mess. Not that that's going to make you feel better."

"Didn't you know he was coming back today?"

"It was a surprise. Don't you think I would have told you? He changed his mind, he flew back late last night after my phone call, when I got so hysterical because he wasn't coming home. He took the Early Bird Special as a favor to me."

"Very nice."

"Don't sneer, Eric. It couldn't be more awful, I couldn't feel worse than I already do. I have to get off now."

"Wait a minute! We have to talk. I'll be right over."

"There's no time left. I'll call you as soon as I can—from Boston. That's a promise. Hate me if you want."

"Don't worry, I will!"

As soon as I heard her click, I ran out of the agency. It wouldn't be easy finding a cab in Harlem, but I started running to 125th Street. I flagged down a taxi. I gave him Marie's address before I could back out of it. In the shadows of the cab, my heart thumping, I had to decide what to do. I was grinding my teeth impatiently at the traffic holding us up. We had to go south a dozen blocks through the projects, and then west across Central Park. I was furious! I had said to Bruno at lunchtime our love could last a lifetime. It wasn't even going to last a day! Ha! It was over in less than twenty-four hours! What a jackass I'd been to believe her. Living in a fool's paradise. Deluding myself!

I looked out the window, and even at that moment I didn't believe that all was lost. My optimism had been so strong that I still couldn't absorb the bad news. It seemed to register slowly outside the window, letter by letter, like skywriting, and then fade in a moment against the blue. I couldn't believe that I had *already* run out of my good fortune. Arrrrr . . . ! I leaned back in my seat and looked out. The taxi entered Central Park, I saw trees, the tops of apartment towers in the west, the sun, fast clouds. Revolting. What did I care? This perpetual slide show that was always going on—I'd rather bang my head against a wall than look at it. I shut my eyes; my eyes were tired. And underneath everything, a feeling of faith in Marie that she would make it right. Ah, irrational faith! What was I going to do when I got there? I had to rehearse my attack. All the way, I thought grimly. Be ruthless. Whatever it took, go all the way. What did that mean—get violent? It wouldn't work; she wouldn't respect that if I tore up the place. I'd look like a fool. I should be suave, James Mason: I think you're making a mistake, dear; don't you owe me a better explanation? No, that wouldn't work. No good to stress my rights in the matter; I have no rights. Well then . . . I'll tell her I love her more than Jack does. It's true, too. At least I'll have my say.

I'll get it off my chest. I'll give her a running account of what I'm feeling.

I started to knock on her door, but tried it instead. It was open. I walked inside. She jumped when she saw me.

"What *should* I have done?" she asked. I didn't reply. I was too rich in reproaches to spend them all at once.

"Where's Jack?" I asked, pushing past her.

"He's not here. He went home to get his things. He's meeting me at the train station in a few minutes."

I walked into the other room to check for myself. She laughed bitterly: "If you won't even believe me on a simple statement like that, we don't have much to say to each other."

"Never mind," I said, brushing her remark away. "I can see he's not here." I sat down on a straight-back chair. I looked around with the air of someone who intends to stay for a long visit.

"You can sit here, but I've got to pack."

"Go ahead and pack," I said absentmindedly.

A mood of lethargy came over me. "What are you going to do in Boston?"

"Stay with Jack's Uncle Cyrus. What difference does it make?" She left the room.

"How long will you be away?" I yelled into the other room.

"Four days. I just need to get out of the city for a while."

"Oh, so you're doing it for a change of scenery?"

"Fuck off!"

"Why are you being so hostile?" I asked.

She ran into the room and said: "You didn't come here to ask me what I was going to do in Boston! Talk about hostility. Why don't you say what you came here for?"

"I don't know what I came here for," I shrugged. "I certainly didn't come here to have you treat me like the villain, when you're the one who did me in."

"What was I supposed to do?"

"You keep saying that as if it's—it's self-evident. You could just as easily have gone with me. Instead, you flick me off after one night, and then you wonder why I feel so hurt!"

"You act as if I did it intentionally."

"Not intentionally, but carelessly."

"Oh, I don't want to hear it!" she stuck her fingers in her ears. "Yes I do," she changed her mind suddenly, and sat at the edge of the bed. "Tell me what you were going to say."

"I want to know what made you choose Jack. Yesterday you told me that I gave you hope again. You even told me you loved me."

"It was true."

"But you love Jack more, is that it?"

"I love Jack *too,* but that isn't even the point," she said, getting up and pacing with her arms across her chest.

"What is the point? You needed me as a stick to hit Jack with?"

"I knew you'd say that!" she retorted with narrow-eyed fury. "You're so wrong. And you're not even original."

"It's an old story; why should I get points for being original? Woman has two men fall in love with her. It must be grand for you."

"It's not grand. I have to pack."

"Excuse me for taking up your time!" I said, following her into the living room foyer, where her coat closet was. "Maybe I can help you pack."

"Oh, stop it! Why are you being so—small-minded and sarcastic?"

"How do you expect me to be? Jolly? One moment we're lovers, we're supposed to go out to a show tonight, the next moment you're off to Boston with another man."

"That's exactly what Jack said! I swear, you two are . . ."

"Exactly alike? There must be some difference between us, if you chose him. Tell me what it is. I really want to know."

"All you care about is what Jack has that you haven't. You don't even care about me!"

"That's an easy way of getting out of answering."

Marie dropped her arms and looked at me beseechingly. "I have to go with him. He needs me so much more than you do."

"How do you know? You're not inside me."

"I feel so terrible that I hurt him."

"Doesn't my hurt count?"

"But he's not as strong as you. It's true, you know it! He's so upset. He hates me twice as much as you do."

"But that's horrible!"

"What's horrible?" she said with a faraway look.

"To go with a man who hates you is horrible. And even more horrible that I should be deprived of my happiness because someone is weaker than I am! It doesn't seem quite fair. There'll always be someone weaker than I am—must I wait for all of them to become happy? And why should you take it on yourself? You're not a Christian saint, are you? No one asks you to make these sacrifices for the emotionally crippled."

"But I'm a cripple also. In the same way Jack is. And we'll probably never be happy together, and he'll probably never forgive me for this. But if that's the way it is, I'm prepared for it."

"Prepared to throw your life away on an ungrateful, unforgiving —weakling? You're getting carried away with heroism. You're playing Joan of Arc!"

"No I'm not. I understand perfectly well what I'm doing. Even if it doesn't make sense to you. I have to finish packing now." She looked at her watch. "I'm almost late as it is."

"So you'll catch the next train."

"No: if I'm not there Jack will leave without me. He already said so."

"Nice guy!"

"He's your friend."

Marie was like a tennis ball machine that kept throwing back whatever I said. I had half a mind to stall her from catching the train, but she had her defenses perfectly in place and knew what she was doing every moment, as she ransacked the closet bottom for a pair of shoes, ignoring me.

"I can't believe how cold you are to me suddenly!" I said.

"And I can't believe how different *you* are from the manly person I took you to be," she threw back at me. "Whining about how I did you in and all the rest of it. Do you know how selfish you sound?"

I was furious enough that my fist rose in the air by itself. Then I answered indifferently: "When you treat me well, you bring out the best in me. When you hurt me you bring out the worst."

"That's not being responsible for your actions."

"Oh, don't give me that crap." I felt she was partly right, though; I *was* being creepy. And she was being rather plucky and brave. I wanted her to remember me with a positive last impression. There must be some maturity left in me to bring out: even if it convinced her of nothing, even if we never saw each other again, at least I could know I had acquitted myself well.

"I didn't come over here to condemn you," I said suddenly. "I came over to tell you one thing. That I care for you very much. That I love you, Marie. I'll still love you after this," I said, feeling my throat swell up. "I want you to remember that." I kissed her on the neck, with a helpless, paralyzed passion that came out as spongy.

She took the kiss passively—numbly, it seemed to me. The perfume behind her ears swam into my nose, waking me up, like smelling salts, to what I would soon have no more. I put my arms around her. The tenderness began spilling out of me.

"Don't," she pleaded.

"I want you to know," I continued, "that I'll still be here for you. And I understand your going off with Jack. I don't hold that against you. It's loyalty. I admire that. And I don't feel I have to have exclusive rights over your love. I can understand how you loved two people at the same time. Maybe it will all work out. If you can find a way to love both of us," I said, "I wouldn't mind. I would accept sharing you with Jack."

"No." She broke away. "It wouldn't work out. I tried that once in Stockholm. With Sven and Mark. I was very happy, but I kept feeling I was making one or the other miserable. And what finally got me down was all that phony camaraderie between them."

"I think we could work it out," I said, trying to hold on to her and to kiss her again.

"I don't like it when you kiss me like that."

"Why, don't you want to receive my affection?"

"Because I don't think you mean it—I think you hate me."

"I don't *hate* you," I said wearily.

"At least Jack was more honest. He screamed at me, he called me a whore! He called me horrible, disgusting things . . ." she suddenly remembered.

"I don't see why I have to compete with that. I *don't* hate you. I'm not going to manufacture that, just for your dramatic expectations."

"I can't stand it when you try to be nice to me."

"Look, Jack tricked you. He tricked you by throwing a tantrum, which you fell for, thinking it was real passion!" I cried. "In my opinion, Jack can't love any woman. He fooled you by making you think he could." I despised myself for this treachery to our friendship. I had really gone too far this time. Yet Marie didn't seem to have heard it, didn't even seem to be listening.

"You hate me, you just hate me!" she repeated. "Get out!"

"I do think you're a bitch. But then again, I think you're simply very young and don't understand the consequences of making someone fall in love with you."

"I know," she said, "that you think I crave that abuse, to be called a bitch. But it's not true. I'm not a masochist."

"No, I'm the masochist—for falling in love with you!"

"Neither of you loves me. Neither of you. That's the terrible truth." Marie turned around to close her luggage. Her back was to me. I hated her. I hated her so much that, when she stood up, I wanted to deliver a blow to that cavity in her chest, the source of all her weakness and privileges.

"I would hit you if I thought it would do any good," I said, trembling with the itch to do it.

"Don't," she said; "it won't."

"I would love to smash you."

"I just feel totally alienated," Marie looked away.

"I just want to smash you like a pile hammer into the ground." I closed my eyes to let the homicidal tremor pass through me. For a second I had come close to being a killer, and then I got control of it. "I hope someday you take Judo lessons," I said, "so that you can defend yourself. But then, if you could defend yourself you probably wouldn't need to spite men by making two of them fall in love with you at the same time and then acting like a confused helpless waif."

"If you hit me I'll just hate you!" Marie declared.

"I'm not going to *hit* you," I said disgustedly. "Pack!" I raised my fist and ordered her. It was ludicrous to put such malevolent force into this command, ordering her to do the one thing I did not want. She stood there, almost disobeying; then she bent down to grasp the case handle. Her two-day bag was already packed.

"I've got to go now," she said. She came up to hug me good-bye, but I wouldn't have it: it was too little. "Nothing?" I cried. "You'll just stand there and give me nothing?"

"You don't know *anything*," she cried, with tears in her eyes, "if you think that was nothing! Would you have been satisfied if I'd kissed you?"

"Don't tell me what you could have done. It's for you to do it, not to make me beg for it."

"Get out," she shrieked. "Get out of here!"

"That's all you can say, 'Get out!'" I mimicked. "'Get out!'" I began shaking her by the shoulders. Her head flopped back and forth slowly, and her eyes got scared; and then she just stared helplessly at the floor, as though she really thought she were going to be murdered.

I took my hands off her. "Just this morning you hung out the window for me when I left. *You hung out the window to kiss me good-bye!*" I spat the words out. "Just this morning!" Then I turned and ran, slamming the door behind me. It had not ended well. There was no way to make it end well any more.

PART TWO

Decrystallization

I

It was an intolerable weekend. I wanted to die. The bridges between moments had been washed away, there were huge lacunae that the second hand had to jump. It had never seemed so difficult to get through a Saturday and Sunday alone; yet I felt too wretched to inflict myself on anyone else.

Monday I went to work. I asked Bruno if I could see him in the evening.

I was propounding my problem to Bruno, Monday night, as we walked up Times Square. Since there was nothing else on my mind and no point in faking other interests, I had been unburdening myself with a description of the whole episode of sleeping with Marie, and our battle the next day. As we were walking, I was aware of the homey, decrepit wash of movie marquees, electric signs and billboards tilting over us; Times Square was in fine form. All the hookers in hot pants were out. Little girls rushed up to us with orchid corsages, and then turned nasty when we wouldn't buy one. They were like gypsy children with their long dirty dresses and suggestion of a mustache, and you felt they would have just as soon stuck the pin into your heart as on your shirt pocket. Added to hot smells of griddle grease from Child's Coffee Shop were the flying cinders, confirming the fact that this weekend had seen the worst pollution crisis in New York City's history. I had heard it on the radio, and it was the only piece of news to cheer me up all day.

We passed a candy parlor with its heavy caramel reek.

"How many times did you fuck her?" asked Bruno.

"Only that once. I told you."

"You should have balled her more."

"It wouldn't have made any difference."

"Might have. It's in the cunt where these decisions are made."

"Oh, I don't believe that!" I said with full annoyance. "That's baloney."

"You told me she said she wanted you to come into her again. Maybe she wanted you to put your brand on her more definitively. Make it irrevocable, so that she wouldn't have to go back to Jack again."

"She had good reasons to go back to Jack, whether it was once, twice, or five times. 'Branding'—that's just macho bull, you probably picked it up in Mexico."

"Hold on. It's folk wisdom," said Bruno, smiling. "What do you think love is?"

"It's not just that. . . . Besides, I assumed there'd be many more opportunities. I had no idea this was the one and only night. I thought this was the beginning of a relationship of some duration."

"You could've screwed her in the morning."

"Oh, come on—look, I couldn't, I was frightened. I thought we would get to know each other slowly. You can't rush intimacy."

Bruno was about to reply, but backed off. "Want to hit the machines?" he pointed to the insides of a penny arcade we were passing, where a strange-looking breed of people were sitting at keno machines, lobbing red rubber balls into round holes.

"I'm not in the mood for pinball tonight."

"That's where we differ: I'm always in the mood."

"That's what makes you such a *sport*," I replied, irritably.

"*Olé!*" Bruno exclaimed, touching my cheek affectionately, like a cat reaching out its paw. He always disarmed me with his gentle gestures. We stopped at a light. "What will happen now?"

"I don't know. I guess I've lost her."

"She should have gone with you. You're a heavier dude than Jack."

"Well, thanks for saying that, friend, but I don't think it necessarily always works that way."

"Maybe she'll change her mind. You never can tell with women."

"I doubt it. There are such things as loyalty, habit. And besides, she and Jack are from the same social class. They've both been to Europe a million times, they both have ill health: they belong together more than she and I do."

"Do you honestly think that's true?"

"Maybe. I don't know," I said gloomily, realizing I didn't. "It's like, once when I was in high school and I went out with a girl who was elected runner-up to the prettiest girl for Miss Venus title."

"What was Miss Venus like? She must have been a piece," Bruno chuckled; he loved stories like this.

"Oh, she was. She was a knockout. She could have been a movie star. She looked like Veronica Lake."

"What happened with the runner-up Venus, the one you went out with?"

"She was quite something, too. She looked more like Rita Hayworth. I went out with her for about three months, and I kept feeling that she was too good-looking for me—too far above my head. I kept making things difficult, from embarrassment at my excessive good fortune. Purposely trying to mess it up. I did *ridiculous* things! What bothers me with what just happened is that maybe I blew my chances because I was feeling Marie was over my head. I can't help wondering, did I have a serious chance with her? Could it have gone differently if I had played it smoother? Or was I always out of the running?—Or am I still in the running?"

"But you're a good-looking guy. What do you mean, she's over your head?"

"I don't know, it's just a feeling. Let's not talk about it."

"Triangles are a bitch," Bruno murmured.

"Have you ever been in one?"

"Sure, I've been in 'em," said Bruno. Sometimes it seemed he had been in everything having to do with sex.

"What are they all about?"

"Usually . . ." he thought for a while, "Usually it's the Oedipal situation. The kid wanting to crawl into bed between his parents."

"Yeah, I guess." I thought he was probably right, but was disappointed because I had expected something juicier, like one of his Mexico City tales; instead he seemed to be quoting from textbooks they gave him in social work school. "Still and all," I said, "I never thought of Jack as my father."

"Any couple. It's the primary *dyad,* which gives way to the *triad,*" he laughed, mocking his own jargon. "The dyad is a relatively stable but deadening form, whereas the triad is a notoriously unstable form. In sexual matters it nearly always resolves itself into another duo: either the old couple balances back, or there's a different combo. You were probably good for them. It sounds like the two of them were headed for a dry spell; Jocko may have even had eyes for cutting out. Now Jack will think more highly of his broad. Her value will go up in his eyes because she made it with you, and he respects you."

"Wonderful."

"Maybe the three of you could even work out a sharing deal. It's not unheard of."

"I think one needs to be more worldly than we are."

"Not necessarily. I have a client—you should see what goes on in these Puerto Rican households."

We stood at another corner light. I found myself looking into the window of the poster shop on my right, with pictures of Marlon Brando on a motorcycle and Richard Nixon with his head on backwards, and Raquel Welch bursting out of a lion skin. "So triangles are always Oedipal?" I returned to the first surmise.

"Not always. Sometimes it's a gay-inspired thing. It often happens that, when two men are homosexually drawn to each other they fixate on the woman," said Bruno, blandly and tolerantly.

"I know, I've been thinking about that," I mused. "Like Frederic and Deslauriers in *Sentimental Education:* Deslauriers sleeps with Frederic's mistress to get to Frederic. But go on— what do you mean, they *fixate* on the woman?"

"Just what I said. They transfer their attraction for each other, to a woman who's going with one of them. She becomes the spoils."

"Do you think that's what's happening here?"

Bruno shrugged: "I'm not close enough to tell."

"It's something I've thought about, but . . . you know, I try to make it real to me. To see if it fits. And it doesn't. I ask myself whether I would want to sleep with Jack. No, I don't think I would. Am I homosexually drawn to him? No more than to any of my friends—all my friends I find physically attractive in some way, or it would be hard to like them as friends. Did I want to go with Marie only because she was a surrogate for Jack? I doubt it: I think I was genuinely excited by *her*. She moves me, regardless of him. I—I don't see how such insights can help at this point anyway, when I'm going through feelings that . . . Even if they were true, they're so abstract compared to what I'm feeling."

"What are you feeling?" Bruno interrupted.

"I'm feeling lousy. I'm feeling in constant pain. My stomach is —kicking at me, it's all fired up. My chest aches, my throat is swollen as though any minute I'll cry. I can't be with people, *or* alone. When I'm with people, it's too hard to carry on the farce of talking about something else, when this is all I'm thinking about. That's why it's such a relief to be telling it to you, tonight. But most of the time it's an inappropriate conversation topic. Like at work. I want to go away and be by myself, and think about it. But when I am by myself I start thinking about, you know—killing myself. I have to have company around me. I have to make sure I don't hurt myself. It's ridiculous—I don't want to commit suicide! I—I feel stupid even telling you; it sounds so maudlin. I only say it because it's been on my mind a lot."

Bruno nodded understandingly. "How would you do it?" he asked in a theoretical tone of voice. My God, he was turning into a real professional! That's exactly what you were supposed to do with someone who made a suicide threat: flush it out, make them picture the act concretely. I had to bite back a smile at seeing the technique played on me.

"I'd use a surefire method. None of this chancy stuff, like sleeping pills," I said, wrinkling up my nose at the memory of sour, vomited powder. "This time it would be by jumping off a building. Or a gun."

"Rifle's the surest. At close range."

"Not if you know as little about guns as I do. Look, it isn't that I want to—I don't *want* to kill myself, exactly, but I would like to *gouge* a piece of flesh out of my stomach to stop this feeling."

"Try liquor," suggested Bruno.

"I don't really like the taste of liquor. That's *your* way, isn't it?"

"It works. There are times when anxiety passes a certain point," he explained, "and the body can't take it any more. It doesn't matter how: when you reach that point, Bro, there has got to be a stop to anxiety or else you've had it. Buy a little bottle of brandy. A pint bottle for a few bucks—I like Tres Secas. Take a swig when you get home. You'll see, it gives you a warm glow in your stomach, knocks out all that static. Seriously, it's good advice. Get yourself some scotch, or brandy. It's good to have round the house in any case, for medicinal uses. It's a recognized anesthetic."

"All right."

"You don't sound very enthusiastic," noted Bruno. "I know you just think I'm trying to turn you into a lush like me. But believe me, you may need it in the weeks ahead."

We were approaching the Metropole Bar, and I started to slow my steps unconsciously as we neared that shrine. Ever since I could remember coming to Manhattan, I had always stood outside the open door and looked inside. Years ago they had had jazz combos, and jazz lovers who didn't have the price of admission would take in the music for free, catching a glimpse of a flashing high hat, or a trombone's sheen. Then they changed the policy, got rid of the live musicians and brought in topless dancers. The crowds grew twice as thick at the windows. Family men smoking pipes would grin, standing next to bums and students, all caught red-handed in their libidinous curiosity. It was a friendly crowd of voyeurs, but it must have gotten too raunchy, or else no one was paying any money to go inside, so the management papered over the windows. But still they kept the door opened—it was a trademark of the Metropole—and you could grab a peep at a tit if you hopped up and looked over somebody's head. Sometimes on a cloudy afternoon, thinking about anything but that, it would give me a lift to see a sultry naked woman from the doorway, without my even leaving the street.

Bruno and I were stretching our necks.

"You want to go in?" he said.

"No, I don't think so."

"Have you ever been inside the Metropole?"

"Once, I think," I started to lie. "No, actually, never."

"We must respect the banalities," he said, taking me by the arm. "Come on. My treat."

Inside the Metropole there were chandeliers with ruby droplets, gaudy wallpaper, pulsating lights and silver mirrors; still, the place looked like some interior decorator's distracted approximation of a honky-tonk. The hall was too spacious and empty to feel carnal. At the railing, a sailor was looking up with pug-faced moroseness at the go-go girls dancing on top of the bar. The women were naked except for silver high-heeled shoes and red plush triangles over their pubic areas. We took a table in front of the center dancer, a brunette with a full shape and an older, more experienced air than the other two. After dancing a song, she got down on all fours on a divan and tensed and untensed her buttocks, managing both to create an image of forbidden pleasures, and to conserve energy. I say she looked more "experienced" because she consistently worked less and made it seem more sexy than the girl on her left, who struck me as a college girl trying to pick up some extra money, rather valiantly projecting all the naughtiness of a skinny ballerina self-consciously switching into a jazzy modern dance. She made salmon-like offerings with her mouth towards her customers, who looked away in embarrassment. Our girl, on the contrary (I already thought of the brunette as "our girl"), had a knowing, goodhumored veteran's expression on her face, and when she wanted to do something sexy, she turned around first to look at herself in the mirror.

Behind us was a table filled, to my surprise, with a party of middle-aged women, probably from the suburbs or someplace like Astoria. They were chatting among themselves as though this was a birthday outing, and showed no particular awareness of the bumps and grinds in their line of vision.

Sprinkled here and there, throughout the club, were solitary men in dark suits, as far away from each other as possible, looking ahead at the dance with stoical, lonely eyes. I tried to promote a little misogynistic disillusionment, feeling how tawdry and pathetic this all was. But it wasn't, really; not especially disillusioning, just a kind of deal between people, with the rules understood. If this were sin, it was so much more innocuous than what one did in one's regular life. (I was thinking of Marie.) Just then I noticed the brunette dancer in the center: she was twirling one of her breasts clockwise like a helicopter propeller, while holding onto the top of her head for balance. It looked so funny that I laughed aloud—who would confuse such a grotesquely unnatural movement with desire? She smiled, permitting herself a broad satiric grin while twirling the breast in the opposite direction, and our eyes caught for a moment, in a recognition that felt so naked I feared she would falter, step out of role. I couldn't bear to engage her eyes again, it would force her to do an unprofessional thing, to acknowledge her disbelief in the ritual. And force me to acknowledge my humanity. On top of it all, I was embarrassed by the suspicion that maybe when our eyes caught she was merely trying to get a tip out of me, to add to the bills in her glass. So I looked away, at the struggling girl making fish enticements on my left, and studied the old limping waiter and the middle-aged broad-shouldered manager with dandruff-flecked, greasy green suit, to try to guess what their society might be like. Bruno had ordered again, he was already several drinks ahead of me. My thoughts were getting light-headed, and whether it was because of the beer, or the "entertainment," or my own reluctance to suffer any more, I realized with a start that I was in a good mood. What can I do? I said to myself; I'll always be a shallow person. There are those who can go to the depths of tragedy, who can suffer magnificently!

But just as I'm getting to it I'll be distracted by a booby whirling, or something ridiculous like that.

I went back to watching the brunette. I had put a stupid grin on my face, and was pretending to look as Yahoo, as much like a typical customer as possible, so that we would not have to go through that moment of shared understanding again. I had probably made it all up anyway. The brunette, who certainly had a lovely body, was stuffing something up it like a feathered boa while looking straight at us. I tried to imagine how she would express tenderness in the bedroom with her lover. I pictured her being quite different, holding the man's head in her hands and stroking it maternally while the moon and the street sounds came through their tenement window.

"She's good, eh?" said Bruno. "She's got something special about her."

I leaned over to whisper to him: "She's the only one who's any good."

"Oh, I kind of like the redhead."

I looked at Fishmouth again. It interested me that Bruno liked her. He often saw possibilities in women whom I tended to dismiss without a second glance—even huge, monstrously homely ones.

The three women dancers got off, went to the side of the stage and slipped on their street clothes, and another trio took their place. This time the center girl was bleach-blonde, the one on the left a Eurasian, but I couldn't find anything to interest myself in their acts. The motions of the go-go dance itself were not that fascinating, and the sensation of seeing bare what is usually draped had worn off some time ago. I realized that what had made the brunette dancer so arresting was not only her sexy shape but her dramatic flair, her ability as an actress to project a character and make one look at her. I turned in my chair to catch her squeezing into a booth, next to the skinny redhead. She had put on a pink middy blouse of polished cotton with ruffles in front. She lit a cigarette, said a few words to the redhead, and laughed briefly. The stooped old waiter came by to ask her what drink she wanted.

After she ordered, she settled into the booth's backrest and smoked her cigarette, pulling a curtain of privacy around herself.

"Oh, he's smitten!" Bruno pounded me on the back. "Smitten *again!*"

"No I'm not."

"I don't blame you. She's splendid! If I had the money, I would love to give you a grant to do nothing but go to these places for a year, and follow your instincts."

"It's a lovely idea."

"It would be good for you to get your fill of this—" he burped, and gestured toward the bar. Bruno must have had a pretty precise idea of what "this" was.

"Somehow, when it comes to the bars and red-light districts," I said, "I'd rather imagine it than do it."

"You're right! That's what puzzles me, *amigo.* You seem to know what something's like, without having to go through it! That's admirable," Bruno said murkily. "That's phenomenal." He was a bit drunk; and when Bruno drank too much he got either admiring or insolent. "It's splendid—I envy that in you. Myself, I have to stumble again and again to learn. But you, you can look ahead, decide that it's not the thing for you, and not do it! And you know why? Because you're a moralist. You have moral values to fall back on—that allow you to anticipate mistakes. . . ."

"Not always," I said, smiling bleakly, thinking of my mistake with Marie and Jack.

"But most of the time, most of the time. This is nothing—this business with—you'll get over it. I'm talking about the global picture. The decades. Sure you make mistakes, but you don't have to keep making them. Once is enough. You do your work and stay out of dangerous situations. Whereas I—I don't have that control. I'm a slave to my cock. But you, you figure out a thing's not going to work out, you leave it alone. I admire that, very truthfully." Bruno had leaned against me with his mouth close to my ear, and I let his warm beery breath and words of praise wash over me.

Suddenly he broke off and said, "I've got to go over and talk to her."

He stood up, pulled himself into cavalier's posture. Then he wandered between the tables to the booth of the brunette. I saw him motion fluently with his hand—Bruno could be very polished when he wanted to be—and he sat beside her. They started talking. Sometimes I thought it was Bruno's Falstaffian belly that enabled him to play out these parts with women. He could treat himself as a joke, a creature of appetites, and women seemed to find that corpulence reassuring, bearishly cuddly. Feeling ditched and alone, I walked up to the bar at the back, toward the red flashing lights and stacks of mirrors where no one sat, past the loudspeakers which were booming a mindlessly repetitive discotheque song, *Don't stop doin' it, don't stop, ugh!* I circled back around the nightclub, giving them a wide berth as I approached their booth, pretending to be a movie camera doing a 360-degree turn around a pair of lovers; and debated whether to join them (Bruno would have enjoyed that), or take the next table over, playing his discreet, gentlemanly foil; but it was too gross an invasion of privacy for me, this business of going up to a topless dancer after her act, I would have to show my disapproval by not joining. Such distinctions have to be made; they add up to a self.

Maybe that was what I needed: to have an affair with a Metropole dancer. I would get all the ascetic garbage out of my system. I was starting to lose patience with Bruno, and thought it was quite inconsiderate of him to chase women tonight when he knew the state I was in (what was he up to anyway? he already had a woman he was living with); but the very next moment he stood up, and came by the table where I was sitting, as though he knew to the split-second how long a rope he had with me. "Ready to go?" he asked me. Bruno picked up the bill, paid it, smiled amiably at me, and led the way out.

It was a breezy night, and Bruno started whistling.

"What did she say?" I asked, finally giving in.

"Her name's Leah. Can you imagine that? *Leah!* I would have imagined any name but that. A biblical name! . . . And she's only twenty-three. That also surprised me. Bright. Dignified! When I asked her her name, she told me and asked me mine right back. Not as a come-on, mind you, but a liberated quid-pro-quo thing. She wanted to know what I did. I told her I was in training to be a psychiatric social worker. She asked me what that was about; I told her. She said she was thinking of going back to school herself. In painting. I asked her when she got off work. She said around three. I asked her if anyone was picking her up. She said yes, her boyfriend. She was fairly explicit about that. I asked her if she was living with him. She didn't answer. I said, 'Do you love each other?' She said yes. 'Does he take good care of you?' She said yes. I wasn't too sure though—there was something about her voice when she said it. I asked her if she was working there tomorrow. She said she works there four days a week: Sunday, Monday, Tuesday and Thursday." He smiled his chubby-cheeked smile.

I pinched his cheek: "*Boychik,* you're so sweet when you're contented with yourself! Do you think you'll come back and visit?"

"I'll probably never see her again. I just wanted to talk to her."

II

At the end of four days there was still no phone call from Marie. Now the suffering began in earnest. I was surprised how much there was of it. I imagined them winding through the shops of Cambridge, kissing, sleeping together, and when I was not torturing myself with such pictures, I turned to my own memories.

One of the privileges of suffering is to go over past events and run them back and forth in the mind's screening room, as many times as it takes to detect a new and more piercing motivation for the other person's behavior which one was too stupid to see at first. So it was with Marie saying good-bye to me at the door, and clinging to me, then watching me from the window: it now seemed to me that she was probably much more aware than I was of how short-lived our time together would be. I thought over our last wild meeting, and my smorgasbord of responses, from sluggishness to anger to mushy amorousness, petulance, sarcasm, pleas—I should have stuck to one strong line. I picked flaws in my performance; I shuddered at both my lack of ethics and my scruples; I reproached myself for everything crass I did, and everything decent I did. And when I got tired of tearing at myself, I started in on her. How I despised that little cheat now! I called her every name that men have pinned on pretty women since the world began.

On Wednesday, having waited a full five days, I called Jack at home. He hung up on me.

I was now even more determined to talk to him. He had moved, in my mind, to the position of dominance. He alone had the power to grant happiness to all three of us. That was one branch of my thinking. The other branch was not thinking at all but simply the urge to throw myself on the bayonet of his disapproval; to make all the excuses I had stored inside me and to hear the dismissals I was entitled to hear. He could say anything to me he wanted, so long as I could hear his voice: that urgent, hot, sensitive tragedian's voice of his, muffled by coughs, toned down by discreetness, but always alive as few voices were to me. I had a yen to talk to Jack, just as when we were college students and I'd imagined him roaming around his house with a telephone cord that took him into the kitchen and back, as we shared our impressions for hours. It had always seemed that nothing could stop us from liking each other.

And now the finality of, "I don't want to talk to you, Eric."

I had assumed Marie must be with him, but in desperation I called Marie at her number, and she was home alone. She sounded very happy to hear from me, and said she had wanted to call me from Boston but couldn't break away. She was just getting ready to phone me tonight. I was so grateful to be allowed to talk to her again that the shadow of our last fight flew out of my mind, out of both our minds. I asked her how Boston was. She answered that they had quarreled the whole time. They had barely gone outside. Jack wasn't feeling well, he had a relapse of bronchitis. They'd slept in separate beds. . . . She seemed determined to let me know this, vaguely as it was inserted into the running account; maybe they didn't make love because of Jack's venereal infection, I thought cynically, but nevertheless I was pleased that she should take the trouble to reassure me that she had been faithful, in however a roundabout way. But the next moment she felt obliged to tell me that she *had* taken care of him and been very loving. She had just left him off, in fact, at his mother's house, and was supposed to go over there later to nurse him and sleep over. What did he say about me? I asked. "Oh, every second word out of his mouth was Eric, Eric. 'You love Eric, don't you?' he kept throwing at me. I told him I did," Marie said.

I pulled some courage into my chest and said to her, "I'd like to see you again."

She came back with: "I'd like to see *you*."

"Do you think we can arrange that?"

"I think it's a possibility," she laughed. "Any time you say."

"When are you free?"

"How about . . . Saturday afternoon? Earlyish, like around eleven-thirty?" she asked hopefully, with a lilt in her voice.

Any part of Saturday was more than I had hoped for. "That's fine. We can have a picnic if it's nice."

"Oh, I love picnics. Terrific! I can hardly wait till Saturday at eleven-thirty."

"Me too. See you then."

"Sweet dreams," Marie said.

I was buoyed up to the sky by this conversation. Not that I had any idea what I was hoping for from the date, but at this point I merely wanted to prolong our contact, to stall for time until something unexpected might occur in my favor.

And, strange as it was, I had every confidence that my troubles with Jack would be resolved as well, after one good talk.

Saturday went like a dream. Marie and I took sandwiches and plums and pint containers of chocolate milk into Central Park, and we walked a ways and sat on a patch of weeds and crabgrass, looking out at the clunky brown fence around the reservoir. It was a quiet, humid late August day. Marie had on a red and white sundress that was adorable; I leaned my head on her lap. We were in such a good mood, and the park looked luscious in its rank late summer overgrowth, as we ate our lunch of plums.

The big elm branch over us, shading us with its leaves, was swaying susceptibly, exactly as we were; romantic suspension, no decisions. I talked nonsense to Marie. We kept laughing at everything: we were able to appreciate our predicament with a gallows humor, looking up at the trees.

"What did his mother say?"

"She said, 'You can't pin it all on Eric, Jackie. It takes two to tango!' "

"That's marvelous. I knew she'd put in a good word for me."

"Well, it's less a good word for you than a bad one against me!" said Marie.

"Don't you get along with her?" I said, rolling over on the side.

"Well, on the surface we do. But she's suspicious of any girl Jack would care about. And I think she's delighted with this turn of events."

"Did she say anything else?"

"Only that. Takes two to tango!" Marie remembered gaily, her eyes sparkling.

"Is she the only one who knows?"

"I think his Uncle Cyrus guessed. Jack muttered about some troubles we were having, but Cyrus may have put two and two together. There was one amazing moment—" She lowered her head laughing.

"What's so funny?"

"I was just remembering Jack kicking me under the table to stop me from saying anything. His Uncle Cyrus is a retired doctor, he's a really fine gentleman from the old school. He told a lot of stories about his past. We were sitting at the dining room table and he started talking about his college days. At old Cornell. He belonged to a special fraternity that he seemed to be very proud of—he said they were different in the old days, not so anti-intellectual—and he started telling about two fraternity brothers. These two fraternity brothers were the best of friends, insepa-rable? Everyone made jokes about them because they were so close, and their nicknames were Castor and Pollux?"

"Go on; I get the point."

"Well, one of them had a fiancée. And he and the young lady were going to get married as soon as he finished his studies. And the engaged one went away on a trip—we'll call him Castor—and Pollux stayed behind. And—I forget how Cyrus phrased it, it was so delicately put—he 'had his way with the other fellow's girl.' You should have seen the look Jack gave me then! So when Cas-tor returned to Cornell the secret came out, and he broke off the engagement; and his friend Pollux was so stricken with guilt that he dropped out of Cornell. But that isn't all he did—as if that wasn't enough! He stuck his hand in the fireplace. And he spent the rest of his life atoning for that one misstep. Boy!" Marie shook her head, impressed.

"Those were the days when men were men," I said, pulling up some grass. "It must be a measure of how far we've fallen off the track of nobility that I'm not even tempted to stick my hand in a fire."

"And I wouldn't want you to."

"Still, it's fascinating to hear what someone in my shoes—the 'scoundrel's position'—would have done in the days when men had honor. Can you imagine watching your hand burn until it's lost its flesh? Then what did he do? Wrap it in a dirty rag and go off to the country to live like a hermit?"

"No, he didn't wrap it in a dirty rag!" she poked me. "That's *your* version. Why would he have done that?"

"To keep the dogs from nipping at it."

"It would be so crusty, I don't think they'd like it."

"You're pretty crusty yourself," I said.

"How dare you? Feisty is what I am, not crusty."

"No, you're like a meat loaf, moist inside and crusty on top."

Marie jiggled her lap with laughter. "Your compliments are so romantic."

"But I am romantic."

"You're outrageous," she said fondly.

I looked up at her, propping myself on an elbow. She was so pretty when she sparkled, like today—that was the thing, she was so *pretty*. Those Bing cherry lips. Her glistening eyes. She presented such a convincing metaphor for happiness. Whether Marie was ever going to be mine or not, she had given me something: an image of what happiness looked like. Was beauty really meant as a portent, an advance swelling of happiness? The more I looked at her, the more I saw there was something absolutely right about Marie.

"I'm so infatuated with you, you couldn't believe it," I said disgruntledly.

"That's such a funny word, 'infatuated,'" she stroked my hair; "because it has 'fat' in the middle. It's like a man with a little pot-belly."

"It comes from my eating too much of you—with my eyes," I said.

She looked down at me with a dubious, dimpled smile.

My eyes were wet—maybe because I was looking into the sun; or maybe because life was so ripe that the tears finally spilled out of me.

Before separating, we made a date to see each other on the next Saturday evening.

How did I think it could work? Yet, in spite of what my mind told me, I had confidence in her—in the larger genius of Woman to keep all the contradictory strands of love in motion. It was the kind of faith an actor places in a really intuitive theatre director to balance all the parts of the production. And if life were theatre, Marie would have succeeded; she could improvise within a scene and make the most of any accidents. One sensed in her incredible reserves of unused dexterity.

I had a fantasy of Marie as the wife in a *film noir,* who suddenly reveals an awesome ability to execute crimes. We would kill Jack; she'd handle the details; then we would get rid of the body, collect the insurance. I would follow her take-charge manner with a fluid passivity of my own, feeling lost, sapped, with nothing to hold onto but the sparkle in her eyes, the dark brazen allure of the femme fatale. . . . Yes, but if only she had been more of a femme fatale! She could have taken care of everything. Myself, I had no idea what to do. I kept calling Jack's number. I did not know what I would say to him in this call, but I told myself I would simply "level" with him.

Most of the time no one was home; twice his mother took the call. I was on the alert (since Mrs. Bogardes and I used to get along well) for any curt or newly hostile tone in her manner. But I heard none. Instead there was a sort of flirtatious curiosity, as though she were excited by all the sexual possibilities raised up dustily around her, and would have liked me to say something much more spicy than "Please give him the message I called." She promised she would: I sensed she rather looked forward to performing this service.

Finally, as had to happen sooner or later, Jack picked up the phone.

"Oh it's you. I don't want to talk to you," he said coldly.

"I think it would be better if we did. Hear me out for a few minutes."

"There's nothing to talk about. You did it and that's all."

"Wait, haven't you ever done anything you weren't supposed to?"

"Yes, and I paid for it."

"I'm willing to pay."

"Well you can't expect us to pick up from where we were as friends after an episode like this. You have to live with what you did."

I had never heard Jack address me in such Old Testament terms. I was thrilled by the new categorical, forceful strength in Jack: gone was the apologetic deference he used to have with me.

"I just want to explain how it happened."

"What difference does it make?" he replied. He broke off, coughing.

"What's the matter?"

"I have tonsillitis, some mild form of it."

"I'm sorry to hear that."

"Look, this isn't the best time for a confrontation. My family doctor examined me and told me that my nerves are shot. I don't like psychodramas, Eric, so count me out!"

"What's that supposed to mean?"

"Just what I said. I won't be sucked into your psychodramas and your confrontation politics."

"Since when have I gone in for psychodramas?"

"I won't be drawn into your past. If you need to retaliate for some other injury, leave me out of it."

"What are you talking about?"

"You know what I mean. You're just acting out what Curt did to you. Now I know that scarred you pretty badly, and I'm sorry about it, but that's no reason to turn around and do it back to me."

"Wait a second, those are not analogous situations. Curt and Natalie were sneaking behind my back for years, whereas I want to get this out in the open immediately."

"You had no choice. Marie told me."

"Even if Marie didn't tell you I would have. I even tried to tell you when you were in California—"

"What did you tell me? You didn't tell me anything. Come off it, Eric."

"I told you . . . that I was growing attracted to Marie and wished you'd come home before I did anything rash. And you said—"

"You didn't say, 'Before I did something rash.' You just said you were attracted to Marie. Who isn't? Guys who pass her on the street, truck drivers. You're not alone in that."

"I know, but you said, 'Marie's a free agent. She can do what she wants, and besides, we don't have that kind of relationship.' "

"I don't remember using the words 'free agent.' But still, that's no reason for taking advantage of the situation. Especially being my closest friend. I would have expected it from anyone else, but not *you*, Eric. That's what hurts so much. Don't you get it? Not just that you made love to my girl, but that you preferred her to me. That's what disturbs me. You made a choice, and you didn't choose me."

"I wasn't aware I was making that choice."

"No, you expected me to continue being bosom buddies with you while you were shacking up with my girl! I was rejected by you, Eric. That's the part that hurts, not only the part about you and her. What were your feelings towards me, then?"

"I was . . . angry at you."

"Well, I'm not surprised! And it won't work, this business of hinting to me on the phone to California. You want me to take the blame for what you did and I won't take it. There's a right and a wrong. You're just trying to confuse things—to muddy the issue. As for you being sore at me, what were you angry about? I haven't done anything to you."

"I was angry, not because of anything you'd done to me—but because I was envious; you always seemed to have beautiful girl friends and success with women . . ."

"That's something that's pure myth on your part—that was made up by you. This business of my having such an easy time with women is ridiculous! I've never had an easy relationship with a woman." He said it so directly that I was stung by the truth. "You abstracted me into a Don Juan for your purposes. You think you could just walk in and take away Marie and I wouldn't care? That it's such a lark for me to find another woman to love?"

"No, I know but—I was wrong about that, what you said is true —but I just felt at the time, *angry* that you had gone off, and started up with Bernadette on the West Coast, which hurt Marie —"

"Leave Bernadette out of this," Jack interrupted. "You have no right to drag her in."

"All right, but I was just telling you what I had thought."

"You're trying again to shift the blame. I've noticed that about you for some time; I've been meaning to tell you. You've great amounts of anger towards yourself which you turn outward by judging other people. You always need someone around to feel superior to. And it's dishonest." Again he was speaking in that *ex cathedra* voice I had rarely heard him use. The dignity and sobriety of it fascinated me. He must have had any number of critiques about my personality stored away.

"I think you're probably right, I do do that."

"Sure; and for someone who makes such a fetish about honesty as you do, you should examine yourself for a start."

"All right, but—the only part that's wrong about what you're saying is—you seem to be dismissing any reality of what happened between Marie and me, by treating it only as a reaction to other relationships. I don't think the only reason I fell in love with Marie was anger toward you, or Curt, or self-hatred. I think . . .

there was more to it than that. I think we were attracted to each other genuinely; regardless of wanting to hurt anyone else, there was a powerful rapport between us."

"I don't want to hear this!" Jack cried out, with a frenzy that scared me. "I can't take any more!"

"Don't hang up!" I pleaded. I felt so awful to hear him in anguish as if he'd been stuck by a hot poker, that it came as an unthinkable, unwanted coincidence to me that I was the cause of it. How could it be that what was hurting him so much was simply talking to me? I would have done anything to salve his pain, but he was covered with boils, and I was the fire. I was shocked by my tongue which had dared to make defenses of myself when his situation was so much more extreme. I began stalling him: my throat swelled up like a boy's when the teacher yells at him—justly. I tried to weep to relieve the swelling. It came out as rapid gasps, like a dog's whimper, and I knew he must be thinking I was only doing it for sympathy. Jack was hesitating on the other end. The fact is, I wanted very much to cry for my own sake, to clear away the congestion in my chest. "Don't hang up yet. I just wanted to . . . I'm sorry," I said, sobbing. "I'm . . . There are no excuses . . . I'm sorry, you're right! I'm completely wrong."

"Well I don't like to hear you cry," Jack said with unwilling compassion. "That doesn't make me feel good."

"I'm sorry. I'm sorry I cried, I was just ashamed of myself for making alibis. Thank you for listening. You were very patient! You don't have to forgive me. Good-bye; that's all I wanted to say." The phone call ended. I felt better now. My heart was stretched and cleansed, as though it had gone through a car wash. Maybe they were only crocodile tears; but even forced emotion has its cathartic result.

Marie and I still had a date to go bowling. I bought a new tan shirt from a French boutique on Madison Avenue, and added a brown velvet tie, and ironed my suit pants to put a fresh crease in them; my hair was washed, my shoes were polished. When I came by to pick her up at seven it was still light, the sky was a tawny rose color. I mounted her brownstone steps, was let in by her buzz, and rose with my hand on the polished black mahogany banister to the second floor, where Marie was standing in the open doorway.

She told me she couldn't go because it would hurt Jack too much. He had come by earlier, and she had told him her evening plans; and he had gone away very upset. She had promised him she would cancel.

"What about *my* injured feelings?" I protested; then I realized it was impossible. I became very calm . . . even clear-headed. All along I had known it could not possibly work. I made my renunciation speech to Marie. It was better not to try to see each other again, than to continue an unresolvable triangle that could only bring sorrow to the three of us. The time for self-discipline and resisting temptation had arrived. I knew it, and she knew it, and Jack knew it. It was up to me to be the one to act on it. We had to make a rule: though we might still talk on the telephone, she and I could not see each other alone again.

Marie nodded wistfully, showing the lovely long slope of her neck. I would have preferred a little more resistance on her part. It was one thing to make a sacrifice, quite another for the other person to snatch it up. In any case it was over. Our love affair was over. I went home, to try to find a way to tear my feelings for her out of my chest.

I had little doubt I could do it. I was a hard worker, I had accomplished arduous tasks in the past, and, while love is not as malleable or as subject to will power as a piece of work, I had faith in my capacity for discipline. It was my pride as an ascetic that I turned to now—not recognizing that this very same vanity of self-denial had got me into trouble in the first place! For what else had I done with Marie if not to congratulate myself at every stage on giving her up, until suddenly I found I had used up all my capital for self-restraint? I had renounced and renounced and renounced myself right into Marie's vagina.

III

I sank into work. Thank God I was good at it: I had started a student newspaper, and was challenging the phony evaluation procedures at the agency. After some incredulity and inertia, people were beginning to come around.

Unfortunately, there were still the evenings, when I had to pursue what is euphemistically called a personal life.

I had now reached the stage where I was talking about my involvement with Marie to any friend who would listen. If the relationship existed in other people's minds, perhaps it would have more solid reality. Bruno and his girl friend Dawn were always interested in hearing the latest installment from "young Lochinvar," as Bruno now called me. There is nothing more enjoyable for a couple getting along than to entertain a heartbroken single friend. But I could see I would soon be boring other people if I kept this up.

Still afraid of hurting myself, I had arranged every night to see —be watched over by— a different friend. The next night was Michael's turn of duty. The day had made me restless; I wanted to rub shoulders with crowds in theatre lobbies, and I almost talked Michael into going to a Broadway play with me. But Michael was not going downtown. He refused to leave the streets around his house, and considered me something of a gadabout, a cultural butterfly, going round to theatres and movies, to concerts in the Village, leaping on crosstown buses. I must say, he had a way of making my subway ride downtown to a Fifty-ninth Street movie sound as adventurous as a White House invitation. "How do you manage to see everything?" he asked me. "How do you know about all these events?" I told him it was mostly in the newspapers but he seemed to feel I was holding out on him. Here I was, a step away from ending it all, at the very least depressed, in love with a woman I might never see again, and he was envying me my mobility.

I called on Michael in his bare apartment, surrounded by dirty dishes and notebooks filled with poems—he called them "rants" —which he refused to type up, or even let me see. This time he read sections of them aloud, lying on his mattress against the wall, with his face in shadows: they sounded full of rage, and quite good in an opaque, visionary way. Michael was talented, no doubt about it, and I will put up with a lot in a talented person.

That night, however, we were not in the mood for each other. We went for a walk on the promenade alongside Riverside Park, by the benches that overlook the fieldstone wall, with its steep drop into leaves and broken glass thirty feet below; and for the first time I confessed I had actually slept with Marie. He was appalled. Unlike Bruno, who reacted so indulgently to sexual peccadilloes, for Michael it was a simple case of betrayal: so simple that he did not even bother to lecture me, but shrugged his shoulders, writing me off as a moral monster. Perhaps I needed to hear this response just as much as I had needed Bruno's absolution. But his censure was delivered with such distracted gravity, as though there were more important matters on the docket against me, that I could see it was going to be a difficult night.

We ended up having a silly fight. He accused me of being too fond of irony, hence showing "bad faith" and lack of sincerity. He told me that I was very devious and complicated, and that he was very simple—and that he was greater than I in his simplicity. Not a nice thing to say, but once I understood my role I played it to the hilt: I was the fork-tongued urbane, he was the moralist peasant with the simple heart. Of course I had rarely met anyone less simple than Michael, so the whole thing was idiotic, but we managed to irritate each other thoroughly.

The next day, when I came home from work, I was attracted to the wall kitchen telephone, like a black widow spider. It seemed to be asking me to use it. I wondered whom I should call. It was early, not even five-thirty; I fixed myself a sandwich and read the mail. There was a letter from the Kroegels telling about their beach holiday and letting me know they would be coming home in a week: i.e., time to find my own apartment.

I kept being drawn to the phone; it seemed a living creature with needs of its own. I knew who it was I wanted to call . . . Jack. I wanted to call Jack and tell him that it was all over between Marie and me, that we had decided last weekend not to see each other any more. Having cleared that danger away, it might now be possible to begin to patch up our old friendship. I had made my sacrifice; I had sacrificed Marie, not Jack. When it came right down to it, there was no one I liked more in the world than Jack, and in spite of the fact that I might have hurt him, I had no intention of ever really losing him. That would be unthinkable; Jack was as much a part of me as—as my brain, as my eyes! I had a moment of doubt, while dialing his number at work, whether part of the reason I was doing this was to keep alive the thing with Marie; but that explanation seemed too harsh on myself, and in any case, it was already too late to stop.

I had to wait through several operators, first the general receptionist at the television network, then another secretary; and as I heard her speaking my name I imagined him making a face and telling her he had "just stepped out." Yet, easy as it would have been for him to brush me off, I had the hunch that because he was in a workplace he would deal with it as one more piece of the day's business.

"Hello, Eric, I didn't mean to keep you waiting. It's really hectic here today. Excuse me . . ." he said, turning to answer someone else's question, and I heard him say exasperatedly, "Where are *what* Peruvian prints? I've been away for a few weeks, I don't know! . . ." Then some scrambling around, and three minutes later he spoke into the receiver again: "Sorry, Eric. The phone's been ringing all day. I'm going to pick this up in another room." I waited, glad for the time to relax; I was also grateful that he sounded more like his old polite self. Maybe it was just the office atmosphere that forced him to be less rejecting.

He gobbled up the receiver. "It's quieter here, in the conference room. Sorry to make you wait. What is it?" he said with sudden steeliness.

"Can we talk for a minute or two?"

"This isn't the best time. But I suppose it doesn't make much difference, it's not going to get any less busy."

"I just wanted to tell you that I value your friendship and I don't want to give it up. Also, that I've broken up with Marie; we've agreed not to see each other alone again."

"That's fine, but what do you expect me to do about it?"

"I expect you to listen to me for a minute."

"Why should I listen to you? You're pretty callous. You just tell me like that that you broke up with my girl friend, and somehow I'm supposed to be grateful, is that it? Well, I don't trust you, Eric. So there's no point trying to work this out, because as long as I don't trust you I can't talk honestly to you. And what's the point of talking if we can't talk openly? I know it's the only way you like to talk; and it's the only way that makes sense for me to talk too."

"What do you mean, we can't talk openly? We've done it for ten years."

"I'm not so sure that's true either. There was a lot in our friendship that got covered up. But that's not the point. I don't trust you, Eric, it's as simple as that."

"Why don't you trust me? I feel by and large I've been trust-worthy. I'm dependable, consistent. If you take the great number of instances of friendship over the years and compare it to this one, you'll see I have a very trustworthy record."

"You're amazing! You just think we can pick up where we left off? You're so sure of yourself! You're consistent, all right, that's the trouble. You're pretty arrogant. Your nerve is incredible. I admire that; I always have—but it's a mistake, I shouldn't admire you, because you're out to get me."

"What do you mean, I'm out to get you? That's ridiculous."

"Don't ridicule my sentiments and call them ridiculous. You always did that, and I'm not going to put up with it any more. I used to take your opinion in everything. That was a big mistake. It's true you have self-confidence but you're pretty ruthless. You do whatever you feel like, don't you?"

"I did one thing. I slept with Marie *once.*"

"I don't want to hear how many times; I'll hang up if you talk about how many times—!"

"Okay, wait a second. All I'm trying to say is—I made an error. Human beings make errors. It's not unprecedented. You don't dismiss ten years of a friendship because of one misstep."

"It's not the misstep, it's that I don't trust you, Eric. As long as I don't trust you we can't be friends again."

"Why don't you trust me?"

"Because, frankly, I think you're trying to get past me to Marie. I think you're just trying to use me."

"That's—" I was going to say ridiculous, but stopped myself; "that's not so. If I wanted to get to Marie so much, I wouldn't have to go through you. I could do it in any number of ways: I could even kidnap her!" I said jokingly. "That's not why I'm talking to you."

"You could kidnap her?" he said, startled.

"I'm not going to! I only said that to disprove your cockeyed idea that I was talking to you just to get to Marie. That's not the reason: we've been friends for a long time, long before Marie came on the scene. I know you think I made a choice between you. But I don't see it that way. I'm not saying you should just forgive and forget, but we could try to work out some of our differences. I'd like to be able to see you sometime. . . ."

"I can't see you now because I'm too upset. The doctor told me my nerves are shot. I don't need this, Eric!"

It was the second time he had used that *nerves-are-shot* expression. What did his doctor actually mean? Could the nerves really "shoot" all their neurons, as it were, and become used up? I doubted it, it didn't sound scientific to me; but this wasn't the right time to ask.

"I don't mean you should see me right away," I said. "Just that you'd be willing to see me eventually, instead of throwing a wall down between us."

"You're the one who messed things up," said Jack. "Somehow now you're trying to make me feel that I'm failing the test of friendship. You have a very romantic notion of friendship, Eric. That whole 'best friends' idea: I'm not sure I can live up to it. I mean it's like the Icelandic sagas, *The Epic of Gilgamesh*— that notion of comrades who die for one another, like in *The Song of Roland* or in Goethe or Diderot—" (I knew when he was nervous his mind flipped from reference to reference.) "I can't think of the name—anyway, *The Epic of Gilgamesh* is what I always connect with you."

"I've never read it."

"You really should read it, it's one of the greatest poems ever written. Well, you don't have to read it, you have it already inside you. I don't think I have that ideal of comradeship so strongly in me. Or I used to but I'm moving away from it. One pays a price for that kind of friendship. I don't want to be tied to you for life, when you keep putting me through tests. You always have to keep me on my guard, Eric! I want to be able to relax around a friend. I admit that I don't have any other really close friends besides you. And it makes me sad to think that it's over. Because you were like a brother to me."

"Why does it have to be over?"

"That's like asking, Why do things end? Why do people die? Why did I lose Victoria? I went back to see her in California, just this last trip, I paid a visit to her and her husband, and she acted like a stranger to me. I'm sure she thought she was being nice, but it was as though we were distant acquaintances; and it hurt to feel such indifference from someone who had been so close all those years. I wish I *could* trust you, Eric. You think I like being unforgiving, holding grudges? I would like to forgive you, sure; I would like to forgive Marie, Vicky, old friends, I would like to forgive a lot of people. But it's not in me to. And I can't sham that. You wouldn't want me to fake what I feel, would you?"

"I don't expect you to fake anything. Just to be willing to see me, to talk to me from whatever your feelings are: wrath, mistrust, anything. It doesn't have to be feelings of friendship."

"Well I can't see you right now. I'm too angry."

"I respect that."

"So there's no point in talking about it any more. When I feel differently I'll let you know."

"Good. That's all I ask," I said.

"Anyway, good luck. You should get a book of your stuff put out by now. I've always felt you deserved that."

"Thanks. I'm a little surprised to hear you say it."

"What's one thing got to do with the other? You're a good writer and that's that. Listen, I have to get off now. I don't mean to rush you but I have to pick up my uncle at the airport and I still have some things to do here."

"I understand. Good-bye, Jack."

We hung up civilly.

I poured myself a glass of milk and tried to sort it out. He had been fairer than I'd expected.

The phone rang. It was Michael. He asked me rather formally if I knew of any job opportunities for him. (It was clear we were not to talk about last night's fight, that this was a business call). I asked him what kind of field he would like to work in. "I was thinking of something in television," he answered. He wanted a job in television, he repeated, as if saying it twice would make it happen. It was hard to picture a misanthropic type like Michael stomping down the halls of a network with Nielson tear-sheets in his hands. But I knew he loved to watch television, the Johnny Carson show, and, like many marginal intellectuals, had a romantic notion about reaching mass audiences.

What part of television was he thinking of? I asked. He didn't care— Programming. Did I have any "ins"? I told him the only person I knew in television was Jack Bogardes. We were not exactly on such great terms at the moment, but since Michael knew

Jack slightly he might give it a try. I gave Michael the phone number. He might not have anything specific at the moment, I said, but he might know of some other lead. Jack had always been very generous in sharing information like that.

Michael thanked me stiffly and hung up.

Something like a half-hour passed. I was glued to the kitchen table. The phone rang again. I reached up and took it off the wall hook.

It was Michael; he was breathing heavily—so much so that I thought he must be winded from an accident. "I wanted to tell you that I don't think I care to see you again."

"Okay," I said impassively.

"That's all I had to say."

"What brought this on?"

"You play with people's hopes and I'm tired of it. I called Jack, and he *wasn't* very helpful. He acted like an hysterical woman in flight. I've never heard anyone so out of control."

"That's funny. He sounded quite reasonable to me when I spoke to him an hour ago."

"Well you have no idea. Or I think you had a very good idea this would happen. Unconsciously or not, you set me up. In any case, I've decided I don't want to be your friend. You're treacherous and you manipulate people and you play with their feelings."

"Okay. It's your right to think what you want. I must admit that it hasn't been going well lately between us."

"I won't be speaking to you again. And if we meet on the street, I'll thank you to ignore me, because that's what I plan to do to you."

"Whatever."

Never one to mush up a moral line with politeness, Michael hung up, pointedly omitting the "good-bye."

"And up yours too," I muttered into the air. *"Next!"* They were dropping like flies. I was certainly getting my knocks today. Everyone had the scoop on my character. I expected my mother to ring next and tell me she couldn't see me any more, she'd decided

I was unfit to be her son. A whole conga line of people: students, my boss, the man who sold me the evening newspaper. . . . 'I don't think I care to sell you a *Post* any more.' Was I really such a bad guy? But I just didn't *feel* so wicked; it didn't seem to me I had the cleverness or the power to be doing half the manipulative things of which Michael accused me. Still, that was no alibi. The monster never sees himself as a monster. Frankenstein's creature also felt he was misunderstood, as he roved the countryside.

I grappled with a bit of guilt—did I merely play with people and hurt those I loved? Was I really that horrible a person—but it slipped off me. I was never in the mood for guilt right after being attacked. Accusations made me too self-preservative and proud: Monster I am, monster I shall be!

I had just lost two of my best friends—ah, well, these friendships formed in college, all that male-male latent homosexual intensity, was getting to be a royal pain anyway. The era of the breaking up of old school ties had finally come.

I made myself a plate of buttered spaghetti. I was not really hungry, but I needed the industriousness of taking care of myself. As I sat down, the phone rang again. Now what? I put down my fork and answered it. This time it was Marie—she was just calling to chat. How relieved I was to hear her pleasant vibrant voice! Here was one person who still liked me. Talking to her, I had the uncanny impression that we were two halves of the same person. I told her about my conversation with Jack, in which she was of course interested. I said he had gotten very Mosaic and stern: the Jewish patriarch side of him was coming out. She said he had a "cash-register" morality—that you do something and then you must pay the price. Sometimes she didn't have the strength to argue with Jack any more, because he made her feel so discredited. She was tired of raking over "old history." She wanted to go away, get away from him, from everyone. And she was tired of her courses; she wanted to drop out. What sense did studying make, when all this trouble between the three of us was going on?

I counseled her to stay in school. She had only one more term.

Marie apologized for dropping all her problems on me. Not that

I minded: even when she griped, she did it with a certain liveliness. After an hour on the phone, we had both cheered each other up. Then we got off because it was eight o'clock and we wanted to watch a special news program.

I went into the living room and switched on the Kroegels' small black-and-white set. It was a cinéma vérité documentary about prisons. I found myself interested in the technical aspects, the constricted camera angles and limited lighting in prison cell interviews —more, actually, than in what the prisoners had to say, which was not so different from what I had heard or read a hundred times before. In spite of the fact that the film portrayed an ominous situation, I felt so comfortable watching television and not having to think about my personal problems, that I was outraged when the phone rang again, calling me probably to a new accounting.

I turned down the television volume and ran into the kitchen.

"Yes?" I demanded. "What?"

"It's me again," said Marie. "I'm sorry, something horrible is happening! I think Jack's having a nervous breakdown. I don't know what to do!"

"Calm down. Tell me what happened."

"He went to the airport to meet his uncle's plane? And when the plane was late he flipped out! He was hiding in a pay booth in the airport. Jack called me from there and he was raving about Peruvian princesses—and junkies in the street trying to get him! He thought that the people in the airport were FBI decoys only pretending to be there to meet the planes. Then he kept shouting at me, 'You love Eric, don't you!' And I didn't know what to say, I couldn't tell him no because it would be a lie."

"Oh my God." I wished she had lied to him. More, I had the urge to order her not to love me any more. If this was what it would lead to, I didn't want it.

"He kept raving on about Peruvian princesses. The craziest part was when he started yelling that you were going to kidnap me! He wanted me to check my doors to see if they were locked."

"Oh, no, that must be—I made some joke about kidnaping you

if I'd really wanted to get to you, and he believed it! He seemed so —sane and understanding this afternoon when I talked to him on the phone. Why did he have to go back on his understanding?" I was asking myself as much as her. All I could think of was that if only he had been harder on me at the end and not complimentary, he would not have shattered. "Did he say anything about our talk?"

"It was hard to understand him sometimes; but he did say the conversation with you had upset him, because you seemed to be blaming him for everything."

"That's not true."

"I know, but—this is what he said. He felt you were blaming him for failing you as a friend, and it was like all his life when he felt helpless and it reminded him of when he was in the car with his mother and her suitor, when he was twelve years old, and his mother's suitor asked her to marry him, and Jack felt completely small."

"Where is he now?"

"Cyrus had to drag him away from the phone booth in the airport. They're driving in to Jack's mother's house. I have to go over there and meet them now. I have to get off. I don't know if it was the right thing to call you or not, but I just had to tell someone. I had no one else to turn to who would understand."

"No, I'm really glad you did. I just feel so helpless! I want to cradle him in my arms, but he would get hysterical if he saw me."

"That's another reason I called. I wanted to warn you not to get in touch with Jack again," said Marie.

"Don't worry, I won't."

"If you want to find out how he's doing or give him any messages, please do it through me."

"All right. Listen, I know this is asking a very big favor, but can you please try to call me sometime later tonight and tell me how he's doing? I'm very worried."

"I'll try to."

"Thanks. I'll be in all night."

I went back into the other room. "How could I know Jack was

so close to psychosis?" I demanded of the walls. Believe it or not, I turned on the television again to see if I could catch the end of the program but it was just going off; the credits were rolling over the prison bars.

I snapped it off and returned to the kitchen, where I made myself sit tight and wait for more hospital bulletins. My punishment to myself was to do nothing but sit.

At midnight I received another call from Marie. Jack was doing better. He had talked for a while more, then he was given some sleeping medicine, and now he was sleeping. His mother was not in town, so Marie was staying over and nursing him. Even though obviously she was part of the problem, Marie still thought she could do some good, and he seemed to want her to be there.

"Did anything else come to light?" I asked, "about the reason for the attack?"

The only other information she had learned was that he had been agitated by a phone call from Michael Probst just before he left for the airport. "It seems your friend Michael called asking for work," she said, "and he made a remark that he hoped his previous relationship with you wouldn't influence Jack against him. Jack took it as treachery on Michael's part—"

"Which it was. Incredible comment! And he had the nerve to say I manipulate people!"

"Jack was suddenly put in the position of having to stop Michael from saying anything else against you. You can imagine what a strain it must have put on him to defend you."

"It's a credit to Jack that he was so loyal. He is really a honorable person. Too honorable sometimes."

"I know," Marie sighed. There was something grotesque about the two of us complimenting the decency of the person who was lying on his sickbed in the next room at this very moment, while we continued to reach out over him to each other. She must have felt it too, because she said: "Listen, I have to get off. I think I hear him waking up."

"It was really kind of you to call."

"I'll keep you posted. Promise!" said Marie.

"I love you. Good night."

"G'night. I love you too. Sweet dreams."

IV

I had found a new home, in the East Eighties, a small studio apartment with two spacious windows that projected shifting bars of sunlight, and a ballet studio floor of polished wood. I was tempted to put in an exercise bar. The place still smelled of fresh latex and varnish, and it had absolutely no furniture. The purity of a cell. White walls, newly laid parquet floor; the wood was still sticky with wax, which I discovered by walking around barefoot. At one end you saw windows and sunlight, which there really was quite a lot of, it being the top floor of a walk-up; at the door end of the white square had been attached a kitchenette, like an extra-squat dining car, and then a squeeze-in bathroom.

The building itself was five floors high and slender as a cigarette case; it had recently undergone renovation, the lobby done up with turquoise mosaics, and the interior shell subdivided and T-squared into skintight "efficiency studios." The efficiency had all been for the owner, not the tenants; but the selling point, in any case, was the neighborhood, which I knew nothing about. I had wanted to get away from the Upper West Side, with its choked air of homey, dingy responsibility, and complacent liberal intellectualism; and, more to the point, where every restaurant was ruined for me by memories of botched love relationships. The East Side seemed frivolous as a poodle in comparison.

I moved on a Saturday, with Bruno's help, and when we were finished and he had left, I wanted to go out at once. My explorations took me past chalky luxury apartment towers, mirage-new, with their self-important fountains and elaborate underground garage entrances, past a discotheque named Barney Google's with artificial grass carpeting its sidewalk. The vulgarity excited me, as vulgarity often does. French bakeries on virtually every block proclaimed a bonbon of a neighborhood where I might walk for miles without encountering another dyspeptic bookworm, another image of myself. I looked through the glassed-in windows of bistros that offered special Sunday brunches of eggs Benedict and sangria, at the clients leaning their foreheads towards each other like penguins, the men in blazers and turtle-neck sweaters, the women with Cacherel shirts and decorator scarves. It was a young or middle-aged crowd—the epicurean avant-garde of the bourgeoisie—who took very seriously their weekend relaxations, their tennis, their sex, their coffee makers, their rock records, their beaujolais-by-the-case. I was both repelled by them and anxious to join them. The neighborhood was spoken of as a kind of dude ranch for stewardesses and kindergarten teachers on the make: singles territory. Very well then, that's what I was, and the sooner I faced up to it the better.

That night I threw my body into a sleeping bag and pretended it was a bed. No mattress, no phone, no lamps to read by: the purity was beginning to pall. In the loud partying midnight, feeling myself in a foreign country, without any optimism left over from my walk, I thought about jumping through the window.

It would take too much trouble to get out of my sleeping bag and kill myself.

On Sunday I walked down to the river, exploring that untried direction near Gracie Mansion. Along the promenade of Carl Schurz Park, fathers with long overcoats addressed their children in European languages, amateur photographers took amateur photographs, tennis couples in spanking white outfits looked courtbound; a woman in a kerchief sat in meditation posture with her legs tucked under, her face arched toward the sun, Sunday *Times* next to her on the stone parapet.

Monday I took the Third Avenue bus uptown to East Harlem, to my job. As I entered the storefront I heard shouting and cursing, which was not unusual: Horace Hinton had decided to "get tough" with a student named Skipper. Horace, whose enormous size and bank guard gun still scared me, was yelling at Skipper to "cut out the nonsense," and the teen-ager retorted something obscene and ran up the stairs—he looked afraid of Hinton too. I shook my head at what naïve faith members of the agency hierarchy put in this *get tough* strategy. Their argument was that the agency teen-agers were street-wise dropouts, ex-addicts in most cases, who needed Structure. "These kids are con artists, they need to be cracked down on," I was told; it was harming them in the long run to go easy. Black and Hispanic counselors especially talked this line, and seemed harder on their own, asserting that they knew the only kind of talk these kids would listen to; but I remained unconvinced. It could be that what they knew was how to pass on the same brutality they had suffered. Of course I never said this aloud, as I would be accused immediately of racism. But I thought it, and some of my positions, such as refusing to give demerits or dock kids any of their (ridiculously small enough) stipend pay, had the effect of beginning to rally another group within the agency.

I came upstairs, and saw Skipper kicking the metal cabinet. He had on his ship captain's hat and a black leather sleeveless jacket with no shirt underneath, to show off his muscle beach arms. Skipper was short and childish though his arms were tattooed blue with anchors: as he swore what he was going to do to Hinton, I asked Skipper what exactly had happened. The head teacher, Nan, sent me a frowning look, and as Skipper began blurting out his story, Nan tried to catch my eye again with a shake of her head, warning me not to give him any further attention. She walked over to us with a white booklet in her hand, like a nurse, and told Skipper to start working on it. That was her idea of handling any tense situation: to give the angry person a multiple-choice booklet, which had roughly the same intent as slipping him a Mickey Finn.

The booklet was part of a package of programmed instruction, a sequence of one hundred dog-eared pamphlets with sample questions, designed to prepare a dropout for taking the high school equivalency examination. The white booklet series was our

Great Wall of China: many started out but few arrived. So far I had not heard of one of our students ever completing the series, or indeed of ever passing the equivalency test (though, in the mists of history, there were said to be a few). Some of the young men and women assigned to our program were at too low a reading level even to start the booklets, full as they were of algebra and essay comprehension questions on Bonnie Prince Charlie. The slower readers were put on elementary school S.R.A. cards, another packaged programmed-instructional series, with little innocuous stories about racing car drivers, the Yukon, and "Rasputin: the Man Who Wouldn't Die," as though these "catchy" themes could sugarcoat the dull, mechanical process. The teacher became little more than a file clerk who handed out materials, saw to it that the students kept quietly at work and checked their answers afterwards. The booklets and the S.R.A. cards were what held the agency school together: they disguised the lack of any educational vision, and shifted the blame onto the "learner," who was told to hold his tongue and keep climbing up the sequence ladder. How I despised the pretense that just because everyone was silent and bent over tests, they were seriously learning.

This morning I gathered my students at the back table: Dewey, Cora, Cha-Cha, Skipper, and Rosa. I was working for the moment with Cha-Cha, a completely cross-eyed, slightly built boy who had to hold the paper an inch away from his face, and was legally blind; to distract me from his reading difficulties he clowned around, pretending to be masturbating. Cora and Rosa were both round-faced, heavy-set women, who already had the weariness of matriarchs. Dewey was an enigma: he had done four years in jail for armed robbery, and had been paroled to the agency. He actually had the most serious attitude toward studying and getting his diploma of anyone there, and would work for hours with concentration on math or reading. But then, without warning, he would go into his "bad nigger" act. Dewey had a black goatee, and an orange nylon shirt, and he would lift his head and intone, "I'm a *bad* nigger. I don't care who knows it. I am one . . . BAAAD . . . NIGGER."

"Hey will you cool it? I can't concentrate," whined Cha-Cha.

"I don't see how you can even *read* with your one eyeball crossing over to the other side. Why don't you take your coat off? Man, ain't you staying with us?"

"I'm cold," Cha-Cha pouted.

"You never take that coat off. That shit's glued to you."

"Hey, tell him to quit picking on me," Cha-Cha appealed to me.

"All right, Dewey, forget it," I said.

"I don't want to forget it. No one gonna tell *me* what to forget. I don't take orders from no Whitey, understand? We gonna step outside."

"All right, we'll step outside. Later."

"I'm gonna cut you. Hey, is it true that Bruno's people killed off all of your people in Germany?"

"What about it?" I asked, guardedly.

"I'm just asking a simple fact! During World War Two, I heard that all of them Nazis killed off all you Jews. Now is it true or not?"

"The Nazis killed millions of Jews. Go on. What are you trying to say?"

"Well you got that German down there, right downstairs, your friend *Bruno,* and you mean to tell me that you don't get a gun and blow him away for what he did to your people? What's wrong with you? Haw haw haw!"

"Dewey, you got a great sense of humor."

"Don't pay him no mind," Cora said to me with a slow smile. "That nigger's off his head."

I let it pass. I didn't feel like being pulled into every challenge: there were too many of them in this place, you'd feel flayed at the end of the day if you listened too hard. I turned to help Skipper with his fractions.

Dewey threw down his booklet. "I don't want to do this shit no more!"

"What would you rather be doing?" I asked curiously.

"What would I rather be doing?"

"Yes."

"I would like to be home right now, *fuck*ing," he said, savoring and prolonging the words. Cora allowed herself a slow, weary smile. "And gettin' *high* on some *coke*."

"What else?" I asked.

"I would like to fuck a young *vir*gin with a tight cunt," Dewey said, sneering. "I will bend this virgin down and drive a yard of dick up her ass. That bitch would be screamin' and hollerin'. . . . Then I get a homo to come over and suck my dick with some coke on it. I'll get a homo like Cha-Cha."

"Hey. Just because you in jail with all the boys, don't mean everyone's a homo," said Cha-Cha.

"You wouldn't know what goes on in jail," Dewey said with dignity.

"What is sex life in jail like, Dewey?" I asked, getting back at him.

"Sex life in jail? I could write a whole book about that. To have to look at men every day, men start to look like women. There are lots of pretty boys who will do favors for cigarettes," he said with a broad grin, "like Cha-Cha here."

"You *should* write about it. We'll put it in the agency newspaper. Here's a piece of paper." I gave him a stack of yellow paper and told him to take the rest of the morning on it. At first Dewey ignored me. Then he set to work. He was writing and covering the paper with his left hand, chuckling to himself. I went back to work with Cha-Cha, who read painfully, slowly aloud from *The Little Prince*.

At lunchtime I was walking around in a daze when I heard someone call my name. "Hey, com'ere, Rick." That was what they called me: Eric shortened. Squinting, I saw Cora and Dewey on a park bench in the projects. Each had a quart bottle of Country Club beer hidden in a brown paper bag and they invited me to join them.

I was pleased that they would want me to sit with them. Dewey had apparently forgotten his earlier threat to cut me; head cocked to one side, in that half-snarl, half-friendly grin of his, he offered me a tug from his brown bag. The great equalizer. It was a sunny afternoon and we passed the warm beer back and forth. I took a swig and closed my eyes in the sunshine and listened to them talk, pretending my presence made no difference. Cora was telling a long complicated story about her cousin and her cousin's baby and everything she had to do yesterday, from standing in line at Welfare down to the fish n' chips she ate. Dewey was trying to tell a different story at the same time, something about the lockup in Comstock and the dumb farm boy guards who didn't know nothing, but every time he started he got talked down by Cora, which wasn't too unusual once she began her inventory of hours and days. I had nothing to say, but it was a treat just to take in their conversation without having to channel it or "teach" anything. We finished the bottle and sat a few moments longer in the sunshine, before going back.

I came home wondering what, if anything, I had taught anyone during the day. Other than getting Dewey to write his paragraph-long opus, "Sex Life in Jail," I did teach one eighteen-year-old boy in the afternoon how to use a ruler. "Lots of people try to explain it to me," Chino said with an odd sort of pride. But in the end I did explain it to him.

Coming home on the bus I kept thinking of his face, and the way it looked when he finally "got" it. He was by no means stupid, that was the curious part. How was it possible that young people who revealed intelligence with every statement and with every wry expression on their faces, could reach the age of eighteen, nineteen, twenty, twenty-one, having passed through a decade of schooling, and not know how to read, or how to use a ruler? Why *couldn't* they read? Were the schools really *so* atrocious? Was it them? I had read many studies about the problem of illiteracy in America, but on a purely secret level that I could not have confided to anyone, it was still a mystery to me.

It did seem to me that this society could, if it wanted to, teach its population to read. Not that I had any deep messianic urge to lessen the store of ignorance in the world, but my sense of professionalism was irked by the fact that the efforts to deal with the problem seemed so perversely tailored to fail. From working in an anti-poverty agency day after day, it became obvious that the federal, state and city governments had no intentions of eliminating the social problems around poverty they were ostensibly addressing themselves to, through these farcical efforts, these dribs and drabs. And the agency leaders themselves were just as dishonest: they put non-existent clients on the list for reimbursement, they siphoned off funds for their own personal use, they had no notion of where they were going and their success rate statistics were a fiction. While this state of affairs, which every newspaper reader knows, did not surprise or "radicalize" me, it did make me feel a little foolish for collaborating in an enterprise which was not meant to succeed.

Once home, I set to work unpacking and rearranging my apartment. I could not bear to sit still and do nothing; at the first moment of idleness, my mind would be flooded with Marie. I was determined to leave that alone for a while. The fruits of my intervention were all too apparent, in Jack's nervous breakdown; if I had any discipline, I would stay out of their path. But no matter what activity I was thinking about, my mind always circled back to Marie.

In unpacking a final carton, I found a sketch I had made of myself when I was a teen-ager, by looking in the mirror. Like all self-portraits done with mirrors, the subject had that solemn, squintily nearsighted look . . . but there was another quality, a sweetness I had forgotten was in me. I was struck by how vulnerable this adolescent was as he looked at the world in his white T-shirt, with just the tiniest hint of reproach.

The face suddenly reminded me of Marie's. So that was it: take away the mustache, move back the clock a few years, and we could be identical twins. Her brown eyes, her squinty moist look. . . . Narcissism! That's all it was!

I was as happy as if I'd found a twenty-dollar bill in the street. This explanation provided a few hours' relief: like all other explanations designed to denigrate my feelings for Marie, calling myself a narcissist had the merit of reducing an unachievable yearning to a petty selfishness. The only problem with reductionist psychology, and with calling yourself names in general, is that it leaves the obsession intact and untouched. The more you explain away your amorous attraction for a person as masochistic, Oedipal, familial resemblance, self-destructive patterns or whatever, the more you are free to play with it in another part of the imagination.

The only way I found I could stop myself from brooding was to write down my thoughts, which had the temporary effect of draining them off. I began to keep a journal about Marie. Stendhal speaks of *crystallization* as that process by which the lover not only falls in love, but "draws from everything that happens new proofs of the perfection of the loved one." I, on the other hand, hoped to fall out of love with Marie through analytically negative proofs taken from everywhere. I was searching for clues that would discredit her; I had the urge to take her apart, shred by shred, like Armenian rope cheese. And this impulse formed the inspiration behind my journal of decrystallization.

V

Journal of Decrystallization

Everything resolves around this simple question: is she a flirt, a coquette, or sincerely torn?

It is entirely possible, I would think, for a woman to be in love with two men at the same time. It is also possible for her to be in love with neither and merely feeling her oats.

"I don't care. I can't be bothered." These two expressions I catch myself repeating so often when I am alone, they might as well be a mantra. I sometimes manage to block her from my thoughts for a day. But she always comes back—stupidly enough, whenever I take a shower. The moment I turn on the hot water I start to think of Marie. I picture the way we made love afterwards, on the bathroom mat, and how slippery and soaped-up she was; and how nice she felt. I can remember now the goodness of the skin contact—which had bypassed my consciousness during the act itself, only to register in my nerves like a genetic memory for a later point, to be recalled at will.

The moment I relax, Marie swamps me.

*

My naïveté was in thinking that you could touch a woman in a certain place and it meant something. To touch M.'s breast, her vagina—what did it mean? She had allowed it, perhaps, because of the power situation at the moment, but in her mind she was untying the strings as fast as I imagined I was tying them.

*

There is, in that Daddy's Girl desire to please, that dependence on others' praise, evidence of undevelopment in the feminine sphere. She is a girl, not a full woman. I am not speaking of her sexuality—which even a teen-age girl can master—but of self-hood, real self-acceptance, which she lacks. And charm is no substitute for selfhood.

*

Half-woman, half-girl: That I could be tortured by a woman who seems so much still an overgrown teen-ager surprises me. It betrays my need for some partner who is underdeveloped, and whose immaturity moves me precisely because of all that is still undeveloped in me. There is a sort of self-pity for my (wounded) adolescence which draws me to Marie.

Nevertheless, it is possible to construct a whole woman from this ingenue. When I was with her my imagination saw, not a young girl, but every woman, the whole edifice: from the child to the grandmother. But it isn't so much my imagination. No, she has the talent to project all women. This very dramatic plasticity is a capacity she pays for in other ways: by not having a regular, everyday work life, a self.

*

It's occurred to me that I like women who are a little *precious,* who carry on like actresses in their real lives. Marie has the quality of speaking her lines in a fresh, heartfelt way which, if it were on a stage, might be quite riveting. Yet what intrigues me in her is precisely the element of phoniness, of performance. Perhaps I view all women as artificial, not to be trusted (and those who do not convey this untrustworthy quality strike me as bland, so it's a vicious circle). By the way, I am not speaking of professional actresses. The few I have met in this line, at parties and so on, seem always to be conserving their energies for a paying performance: they hold back, knowing they don't need to be dramatic except when it counts.

No, with Marie it's different, she's always being animated, she doesn't need a script to start acting. Coy, arch, self-conscious, turning everything into an occasion to rise to. The problem of adrenalated effervescence falsifying the blankness of life.

Effervescence as a bubbly, charming quality which goes no-where. Carbonated moments. Like those old cafeterias that served seltzer instead of plain water—the denizens couldn't drink a glass of water without having that sharp tickle in their throats.

*

The *insecure* pretty woman does most damage not by her se-ductions, but by refusing to believe she has actually moved men's hearts. Because she knows so well the backstage part of her per-formance, the makeup, etc., she distrusts the effects it causes. Like Marie with her Sven—refusing to believe he might actually have been in pain when she left for the airport. If only these women could know their power, they could be more gracious to the men who surrender to it! If not necessarily by obliging, at least by un-derstanding. Instead they treat a man's declarations of love as low comedy, involving his own hyperactive imagination and ego.

*

Today I thought: I *could* kidnap her. I could wait by the banister with a gun, force her to go upstairs with me, and tie her to a chair. And then the fantasy goes strangely chivalrous. I beg her to listen to me, and I pour out my love in ornate, desperate speeches, until she, with the gag over her mouth, is forced to real-ize how much she hurt me by rejecting me, and tears come to her eyes. The rest is pornographic.

*

To renounce what you never had a chance for is ridiculous.

But, on the other hand, maybe that is precisely what is most difficult and heroic to renounce.

*

Suicide is a thought that thinks itself. It waits for a time when I am low, to sneak in; it loves a vacuum; it fills my mind for days. What I despise about suicide most is its limited intellectual con-tent. It's like a jingle that you can't get rid of, a corny hamburger commercial. I no longer think of cure, but of fighting it to a stand-

still, every day of my life. One suicide attempt is enough to tinc-
ture a lifetime: like certain diseases, malaria or hepatitis, which
leave a parasitic remnant in the bloodstream, and can flare up at
any moment if you don't watch them.

*

No, something more extreme is needed this time to check our
despondency; this cue-person's familiarity with every change of
scenery. We must animate the corpse! To begin with, pick an argument with a waiter or a postal clerk; make a scene in public.
The more unmerited, the better.

Above all, remember never to miss an opportunity to fly into
rages.

I know a man who goes around in a continual boil. He prides
himself on being a man of feeling. We are no longer friends. . . .
Naturally.

What a mistake to think that rage is therapeutic!

*

Anger dwindles to annoyance. A cranky peevish pettiness the
opposite of emotional living. Like running a low-grade temperature to convince myself I can "feel." Better to cultivate the
coldness of the tomb than pride yourself on this post-nasal reac-
tivity.

*

After several weeks of telephone isolation, my white studio a
space capsule cut off from all telecommunications, finally I received a letter saying that my name had floated to the top of the
phone company's installation list. I took the day off to be home
when the hookup man arrived. After he was gone, I picked up the
receiver and, with a thrill of power to do mischief of all kinds,
heard as though it were a new sound, the dial tone.

The first person I called was Marie. I told myself I was only
calling to give her my new number; but as I rejoiced at her voice,
I knew there was more to it than that. She said in a rush she'd
been trying to get in touch with me. She'd called the Kroegels—no

one knew where I was! She'd even called the phone number for new listings and had thought of phoning my mother for the number, but decided against it. I listened to this tale of her wild-goose chase with a partial suspension of disbelief, knowing all along that Marie had my number at work and could easily have reached me there.

She had so much to tell me. She was thinking of dropping out of school. Jack was out of danger, still very agitated, but much better. They were fighting a lot. About what? I asked. Marie didn't want to go into it.

*

It finally came out. Marie thinks she's pregnant. She hasn't gotten her period yet and, though the chance is very slight—I slept with her when she was at the end of her period—it's possible I am the father.

Jack is relentless in his suspicion. "I don't love you enough not to care who the father is," he says. Nice statement.

Marie thought of going to Pittsburgh, leaving us both and having the baby. It rather hurt me that she didn't even consider I might take care of her.

Why Pittsburgh? I asked.

She says she likes the sound of the name, and has never been to Pittsburgh. I can only guess that the word "Pittsburgh" has romantically downfall associations for her, like Steel Town, where she and her baby can live in a cold water flat, turned out of society, a Griffith heroine.

*

Another phone call. I offered to take care of her and the child. We could all live together in the same apartment on my salary: I would work for both of them.

It was one of those generous offers which you don't know if you really mean, and you make because one road looks as good as another, at a moment when you don't have clear faith in your future; if the other person were to take you up on it you'd have to go along, being a man of your word, and then your whole life would be changed, and that was part of the excitement of making such gestures. So it was offered partly in the spirit of a self-pitying gambler, though it was also meant quite sincerely. I would marry Marie. But she doesn't believe me, I guess. She thanked me in a distant, distracted voice, as though she were already on the train to Pittsburgh.

*

Marie saw her doctor. Not pregnant.

The false pregnancy depressed her. She is still thinking of going to Pittsburgh. I told her we could both move to Pittsburgh, and I would get a job in a factory. We made it into a tender fantasy: I with my lunch pail, my flannel shirt with rolled-up sleeves (and new muscles); she in her shirtwaist dress, waving to me, a perfect workingman's wife. It was the nicest ten minutes of the day, that mutual daydream. . . .

*

Marie surprised me yesterday by saying that no one wanted her, that no one would ever marry her. "No one wants a bride with holes in her lungs," she said with bitter conviction. Where did this come from? Such certainty of her own unhappiness disturbed me to the point of really worrying about her. But then in today's phone call she was lightweight, carefree, with no reference to the dark mood of the day before. I felt cheated. I wanted to get back to that moody side, and find out if it held the truth about her; but she had already skipped off to her more characteristic cheeriness. The more "up" or "on" she sounds, the more I distrust her now.

*

Perhaps what bothers me most about her high spirits is that I suspect only one thing could make her happy: Jack's love. It's so obvious how much she loves him. And how closely she watches him for signs of favor or disfavor. Last Friday she told me how excited she was because she was getting ready to go to a fancy party he was taking her to. She expects me to share her happiness, because he's been good to her! That's carrying empathy and my platonic role too far. Of course it's understandable to hope that someone who cares about her would rejoice at her good fortune; but somehow, the whole thing seems to be at my expense.

Last time, I drew her up short with a hard remark, which asserted my own lover's claims. It threw her off-stride. In the whimsical landscape of these telephone tête-à-têtes, there aren't supposed to be any thrusts of hurt. She treated it almost as a lapse of sportsmanship, like changing the rules in the middle of the game. "Be nice," Marie seemed to say. "We were playing nicely, and now you've turned into the kind of boy who throws spiders on my dress."

How can I be nice, when every time I hear her voice I'm reminded that *she rejected you for Jack*. That is the thought underneath all this ebullience, the rotten cherry inside the chocolate. And I can never take my eyes away from it for long. Or allow her to forget it either.

*

Marie has dropped out of school. I tried to argue her out of it: it seemed such a waste to throw away all her previous work and quit in the last term of college. She had already dropped out once or twice before, which explains why she is going on twenty-two and still hasn't got her bachelor's. It's as if she's terrified of crossing the finish line. Marie claimed she didn't care about "that piece of paper." She said a diploma wouldn't make her a better human being. But I couldn't help feeling it was all spite. She has no ability to stick to things; she has lousy work habits. Her father and mother seem willing to support her for life. Well, why not? They have the money, and only two children. Her ill-health confuses the issue of whether her inability to prepare herself for a career of any kind is justifiable or is pampered self-indulgence.

She said to me recently, regarding the biography of Zelda Fitzgerald, "All Zelda ever wanted, the one thing she wanted most in her life, was to be able to support herself." Then she sighed, as though with total identification. I didn't say anything, but it seemed a simple enough thing to do: Why couldn't she go out and support herself and make her own living? I mean Marie, not Zelda.

*

She likes biographies: Cole Porter, Zelda, Tracy and Hepburn, Madame de Pompadour. I wonder what that means. (Maybe that she only likes light reading.)

*

Gamine: a condition of arrested development; a disease of the soul's chirping thinness. On screen it can be charming, like Katherine Hepburn in *Sylvia Scarlett,* dressed in boy's clothes, masquerading as a page. Then flipflopping into womanhood—as if it were that easy! Caught in the transition from one sex to another: a chrysalis that has not made the leap, resulting in a mutant, the eternal fresh dewy feisty spunky Kid, wanting just to play. The gamine seen as a disease of a certain class—the way hemophilia used to be associated with royalty, or rickets with the undernourished lower classes. This is another kind of malnutrition. How much family wealth goes into the production of one gamine!

Marie seen sociologically as the perfect bloom of Greater New York's comfortable Jewish middle class. The grandfather was a Russian immigrant and slaved to start a business. The father was more successful using his brains, and didn't have to work as hard. He married a self-indulgent neurotic wife with artistic pretensions, and had two hysterical children, including a daughter whom they treat as a work of art, as lovely and as useless.

*

M. is incapacitated so easily! I don't understand how she gets through her days. She told me that a huge moth flew in her window and lodged itself in her bedroom closet and she tried to get it out for hours, but was terrified. She had to call the Museum of Natural History to have someone catch it. It was "so enormous" that she thought it must have been a rare species and the museum would want it. These people must have endless time and leisure to support such luxuriously frantic incapacitations.

*

By describing her I am attempting to kill her. Or, put less luridly, to pin down what is already past, fixed and ruined in her nature. Tomorrow she may be entirely different. Am I even interested in her potential any longer, or am I already too consumed with the job of remembering and cataloguing?

*

I can't picture her so easily any more. She's beginning to seem disembodied to me: a telephone voice, full of artificial coyness. There is, in my way of listening to her now, an almost chronic threshing system by which I separate out what I take to be hyperbole from truth. Not that she lies (she's rather scrupulous that way), but she does flatter, or say what she thinks someone might want to hear. Partly she's afraid of being disliked, but it's also that, as an artist of sympathetic conversation, it delights her for the "good" answer to leap into her mind, like a telepathic flying fish straight from the other person. How I distrust all this telepathic stuff! We were wrong to make such a fetish early on of our "empathy." A conversation between us is always in danger of roaming toward too hasty agreement; a stubborn part of me feels like putting a wrench in the machine, while another part is seduced and flattered into pleasing her with having seen things the same way, and thus joining her little aristocratic group of understanding spirits (which I detest).

*

Marie hits back at me in her own way: dropping hints of their sleeping arrangements, telling about their adventurous weekend camping in sleeping bags. Our rule of candor is an invitation for her to use spontaneous narrative as an excuse for inflicting pain. It is part of our macho attitude toward the truth that neither of us wants to be caught saying, "Don't tell me, I don't want to know that." But she's always as quick to let me see the flawed side of her relationship with Jack. Does she do it to keep my hopes up? Or is it purely unconscious, the balancing instinct of a flirt?

Sometimes Marie seems to be shaping a Metternichian balance-of-power among the three of us. She likes being the go-between, through whom Jack and I have to communicate. (She relished telling me that night not to get in touch with Jack!) I wouldn't be surprised if our old friendship were still a threat to her; it's in her *interests* to keep us separate.

*

Today when I had just come home from work, and had thrown myself on my daybed to take a nap, in the middle of my dreamy going-under I got a phone call from Marie. Her voice pulled me up through sleep. I pretended I had been awake all along, so as not to make her feel bad about disturbing me; but I was still in a delicious sluggishness which made me say whatever popped into my mind. Marie is one of those people who is great to talk to when you're half-asleep. She can fall in with any free association. My voice had a low growl when I awoke, which helped me to feel manly, sexy and supportive; and with her spacy animation mixing properly with my growl, we generated an amorous field, in which even the most ordinary statements were shaded with double-entendre.

The only problem is, that we are so quick to express in a playful sense what we think the other would like to hear, that I question whether we are really talking to each other, or only sending out shadow-emissaries to converse.

*

Her voice: A shocked, open freshness . . . like a Miro painting. No, that's not it. Tingly. A teasing buoyancy. Seltzer. I wonder if that "on" quality has something to do with the medication she takes. Bruno tells me that asthma drugs often contain amphetamines besides belladonna . . . which would explain why she has such a need to talk a lot sometimes.

*

Yesterday Marie was saying, "I feel sorriest about you and Jack. To have been close friends for ten years, and then have it ruined because of something that had to do with me—I feel sick about that. I'll never forgive myself."

"Don't feel so bad," I found myself saying. "We were due for a falling-out—maybe not this year, but the next."

"I know you're trying to make me feel better. But it's something I can never forgive myself for," Marie said again.

She seemed to be telling the truth, and I did not object to her guilt. Guilt is what civilizes. Besides, I like Marie when she is a little chastened with guilt; she becomes more womanly.

Everyone's being so damned *noble* except me. Marie's being noble. Jack is noble in his anger.

Well, perhaps I am too—but can't see it because of a need on my part to feel baser and more earthy, lower class.

It's another way of grouping them together in my mind. As I have to do, to reconcile myself to their going off together, leaving me alone.

*

I keep dreaming about Marie. This time I dreamed I visited Jack and Marie together. Jack left to pick up some people at the airport, and Marie proceeded to take off her clothes. She jumped into bed, looking absolutely delicious. "Marie, this isn't a good idea," I said. I struggled against the urge to hug her; I tried to make myself not do anything but sit beside the bed. Then I began touching her; her vagina was hot and sopping wet, she was romping up and down while I sat there fully clothed, rubbing her clitoris, enjoying her lubrications, which kept peeling off like bran flakes. I began to feel wonderful—but terrified that someone would see us. The buzzer rang. "Marie, we have to hurry!" By this time I had taken my pants down, still touching her. "You're doing it too hard and too fast, like last time." To satisfy her, I slowed down my finger, and Jack walked in with his guests. I turned away to buckle my pants but he saw.

"I don't like that," he said.

"No, Jack, I didn't do what you thought—" (meaning I didn't go all the way, didn't penetrate her) but he cut me off. "I don't want to hear it!" he literally plugged up his ears. Marie had meanwhile hopped onto a chair and was sitting there with perfect aplomb. I tried to explain that we hadn't *fucked*—always that technicality, which seems such a hang-up with me. Then it dawned on me that she had planned all this: she had purposely forced me to take more time so that Jack would catch us in the act. "She was the one who started it," I said. "It was a trap! Now I understand: she did it the first time too!"

"Why do you always have to blame other people?" one of Jack's guests said reasonably. I was silenced. Then, realizing that Jack wanted to pretend that nothing had happened (for reasons of decorum I could only guess at), I refused to let it drop. I threw a fit in the middle of the room, like an epileptic.

That did it. Marie said: "It's clear that I should go," and hurried out in her nightgown before we could stop her. I turned to the others and said: "I'll run after her and bring her back. You'll have to trust me that I will, Jack."

Outside, she was nowhere around. I ran into a train station and got rammed into a crowd of merrymakers who prevented me from getting off until Yankee Stadium in the Bronx. There were signs: "Big Peace Rally at Yankee Stadium." I walked to the stadium and stood by the ticket windows, not knowing what to do next. Someone came behind me and put hands over my eyes. I turned around, and was so relieved to see Marie that I forgave her everything. I pretended that our meeting was no coincidence, but that I had guessed she would come to the Big Peace Rally at Yankee Stadium. "It's because I know what you're like and how your mind works," I said.

"I'm glad!" she said. "Do we have to go anywhere else first?"

"No. Let's start back right away." I was so happy to have found her again that I woke in a mood of euphoria.

*

VI

Fall had come, but I hadn't noticed. Someone told me that the leaves were beautiful around Great Barrington. There was talk of getting hold of a car and driving up to look at the turning of the leaves, which was supposed to be spectacular that year. Somehow the thought that a New England autumn was so close to me sufficed; I didn't have to see it.

When I looked almost by accident into Central Park, running to catch a movie, and saw orange and vermilion instead of green, it took me by surprise. I must have expected New York City trees to defoliate in not quite such a natural way. Fall in New York meant getting inured to the oncoming cold. The sun set earlier, through cloud banks over apartment towers; the sky was the color of weak tea bags.

I had furnished my apartment bit by bit from castaways that the superintendent told me about, finds in the street (the East Side was rich that way), and a few reluctant purchases. My best discovery was a card table which I used when dining in the studio room; at other times it became my typewriter table. I began to unpack my cartons of books, using metal milk crates from supermarkets for bookshelves, and spraying everything for roaches. This Robinson Crusoe resourcefulness, this taking care of myself, had a grimness to it, like a child who is left to play by himself, and doesn't really know how to play, or even how to be a child.

It reminded me of a time once, when I was around seven years old, and my mother set me in a beautiful rolling park outside her doctor's office to play. I had wanted to go in with her and sit in the waiting room, but it was a psychiatrist's office: somehow that made it more of a sanctuary for adults. Stationed near some benches and soft grass, I spent half the time trying to figure out what a "regular child" would do in my situation, to entertain himself, and I hit upon the idea of rolling down the hill, then climbing to the top and rolling down again, all the while hoping that this would be appropriate. At a far distance, some children were chasing each other and yelling, and I watched them, thinking, "So this is how children in this part of town play."

Just as I had waited what seemed like forever for my mother (greeting her with punishing silence when she finally came out of the building in her mouton coat), so now I waited for another woman to come along and take away my need to continue "playing house." Of course I was a spoiled only son, spoiled first by my sisters and then by Natalie. My housekeeping skills were a joke. But I had gotten a little better as an adult at taking walks by myself, and at spending hours in parks.

My favorite walk was down by the river, near the mayor's house, Gracie Mansion. I would look out left to Queens, to a factory across the water with a scarlet neon sign which kept blinking, alternately, *Pearl Wick Hampers . . . Bathroom Hampers . . . Pearl Wick Hampers . . . Bathroom Hampers*. It was as though God were whispering something in my ear. Downriver were the three Con Edison Electric Company smokestacks, a comforting triptych painted white, red and gray, with their spires narrowing to a flat pudgy top. Aside from being ugly monstrosities, they had the quaint honesty of antique industrial totemism, iron and foundry works of the nineteenth century, innocence itself, as they stood in the blue-gray light surrounded by storm clouds that had earlier unleashed rains, or were just about to. Across the river to their left was an old piano factory, grimy-sooted but with a green cupola, surprisingly like Paris. Sometimes a tugboat would start out from the basin a few blocks north, thoughtfully smoking its pipe; would round the bend, pulling three barges capped with dirt like funeral mounds strapped end to end; and then there was nothing else to do but follow it for as long as it passed. Its white spume started the dark green waves slapping against Manhattan Island; and, leaning over, one could see jimmied-loose pads of black tar floating along. I preferred the East River to the Hudson: the East River was a real city river, it seemed more grittily human, like Broadway, cutting a channel between concrete-slab shores.

I liked to lift my head northeast and watch the dinosaur Triboro Bridge, with sixteen-wheel freight trucks crawling up its triceratops bones—the traffic thrown high in the air, like ants removed by prank from the ground to a tree limb, and just as stunned.

Directly across from where I leaned over the railing were the city islands, whose names I can never connect with their land mass. Which one was Welfare Island? Riker's? Ellis? The one in front of me had a collection of buildings that looked like a cross between a housing project, a hospital and an army barracks. There was a bus that made a loop around the island; though from where I was standing everything on the island appeared close enough to be within walking distance. I would follow the bus with my eyes: the landscape immeasurably improved by anything that moved steadily and slowly through it.

Cora strolled into the agency at eleven, two hours late. Her round sagging face was creased with the troubles of the world; her yellowed eyes said, Don't you mess with me, I don't want complications today. She sat glowering in the corner with her coat on. Little by little I got her to tell me what the matter was. It seemed the manager of her welfare hotel had taken away her hot plate and wouldn't give it back to her.

"It was the hot plate my boyfriend gave me. My boyfriend said, 'I'm going to go over to that sucker and show him what a man is.' He was a Whitey, too," she added. "So I akst the man very sweetly if I could have my hot plate back. And he said, 'Sorry young lady, we can't have any hot plates in the rooms.' I didn't even get angry at him, I just walked away. Because I kept thinking I was gonna get a gun and shoot him in the head and go right up to my room after leaving the gun on the counter and nobody would know the difference."

I took in this confession of intent with a speechless nod. What a life it must be, I thought, where daily frustrations closed in on her so, that she might murder a man over a simple thing like a hot plate! On the other hand, I sensed it was just a way of talking.

"So that's all that's bothering you, is the hot plate?" I said finally.

"I don't want to talk about the rest of it because it just gives me more aggravation. Give me heartburn. You ever have trouble with your stomach?"

"Sometimes."

"Did you ever love someone and wanted to stay with that person and no matter what it just wouldn't work out?"

"Yes," I said, and would have said more; but Cora was already going into her scowling cocoon. She pulled her cloth coat around her, stolidly scraping off a dirt smudge on the mother-of-pearl button.

Finally she said, "I be thinking of killing myself." That was the way she talked, with long impressive pauses and a deadpan face, looking at the person to see how he was taking it. "I tried it a few times. Next time I try it'll be real."

"What was the same about the other times you tried it, and this time? What made you think of it each time?"

"If I don't get my way. See, I'm the kind of person who has to get her way. You see what I mean? Or I'm gonna make it bad for someone or make it bad for myself."

This showed a fair amount of insight. "Why don't you make it bad for someone else?"

"I'm thinking of that too," she laughed oddly.

"I know just what you mean about not getting your way and immediately thinking of suicide. That's often happened to me. Fooling with suicide is for people who are spoiled—like you and me."

"Hardheaded," she corrected me.

"Yes, hardheaded, stubborn. Only you know what stops me? I ask myself, Why do I think I'm so special? Everyone's suffering. Why should I think that my suffering is so much *grander* that it merits putting an end to myself? You know what I mean? Why should I get my way? We're all suffering."

"I wish I had a dollar so I could get me some fish 'n chips."

"You brought your lunch, didn't you?" I asked, looking at her brown paper bag.

"I ate it. But I'm still hungry. I wish I had some fish 'n chips right now."

"I'll loan you a dollar."

She was so surprised that she grinned: "Why don't you take me out to lunch?"

I hesitated, looking forward to my lunch hour privacy, but also thinking that it might have been a big step for her to ask me.

"Aw, why don't you take me to lunch?" Cora said coquettishly.

"Sure."

We entered the sweltering fish 'n chips shop and I ordered two portions and two orange sodas, the only kind they had chilled. The portions were gigantic: I could see why she always had heartburn. Cora was laughing softly to herself. "What's so funny?" I asked.

"I like to go out with white people. I wish I could go out with lots of white people and everybody be looking at me. See that man passing by the window? He see me and you, he be saying to himself, 'What the hell's going on there?'"

Debra, another student, spotted us from the window and stepped inside the shop. "Hey, how come you took her to lunch and you din take me."

I pushed my plate over to her. "Want some?"

"No I can't *stand* fish. You shoulda ordered chicken. Next time take *me* to lunch and make it chicken!" she roared, and wheeled out of the doorway.

After this discussion with Cora, I became conscious of some male-female tug going on between us. There was definitely an attraction of a low-key sort, and I dimly wondered what it would be like to act on it. But in that atmosphere it was hard to separate out flirtations from racial mockery. One day I came upstairs during lunch break, and the kids were gathered around the agency phonograph. Seeing me, Debra threw her arms out, nudged forward her enormous tits and yelled, "Fuck me, baby, O give it to me!"

I was embarrassed, everybody cracked up; I tried to pass it off with a smile, but Debra, with Amazonian ferocity, began humping against me and, when I moved aside, made as though to chase me around the room.

This was the time of the big hit "Pecan Pie." It was played so often that it moved into my brain like an unwanted boarder. Whenever the song came to the chorus

> Groove me, baby
> Oh ye-eah
> GROOVE ME NOW

all the kids would slide into that grroove me, their faces wincing with pleasure, crying, Screw me, baby! At such times it seemed pointless to try to teach.

I won't say it didn't amuse me. But it also made me feel like an interloper. I wondered if I were jealous of their sexuality—or if that in itself were only a false stereotype. For days at a time, I seemed to have to struggle to hold onto my measure of things, in the face of their powerful version of reality as a concrete set of knowable street experiences, codes, frustrations, repetitions, hassles, defiances and pleasures. I needed to remind myself sometimes that their conviction that the world was thus-and-so came not only from shrewd experience, but from provinciality and a fear of extending their boundaries beyond the ghetto.

This became clear to me one day when I took a dozen students downtown with me to a museum. On the Lexington Avenue bus, Debra, Joanne, Cora, and Rosa were playing their favorite game, Goofing on Whitey. What they did was to pick out a white person on the bus, and shout gross remarks about her until she realized she was being talked about and had to get off before her stop. When the passenger left, they would let out a righteous war cry. Debra excelled in remarks like "She sure looks stupid in that short dress with them dumpy legs." Joanne's pleasure was to parody the way she thought white people talked. Honestly, darling, the very idea! I would be flabbergasted to consider it!

I began to get an uneasy and yet prideful feeling as we came into my own neighborhood. We passed Rosedale Fish Market, the chocolate store, the florists, the china shops, Versailles Bakery, the boutiques with tweeds. Everything was cause for a putdown. At Seventy-ninth Street Joanne cried: "Oh look at that ugly old thing trying to call a taxi!"

We stared at the wrinkled ancient wrapped in blue furs, knocked silly by the wind, her gloved finger pointing and jabbing the rain, her pillbox hat with veil flying off, until a cab finally drew up and she threw herself inside, with the sense that this had been a great indignity and the worst ordeal of her week.

"White people are unreal," said Joanne.

For a moment I was caught between seeing through their eyes, seeing this neighborhood as insipid and doll-like (although I lived here), and—feeling sorry for the old lady. How often had I tried to flag down a cab on Lexington Avenue?

"There's nothing unreal about white people," I said. "I'm white, and I'm as real as you are."

"Oh shoo! I knew you'd take it the wrong way. We didn't mean you, Rick—you fly."

"Yeah, Rick, you together. We like you."

"But I'm white," I protested whitely, "just like them."

"But it's different."

"Look, I don't like it when you hurt other people's feelings. Let's stop goofing on other people, okay?"

"Damn, we were just having some fun," said Rosa. "He gonna catch an attitude. . . ."

Working through the last hour of an afternoon, I would suddenly imagine Marie coming to visit me here. What would happen if she walked up the agency steps right now? She had once promised to pick me up at the storefront some afternoon, when I least expected her. How she would transform the back room, with its metal tables, laughing in her spotlessly stylish outfit, and everyone wondering who she was and why she would want to visit me, of all people—Marie's arms bending to examine the math games in the front room, Marie turning the other cheek, that lovely cheek, to insults—turning them into compliments . . .

Going home that evening I heard a conversation between two women on the bus, sitting across from me. Both were black: one rather strait-laced and prim, with marcelled hair, the other one a hang-loose, big-legged woman in a housedress, with a loud voice. The one with the loud voice was saying, "If you want someone you'll go back to that person. And right away."

"Not necessarily," said the cool, severe one.

"If he *want* you—I'm not talking about the funny stuff now, I mean if he really want, he won't stay away long. Because people can't control their emotions that way."

"Some people can," said the strait-laced one, in a low voice.

"What you tellin' me? If someone really misses someone he wants to be with that person right away. And he find a way to do it!" She caught me listening: "Ain't I right?" she asked. I nodded in agreement.

The other woman was not so much disagreeing as resisting for a moment, withholding assent. "It's more complicated than that."

"You don't understand what I'm saying!" cried Big Leg.

"I understand perfectly."

"Then what are you shaking your head like that? Check yourself out! You blind to the facts."

"It's different for some people. Sometimes a person goes away, and he might want to come back, but he meets someone else."

"What am I saying? If he loves you enough he'll come back to you."

"But sometimes it takes a long time. You can't predict how long a thing like that will take."

"Right away, if he's serious."

"Not necessarily. He may have to work out something for himself first."

"You don't understand what I'm talking about," said Hang-loose, the voice of folk wisdom, and I agreed with her. Marie will never come back, will not visit me by surprise at the agency.

The cool, marcelled woman shrugged. They both got off the bus at Ninety-eighth Street.

At my own stop, I treated myself to a hot dog at the papaya stand on Eighty-sixth Street, and continued walking east. I was beginning to know the neighborhood well. People always seemed to have packages in their hands when they walked on East Eighty-sixth Street: they lived in a perpetual state of Christmas. I passed the German sausage shops and glanced inside at the customers from the Old Country lining up with their mouths watering before the delicacies of their childhood. The street was legitimately called Germantown. At the corner of Eighty-sixth Street and Third Avenue was The Berlin Bar, and, curiously enough, one block further down on Second Avenue was another Berlin Bar. Also on that street were the elegant German pastry restaurants, the Café Geiger and the Kleine Konditorei. I loved to wander into their satin lobbies past the reservation desk, see the pink tablecloths and sailboat napkins, a dowager about to decapitate an éclair, the maître d' advancing toward me with a shiny menu, and then change my mind and walk out.

I took my meals further east at the Hofbrau, a noisy beer hall with a bar in front, sometimes featuring live accordionists, elderly men in gray chamois lederhosen, and dining rooms up a short flight of steps in the back, where middle-aged waitresses with haggard, horsey faces and German accents and knotted lower legs would fly between tables in their running shoes. I would eat the same meal every night: Roast duck with red cabbage. It was fatty and cheap. I would take a ringside table, in the middle, so that I could still hear the noise and merrymaking at the bar, and pull out my book or evening newspaper. Sometimes I would eavesdrop on the German-speaking tables around me, imagining—as is so easy to do in New York—that I was a tourist in Europe; it was relaxing to eat to the lapping sounds of a language I could not understand. Then I forgot all this, and got down to my roast duck and cucumber salad.

The nights were colder; I still preferred to stay away from my small apartment. I had the feeling as soon as I went inside it that I was in mourning.

VII

One Saturday afternoon, when I had done my laundry and finished my walk, I was suddenly filled with a crazy energy that meant the end of my patience with elegy. I had to see Jack and Marie. If I had been depressed, I could have gotten the better of the impulse; but on the contrary, I was all at once alive, and full of hope that everything would work out somehow.

They would be confronted with a *fait accompli:* they would have to deal with me. I wanted them to make this intolerable feeling of banishment cease. The pariah, the untouchable one was thrusting himself into their sight; the leper was showing his stumps.

I made the phone call from the corner near Marie's house, so that no one would have time for a getaway.

I ran up the steps of her brownstone, and called, "It's me, Eric!" through the intercom. Someone buzzed me. At the foot of the stairs Marie stood. I had almost forgotten what she looked like. She opened her eyes wide. I saw her fear that perhaps I was out of my mind, coupled with something else, which became clearer the closer I rose toward her. It was a blazing, giddy look that meant the disaster had finally struck, as when one smiles involuntarily at the smell of sulfur escaping from a test tube that has just exploded with a wry pop.

"I just had to . . ." I explained (or didn't explain).

She nodded and led me by the arm. She was wearing the wine-red sweater which made her breasts tantalizingly vivid and close.

"Jack's here?"

"He's gone into the last room," she said amusedly, meaning, the furthest extremity to which he could run.

My heart was beating as it did around Marie. She had the effect of quickening my adrenalin. I followed her into her bedroom where Jack was slumped in a low-slung chair, studying an orange calendar of Museum of Modern Art events with single-pointed attentiveness, as though it were an orange inflated raft he was holding onto for life.

"Hello, Jack," I said.

"Hullo," he replied hollowly, from the inside of a cave. He looked like an invalid. His legs were bunched up to his chest in an uncomfortable attempt to hide; the look of suffering on his face was so contorted it approached a German Expressionist caricature.

Marie smiled at me reassuringly, as though to say, "He's all right. Just give him time."

Now that I was there, I had no idea what to tell them. I had no eagerness to look at Jack in that state; and I had to keep tearing my eyes away from Marie, who was so winsomely, achingly lovely, more than I had even remembered. Her whole being, so beautiful and full of vitality, was a curiously fascinating mixture of carelessness and cunning, artificiality and simplicity, calmness and vivacity; there was a subtle, delicate charm about everything she did or said, about every movement of hers; in everything there was a peculiar, sparklingly vivacious force at work.

"I just came by to see how you were doing.—Nice day, isn't it?" I laughed.

"It's a brilliant day, it's so sunny, we were just going to go out," Marie said enthusiastically, then ran out of words.

"What were you doing before I came?"

"We were sitting around the house having a lazy Saturday. We saw a bit of the game on TV. I wanted to go out for a walk before, but we kept dawdling with this and that, and now it's time to go to a movie we're seeing at Lincoln Center—"

"We were just going out," Jack cut in. "This isn't a good time to visit, since we have to be there by five-thirty."

"What are you seeing?" I asked.

He answered, reluctantly: *"The Mystery of the Wax Museum.* It's a revival."

"Oh, that old Michael Curtiz version. That sounds like fun."

"It's supposed to be full of wonderful special effects and things," Marie said, gallantly trilling. "And Fay Wray's in it!"

"Mind if I come along?"

"I don't mind!" volunteered Marie.

"We only have two tickets—I'm sorry, we didn't know you wanted to see it," added Jack, with those apologetic manners which were so much a part of his training, and which slipped in despite his outrage (or were the expression of his outrage).

"Well, if there are any tickets left to buy, is it okay if I join you?"

"If there are tickets left," Jack said with a shrug, implying, It's a free country, anyone can buy a ticket.

I waited for him to stand. I didn't like hovering over Jack this way, it made me uncomfortable; but inertia or obstinacy kept him a prisoner of that chair.

"We may as well get started if we want to go. Right?" Marie broke the silence, looking appealingly from one to the other. There was something festive in her manner, as though I were the prodigal son who had come home and she were the mother trying to reconcile her two men, the grim unforgiving father and the errant boy—who really did love each other, only they were too male-stubborn to fall into each other's arms. She came behind Jack in his chair, and put her arms around him, almost to help him up.

"Maybe I should just leave," he said suddenly.

"Why?"

"You two want to be alone, it's obvious I'm in the way."

"If anyone's in the way, I am." I said.

"No one's in the way! Don't be like that. Come on now, let's all go down there together," Marie said. "We've got ten minutes, so we have to get a move on."

Jack stood up stiffly, turning away as he did, as though buttoning his olive jacket were too private and vulnerable an act to let me see.

We flagged a taxi on Columbus Avenue and told the driver to take us to Alice Tully Hall at Lincoln Center.

There was no problem getting tickets; the theatre was one-third empty. For better or for worse, we were able to sit together, I took care to sit, not beside Marie, but next to Jack, with him in the middle. We were all facing straight ahead now, with no possibility to talk. Tension rising from the three of us tightened in waves on my shoulders. What a stupid idea this was, to sit in a theatre—not at all what I had wished for! The movie started: I felt as though I were being cast in cement. The violent tousling of two men on the floor while flames melted the beautiful wax statues of Marie Antoinette and Robespierre paled beside the anxiety in my stomach. I remembered that the historically interesting thing about this particular film was the two-color Technicolor process, which made the frames look almost hand-tinted. Ordinarily this would have been enough to hold me. It was no use; it didn't interest me in the slightest. I kept wanting to look over sideways at Marie and Jack. The wise-guy thirties newsroom dialogue and the theatrical horror which the Lincoln Center audience responded to with campy appreciation required a tolerant looseness which was not in me at the moment. What special torture to have to watch a light piece of fluff in this situation!

I couldn't take it any longer. To my surprise, and theirs too, I got up and left without a word.

The lobby was empty, except for an usher. I sat by a bronze cigarette urn on a flat polished wooden seat, and stared at the red concert carpet.

Five minutes later Marie came into the lobby, looking all around her. Her face lit up when she saw me. "I was afraid you'd left!"

"No."

"I came out to see if you were still here."

"I—couldn't get into the movie."

"It's a silly picture," she agreed. She sat down next to me on the polished bench and took out a cigarette. We grinned bashfully at each other. I kissed her. She let out a dying sound, and leaned her head meekly on my neck. We both stared at the red carpet.

"I'm so glad to see you again!" I said.

"You certainly can come up with some surprises! You scared us half to death," said Marie, laughing.

"I'm sorry."

"Don't be. I'm glad it happened. It's something I've been wishing for weeks, but I couldn't ask for it."

"What?"

"To get you two together."

"We're hardly together," I replied.

"No, but he's—he's taking it pretty well, don't you think?"

"I don't know. I'm not optimistic."

"If there were any way for you two to be friends again, I would give *anything* to make it happen," she said. "I would even drop out of sight if I thought that would help. That's why I almost went to Pittsburgh."

"Don't you think it's in our power to patch it up, Jack and I, if we wanted to?"

"Believe me, I so much think it's in your power that sometimes I feel invisible in this whole affair: I don't seem to have any reality, it's all you and Jack fighting," said Marie.

"That's going too far the other way."

"But that's how it feels to me, sometimes. That's why I wanted to go to Pittsburgh—to get back my own reality."

"You're real." I caught her in my arms and kissed her on the lips: this would be the last time, I cautioned myself.

"No more," she said.

"I know." We moved an inch away.

Marie put out her cigarette, and started another.

"How have you been?"

"Not bad."

Just then we noticed Jack had come out of the theatre, and, seeing us together, squinting to make sure it was us, he traversed a wide circle away and continued out towards the street doors.

"What's he doing?" I asked.

"I don't know!"

"We'd better stop him." I ran across the lobby, yelling *"Jack!"* with Marie following alongside. As we caught up to him, asking him to wait, he turned his head and answered with unassailable dignity, "I'm going out to get some cigarettes."

Marie and I looked at each other with misgivings. We followed behind him, seeing where he would go. He crossed the street and walked along a narrow construction-site path sided by door boards, under a makeshift roof of timbers with strung electric bulbs. There was only enough room to walk one abreast; Marie and I were already making it into a spy game. The walkway was strangely damper and colder than the street, with puddles we had to step around. I caught up to him at the next light. "Jack, wait!"

"This is absurd," he said. "Stop following me. I'm taking a walk to get cigarettes."

"I know, but I was afraid you wouldn't return."

"And if I didn't why would that disturb you? You came to see Marie, not me, and I was giving you a chance to be alone with her."

"That's not true. I came to see you as well."

"Look, before when I came upon you two sitting alone. . . . I saw you with my own eyes, Eric! It was perfectly obvious that you wanted to be alone and that you were enjoying talking to each other. I'm sure you have a lot to talk about. You haven't seen each other in a while. I'm trying to make it easier for you."

"Your running from us isn't making anything easier."

"I don't like to be a third wheel," Jack replied.

"How do you think *I* feel? Only I feel it day in and day out, week after week!"

"I'm sorry to hear it, but there's nothing I can do about that."

"Let's just go in there for some coffee, or something to eat." I pointed to a restaurant which was coming up on our left.

"If you want to discuss this business, I don't think I'm up to it."

"All right, then we'll just go in there and have some coffee. We don't have to discuss anything." I looked at Marie. "Is that all right with you?"

"That's fine with me."

We had come to the coffee shop I had in mind, The Pink Cloud, chosen by me for economic as well as poetic reasons. Marie and I took a table, while Jack fiddled with the cigarette machine. The next thing I knew, Jack was heading out the door.

"I'll go after him. Why don't you wait here?" I told Marie. I caught up as he was stepping off the sidewalk, squinting at the traffic light in his nearsighted Mr. Magoo manner.

"What's going on? I thought you were sitting down with us."

"I decided to go for a walk," he answered. "You came to see Marie, and I'd prefer to stay outside, if you don't mind." I decided to walk alongside him, wherever he chose to set his feet. As it happened, we did not get far at all: we reached the bench island in the middle of Broadway, where a few senior citizens and bums were taking their early evening rest. In this concrete limbo we stood, momentarily, without my having any idea to which shore of Broadway we were ultimately headed. Jack cupped his hand to light a cigarette, turning away to block the October wind.

"Why do you keep running away?" I demanded. "Are you going to make me chase you all over New York?"

"I figured you two wanted to be alone. Three's a crowd, as they say."

"Why are you being so *petulant* by insisting that I don't really want to see you? It's just perversity on your part. I told you I wanted to see you. I made a solemn promise to you that I wouldn't try to see Marie alone again; so if I'm here, it's because I wanted to see the two of you."

"What am I supposed to do, feel flattered?" said Jack.

"No, but just don't distort the truth by acting as though you're in the way." I was angry now—and self-righteous.

The loud passing cars emitting fumes on either side of us were getting on my nerves. "Can't we talk somewhere else? I can't concentrate with all this traffic noise."

"Why? I'm used to noise. It's contemporary," said Jack. "Like the Straub film, *Othon*—actors in Roman togas reciting Corneille by a freeway. I didn't see it at the festival but I heard it was good."

"I saw it."

"I'm sorry I missed it. I'll bet it was terrific."

"It was interesting," I shrugged. "It managed to be both magical and tedious, like most of the avant-garde. But I didn't come out here to talk to you about the avant-garde."

"Well I don't have anything personal to say to you any more, Eric."

I shook my head disgustedly. "How can everything personal dry up between us? It's so easy for you to act as if we were never friends. You know, I can't help feeling you're hiding behind this thing with Marie. Pretending that I don't have any interest in seeing you—as if there weren't ten years' history of friendship to the contrary!"

"What difference is it if it's ten years or fifty years? I don't trust you, Eric, and that's that."

"What can I say? You certainly have a way of silencing discussion."

"It's how I feel. It comes out everywhere, comes out in my dreams. I'll tell you, I had a dream about you last week, that I had to discuss with my analyst, you'll be happy to know," Jack said.

"It doesn't make me happy in the least. But go on."

"I dreamt we were in a wrestling match. We were like two brothers locked in mortal combat. One moment we were snakes strangling each other, the next moment it was turning into an embrace. . . . But I didn't like it. We each had fangs. It was very bloody and it seemed to go on forever. Now I don't need that! I have enough problems keeping sane without deadly combat."

"It's a dream. Don't blame it on me, it's your subconscious! Maybe it wasn't even about us."

"I think it was. And that's not it. The point is I feel that way in my waking life, right now toward you."

"You feel I'm making homosexual advances toward you?"

He bit his lip. "In the dream it wasn't even clear who was who.

We were both merging too much to tell; the struggling would turn into hugging and back into struggling. We were two boa constrictors—or more like a cobra with two heads. Now I don't need that!"

"You're being rather superstitious," I said. "Letting your life be ruled by dream-omens, like the Egyptians."

"I don't need you to tell me I'm superstitious. You can't control the situation by putting me down. What I feel, I feel. Besides, these symbols have meaning; you've always undervalued the Jungian side of things," he said, as I rolled my eyes impatiently, "and you're wrong about that; like what Dylan said about the cobra—"

"Can we leave Bob Dylan out of this for once?"

"Now, see, *that's* why I don't trust you! I was speaking about something that mattered to me and you put me down for it because it's not up to your taste standards. You always have to keep me on my toes," said Jack, with real bitterness.

"I'm sorry; it just hurt me to have Bob Dylan become the final arbiter of our friendship."

"You always turn things around so that it's my fault. First you do a thing like that, and then you treat me as though I'm failing you because I can't accept it immediately."

"I didn't say you were failing me. That's your word."

"Listen, I always feel I'm failing you because I'm not doing what you expect of me as a real friend. But I don't know how to, it's not in me. You picked the wrong person for this experiment, buddy," said Jack.

"If I picked the wrong person, how come you were able to satisfy me all these years?"

"All I was doing was acting according to what I thought you wanted. You were always trying to force me into your ethical system, like not running away and not withdrawing," said Jack. "It's true I'm always withdrawing but that's the way I am. Maybe I needed reminders all the time. I'll admit I got a lot out of it; I learned a lot from you. You're a great teacher, Eric. That's what makes you a good organizer. But you teach by dominating the person with your values. I'm not saying there's anything wrong with that. It works, usually; it's the shortest, fastest way to change people. But you've got to expect trouble when you break one of your own rules, like sleeping with my girl—"

"I refuse to accept this version of our friendship which reduces it *ex post facto* to my manipulation. I can't agree that for ten years there was nothing but my dominating you. I remember it as quite a give-and-take," I said. "You were often the teacher, not me. Have you forgotten all you introduced me to? If you don't remember that, that's your neurosis! Rather than my being the one with such inflexible moral standards, I think you're being the inflexible moralist here."

"I may be inflexible," said Jack. "But if I'm rigid, that's the way I am. You shouldn't try to make me feel bad for failing your standards of flexibility."

"Why do you keep putting it as, *I'm* trying to make *you* feel bad? You don't accept any guilt for your own bad feelings. You want to push the whole thing on me. You're making me out to be the active agent and you the passive agent, and then you complain of being dominated!" I cried. People were beginning to listen to our raised voices.

Jack shrugged. "It's a kind of fencing we're doing," he remarked. "It doesn't lead anywhere." He looked longingly toward the other side of the street, trembling a little from the cold. The wind suddenly blew his hair.

"All I'm saying is, can't we go beyond this dimension of your failing me or my failing you, or what we should be doing or what's expected of each other? I don't have a script. There is no script. I've never been in this situation before. I have to make it up as I'm going along. This jazz about failing each other for not living up to our expectations, in a new situation where there *are* no guidelines—it doesn't make sense."

"There's no point in going through this, Eric. What's done is done."

"All right, it's done, but maybe we can begin to heal things."

"If I were a forgiving person, fine. If I could forgive, I would have done it long ago. I would have forgiven my father, I would have forgiven Victoria for what she did, you, Barry, lots of people. It's sad to realize the people I care about are gone; all those people are locked doors to me."

Jack frustrated me so much I couldn't speak. This was the second time he had reeled off this list, and I suddenly understood he had already annexed me into his mythological kingdom of Loss. I was in Hades, the past tense. Not only didn't I like being "dead," I also did not appreciate having lost all uniqueness in his eyes, to become merely another name in his litany of transience.

"You talk as if all this were *Fate,* finished! *Okay,* there's been a rift. Feelings have been hurt. But we don't have to accept that as the final stage. We can do things to heal it!" I said.

"You don't want to heal things, you want to take my girl away from me, don't you?" he looked at me sharp-eyed, his nose pointed like a fox. "You just want me out of the way, don't you?"

I laughed. "I'm tempted to agree with you. It sounds so harsh, so it must be true. But then why doesn't it ring quite true to me? I wish it *were* that simple: I could have acted much more decisively with Marie, and been the ruthless fellow you take me to be, instead of pulling my punches."

"I don't think you're ruthless, just that you believe in Will, in the Nietzschean sense. And you go after what you want until you get it."

"Don't you?"

"I'm no Nietzschean superman," he said gloomily.

"Neither am I. You're being unfair, throwing that at me, just because I liked Nietzsche in college."

"Well, don't make me out to be a Jungian simpleton."

Marie came out of The Pink Cloud. She shook her head with amazement when she saw us standing in the bench island, and called something over, but it was too noisy to hear. We crossed the street to Marie.

"I thought you two'd run off together! The waiter wanted to know what happened to my friends."

"Can we go in and have a cup of coffee?" I asked Jack, gently.

"All right, but I don't see the point of it."

We re-entered, the Greek waiters looking at us closely. They must have made up their own good version of what was happening. We sat at a back booth with a red formica table, Jack and Marie on one side, I on the other. The waiter handed us two large, greasy menus. After he had taken our order, we waited until he was out of earshot.

"We don't have to beat around the bush," Jack said. "All right, I'll come right to the point. Marie, what do you think Eric wants from you?"

She looked at me, blushed like a rose, and—giggled. A remarkable answer.

Jack said moodily, "Well at least we all agree on that."

"No, no, you don't know what I mean!" Marie snapped back at him.

Jack started coughing. "What did you mean?" he said, covering his mouth between coughs.

She shook her head from side to side, enigmatically, her brunette-reddish hair swirling. I wondered how she was going to get out of this one. Marie continued to smile, wordlessly full with her secret: her dimpled expression was by turns provocative, prim, maidenly, and disenchanted with the paltry suspicions of men, who needed to project onto every girl the age-old role of Jezebel. Jack drank from his glass of water, to stop his cough. He spoke up again:

"If Marie loves you and she doesn't love me, then that settles it. And if it's the other way around, that's the end of it too." He flung out his hand towards Marie: "Let her be the one to decide."

"You can't do that to me," she said.

"Why not? *You* decide. It's the woman who usually chooses in these cases. It's always been like that," Jack said.

"You can't put that on me. I won't."

"Why not?"

"It just isn't fair," declared Marie, appealing to some invisible Bill of Rights for women in these straits.

"Why can't you ever make up your mind?" said Jack, lighting a cigarette.

"It's an impossible situation to put someone in," said Marie.

"You brought it on yourself. Why ask Eric or me to decide for you? We both want you. You have to be the one to pick. It's like *Morte D'Arthur,* except that's not a good comparison. . . . Let it stand. Which one is King Arthur, which one's Lancelot? Maybe we should have a jousting contest. Settle this the old way. All right, Eric, you choose between the mace and the longsword. Only we'll update it: car antenna and switchblade in Central Park, he said sarcastically. "If the lady can't make up her mind, we'll have to do it for her."

She laughed, icily.

"Well? Let's have it, Marie," he insisted.

"Don't make me do this," she whispered, pleading in a voice that had suddenly lost all its power.

"You've got to. There's no other way," said Jack.

I couldn't understand why she was so hesitant. She had already chosen long ago—Jack! Unless it was the humiliation of having to declare it publicly, the effect was going to be the same, I thought bitterly.

"I can't."

"You have to," he said.

Now it was turning into a kind of lovers' quarrel between them, and I wondered if this was the way they usually argued, with these words, this pattern. I could see Jack almost legalistically forcing some sort of admission from Marie, and she just as stubbornly determined to withhold it.

"I love both of you," Marie declared.

"Your love is only half a loaf then."

"No it's not half a loaf!" she asserted with great passion. (Again, I wondered why this particular charge should set her off. Was it something he often accused her of?)

"Well, if it's not half then it belongs to one of us. Now which one is it? If you love Eric, just tell me. Don't beat around the bush. Either you love Eric and you don't love me—"

"You know I love you," she reassured him.

"But you still can't make up your mind."

"It isn't that," Marie said. "When I love you, I love you totally, and completely. I don't cheat you out of anything because I also love Eric."

"I wish I could believe that."

"You can. I think you can stretch yourself that far."

"Do you realize Eric's probably in pain at this moment?—I don't like to see you hurt," he turned to me; "that only bothers me more."

"Thank you," I smiled faintly.

"I can feel your pain from what was just said. I could be you. That's the trouble; I keep identifying with everyone at this table and losing myself. That's not good for me, I have a tendency to lose my boundaries already. My doctor says I should look out for my own feelings, instead of worrying about everybody else's."

"You seem to be doing all right," I responded.

"I'm just trying to put everything on the table. Everyone keeps telling me to talk things out!" he muttered.

We fell into a moody silence.

Finally I spoke up, to break the tension:

"I'll tell you what I want from Marie. I want everything. I admit that I'm still in love with Marie. And I might be using you, Jack, to get to her. That could be part of it. I won't deny it," I said (wondering where all this honesty was headed for). "But it's not the whole of it. I also need you as a friend. Now I have to negotiate in my own mind between these two needs. Obviously I want both, I want everything. But it's just as obvious I'm not going to get everything. One usually doesn't. So I'm prepared to settle for a good deal less," I paused. "I think I would be willing to go back to the way it was before you left for California, with you as the couple and I the single friend. That was attractive to me. I was happy being around you two, that time we got together, and you made veal Marsala," I said to Marie. "I think if I had both your affections again, on whatever terms, I would be satisfied with that."

"You're asking a lot," said Jack, frowning. "How can I trust that you wouldn't try to sleep with Marie again behind my back, after you were accepted as a friend."

"Well, I'd want to, of course," I admitted. Marie permitted herself a saucy look of bravado. "But I wouldn't, because I wouldn't dream of making the same mistake again, now that I know what the consequences are. I wouldn't be that stupid twice in a row."

"You'd be tempted," he said. "How do you know you'd be able to resist the desire?"

"What do you want me to say? How can I prove it—stick my hand in the fire? I tell you I wouldn't do it again!"

"You'd say anything to get closer to Marie. I understand you, buddy. You said it yourself before; you're in love with her. A man in love will do anything to keep his chances alive," Jack said warily.

At the word "anything" I saw Marie's eyes dilate. This was romantic stuff to her. What enthralled her, I thought, was not so much that two men were fighting over her, which, out of some corrective modesty, she never quite treated as real, but simply the chance to hear in life the vocabulary she had only encountered before in fiction and films. My own response was also to be flattered. Jack's interpretations of my motives seemed to grant me more sense of purpose than I had. Suddenly I was that heroic character, the desperate man-in-love who would stop at nothing. The actual fact was that at the moment I was content enough just to be in their company. I didn't need more: you could call that a failure of imagination, if you will, or a failure of passion, but Jack couldn't understand it because he was so much more of a worshiper of Venus than I was. Of the three of us—I, with my doubts in the first place about the primacy of love, compared to one's lifework; and Marie, who took romantic courtship with a grain of sand, though she liked to hear its language—Jack, in his morbid and fatalistic way, was the only one among us who sincerely believed in the all-consuming power of Eros.

And yet he was also right: I would do anything to keep my chances of love alive.

Jack excused himself to make a phone call. "I'm not running

away or anything. I just have to take care of one call." He wedged between two tables and went up to the front of the restaurant.

"He's probably calling Bernadette!" Marie said with a wink.

"Is that . . . still going on?"

"Sure. She's been in town since last week. Jack says it's different." She laughed airily to herself.

"Where does that leave you?"

"I'm all right."

Marie and I began smiling at each other like conspirators. "What do you think?" I asked.

"I think it's going well. Don't you?"

"He's listening, at least. But I'm not hopeful. I've never seen him so jumpy! What did you mean when he asked you what I wanted from you, and you just laughed?"

"I looked in your face and I couldn't stop laughing. Don't be hurt," she said, touching my hand; "I mean it was a lovable look, but you looked so worried that it made me crack up."

"What did you think, in fact, when he asked you what I wanted?"

"I thought . . ." her face went luminous, "he wants the Marie!"

I felt a cold chill go down my back. For a second I detested her. She seemed so smug that everybody wanted her—and the affectation of putting a definite article before her name as though she were an ocean liner! Then, in a turnabout, I suddenly pitied her. No, maybe she put it there because she felt like a thing, some chattel we were fighting over.

"What are you thinking?" She broke into my reflections.

"Oh . . . I'm wondering what it feels like to be the Marie."

"And do you think you know how it feels?"

"Not necessarily. But I'd love to be in your shoes for an hour to find out."

"I think they'd pinch. I wear a six-and-a-half!"

"Well I could put my toe in and find out that much."

"What do you want to know? Ask me anything," she said bravely.

"How do you feel right now?" I asked.

"Confused. Sick to my stomach. I wish I was leaving for Venezuela."

"Or Pittsburgh."

"No, not Pittsburgh. That's something else."

"I wish I could really kiss you right now," I said in a low voice.

"You can't."

"I know."

She said, "Someday I'll tell what it feels like to be me."

"And the world will split open."

"Not that," she said incredulously. She smiled. "You say the strangest things sometimes."

"I was only thinking of the Muriel Rukeyser line, that if one woman ever told the whole honest truth about her life, the world would split open."

"Do you believe that?" Marie asked excitedly.

"No, but it's a nice thought."

"That's the trouble with you, you like all these nice thoughts but you don't believe them."

"I believe in some things," I said.

"I know you do."

We looked down at the table, blushing.

"Here comes Jack."

I wondered what we would talk about now. I hoped we would be able to make some ordinary conversation, to smooth things a little before leaving. But after Jack rejoined us he looked shaken, haunted; the change was remarkable. Before, he had been edgy, but at least he had been willing to hold up his end. Now he refused to look at either of us; he twisted a forelock of black hair as though he wanted to grind it into his temple.

When he went to the counter to pay his bill, I asked him if something was wrong, but he pulled away. "I can take care of myself!" He handed the bill to the cashier as though he were in a foreign country and not used to the currency. He seemed transfixed by the counter-sitters eating their food.

I had never seen Jack be so catatonic. I gave Marie an alarmed look, which she shook off, seeming to say she knew what to do.

She walked with him out of the coffee shop, and I said good-bye to them in front. It was dark by now, and we shook hands mechanically; Jack roused himself for a second to engage in the formalities of good-bye.

I walked home slowly, trying to figure out what had gone wrong. The only explanation I could think of was that when he came back to the table the sight of Marie and me alone together must have thrown him into a jealous fit, like coming across us in bed. And yet, I thought obstinately, he had done nothing all afternoon but try to arrange it so that we would be left alone.

VIII

What happened between them after I left, I later learned from Marie. They had had a big fight; Jack said he was through with her, Marie accused him of treating her the same suspicious way his mother always treated him, and this charge made him so upset that he locked himself in her bathroom. Marie asked to be let in, at first sweetly, "Please open up?" and finally like a marine sergeant: "HEY OPEN UP IN THERE!" When no answer came, she figured she would have to break in with a hammer. Marie began to hammer at the hinges. The door eventually gave, and she found him sitting on the lip of the bathtub, crying to himself: "Where's Vicky? She's the one I love. Where's Sara, I want Sara.—I hate you!" Then he looked up and said with surprise, "How did you get in here?" She told him, "I broke the door down!" They both started laughing. There was a reconciliation.

Then they went off that same evening to a party for the Venceremos Brigade, which had just returned from cutting sugarcane in Cuba. They got drunk, she met an old friend and talked to him for an hour, then Jack and she went home. I presume they fell into each other's arms, though her account raced over that point. In the morning he was perfectly loving; and since then, she said, things had been pretty much fine between them.

The upshot of my ill-starred surprise visit was a kind of honeymoon period for the two of them which lasted some months. I had helped the couple come together again. There was nothing I could do, it seemed, that would not have this effect. I was the outside threat which united them. And getting Marie to leave Jack would have probably bothered me equally as much, since I was playing to lose, like the United States in Vietnam. I had run out of offensives or moves of any kind. To summarize: there was no point in barging in on the couple again, I had already played that card; I could not see Marie alone, because I had given my word I wouldn't; and I was no longer under the delusion that Jack would get in touch with me of his own free will. As for my crazy but sincere offer that we go back to being friends the way we were in the veal Marsala days, this was never mentioned again, never even taken seriously.

I had lost them both. Though I lived in the same city, the same Manhattan, I was exiled from their company as though I were on Elba. All I had left of the two of them was a telephone voice; and without the possibility of ever seeing Marie again, this mode of contact brought less and less satisfaction. Finally, that went too. I was quite curt with Marie on the phone one day, and after that, the calls stopped.

I had made up my mind to forget them both. But first, there were quite a few pages added to my *Journal of Decrystallization*.

And as I walked the streets, carrying grocery bags home, or holding clothes from the dry cleaners over my arm, I would sometimes compose poison pen letters to Marie. In these missives, never sent, I would curse her for blocks: *Dear Marie, I just want to tell you what a shit you are. After that latest phone call, full of bubbling good spirits because Jack was loving to you when you went to your parents' country house for the weekend—I don't give a shit about any of that! I'm sick of you. Jack is a pain in the ass too. Always checking his hospital chart. . . . I don't give a damn if he starts being "loving" or not. The two of you deserve each other. You're the Black Plague. What a phony! Like the time you told me how sorry you were for the ugly girl in the corner because you were having such a wonderful time and she was having such a miserable one. You dash through people's feelings like Lady Bountiful, you have no idea of the price. Spare me your "affection." Even a rat learns to stay away from electric shocks. . . .* In the middle of the epistolary rage I was directing at some metal piping, I would suddenly come to and see the scaffolding of iron, the yellow hydrant, the snow, the lending library, and feel ashamed of myself for letting my mind be filled with such obsessive, vengeful garbage. The real world, which could be sustaining me every second, was passing me by.

My city walking consisted of this red light, green light alternation of interior fury, with dazed attempts to come out of it into pure observation. What triggered the switch from obsessing to observing would be a little kick of guilt: "Come on, it's all getting by you!" In the mornings, when I took the bus to work, I would force myself to look out the window at Third Avenue and wonder at what street, at what precise building, the neighborhood began to turn into slum. Further on, there was the movie theatre with a Spanish marquee which promised three different films a day, *Hoy*, that I always wanted to try but never did, and a few blocks after that a jewelry store with a diamond-shaped hanging sign, *Joyeria* (I liked that word so much better than "jewelry store"). Always the same four or five stores I'd notice, and then my mind would wander; and even when I tried to force myself to note each storefront, I would drift off in the process, and be struck with the same five familiar landmarks: the theatre, the *joyeria*, the driving school, the photography store with wedding pictures, and the Blue Jay Bar.

Coming into East Harlem, with the domino players, sidewalk vendors, the people on the street corners, I always felt as though I were on a bus going into an island village. It gave me a sense of placidness, of diminished tension, peculiarly at odds with the rough reputation of the neighborhood.

The sleepiness followed me into the agency, where, for all the loud shouting matches and bravado, nothing was really happening. Nothing was going to change. And everyone knew it. I began to find this passivity enjoyable, even as I fought against it and insisted vocally that everything must be stirred up, and made better.

I was doing a lot of exploratory work at the time, experimenting with different teaching materials. Suffice to say that at the time all this Marie-Jack business was dying inside me, I was at the first stages of developing my method for teaching reading to high school dropouts, which I have described at great length elsewhere in my books, *Inner City Youth* and *Decoding*. It had not yet coalesced conceptually, I was still not confident that anything useful would come out of it. In fact, what I remember most from this period is feeling uncertain and anxious, tapping forward in the dark. But I was engrossed. In any case, I no longer loved Marie.

PART THREE

Humiliations Unforgiven,
Compliments Received

I

It was August; I was traveling to London for pleasure. I had no work to do, no family to visit, no programs of self-improvement to meet. After a long year at the agency I had promised to refresh my eyes with new landscapes and sensations. If a friendship-of-the-road happened to be struck, and the friend turned out to be a duke who put me up in his castle for three weeks I would be grateful but not astonished, since my only purpose was to search for the miraculous.

It was summer again. To my surprise, in England this meant rain. The backs of pedestrians hurrying for double-decker buses were sleek with it; the ubiquitous umbrellas, the newspaper headline sheets, the green-grocer awnings leaked it as casually as sunlight. It was not exactly a downpour, but a diligent vaporization, with a chill that forced people indoors for teatime (now a perfectly understandable custom to me). The rain gave the opportunity of watching a civilization going about its business, carrying on in a routine unfestive way—which was fine for one like me, there on holiday myself. Everything was quite unspectacular, and yet through American eyes looked strange, a tiny bit off-register. It started with the typefaces on traffic signs, which were somehow exotically understated, and continued to the lingerie ads in the train tubes, which slid by one after another alongside steep escalators—ads that seemed sexier and more unashamed than their American counterparts. Contradiction by contradiction, the way a tourist cannot stop playing anthropologist, I was putting together English society in my head.

From my bed-sitter rented near Victoria Station, on an off-street of row houses turned into hotels, I would strike out with my umbrella, take a bus anywhere, get off and start walking through a new district, carrying a book along to read in restaurants when my legs gave up. This agenda of happy self-reliance crumbled after two days when I suddenly found I wanted to talk to someone.

I had been given a few names to look up, and went down the list, with various degrees of success. My best luck was linking up with Teddy Forster, whom Jack, of all people, had told me to call. Not that Jack and I had made up: on the contrary, he always ran away the moment he saw me. But once we were trapped in the same party and surrounded by other people, and I happened to blurt out that I was going to London; and he gave me Teddy's name and address. "You'll like meeting those people and I'm sure they'll be crazy about you," he said, not without a trace of self-defeating bitterness.

Teddy Forster turned out to be a Canadian who had been living in England for over seven years, and, like certain émigrés, knew everyone. He was a garrulous, scrawny, shaggy, drifting young man, Jack-of-all-trades, from talent agent to drug dealer, and at first it was a little difficult for me to put my finger on the source of his popularity. But he had a fast punning sense of humor that deflated tension, and I could see how he might come in handy as a catalyst and universal mascot in awkward social situations. A typical evening with Teddy consisted of making the rounds, in his little Volvo, from one corner of London to the next. Dropping in on upwards of five households a night, I would hear a dozen names, shake a bunch of hands, be taken aside by the hostess and offered hashish, liquor or food, participate in ten minutes of topical conversation, listen silently to fifteen minutes of malicious gossip about people I didn't know, and be taken to the next house. The houses were generally rather graceful and comely, the women also, the men red-faced, boisterous and witty and well informed and constantly drinking. I gathered it was a sort of circle of New Left journalists, who were always about to go off to another European capital to do a muckraking story or a "shoot," and meanwhile were celebrating. Sometimes it seemed as if half of Europe was going around shooting documentaries on the other half. Although I was ignorant of the rules of this journalism world, I found that all I had to do to be accepted was to cover my fright, insert an intelligent or clever-sounding remark from time to time, and keep quiet the rest, with an ironically amused look on my face. The general air of smoke and bonhommie tolerated nearly everything, except perhaps intimacy.

Teddy seemed to have the function of a go-between, bearing gossip from house to house, as well as quietly accurate information about the prices of dope. His entry was always greeted with a shout and an explosion of merriment, implying that the party could now begin. Yet when he left there was no great sense of loss. It took me a while to connect this rather ungalvanic young man with the English lover Marie had told me about. But we discovered in talking that we had something very much in common: we had both lost Marie to Jack.

By far the most interesting household Teddy introduced me to was the Princess Anna's. Teddy was actually the only one who ever called Anna Vilardes Hodgkinson a princess; when I asked her directly one night if she was royal, she smiled charmingly, saying that her family merely owned a good deal of land in Indonesia. "They are one of the powerful oligarchic families who are destroying the country," were her words. The next day I told Teddy that Anna had denied possessing royal blood. "She's entirely too modest," he said in his sly, mysterious way, leaving the matter still open. I preferred to think he was right, because there was something anointed about Anna. She was rather small, with quite a voluptuous figure, almond eyes widened by curiosity, straight shiny black hair and a graceful way of advancing which seemed to emanate from her pelvis alone. Her ancestry was half-Javanese and half-Spanish, and you could see the Javanese in her cheekbones. While she did not go about in island costume, there was a trace of native dress in her liking for floor-length red mumus, and hair flowers.

She was married, alas, to the successful television producer, Christopher Hodgkinson, and they and their children and children's nurse and a servant or two managed to live in comfortably casual-bohemian style, all together in an elegantly trim house near Hampstead Heath.

Anna and Chris made me at ease the first day in their polished living room—though I was not sure why these people would bother putting themselves out for me at all. And when they kept inviting me back for dinner parties and extending their hospitality, I wondered if maybe they were bored, or if their ignorance of American types was such that they failed to see that I was not at all of their social class: I kept expecting some crude Brooklynese to betray me; and, once I thought of it in those terms, I knew I would have to make sure they saw that side of me—to do less would be like trying to "pass." Yet whatever I said seemed to make no difference in their acceptance. I then suspected that my rough-edgedness itself was entertaining to them as a source of vitality, their diversion-of-the-month. This would have made more sense if the Hodgkinsons were bored, dried-up people who needed to feast on any new stranger, but they were not; they were in the world and leading stimulating lives and I finally had to come to the anxious conclusion that they simply liked me.

The truth was I had changed, though I was perhaps the last to see it. While still feeling myself a boy from the slums, I had gotten a university education, acquired a taste for esoteric culture; and now, when I thought back to East Harlem, to Cora and Dewey and Cha-Cha, where I felt I should really belong, it seemed that I was a stranger there as well. To return to that same ghetto of my childhood as if it were and would always be mine—had proven close to slumming. Yet I did not fit in with people born to middle-class comfort either. It seemed there was no group at all in which I could feel at home. Perhaps anyone of the tiniest sensitivity comes to that banal conclusion. But what I was seeing now with horror, in the accepting eyes of those a class above me, was that I had already partly metamorphosed—into them. My only hope of growing seemed to point in an upward social direction; but that direction aroused in me a characteristic disapproval and distaste; I was by no means attracted by everything I saw in well-off people's lives, and the momentary need to accept their hospitality and keep secret my criticism of them made me feel like a hypocrite.

I also felt under false pretenses because I came introduced as a friend of Jack Bogardes'. This sponsorship immediately won me the company's affectionate trust—and I found myself stuck in conversations about Jack, his rare qualities and lovable idiosyncrasies. I was expected, of course, to supply the latest details. How could I begin to explain that my relationship with Jack had turned sour, and that to him I was something like the Judas in his life? So I did what was expected: I joined the chorus of praise and toasts to Jack.

Among Teddy's many services was to put me in contact with a couple who had a spare guest room, cheaper and much nicer than the bed-sitter I had been staying in. Hugh Wall was a Welshman who had once been a union organizer and still loved to talk about those times, while cheerfully boozing. His wife, Janet, was a highly paid copywriter for an ad agency, and at home, an extremely complaisant soul. They lived in a Grecian house near Holland Park, in a basement flat which was quite sprawling, offhandedly disheveled, chilly and yet full of charm; my own room gave out onto a lovely garden that was shared by all the houses on that courtyard.

Hugh and Janet were perfect landlords; most of the time they left me alone, except to offer me tea when a pot was on, or when they were talking politics, and then Hugh could not resist the itch to draw me into it. Like most English leftists I had been meeting, their outlook was so Internationalist, informed and cosmopolitan, that they never seemed to get around to local London issues: a Free Angela Davis poster hung above their marble fireplace. They wanted me to tell them all about the latest black organizations, American police tactics, wildcat strikes in the auto industry. While I was hardly an expert on such matters, I did what I could—inventing when I had run out of facts.

Teddy Forster was coming over to their house for a drink, the night after I had moved in, and I was glad for the opportunity to thank him in person for the happy improvement in my living arrangements. Teddy let drop, in his oblique, sly manner, the information that a friend of mine had just arrived in town. "Who?" I asked, dying to know. "You'll find out," he said. The friend was meeting him for brunch in a certain restaurant near Regents Park, and if I wanted to surprise the friend I could join them there.

At the Silver Dollar Café, a new London emporium done in Western saloon-style where many Americans seemed to gather, I waited with Teddy by a booth facing the door. Enter Marie, fresh and dewy and plucky as always. She waltzed up to the table and said: "I recognized you right away!"

"I saw you the first moment you came in the door."

We both laughed. So it started again. I was jubilant to see her in this foreign city where I had no old friends. What was she doing here? Oh, just seeing some people she hadn't in a long time. She just decided at the last moment to get on a plane to London. Nico Reeves—did I know her? She was an up-and-coming painter and she wanted Marie to sit for a portrait. "So let's just say I flew into town to get my portrait painted."

"When did you find out I was here?"

"Just now! Teddy wouldn't tell me anything—right?"

Teddy nodded like an alligator. He was watching us, cannily. We had so much to tell, to fill each other up-to-date on. Teddy had some errands to run, so we said we would meet with him later. We started walking across the fields of Regents Park; it was sunny—it had actually stopped raining—but I failed to take notice of this, so logically did it seem to belong with the rest of the miracles of the day. What a pleasure it was to be with Marie! And when we had talked to our hearts' content, we started kissing on the grass.

Edible, she seemed. It had been so long since we'd had the freedom to explore one another. We were lolling in one of those charmed states, when all touches seem delicious, and all words are both funny and true.

What had given us the freedom to lift the embargo on our being alone? Two things: the coincidence of our meeting in this same alien place (an *accident,* hence exonerating us from blame); and the fact that Jack and Marie had "tentatively" broken up. If I thought of my promise to Jack for more than a moment, before pressing Marie's lips, it was only to tell myself that the deadline date of the vow must have passed. Especially since he gave me no hope of ever returning my offers of friendship, I had nothing to lose from that quarter in taking up with Marie again.

It was premature to ask her: "What's supposed to happen now?" We were floating; I said good-bye to her that afternoon, not wanting to press my case too fast, and we agreed to meet the next day at the house of Anna Hodgkinson, who had invited us both for lunch.

I had no idea what great friends Marie and Anna were. Both women grew so animated around each other, with brown eyes flashing, and hands clapping in sisterly glee, that I had only to sit back on the sofa and watch the two of them spiraling to new planes of giddiness. To be entertained by the conversation of two such delightful, malicious, fetching women was heaven for me.

Nevertheless, I also wanted to be alone with Marie, and we excused ourselves for a walk.

Marie held my hand; she was in a happy mood. As soon as we were out in the street she said: "Anna took me aside and told me she thought you were terrifically attractive, and she was beginning to fall in love with you."

I was already used to this circle's flirtatious hyperbole; and yet, I wanted so much to believe that I might actually have had a chance with a woman like Anna, a creature as splendid as that, that my mind started whirling when I heard the news. "What did you tell her?" I asked.

"I said, 'Hands off him, sister, he's mine!' "

"Did you really tell her that?"

"Not in those exact words, no, but I did tell her about you and me. She was fascinated and wants to hear all the details."

"I am half in love with her myself."

"I'll be jealous in a minute. She's so good-looking! She's twice as pretty as I am."

"She is lovely."

"You're supposed to say, 'But not nearly as much as you, dear,'" Marie elbowed me.

"Always excepting you, of course: the prettiest of them all."

"That's better."

"You're not the only one who can be in love with two people at the same time," I said.

The street was bordered with antique shops. We passed a trio of teen-age girls who had short cropped hair, and wore men's shirts and pants, looking rather "butch."

"They're cute, don't you think?" said Marie, turning to follow them with her eyes.

I wondered what she saw in the trio.

"Girls make such pretty boys," she sighed.

"You do."

"Do you really think so? I'm too old to make a convincing boy."

"No you're not."

"I used to love to roll my hair up in a jockey cap and go around with Carolee in the Village and pretend we were a couple." She took my arm and swung it. "Let's be joyous! I love being light-headed. When I'm with you I always feel I'm in a screwball comedy, and you're Cary Grant and I'm Katherine Hepburn—"

"I feel more like Ernest Borgnine at the moment."

"No you don't. You just like to pretend that."

Ordinarily I would have let it pass; but I was a little bothered by her blithe refusal to see me as anything but fantasy. "I'm no smooth Cary Grant. At the moment I feel sweaty, clumsy and insecure, like a butcher on a date with a pretty girl. That's why I said Ernest Borgnine."

"I know why you said it. That's just your way. It's like, you need to do it to be manly. But by denying your suaveness and your delicacy," offered Marie, "it just comes out twice as clearly. Like Cary Grant with a Cockney accent."

"But I'm not Cary Grant!" I said doggedly. "And it's frustrating to have to keep up the part. That's the trouble with us, Marie. We can never situate ourselves in reality."

"I'm not asking you to keep up any part.—Don't spoil it!" she begged suddenly, with pained eyes. She was appealing to my intelligence, saying, You understand everything about this already; why must you belabor this? But I wanted to spoil it. It was so perishable, our happiness, why not go at it with blunt hands like a butcher and kill it with one hack?

Nevertheless, I controlled myself, I "behaved," sensing that Marie had a point, or that she knew how these things were supposed to go; and we rounded our tour through the streets and came back arm-in-arm to Anna's house, presenting ourselves to our hostess as two lovebirds.

The next night, Anna Hodgkinson was supposed to go to the theatre with her husband, but Christopher had work to do, so she invited me to be her escort. It was a treat to be seen with Anna in the lobby, in her coral evening gown and mink. "You do look like a princess," I said. My fantasies reached the skies, and I could not forget for a moment Anna's statement to Marie that she was almost falling in love with me. To be truthful, of course, Mrs. Anna acted not at all like a woman in love; I think the chief object of the evening for her was to get out of me the full story of Marie, myself and Jack. After watching the play (a well-made English comedy which failed to dent my mind in any way), I obliged Anna's interest by walking her home from the theatre and telling her the whole bittersweet tale of our triangle, updated to the previous afternoon. Anna listened with that curiosity for details of the heart, and that suspended judgment, which characterizes a worldly woman: it might be said that she was rooting for all three of us. As I walked Anna across black London in the suddenly enchanting rain, holding her umbrella and unburdening my heart to her, I thought to myself that this was the kind of woman I should be going after.

My next date with Marie was for noon at the British Museum. I was to meet her in the museum gift shop. There was something about the tone of this date, in our making the arrangements, and the drift of events, that made me see it as a crossroads. Were we, or were we not, going to resume our love affair?

I was tense with the knowledge that things were about to be decided. I leaned against the postcard racks, looking up each time the museum door opened, waiting, biting my nails, working myself into a foul mood at Marie's lateness. The old clock showed it was already thirty-five minutes past our meeting time. I would give her another half-hour. Ten minutes later she burst into the gift shop in a brilliant yellow tailored suit with white silk blouse, like a canary, and flew up to me and kissed me on the cheek; she had on white gloves and a wide-brimmed canary-yellow sun hat; I could see the effect she was after, I could appreciate its matching effects, the enthusiastic smile, but somehow I didn't care. In the extra forty-five minutes' wait, I had used up my desire. Her tailored suit annoyed me: it was *too* perfect. Moreover, I was looking for a sign of sexual consent, and this yellow-and-white was virginal. I could not help comparing her daisy-like costume with that of Anna Hodgkinson's last night. Anna who had looked so mature and womanly, while Marie hung back in girlhood, still a gamine.

"Shall we go?" I asked.

"Let me buy some postcards first. You're angry at me, aren't you? I'm sorry. I had to iron my blouse and there was something wrong with the cord. I *knew* you'd be furious. I was trying to go as fast as I could. And then there were no cabs for fifteen minutes, on a street where there are *always* cabs."

"It's okay. Buy your cards."

She moved through the postcard racks, humming, taking a vase reproduction here, an Arabic arabesque there; occasionally she would murmur something like, "This one my mother will love," or "That's for Beth." Meanwhile I prowled the other end, filling my hands with the most rigorous paintings I could find: Holbein, Roger van der Weyden, Dürer. When she was done and waiting at the checkout counter, she said, "Want to see what I have?"

I looked through them unenthusiastically. "You missed some good ones."

"No need to get huffy about it!" she laughed, correctly
sniffing my attitude. I realized I was being ridiculous; we had a
whole day together, and I had better start being more sympathetic
or it would turn into a disaster. Marie looked through my own
postcard stack: "I love this one. Where did you find it?"

"I'll get it. You stay on line."

Marie kept adding souvenirs and posters to her pile; the final
bill came to ten pounds. "I'll carry it," I said, as we left the museum. We had decided not to see any galleries after all, but to go
directly to lunch, since both of us were starving.

It was threatening rain, and we ran into the first restaurant we
could find. Wedged as we were into a tiny table, crowded by
fellow diners on every side, eating beef stew and cold peas, it was
hardly the place for a romantic tête-à-tête. But then, I was not in
exactly a romantic mood. I listened to Marie gush for a while. I
had put on that special diminishing lens, which made me see her
as a series of tics and affectations. Affected she was, certainly—
coy, at times precious—but usually, I was also able to see her
force of character. At that moment, however, nothing in her
behavior seemed real to me: everything had turned into man-
nerism.

It occurred to me that I was foisting onto Marie the blame for
my own fears. Instead of thinking of how she had *made* herself
unattractive, I might have admitted that I was worried about how
I was going to "make" her. Would I have to seduce Marie all over
again? Where would we go? Not to Hugh and Janet's—I would
have to rent a hotel room. Would she feel that was too tawdry?
Was there a suave maneuver she was expecting, some trick to get
her gracefully into it? These procedural questions weighed on me.
Being in a foreign city only made it more complicated. I felt
strangely, lethargically incapable of making a move toward her
that would get us to bed. Perhaps because I was still waiting for a
decisive sign from her that she really wanted me. . . . And, underneath it all, was that old nemesis of ours: the difficulty we had
in going beyond flirtation to create for ourselves a calm, even
space where sexuality could take place. Why could we not meet as

two consenting adults? Why was everything always brimming with promise, and simultaneously unnatural?

"Why don't you say something?" she laughed nervously. "I feel like I'm talking to a wall!"

"I'm sorry. What do you want me to say?"

"Say you're happy to see me; say you can't stand my guts—I don't know, anything! Your face looks so judgmental."

"I was wondering where all this was going. I keep asking sober questions, like: Is this serious? Are we going to be lovers? The whole thing's a bit artificial to me because we're meeting in this social milieu which feels more yours than mine. I don't know what's real in this milieu. There's a language of gallantry and social flirtation which you use, and Anna uses, and everyone else here, and it confuses me—I'm not sure where I stand."

"You stand where your heart is."

"But where is your heart?"

Marie looked down modestly. "Here."

Somehow I didn't believe her.

"Maybe the problem is we're from two different social classes," I muttered, under my breath.

"Why do you keep *saying* that? My parents aren't wealthy. I'm from the same class you are, middle class!"

"I'm from the lower middle class," I said with excessive dignity.

"It's the same thing, middle class, lower middle class. My parents aren't rich. You're so wrong about this!"

"They have a house in Long Island, with acres of green around it, you told me. Your father owns a factory. My father works in a factory."

"Oh, this obsession you have about social class!" She broke off impatiently. "Really! Grow up!"

"Social class is a very real thing in the world. You can't just sweep it away—"

"I know that as well as you do—and I'm not denying it. I could never deny it. I have scars to prove it, as well as you do. But in your case it's become just a—way of hitting at people when they get too close. And it's *adolescent,* like acne or whatever teenagers are ashamed of."

"I'm not ashamed of being lower middle class. I'm proud of it."

"Oh I know, that's what you *say.* But you are ashamed: it's associated in your mind with certain humiliations that you can't forgive," Marie said, with a clairvoyance which stunned me.

"All right."

"It's so unfair to judge people on the basis of their incomes," she said bitterly.

"But I still can't help thinking there's something in it—besides my immaturity. You and I don't come from the same world. You come from Jack Bogardes' world, or from Anna's world, with comforts and codes of manners that are taken for granted."

She looked at me with scorn. "Let's not talk about this subject any more."

"All right," I said. "If it's such a sore spot."

"That's right, let it be my sore spot. Let's leave it at that."

I wanted to go into it more and more. Why? It seemed to explain her choice of Jack over me, in terms that would preserve my ego, and keep me impersonally angry at her. But why was I even stuck on that old rejection, when I had a chance for Marie at this very moment?

"I think we started off on the wrong foot today," I confessed.

"I think *you* did."

"Well, it's just that I couldn't stand the suspense any longer. Why don't you just tell me?"

"I will if I can."

"Well, what shall it be?" I said. "Are we going to be lovers or not?"

"How can I answer a question like that point-blank?"

"You can say yes or no. Look, I don't know if my nerves can take another long siege. One of us is always advancing while the other's retreating—this could go on forever. It's like battering my head against a wall."

"Have you noticed how all your metaphors are martial?" she interrupted.

"So?"

"You speak of battering, advances, retreats, sieges. You talk about me as if I were the enemy, to be captured. There's no tenderness. How can we be lovers when one of us hates the other?"

"I didn't say I hate you."

"But you *talk* as if you do."

"I was angry—first of all, because you were late and that pissed me off to have to wait around three quarters of an hour!"

"I'm sorry! I apologized for that already."

"And second of all, I don't like your having so much power over me. It seems my fate is in your hands again. I don't like that. It disturbs me."

"That's what love is," she said with a shrug.

"I'm not so sure."

"You'll never love anyone until you can put yourself willingly in another person's hands," said Marie.

"Can you?"

"I think I can."

"All right—put yourself in *my* hands," I said sardonically. She smiled, without answering. "You first. I'll follow. Real love shouldn't be contingent on the other person reciprocating at the same pace. You should be willing to go out on a limb."

"How would you want me to go out on a limb?" asked Marie, for the sake of argument.

"Agree to be lovers."

"It's so cold-blooded to talk about it this way, in this place— you're making it into a duel of wills, rather than trying to bring out my feelings of love," she said.

"Are you afraid that if you sleep with me, you'll spoil your chances of getting back with Jack?"

"Maybe," she said, then there was a long pause.

That was all the admission I wanted. The rest, I decided, was window dressing.

Marie wanted to look at some antique shops, to buy gifts, so we made the rounds along Museum Street.

"What shall we do now?" I asked.

"Well, I have to be somewhere at four-thirty," she notified me for the first time. "But we can walk till then."

"I was thinking we could rent a rowboat and go rowing in Hyde Park."

"That's a wonderful idea. Let's do it some other time, okay? I'm a little tired today, and it looks like it's going to pour."

"How about Sunday?"

"Great! Sunday is our date for rowing."

"Where do you have to be at four-thirty?"

"At Fortnum & Mason's. I'm meeting Jack's mother for tea!" Marie announced.

"Mrs. Bogardes is in town too?"

"She just got in. I couldn't believe it either. All these coincidences," said Marie, looking distractedly around.

"What are you looking for?"

"I have to buy gifts for everyone in my family. Do you mind if we go into that print shop and look around?"

"Not at all."

The doorjamb bell rang as we entered. There were stacks of mounted prints, and Marie immediately made for a set of hunting scenes: black geese and ducks.

"My brother loves geese," she said.

I found some frayed-looking political cartoons, with fat balloon texts above bewigged politicians' heads. I was looking for an accidental Rowlandson or Hogarth left in the bin, but obviously the proprietor knew the value of his trash. He had even mounted old *Punch Magazine* pages, chocolate ads and theatrical notices, and was charging one pound fifty apiece.

I had no idea what I was doing in this shop. All this desultory gift-shopping was not my style at all. And yet I had fallen into a mood where, in spite of getting little pleasure from being with Marie, I could not bear to part from her; I would have trailed along with her anywhere to drink the last dispirited dregs of this day in her company. Who can explain that sluglike shadowing of a pretty woman on her errands, which has nothing to do with desire or even expectations of a carnal reward?

Perhaps I was only collecting more evidence to condemn her, to lay the affair to rest, I told myself.

I hurried along with Marie to the department store where she would be meeting Mrs. Bogardes. Even now I had not the spine to bring myself to separate from her. "What are you doing afterwards?" I inquired.

"I don't know. Back to my room, I guess," said Marie.

"How long do you think you'll be at tea with Jack's mother?"

"Probably an hour or so. You can wait around, if you like," she offered, reading the request on my face.

"While you're in the department store?"

"Sure, if you want to."

I squeezed her hand gratefully. "I think I'll do that. Would you mind terribly?"

"Not at all. If *you* don't mind."

"I somehow feel there's more for us to talk about. I'm sorry we got off on such a bad footing today."

"It's my fault for being late," she hung her head.

"And it's my fault for being such a grouch."

"We'll make up for it," Marie said with sudden, brilliant resilience.

Nearby Fortnum & Mason's we found a U-shaped complex of old embassy buildings with a garden courtyard in the middle: something like the Villiard Houses in New York. I was to wait there, behind the gate. Marie said she would meet me back there in an hour, on the dot; and slipped off.

At the embassy, I stationed myself behind a rather large geranium bush to wait. They must have thought I was a spy. I watched the black limousines and Rolls-Royces drive through the gates, park in front of the central door, and men in black homburgs get into them. They looked unperturbed: it was the end of their workday. As the clock hand above the gates approached five, more and more of them left the building, a processional evacuation of neat men in homburgs and tie clasps and collar pins, with briefcases which they threw in the backseat. I was worried that the embassy gates might be locked, with me still inside. From time to time a chauffeur or a building guard would look at me, but I would turn to gaze intently at the red-flower geraniums, like a botanist. Those geraniums were, in truth, shockingly healthy. They certainly got enough rain!

Where was Marie? Oh, where could she be? I stuck my head out past the gates and looked down the busy mercantile street. It was such a ridiculous position to be in; and yet it amused me, I knew I would remember this always. Finally she came running up, looking surreptitiously behind her and waving me back inside the gates.

"I can't get rid of her!" Marie exclaimed. "She suspects something. She's so sharp, that woman. She wants to know where I'm going now—she wants to come along!"

"Can't you make up a story?" I said, thinking to myself: That shouldn't be too hard for you.

"I can't! My mind's a blank. I just excused myself to go to the bathroom, then I ran out here to see if *you* could think of something," she said frantically. "She must be wondering what's taking me so long in the ladies' room."

"We'll figure out something." I paced back and forth. "Just tell her you're not feeling well and you have to lie down."

"Those were my exact words! But then she insisted on accompanying me back to the hotel in case I fainted."

"Aiee! . . . Well, tell her—you're going to see a friend."

"She knows something's up. She thinks she's going to keep an eye on me, to protect Jack's interests. Only it's Teddy she suspects. What if she found out it was *Eric!*" Marie slapped her head. We started laughing till our sides ached.

"I have to go back," Marie cried.

"What will you tell her?"

"I'll think of an excuse."

"Wait—look at these geraniums."

"They're really red!"

"Wait—" I said. "Just one kiss." With the two of us hiding

behind geranium bushes, and Jack's mother around the corner, at a tea table, it was too good an opportunity to pass up.

When she was gone, I paced around the courtyard in a happy mood, thinking to myself: Now she's in her element. This is really Marie's métier, conspiracy and confusion, this lover-in-the-closet farce.

Marie came back a quarter-hour later, looking behind her. "I finally got rid of her. But if she sees me now! What if she decides to walk right by this building?!"

"I'll check to see if she's coming," I said.

"Don't! Get back! If she sees you're in town, she'll put two and two together!"

"She won't see me. I'll do it so that only my eyes stick out."

"No—let's wait a little while. Do you mind? I want to smoke a cigarette." I put my arm around her waist while she lit one. "I never felt so scared in my life!" she said. "It's so crazy. She wouldn't take no for an answer."

"What did you finally tell her?"

"I said I *was* meeting Teddy, but that I would see her afterwards, in the evening. That seemed to satisfy her, my keeping the night open for her."

"Clever girl. The coast must be clear by now—I'll check."

"Be careful!"

I could see no sign of Jack's mother. I pulled Marie by the hand, and we ran down the street giggling, as fast as our legs could carry us.

As we rounded the corner, Marie said, "Let's sit down somewhere. I'm out of breath."

"Are you honestly not feeling well?"

"I'm a little feverish," she admitted. "Nothing serious. I just get tired easily."

"There's a park right around here, isn't there?" Sure enough: one of those perfectly groomed London parks, where I'd remembered it, at the end of the block. The weather was quite hot and muggy now, as we found a bench alongside a lush green field, just inside the park entrance. A woman in a gray uniform came by and collected a few pence from us.

"That's odd, how they charge you to sit on the bench," I remarked.

"They probably use it for the park's upkeep," said Marie, in a faraway voice. She had lost most of her color; she looked spent. I asked her if she were going to have an asthma attack. She denied it; she said she could tell. But there was a remoteness about her; all at once, as sudden as the muggy change in the weather, she had become distant. Or perhaps it was only a return to that self-consciousness of before, since we were once again coming to the moment of decision. I found it hard to get a conversation started. I began looking at the other citizens in the park.

A lame middle-aged woman in a tweed suit struggled past us, throwing one stiff leg out from the waist like the leg of a rusted pair of scissors. I watched her until she was some distance away.

"I once went out with a lame woman," I said, just to say something.

"What was she like?" Marie asked with frail curiosity.

"It's a long story. She was blonde—rather pretty, actually. I picked her up in a bookstore. She was looking at some books on the poetry rack, and I recommended a poet she hadn't heard about. We got to talking; I invited her out for a beer. She started walking toward the cash register, and that was the first time I noticed she was lame. One of her legs was much bigger, more blockish and muscular than the other. The other leg was shriveled —" I could see a look of hurt come over Marie's face. This story was not going to put me in her good graces; and yet, I had the defiant urge to tell it, no matter in what light it placed me. "The other was like a stick. She had to drag it along after the good leg. We went for a drink, and she never said a word about her lameness. She talked about relationships, lovers, that sort of thing. I walked her home, careful to slow down my pace. She gave me quite a passionate kiss good night. So I called her up and made a date for the next Friday.

"I decided to take her to *Elvira Madigan,* a movie I knew I would despise, but which would be very mushy and good for getting her in the mood. And also, I figured she would like the movie." The same wince came over Marie's face: I went on. "It worked. *Elvira Madigan* was so sloshy that we made out the whole time in the theatre without missing much. We went to her house afterwards. It was in the middle of summer; she took me onto her tarred roof. She told me that she was going to Europe that Sunday, for a year. Now I remember something very odd: she said she was going to Luxembourg—not only because her charter plane was landing there, but because she thought she might want to live in Luxembourg for a while. She was the only person I ever met who had that ambition.

"In any case, she was going away immediately afterwards. Her bedroom was right next to the roof. We climbed through the window and undressed in the dark. She had a very violent way of making love, I remember, like thrashing around and crying out. She had a whole routine for reaching her orgasm, and I felt almost incidental to it. There seemed to be a disparity between cause and effect. Afterwards, when we were just lying there, I started stroking her legs, first the muscle-blocked one, then the stick one. It gave me a shiver. But I liked being able to touch it.

"I only saw her one more time after that. It must have been a year later. I was with another woman walking up Broadway. She came toward us, hugging the walls and storefronts like a sleepwalker. She passed. We didn't say a word to each other. Her limp seemed to have gotten worse."

"I don't like your story," said Marie finally, shaking herself with a tremble.

"I didn't think you did."

"Then why did you tell it?" she demanded.

"You asked me what she was like. Why should it upset you?"

"It just does. It upsets me because it exposes the way you feel about women."

"Which is?"

"Contemptuous. Hostile."

"Possibly. Actually I liked her, more than I've conveyed. She certainly wasn't that intelligent, and she had lousy taste in movies, but there was something moving about her." Suddenly I stopped: another picture had entered my mind. "I know why you're upset. You think—that because I'm talking about this lame girl I'm talking about you."

"That has nothing to do with it—" said Marie, but I interrupted impatiently:

"You think if I notice something physically damaged about one woman, I'll be judging you soon in the same terms."

"What do *you* know? What gives *you* the right to speak of other people as damaged?" She stood up, suddenly furious, and stamped the grass like Rumpelstiltskin. I had never seen her so enraged—which convinced me that I was onto something.

"Look, you told me about my blind spot for social class; I'm telling you about your defensiveness over illness. I'll tell you what just popped into my mind. I suddenly remembered the time we were in the shower, before we made love. It was the first time I noticed that little indentation in your chest. . . ."

"So that was what you were thinking of then!" said Marie, furiously.

"That wasn't all I was thinking of . . ."

"So *that* was what was going through your mind. If only I had known I would never have made those sacrifices for you."

"What sacrifices? You didn't make any sacrifices for me! You just went with Jack."

"You don't know anything. I can't believe it. I can't believe"—she leaped away from the bench—"that you could be thinking of *that*—that scar, and that you could say such cruel things to me. I can't believe what a sadist you are! First telling me that story, and then saying what you just did—"

"Well what's so *terrible* about what I just said? All I admitted was that I had carried away with me an image, a memory of something the matter with your chest. That doesn't make me like you less. I'm glad I told you finally!"

"I can't believe how men think they have the right to say anything! It's like Jack telling me that my ass is flat. What gives men the right to say these things?" She was foaming at the mouth. "Why do you make such a fuss if a woman's body isn't perfect? You're not such a perfect physical specimen yourself, you know. I could say something about the way *you* looked naked or how little *you* were!"

I laughed involuntarily at the dig. We had gone too far again. "This is getting unworthy of both of us," I said.

"It certainly is unworthy . . ." She passed a tear onto her new yellow suit. The next moment she was weeping, holding her wet-flushed face in her hands.

"Marie—I'm sorry. I . . . I tried to make a point but it came out all wrong. I didn't mean that you were ugly because of that hollow in your chest. All I was trying to say was that you're too self-conscious about being sick and you shouldn't be. You're always trying to pretend that you can do everything and then your body breaks down. It's all right that you get ill; I understand that. That's all I meant. I didn't mean to hurt you, but I made the point crudely. I was clumsy! Forgive me."

"I know," said Marie, sniffling, "you were saying whatever came into your head, like you always do. Just being honest."

"Forgive me. I was stupid."

"I forgive you."

I stroked her perfumed hair. I no longer felt any anger toward her; it had all been purged, converted into a guilty tenderness.

"Let's go," she said. "I'm getting chilly."

"All right." I helped her up, and walked her slowly to the street, lending my arm for support.

"I'm sorry," said Marie. "I got hysterical, didn't I?" she asked in a wondering voice.

I put us in a cab, one of those high London kinds, like a room, and sat down beside her. Marie gave the driver the address of the family's house where she was staying.

"Look," I said wearily, holding her hand in mine, gazing into her eyes, "let's forget about our being lovers for the moment. I think it's making us crazy. I don't want to coax you into bed. One day we'll be in the right situation at the right place and there will

be no ghosts around and it will be something we both want and—
we'll just do it. But now let's leave it alone for awhile."

"All right, but—" Marie searched for the proper words. "You
won't blame the whole thing on me and just be angry at me?"

"I won't blame you. I may blame myself, but that's another
story."

"Don't blame yourself." Marie looked sorrowfully and sympathetically at me. Then she kissed me—the sweetest and only real
kiss of the day. She did it so impulsively that I knew it came from
her.

"Okay, I won't even blame myself," I smiled.

"And you'll still see me?"

"Of course I'll still see you."

"And are we still on for Sunday in Hyde Park?" she asked, with
wide eyes not even daring to hope.

"It's a date. Twelve noon."

"This time I'll be there at the stroke of the clock. Promise.
Great!" She hugged me as the cab stopped, then turned zippily to
leave. "This is my address. I have to get out. Bye, Eric. See you
Sunday."

II

I was at the boathouse dressed in my rowing best. But she was not there at the stroke of the clock. She was not there at the stroke of the half-hour either. I decided to wait for another hour, trying to pass the time by poring through the only magazine at hand, *Country Life*. It had a thoroughbred horse on the cover, and articles about racing pedigrees and gardening and society events; pictures of country cottages; ghost stories, recipes, crossword puzzles and medical advice. I think I read every word.

The earth is divided between the punctual and the unpunctual. Some of the most sympathetic and attractive and *human* people are in the second camp, but we of the first camp will never fathom or forgive them.

At one-thirty, bored and, I must say, not surprised, I told myself she had stood me up. I found myself a pay booth and dialed Marie's number. The woman at the house gave me another number to try.

A familiar voice picked up. "Yes?"

"Is this Teddy?"

"Right. Is that you, Eisner?"

"Yes it's me. Is Marie there? Can you put her on?"

Marie came to the phone. "Oh, Eric. It's so awful! Have you heard about it?"

"Heard what?"

"George Jackson's been shot! He was killed trying to escape. At least that's what the guards say. They probably just shot him to death and planted the evidence. I couldn't believe my ears the first time I heard it on the radio—"

"I'm sorry to hear it, but what's that got to do with you standing me up at Hyde Park when you said you'd be here at noon? I've been waiting an hour and a half out here!"

"I wasn't feeling well. Give me a chance to explain! I had a real asthma attack last night, and another one this morning. Teddy's been taking care of me."

"That's terrific. You can thank Teddy for me."

"It isn't what you think."

"I don't think anything. I just don't like being stood up."

"Well how could I have gotten in touch with you? I was planning to come this morning, but we got up late—because I stayed up all night. I couldn't *breathe* and Teddy was showing me his family album pictures to calm me down. They were the most fantastic funny pictures! And then we woke up late and by that time it was too late to catch you at your house, and I didn't know how to reach you at Hyde Park. Be reasonable! And still I was planning to go out because I knew how angry you'd be if I got there late. But Teddy wouldn't let me leave the house because I was too sick. And then this tragedy with George Jackson. The radio's full of it. It's so upsetting. Did you read his book, *Letters from Prison?*"

"Yes," I lied.

"Isn't it the most beautiful, heartbreaking, well-written book? and to think that he's dead right now! I don't know if I want to go back to the United States. It's such a brutal, fascist country! There's a demonstration at four o'clock in front of the American Embassy and if I'm feeling better I'll go to that. People have been phoning here constantly from the American community calling Teddy for information, and they say there's going to be a big crowd of people at that. It's at four o'clock. Try to make it if you can," she said, as she might have to any of these anonymous callers.

"Sure," I said. "Good-bye."

It was too unbelievable. I couldn't get worked up about George Jackson being shot: I mean, I would have preferred that he hadn't been; but at the moment he seemed like a red herring being used by Marie for sleeping over at Teddy's. Historically, I will always feel a grudge against him for having been shot and killed on that particular day.

I went out looking for a copy of George Jackson's book. Unable to find one, I sat in a tearoom reading the London *Sunday Observer*. Then I went to the demonstration in front of the American Embassy, just as I was told. About twenty people, most of them white, had gathered there; and we shook our fists at the cold gray eagle atop the building, which had never looked more imperial and indifferent, or ominously powerful. The American Embassy was on a deserted bureaucratic street, and that added to the sense of unreality of the demonstration, as slogans were shouted by three Spartacist rally leaders and picked up by us followers and hurled and chanted at the pigeons, the unhearing stone walls and a marine who patrolled back and forth. It was Sunday, no one seemed to be in the building anyway. I was beginning to feel a little sorry and melancholy about George Jackson.

It would be almost a redundancy to note that Marie did not show up at the demonstration, nor did Teddy, nor any other of their friends, the concerned Americans and political Englishmen she had predicted would come. Not that I blamed them: the rally was a futile experience from beginning to end, and, who knows, they may have sensed that in advance, old hands that they were.

It did me good, however, to yell at Fate. After the demonstration was over, I went into a phone booth and called Marie again. I inserted my coins: they dropped with a musical clang.

"Yes?" she said expectantly, brightly. "Who is this?"

"This is Eric. I just want to tell you you're so full of baloney—"

"Oh I don't want to hear it!" She slammed down the phone.

I inserted my coins again. This time Teddy picked up the receiver. "Miss Curtin doesn't want to talk to you," he said in his adenoidal Canadian-English accent.

"Since when are you screening her calls?"

"I'm only transmitting a message from Miss Curtin. She doesn't care to talk to you. And I think you're making an ass of yourself, if you want my opinion."

"That's the last opinion I would ask for. Don't give me your garbage. Tell her to pick up the phone!"

"She does not want to—"

"Tell her if she doesn't pick up the phone, I'm going to come over there right now. And she knows I would do it too!"

Teddy reluctantly set down the receiver. A minute later, Miss Marie came to the phone, saying snappishly:

"Yes? What do you want?"

"I want to know what makes you so huffy when you're the one who stood me up and is in the wrong."

"I was born huffy. Anything else?"

"Yes." I cleared my throat. "You're a self-indulgent little bitch, a cheater and a snob. You've been spoiled rotten and it's affected your character."

"Thank you. Anything else?"

"Yeah . . . wanna go bowling?" I laughed grimly.

"No I don't want to go bowling or anything else! Good *night!*"

III

That was that. I stayed on in England another week, among other things trying to figure out what Marie's game had been all along. I came to the conclusion that Marie had at first really intended to have a fling with me (she had led me on enough), but at the same time she was going out with Teddy; and when that comfortable old arrangement beckoned, she switched in midair and decided to go with him. He was safer. Also, once she got sick, she might have felt he would take better care of her than I could. I wondered why she thought I was such a poor nurse. (Not that I necessarily disagreed with her.)

The night before I left for New York, there was a party at Hugh and Janet's. I stayed in my room most of the time, reading—it was *Ravages* by Violette Leduc, a modern novel about unrequited love. What bitter pleasure it is to be buried in a book, while all over the house grow sounds of a party getting bigger. Hugh came into my room after a while to get me, thinking he was being kind. "Come on, Professor, this isn't New York, you know. You can't be reading a bloody book in the corner. There's a party out there, we need you." I went out to mix with the others. And just then Marie arrived, with Anna and Chris Hodgkinson. Marie gave me one of those comical looks of surprise, and I went up to her and tentatively, then less tentatively (seeing she held no grudge at all), embraced her. Oh, but I was glad to see her! It was my last night in London, and I needed to tie up the loose ends of feelings. She had done a brave thing to come to the party, and without Teddy, exposing herself to my possible scorn.

I asked in her ear: "You knew I'd be here?"

"Of course. You live here."

After talking with Anna and Chris for several minutes, trading farewells, and allowing Marie to circulate, I came alongside her and suggested in a whisper that we go into the garden where we could be alone for one last chat. Marie agreed immediately. "Excuse me," she said with an enchanting smile to the man she was talking to. I took her by the hand; she looked about my damp room with wonder, and I could see that for her it was already metamorphosing into an adventure. I led her through my basement room up the steps to the back garden.

It was a large common garden, shared by all the houses whose back entrances faced the courtyard; the commons had been divided informally into separate allotments of vegetable plots, with gateposts that seemed more to decorate than keep out, and there were dips in the ground that made it even more pleasant: something quite civilized, unpretentiously communal and neighborly, the best that I would take away with me of English life. We made for the swings, and sat together on a long, flat greenwood seat with rope suspensions tied to the trees.

"It's wonderful out here," Marie said, looking around.

"There should be backyards like this in New York," I said.

"Oh, it's really special." She sighed, and took out a cigarette. I reached for one too. "You don't smoke," she remonstrated.

"Just tonight."

Marie shook her head, amused. She lit her cigarette, and I took the end of hers to light my own. We rocked in the swing in silence.

"You seem so quiet tonight," she said.

"I'm all out of words."

"Good, I feel like talking," Marie exhaled. "You mind?"

"You talk," I urged her.

She looked at me closely. "Are you sad?"

"No. I'm fine." I said it calmly, evenly, and meant it.

"I love that plaid shirt. You have such nice shirts."

"Thanks."

"This green with the black-watch plaid is my favorite. So subtle." She looked up hazily. "Not too many stars. I guess it's overcast tonight. A few stars. . . . The moon. I heard from Jack." She looked sideways at me, quizzically: should I go on, do you want to hear this? I nodded assent. "He sent me a card. It had a very touching note. He wants to get back together again. He said it's been a bad year for him, except for some brilliant moments with me, and that he considers the whole last year a waste. He said he only feels real with me. He said that I bring him back to himself, but everything else makes him feel counterfeit. He used that word —'counterfeit,' it's a funny word. That was going a long way for Jack to admit the part about only feeling real with me. Usually he won't even say he loves me. Although in the last six months his statements have been picking up. He's beginning to accept his dependence on me. Now I'm the one who wants breathing space. I don't know whether to go back to Jack or not. I can't make up my mind. He feels in love with me now, because I'm gone. This is what I think," she said confidently. "Want to hear my theory? Women feel things when they're going through them. Men feel them after. That's why a man, *after* he breaks up with a woman, often starts to fall in love with her. Everything he should have been feeling while they were going out, he does later, but by this time it's too late; it's all in his head. It's not based on a real situation between two people any more. Jack loves to live in his head. He's a totally childlike person. That's why he has such a hard time managing simple everyday things in the real world, like finding an apartment. We're both like that. We were supposed to have a dinner party, and we couldn't decide for five weeks what wineglasses to get! I mean, I'm making it sound sillier than it is—but we do carry our ambivalence into the most ordinary operations. You're not like that," she stopped, and looked me over with curiosity. "You're so entirely different. And when you came along . . . You're such a pragmatist, your approach is, 'All right, if this is the problem, let's see, there must be one-two-three ways to solve it.' You behaved in a way that I'd almost forgotten about. You use your energies to make things happen. You're an activist. I think you're sane. You represent what I desperately need. Some security and balance. But I don't think we're at all alike or really suited to each other. It would never work out. I'm much more like Jack: he and I both fantasize, we make up fictional worlds and try to live in them as long as we can get away with it. We're spoiled, as you say, and we don't do things step by step. Cigarette?"

"Thank you."

"The way you hold it in your hand, it looks so strange. Were you never a smoker?"

"Never."

"Why are you smoking now?"

"I want to feel . . . what you're feeling," I said. "In your mouth, in your lungs."

"I understand."

We looked at the night sky, swinging back and forth, and thinking.

"Why did you and Jack break up?" I asked.

"Oh—that's such a sad story. He humiliated me. We went to a party with friends of his? Orin Shauffen, he's a music critic—do you know him?"

"No. I mean, I know *of* him."

"He writes a culture column for *Newsweek*. And he and his girl friend or old lady or whatever you want to call her had Jack and me over for dinner. Her name is Alice and she's a real scheming bitch. I don't often use that language about other women but this Alice really—she was playing up to Jack all night. And we got into a political discussion, and I took one side and Orin Shauffen and Alice Whatever-her-name-is took the other. She said some really insulting things to me. It's not important what it was about any more, but they were both accusing me of being naïve. And Jack didn't defend me. In fact, he agreed with them, and he took their side against me and told me I didn't know what I was talking about. And I knew what I was talking about—he was the one who didn't know what he was talking about! But from the way he was acting, I suddenly realized that he didn't take seriously what I thought. He never respected my opinions. And he'd been holding back all his criticisms of me to wait for a time when he could shame me in public. And all this buddy-buddy professional stuff between him and Orin, oh it was nauseating, all the flattery and flirtations, the whole subtext of two men fawning on each other which was the real romantic thing that was operating, suddenly I couldn't stand it, and I started talking about what was *really* going on at that table. And Jack got very mad, and he accused me of being hysterical and always out of control. That's a man's favorite word when a woman starts saying how she feels. Hysteria. I know a lot about hysteria. My mother is an hysteric. And now I know what drives women to hysteria. It's men! My father is so rational all the time, and the only way my mother can get through to him is to become frantic. He won't confront emotional things, like when she's starting to feel insecure, little things but they're important to her, and it makes her hysterical that he won't see them as important. He keeps pooh-poohing them, and of course she goes *wild*. I didn't used to sympathize with her but now I'm coming around. Men are so controlled that they can't feel while they're going through something, they can only feel afterwards. And then what they feel is regret. Women feel things as they come up, like being terrified of a certain shade of light in a room, but we can't convince the man that it's there. Of course we get hysterical. But underneath the hysteria there's an intelligence working something out.

"I'm not a big women's libber," she said, gesturing towards the trees, "but I do believe in some of what they say. I marched in last years' Sisterhood Parade on Fifth Avenue. It was great! I felt I was really part of something for once. And to see all those women with soft arms and boobs wobbling under their shirts—no bras, of course!—with those soft arms raised in closed-fisted salutes. There was something so jolly and touching about that parade, it moved me to tears. I grew up being taught never to trust other women. But if you could have seen all that militancy in those soft bodies! Men are so hard. I want to walk down the street some day and touch a man's arm and have it be soft, and myself feel strong and protective. That would be progress! . . . I went to a reception for Anaïs Nin, with Jack. And we had a long talk—she asked me all about myself. I was brilliant, I outdid myself; it was really one of my greatest performances. And at the end of it she said, I can't imitate it, but something like, 'It's this young woman who gives me faith in the future of our sex.' She took Jack aside and told him, 'You have no idea what a rare diamond you have in her, young man.' I was so thrilled: Just think that I was the chosen example of the future of women. And somehow I believe it. I *am* very strong. I'll bet I could be a great women's leader. Like Joan of Arc! Don't you think?"

I nodded agreement, not wishing to contradict her or impede her thoughts. Marie was speaking a little as if in a trance. Her eyes were shiny. I wondered if her medicine were having this effect, of making her words tumble out in a rush without mediation, like a prophetess receiving oracles. Her voice would trail off; her sweet lower lip had a fever scab. I put my hand on hers. She continued the soliloquy, which was coming out of her in an unstoppable flow, a mixture of humiliations unforgotten and compliments received: triumphant first impressions she had made on one or another notable, which were undercut the next moment by rebuffs and treacheries suffered from those closer to home. I heard a bird's screech nearby, in the leaves, then was called back by Marie's urgent drowsy voice.

"Did I ever tell you *why* I dropped out of school?" she said. "I was in an advanced seminar on Melville; only the best students could get into it. And I was the star of the seminar. The professor gave me all A's on my papers and said I should try to get them published? And he would listen with much more attention to when I spoke than to the others. He was a nice guy and a very good teacher, but I didn't get along with some of the people in that class. They were talking one day about Melville's long silence, when he didn't write anything for twenty years? And everyone was blaming Mrs. Melville. All those snotty advanced-seminar students thought she wasn't good enough for him, because she was uneducated. They said she had held him down?—Oh, it gets me so mad! But I thought she was what he had wanted all along. She was his Moby Dick. She was the best thing that ever happened to him. Mrs. Melville was a treasure! You would have liked her a lot! She said the most wonderful things; he put them in his letters. Oh, they didn't have intellectual discussions. They were a pretty quiet couple! But Herman wrote love sonnets to her every year on her birthday. Doesn't that sound like they really liked each other?"

"It does," I said, wondering whether she was talking about Melville or Jack.

"And what's so bad about not writing for twenty years? Maybe he'd said what he wanted to. Maybe he was waiting for new experiences. Why blame it on her? Those young people were so smug. Finally I just walked out one day, in the middle of class, I got so *angry* at them, and I could never bring myself to go back again."

"You could probably write an extra paper and get your degree that way," I said pragmatically.

"I know. But it's not important any more. It's not what I want."

We rocked in silence; the swing creaked. I looked over at her, at Marie's face, so vivid I could stare at it forever. The light from beyond the trees, flickering over her brow darkly, picked out just those spots that would make her prettiest; and yet there was something untouchable about her perfect cheekbones, like a yellowed wax mask. As I was listening I had been rubbing the rope in my hands, between my fingers, and now, when I realized what I was doing, it seemed to be a secret way of touching her, and also anchoring myself. Her hair had come undone; it was no longer in a summer barrette, but loose around her shoulders. Inside my chest I felt some achy cloudiness. I took my glasses off so that that last pane of defense would be gone between us. We were silent a long time; it was just as if we were still talking. This time the talking went on inside.

"What *do* you want, Marie?" I asked, finally.

"I know what I want, but it's not considered the thing to want it."

"Why should that stop you from telling me?" I smiled, prodding her.

"I want a real home, babies, and a man's respect. Most of all in the whole world—I want a *baby?* But I don't like talking about it aloud because I'm superstitious. Also I may not be able to have one, because of my health? But it's really what I want more than anything else in life." She smoked her cigarette for a while, thinking, then spoke again. "Second to that, if I couldn't have a baby— and even if I could have my own baby—what I want is to help others. I want to be of some use in this world. I don't care any more about going to parties and getting dressed up. It's so empty." She looked around her, indicating the party inside. "You know? I want to be of service of some kind. I think it would be really beautiful to be like Florence Nightingale?" she said with a rapidly interrogative inflection, as though afraid she would be attacked. "I would like to go and work in the International Red Cross in disaster areas. Even though I'm not so strong, I would find the energy to drive myself day and night. I *know* I would. I know I can drive myself more than most people. You don't believe I could, do you —make big sacrifices for other people?"

"No, I do, I do completely," I answered. "In fact, the way I see you is as—a heroine at the wrong time, someone who's been born into the wrong epoch, and who would rise to great occasions if that was what was demanded of you. The problem is, it's not demanded of you; nothing is, except daily life."

"And that could be the most heroic."

"Well, sure, but . . . maybe if there was a civil war or an epidemic in America you would find your role. This way, you fritter away your energies in arenas that aren't worthy of you, in love affairs and so on."

"That's what *I* think!" Marie laughed. "I've always suspected I was going to be a hero later on in my life, and that all this stuff was just preliminary preparations, to toughen me up."

"Still, it's possible to seek out jobs now in which you could serve people, without there having to be a war on."

"I know," she said. "I've been thinking about that." She sighed, Marie continued to spell out her plans. Her ambitions hopped from one field to another. . . . I had become like a mirror sitting next to her, a reflector of her thoughts, which seemed to be unraveling aloud without the usual effort of hers to be winning or well liked. It was not so much that she had forgotten I was there, as that she trusted me, for perhaps the first time. I had become objective by relinquishing my claims on her. As a result I could see her now, with a clear view that was both detached and fond: that is I could still hear the alibis behind her speech, at the same time that I could see what was so moving in her. She was a nice, brave girl; a gallant spirit on the right path. As I sat next to her on the swing, I felt as though I were breathing in her way of seeing things. It was a privilege—and all because I had given up my hope of having her. For the first time I had honestly released her. She was flying like a freed canary around my head. No wonder she was talking so openly! She knew my intentions were pure. I wanted only to pay attention to her. And if she should suddenly stop, I would accept that too. I had discovered one of the great, powerful tricks in life: that releasing hold of a desire was a prelude to entering the larger moment. Only now did I realize what an idiot I had been to make such a fuss about sleeping with Marie. What she was giving me was much more important. And I had no doubt that she herself knew this was a present to me, even if it was only the mixed-up drift of her private mind. I could not get over how exquisite and acute it was to live life this way, without any expectations to be satisfied! I was conscious of the creaking ropes, of the people in the neighboring yard chatting through the evening; of Marie's lullaby voice; of sounds from the drinking party; of the harsh taste of the world in my mouth from cigarettes I'd been smoking, one after another, to keep up with Marie; of the swing's gentle motion, the warm night air.

I feel foolish trying to explain why this particular event, listening to Marie on the swing, should seem so unusual. All epiphanies are the same, there is no point in describing them; they always have those predictable lifts of lyricism, and then the universe somehow clinks together.

"Where's Teddy, by the way?" I asked eventually.

"Teddy? He had something else to do first—another party I guess. He said he'd be here later on."

"Are you seeing him regularly now?" I asked.

"No! Teddy's not serious."

I did not know whether she meant, Teddy isn't a serious person, or that Marie did not take him seriously. Either way it didn't matter; her reply reassured me.

"Were you jealous?" she asked joyously.

"Of course I was jealous. I'm always jealous where you're concerned."

"You shouldn't be. Teddy doesn't mean as much to me as you do. You're special; I hope you know that."

"Okay," I grinned bashfully.

"You are, you know. And this place is special—*really* special. Thank you for showing it to me."

"I'm glad we had a chance to talk."

"We? You didn't say a word! But I *am* glad, you don't know how glad I am for this talk, Eric." One of us stood up. "Shall we go inside? They're probably gossiping their heads off about us disappearing so long."

"Let them."

"I know. But I feel kind of bad about leaving Anna and Chris," explained Marie gingerly.

"Fine. I'm ready to go inside now," I said.

IV

That last, understanding talk in the rear garden in London would have made such a nice formal closure to our relationship.

If only we had been satisfied to leave it there: she thought so well of me, and I of her. But life is sloppier than art, it runs through all the red lights of good taste, spoiling the pure endings: like a movie you're watching and saying to yourself, If only he had ended it—*here* . . . if only he had ended it five minutes ago, that would have been a clean ending. . . . Idiot, why is he going on and botching it?

I worked another year at the agency before it started to fold. Around that time, fortunately, a chance was offered me to head my own program. I took it, and have been happier ever since. I had finally found a work situation I could believe in completely. With what time I had left from organizing the new program, I began to write a series of articles describing my experiences with high school dropouts, which grew into my first book, *Inner City Youth*.

On weekends I started going on dates, forcing myself to take out women I met, as a recognition that the business with Marie was over. They were the kind of women one meets in social service agencies, upfront and responsible and a little depressed, tired, usually divorced, ambitious, pursuing professional degrees and yet wanting to be protected; moral and sympathetic and reasonably attractive, and they satisfied certain physical and psychological needs at the time. Looking back, I see how kind they were to me; but nevertheless I felt muffled in their presence, and the moment I got away from them I became as happy as a schoolboy let out of class early.

It wasn't their fault, but they weren't as much fun to talk to as Marie, and they didn't have her stylishness, her talent for shining.

In May, just for old friendship's sake, Marie and I got together for lunch. We met at the Kleine Konditorei, a restaurant on East Eighty-sixth Street I suggested because it was a hangout for old ladies. The toasted sandwiches were cut into easily manageable sixths, and we had no trouble imagining ourselves meeting in our dotage to reminisce.

"What's new? I asked.

"I'm moving right up the street!" Marie announced.

"So we'll be neighbors."

The conversation at lunch went wonderfully, as it always did when we had not met for a long while. Afterwards, I escorted Marie toward her new apartment. Maybe we could learn how to be friends this time.

"I'm so happy today. I mean not just contented, but *happy*." She took my arm. We passed a fruit stand on Lexington Avenue, and I realized that something more was needed to send me up to her orbit. A peach. "Hold it," I said. I bought us two peaches.

"That's the finishing touch," she said, biting into the fruit. The juice ran down our chins and we laughed. Marie was saying: "I'm so excited about my new apartment. My mother's waiting for me there now. She wanted to help me move, and I told her it was all right because I didn't know how long I'd be with you?"

"It's perfectly all right. Do you want me to leave?"

"No, come on up. My mother's—boy, wait and see! It'll be a meeting of the giants."

"I hope I say all the right things."

"You will. I just hope *she's* in a good mood."

We turned in on East Eighty-second Street and Park Avenue. Marie's mother was waiting in the luxury apartment house lobby. She did not appear to be in a particularly good mood. She was a small woman in an orange suburban outfit, with beady, mistrustful eyes, and a perma-spray honeycomb.

"Eric—Mother, Mother, meet Eric."

"I don't like this doorway. It's too easy to get in."

"They have bells! You have to announce yourself," explained Marie.

"I've been standing down here watching people go in and out. It's a cinch to get in. The security's lousy," Mrs. Curtin stated. Marie winked at me, like: Isn't my mother a great character? "Shall we go up, Mom?"

"Let's not go in yet. We have to buy honey, salt and bread at the supermarket. You always do that with a new house."

"Is that a superstition?" I asked.

"Not superstition. Custom," her mother said. "Yes, it's a custom. Don't laugh at me, young man. I know more about these things than you do."

We started out for the supermarket. "I'm sorry I'm late. Did you have fun at the department store?" Marie asked brightly.

"No I had a miserable time. I've been running a thousand errands. It's been a very upsetting day. Oh, your father bought the most beautiful suit. Gray velvet, with legs slightly flared."

"I can't wait to see it!"

"Are you sure this building's safe?" said her mother.

"It's safe."

"What's the super like?" Mrs. Curtin asked suspiciously.

"Julio? He's *really* nice."

Her mother seemed to doubt this.

"No, really. He's helped us so much already. He's the one who got us in here."

"Not Gristedes. They charge three cents extra on every item. Try the A&P next door." Mrs. Curtin guided us into the right entrance.

"Oh boy, isn't this great?" Marie winked at me. "We can have a picnic in my new apartment." She started to put a loaf of bread in her shopping cart.

"You don't want package bread, the flour ants will get in it. What you need is bread in a can."

"Oh, bread in a can, Mother!" Marie laughed lightly, as if it were the most outrageously witty suggestion she had ever heard.

"Or tightly sealed crackers. Over there. Let's see, Swedish crackers. That doesn't look well sealed. The ants will get into that too. Flour ants can be very troublesome."

"Flour ants?" I wondered, in an undertone so that only Marie could hear. "Are they anything like eyelid worms?"

Marie gave me a pinch. "I'll go get the honey, Mother. You get the salt, Eric."

"Any special kind?" I asked Mrs. Curtin.

"Just salt," she said absently, looking past me.

She seemed to detest me on sight. Could this be the lovely Marie's mother?

Marie's apartment on the eighteenth floor was a large and bare two-bedroom suite, modern, not unusual in any respect, so far as I could see, except for the step separating the dinette from the "sunken" living room. It did have quite a view.

"What's the rent here?" I asked Marie.

"It's $550 a month."

"Affluent."

"I'm not affluent at all. I have to have a roommate because I can't afford more than $275. I don't want to apologize—you pay rent too."

"Okay, I'm sorry."

"Want to see the closets?" asked Marie.

"Show me the closets."

"They're what I love the most. Walk-ins," she said with a mischievous little wink.

"Marie, give me a hand for a moment," her mother called in from the kitchen. "I can't do everything myself."

We quickly joined Mrs. Curtin. "I'm sorry," Marie said docilely, awaiting orders. I had never seen her so young and chastened.

"You seem to expect me to make tea *and* lunch and put away the groceries—"

"We don't want lunch," Marie cut in quickly. "We just had lunch."

"It's not necessary, Mrs. Curtin," I agreed.

"Well, at least you can help me put the groceries on the shelves.

I can't reach that high, you know that. What about *you?* We need a good, tall man for this job," she inspected me, with that oddly grudging, matronly admiration for men's physiques. I could just barely see the seeds of Marie's flirtatiousness in her at that moment. I reached up and put the honey jar and canned walnut bread on the second to top shelf. Then, when Mrs. Curtin wasn't looking, I climbed up on the counter, ready to receive new provisions.

"What are you doing up there?" Marie laughed.

"I don't know. Just felt like being near the ceiling."

"You're too much."

"Come down from there!" Mrs. Curtin said, scowling, with considerable less tolerance than her daughter. I was beginning to like this woman.

"What's the matter with him?" she demanded of her daughter.

"He's an eccentric," explained Marie.

"I'll bet," she said, and turned away, this time scrutinizing Marie. "Why are you wearing a black bra with a white blouse?"

"I just put it on this morning in a rush. I just grabbed any old bra because everything was packed."

"Listen, your father wants you to have dinner in town with us and the Sutters. You'll have to go home and change."

"Just because of *this?* I'm not going to go back to my old apartment just for a bra. The Sutters won't mind."

"Yes, they will. Only they're too polite to say anything, and that makes it even worse. What do you think?" she asked me (now that I was on *terra firma,* she was talking to me again).

"Is the problem that a black bra is too risqué, or too old-fashioned?" I hedged.

"Not risqué, that's not the point—I wouldn't care if it were ten times more daring than that. Just that a white blouse doesn't go with a black bra. It looks wrong. Especially with that blouse; it's practically see-through."

"To be honest, I like looking at it," I said.

"You don't always have to be honest," said her mother, turning away as if I had slapped her.

Shortly afterwards, I made my departure, leaving them still fighting about Marie's black brassiere.

Since we were neighbors, I had to come by and see the new place once it was fixed up.

Marie took me on a tour. She had had her childhood bed moved into her bedroom from Long Island. It was an antique gingerbread, four-poster affair, with a fringed silk canopy on top, and a quilt whose motif of green elephants gave off echoes of a children's room.

"I know it's silly, but I feel so comfortable and safe having my old bed back."

I espied the wicker wheelchair in the corner. And a pink chest of drawers, with rows of cosmetic bottles.

On the dresser was also a framed color photograph of Jack and Marie in a rowboat. It had been taken by her father, whom Marie said was almost a professional-caliber photographer; and, indeed, the picture reeked of craft. It showed Marie leaning her head fondly against Jack's shoulder, while the water sparkled with sunspots. Curly-haired Jack, holding the oars, appeared to be frowning somewhat against the sun, staring straight ahead but conscious of her love, as though it were her hot attention and not the solar glare that made him wince and smile a shade, though modesty forbade him to acknowledge her staring straight at him with smitten (not daring to hope for) possessiveness and adoration.

It was a religious picture: an icon of their love. And the fact that the photographer was the girl's father put the final papal stamp on this engagement.

But anyone who wanted to notice (and I was one of these) could see what a saccharine, dead image it was; and what it told about the flaws in the subjects' relationship could fill volumes. Staring at it gave me a private satisfaction, a premonition amounting to a conviction that these two would never marry.

V

Shortly afterward, Jack was off to Paris. Before he left they had a quarrel, neatly timed: they always broke up before one of them was about to take a trip, giving them their "freedom" during the separation period. Jack had not lost any of his Prince Genji quest for amorous adventures; he had his eye on a French film actress. Marie said she had no desire for new lovers, but she was tired of waiting for him to be done with all his stupid indiscretions. This time it was definitely the end.

One Sunday night, I called Marie after ten o'clock and we had a serious talk. Feeling lonely and opened up to her, I asked if I could come over and visit. Sure, she said. I told her that I would want to stay. That was all right, she said too.

At Marie's building, I called up through the intercom; and as soon as the elevator had stopped at her floor, she opened the door to me in a pale blue nightgown. We went to bed and made love. In the morning, her clock-radio woke us; Marie clung to me in her half-slumber, and I remembered my running off the last time, and what troubles had followed from that. This time I called the office and told them I would be an hour or two late. We lay around in bed, made love again, showered and went out to eat breakfast at a quaint luncheonette on Eighty-fifth and Madison with a Louis Sherry ice cream sign in the window. All the seats were covered in pink plastic, and the whole place reminded me of strawberry ice cream. I held Marie's fingers in mine, while we waited for our eggs; and when we finally had to separate I skipped off to work, too bursting to walk to the bus.

We settled into seeing each other regularly. In the evenings I would pick up Marie at her apartment and we would go to a movie or dinner, then back usually to her house, which she didn't like to spend the night away from, and which in any case was rather nicer than mine. We would talk to her new roommate Janie for a half-hour and then go off to bed. Each time we made love it was less shocking. One advantage of becoming steady lovers was that we were comfortable with sex (as I had hoped we would be if we were ever together long enough). I had finally put to rest that old insecurity. If she were going to jilt me again, it would have to be for some other reason than sexual incompatibility.

I had forgotten what a relief it was to relax in bed with someone I was really fond of.

"What I like is the cuddling part," Marie said. "I mean, I like the other part as well, don't get me wrong! But it's so dramatic, like opera! It's exhausting. But I could spend all day cuddling up like this. Whenever I was feeling blue my mother used to say, 'It's cuddling time' and then we would all climb into bed with her. I love nuzzling. I think I must have been a deer in my past life."

"Or an anteater."

"No, not an anteater, they're obnoxious. A doe. Be nice. A nice freckled doe. Bambi."

"Bambi, eh?" I started licking her nipples. "I've always liked Bambi."

"Don't," she said suddenly.

"Why?"

"I don't want you to do it any more. It makes me lonely. I feel they're trying to steal you away from me. They're two sly little misses who want all your attention."

I laughed at this fantasy; Marie could be so whimsical. "You told me you liked it when I touched your tits."

"Usually.—I never can get over men calling them tits. That's such a funny-sounding word. 'Hey, baby, where'd ya get those tits?' Women would never call a man's private parts something like that. Do we call your balls 'pits'?"

"No, but you say worse things about men behind our backs."

"How do *you* know?"

"I eavesdrop. Besides, I have sisters."

"I'll bet they don't tell you everything."

"Probably not." I rubbed my eyes, yawning, ready to get up.

"What does it feel like when I touch you there?" she asked, stroking my nipples tentatively.

"Why are you so interested?" I asked.

"I'm just curious. Can't a girl be curious?"

"A sensation of rainbow colors floating and then my rectum starts fluttering off. Is it the same for you?"

"No, nothing like that!"

Her hair was growing long again. Marie was excitedly looking forward to a show of Nico Reeves's paintings at the Whitney. Her portrait was among them. She couldn't wait to stand next to it at the opening; she would wear the same dress, and have fun watching people do double takes.

Carolee was coming over for lunch. I was getting pulled into the world of Marie's friends, who had begun to take me seriously as Marie's man. I enjoyed having long talks with Carolee, coming to know quiet Beth better, advising roommate Janie on her unhappy love problems, spending idle hours with them representing the male point of view. As much as I knew how dangerous it was to become complacent with Marie, there was something so domestic and tranquil about her attitude this time which encouraged me to feel I really belonged with her.

Of course, I would have doubting moments.

"What's going to happen when Jack comes back?" I asked her later that day.

"I don't know. He should be getting back soon."

"Are you still going to see me?"

"Why shouldn't I?"

"Because it will be difficult," I said.

"Don't worry . . . I won't desert you," said Marie.

"I think you probably will."

"You think that's what women always do, don't you? Where did you get that idea? Why do you think women will always betray you?"

"Because—I've had experiences," I said somberly.

"But if you think they'll betray you, you make it into a self-fulfilling prophecy. Don't you see that?" she asked.

"No. I don't see that," I smiled wanly. "A woman still has the power to act in such a way as to contradict my prejudices."

"But you make it so hard for her."

Another week went by. We had a date for Sunday night. Coincidentally, I had finished the final draft of my book and was feeling like Superman. Nothing could take away from my achievement. I had just put down my pen, when I heard Marie climbing the steps to my apartment. We were meeting for the first time at my place; and she had arrived just at the right moment. You know that feeling of having just completed a solid day's labor, and, in the flush of that tranquility and clear blank brain, wanting someone to be there on the couch to pounce upon? Marie, as I said, had arrived just in time. I opened the door for her.

I could tell something was off from her face; the way her cheeks flushed could not only have been the result of climbing the stairs. Marie had that look of advance sympathy for the heart she was going to break. But I was so cocky from finishing my book, all I wanted to do was take off her clothes. I ignored the signals: that peculiarly tender, thoughtful sadness, that muted, horrible gentleness. I knew it when I took her in my arms, pulled her down on the mattress with me, and instead of letting me touch her she began folding up her body, like a flower closing, and stroking my hair. The sorrowful tentativeness in her fingers somehow implied decision.

I backed off and listened to what she had to say.

What had happened was this: Jack had returned. That first night back, he told her guiltily about his affair with some press secretary in Paris, in detail; she screamed at him, and they ended by throwing dishes at each other. (I could never compete with these outbursts of irrational destruction, which was unfortunately Marie's idea of true passion.) She had started to call the police to have him thrown out of her house. Then Jack had broken down and sobbed in her lap, begging for forgiveness, and she had decided to take him back. A simple tale. Not an element in it to astonish me. The only new part, perhaps, was how I took it. I was so serene and in such a good mood at having come in ahead of my deadline, that I could have borne anything in order not to let that feeling go. I showed her how fat the manuscript was. Marie was grateful for my pride; it gave her an excuse.

"Jack *does* need me more."

"Don't you think I need you too?" I offered.

"Not in the same way. You don't! Be honest now," she said, flattering my autonomy.

"I suppose not," I answered.

We still had the right to a last evening together. I had wanted us to go for a walk, and that still seemed a good idea. I took her down to my favorite spot by the river, across from the cherry-colored sign that blinked *Pearl Wick* Hampers . . . *Bathroom* Hampers. We looked out quietly from the promenade bench. It was a repeat of my calm mood in London on the swings: I would release her, and acquire the power of the universe. Not a bad exchange. Whatever happened, it was structured to work out somehow: either she would change her mind and come back to me, in which case my magnanimity would be rewarded with happiness; or she would fly away, which would be another kind of perfect sadness.

I was getting to be an adept at these scenes of releasing the other from all expectations of behavior. Whereas Marie kept prodding me to reproach her, it seemed to me that she could not do other than what she had done. The very notion of accusing someone of being a cheat or a flirt struck me as subjective fallacy, since it depended on a rigid demand that the woman deliver according to X-Y-Z expectations aroused by A-B-C behaviors. But if one had no expectations, then all behavior became free.

It was an orgy of stoical renunciation, what with the river-flowing symbolism and so on. Of course there were threads of self-indulgence, and of wounded pride displaced into detachment; but on the other hand, I was also being sensible for once and accepting responsibility for my knowledge. I knew all along that Marie would return to Jack. If I had been foolish enough to get involved with her again, it was only because I wanted to grab off a little loving while I could. And in that I had succeeded.

Again I was showing her a place that meant something special to me, with the intention that, by some subterranean code of appreciation, this vista would explain what I felt. Tonight, however, Marie was less susceptible to environment; not as taken with the *mise-en-scène* as I was.

"I'm sorry most of all," she said, "because you'll feel I've disappointed you again."

"I don't feel you disappointed me," I said, looking at the peaceful water.

"I know you do. And I know how you think women are always disappointing and unfaithful. I hate to be giving you support for that. It's such a trap, and I fell into it."

"Not at all."

"I know what you think. You think I've let you down again."

"But you have to disappoint one man or the other, when you go out with two men at once," I said, thinking: *How reasonable my voice sounds!*

"I don't know. Then why should it always be you? Why can't it be Jack this time?" she demanded.

"Because you love Jack more," I said sensibly.

"I don't know if I *do* love Jack more than I love you. Sometimes I think that I hate him."

"Then why go back to him?" I asked. I answered my own question: "Because you have to play it out. . . ."

"Why are you being so saintly about this?" she asked suspiciously.

"Because, it's what I expected. You're tied to Jack in a real way, and you have to play out that tie to the bitter end." We were silent for a while.

"I'm not the only cheat," Marie said, from out of nowhere, as if answering someone else's reproach. "Jack always cheats by holding a chunk of himself off from me. Only he calls it memory, the past. You call it work. Some women can't do that as easily. We think about love, we brood about our husbands or our lovers, our families too much. That's just the way we're built: if it doesn't work out, we don't feel we're real, we have to start looking elsewhere. Why is that promiscuity? You're ready to cheat on me all the time, and not take me seriously; only instead of going off to another lover you go off to your work. Work is your mistress."

"I guess so."

"I figure I'm not being any more immoral by having two lovers at once when that's what's important to me—love is—than a man for whom work or the past is important, like you or Jack. Why do you both try to make it seem like one is dirtier than the other? That what I do is dirtier?"

"I didn't say you were dirty. But sex *is* different from work," I reasoned. "It hurts someone more to find out his lover is having intimacies in bed with someone else, than to find out he or she is reading a book or working late."

"No it doesn't, it hurts just as much. You don't know how much it hurts to know that someone you love doesn't take you seriously because you're not a part of his work. It's like banging against metal."

"All right. I can see that," I said slowly. "It's strange though, the way you talk about life as a mechanical equation: X-amount of work withdrawal equals Y-amount of taking other lovers."

"When it's *your* needs it doesn't seem mechanical. It seems very important then. When it's someone else's needs it seems mechanical," Marie scoffed. "I know. Men don't like equations in emotional life because that implies equality. Justice. The opposite of equality is pure double standard, which is what I was talking about. If you use work for a mistress, or if Jack sleeps with someone else, it's all right, because he's a man; but if I do I'm bad."

"I don't think you're bad, Marie," I said, looking candidly at her. "I wasn't even suggesting that you are."

"I think I am," she bit her fingernails.

I would not permit myself to feed anything into her machinery of accusation and self-reproach, though it was clearly what she wanted. Such are the minor satisfactions, perhaps even the sadisms, of someone in my position.

I walked Marie back to her house. For a minute downstairs, by the awninged door, she was debating whether to invite me to come up. It would mess up her life with Jack if she did, but on the other hand, she felt hypocritical about saying good-bye to me outside the street door, when we had been lovers so recently.

"If it was very important for you sleep with me tonight, I would do that?" she offered wistfully.

"It's not that important," I said, giving her a gallant kiss good night. She went inside. Walking away back to my house, I felt intact, with the dignified manly power that can come from having exercised self-restraint.

VI

The pleasures of sublimation may be more lasting and often more exquisite than gratification of one's instincts, but unfortunately they cannot be as intense.

I had learned to use relinquishment as a drug, to give quick color to the universe. But in Monday's dirty light, it now seemed to me that I had merely played a mental trick on myself: my spiritual pride had gotten the better of me, while Marie had slipped away again.

"Ah, here's our young Lochinvar!" Bruno greeted me a few nights later.

"Don't call me that. I'm not in the mood."

"Why, what happened?"

"It's over," I groaned.

"So soon? I thought you were going great guns this time."

"We were. It's always like that, we never break up because of an argument. Listen, do me a favor. If I ever tell you that I'm going back with Marie, I want you to break a chair over my head."

"That I won't do," Bruno said, smiling impishly.

"I'm serious. If you want to be a good friend, and you hear that I'm dating Marie again, don't temporize, don't cautiously raise objections, don't lure me into psychological conversation. Just tie me down and smash a chair over my head!"

"You're so hardheaded it won't make any difference."

"It might."

"What happened? You don't have to tell me if you don't want to. . . ."

"The usual. Jack came back."

Bruno whistled. "I can't figure out that bitch." He poured himself a brandy and offered me one.

"No thanks."

"You sure? Maybe you need it tonight."

"I'm okay. I'm in pain, I'm fine. It doesn't bother me so much any more. It gets to me less and less."

"Why do you keep going back? There must be something real there."

"There is something real," I said vaguely, biting the flesh around my thumb and thinking. "It's always been my desire to be destroyed by a pretty, heartless woman."

"You have a long way to go before you're destroyed," Bruno said. "You seem in pretty good shape."

"It's my prudence that gets in the way. I have no real talent for collapse," I said regretfully.

I lost track of Marie for a half-year. Then I ran into her by accident in a restaurant. She was very happy; she wanted me to know that. Everything was working out well. How was her love life? I asked. That was the best part: she was playing the field, like a man. She had decided that all her sorrows came from putting her eggs in one basket. Now she just dated.

What made her most enthusiastic was that she was going to write a history of the American space program. She had talked to several editors—Jack knew lots of people in publishing, and the least he could do, as Marie put it ruefully, was to "let me use some of his contacts."

"Why the space program?" I asked, never having heard her express any interest in it before.

"I believe in heroes. Everyone's been putting down the U.S.A. so much and I think it's time to celebrate the heroes."

"But don't you have to know a great deal about science to write a book like that?" I wondered.

"I was good in science. Biology!" her voice jumped. "And you know, my father helped develop some of the radio parts they used in the *Apollo*. I practically grew up in the space program! I would have some great inside leads to start with."

One of these leads, she said, was Senator Donnelly's legal adviser, Page Daniels, who had drawn up some of the original legislation for NASA. (Marie's expanding circle never ceased to amaze me.) She said she had gone up to his office, Daniels', that is, which had a breathtaking view of Manhattan, and a magnificent floor-to-ceiling mirror on one side that reflected the skyline. She was very taken with the decor. She also let me know that this big attorney Daniels, who had a family in Washington, was so smitten with her that he offered to throw over his wife and children and marry Marie.

"Are you going to take him up on it?"

"I couldn't do that," she said moralistically. "Let him leave his wife and children?" But Page Daniels was very supportive and she was sure he would help her talk to some of the big honchos of the space program. It was not only going to be a history of the science effort, but the administration part, Washington politics, economics and so on. It would be a major research job that would probably take her years in gathering data and interviewing alone. "And it would sell, that's the best part."

Apparently she convinced some editor that it would, because she had already gotten a tentative offer for a book contract. She just had to do a few exploratory interviews and transcribe them, to get the contract.

I felt quite good about this encounter. Marie was in fine shape, as fresh as a daisy, pretty as ever, but I had no desire to become part of her harem. There was not even a twinge of the old jelly-legged, knee-buckling sensation in her presence. I was over my love for her; I felt wonderfully cold! As for the space project, it struck me as a ridiculous idea, and it was no surprise when I later learned that nothing ever came of it. In short, I wished her well, knowing that her life would never straighten out.

How did it come about, then, that a few months later we were back at it? Enough is enough, one would think. But in love there may be no such thing as quitting while you are ahead. As long as the possibility exists for more love, you have to push for that little more, and little more, until everything is utterly ruined.

Besides, it was May, time for our annual summer involvement. Once more I threw off the stern coats of winter. I wanted, I told myself, what every man wants: love. Why should I think I was so different as not to need the loving pleasure of a companion? This time, I told myself, I would keep my eyes open. I didn't need oceans of affection, but just enough to tide me over the summer. By now there could be no surprises. What Marie had done the first time she would do again and again; I knew that. But at least our affair would have the reassuring merit of following predictable patterns.

VII

But this time something had changed. It took me a while to understand it: Jack and Marie had definitely broken up. They were through this time; their own strange relationship had run its course. How would this affect me and her, now that the main historical obstacle had been removed? I was both hopeful and frightened that she would turn now and love me with full force.

I had nothing to be afraid of. Marie was in no fit condition to love any man. At first she tried to put a brave face on, but whether we were in a restaurant or on the street or at home, it was impossible for her not to express grief. She was unhappy in a new way I had never seen her: like a widow. Moreover, her brittle health seemed to be getting worse. She would sit with glazed eyes in her wicker wheelchair, as though confined to it, and smoke cigarette after cigarette and talk in a scattered way. Now that she had a job—which she had gotten to take her mind off things—she came home from work so tired that she needed to sit in one place, she said, and simply collect her thoughts. She would smoke and lean her head to the side and start telling me in stream-of-consciousness about the things that had happened at work. She was filling in as a bookkeeper for a tailor, a friend of hers. The tailor's name was Harold Holt, and he had a select clientele of bankers, actors and society people, who came to him for their custom-made suits. In his midtown shop, not only were there bolts of material and racks of suits, but a very pleasant sitting area with plants and Eames chairs, where you would be served tea with cakes. This Harold liked young people; he would take time off from his business to discuss their problems or gossip with the young set (which included Jack and Marie) who dropped in on him. They were not customers, they never bought a suit from him, so what was involved was not mercenary interest but the sympathy and vitality that certain older people feel only in the company of the young. Harold Holt could be endlessly tolerant of the false starts and mishaps of his young friends, while those of his own age group bored him.

It was here that Marie went to work, when she needed a job. Holt's wife used to do the bookkeeping, but he convinced her to let Marie take her place, as a favor to this hard-pressed young girl. And now his wife never wanted to come back. Harry Holt's production assistant was a black tailor named Jessie, who was having a nervous breakdown because his wife was sick down South, and Jessie wanted to run away both to be with her and because he was in debt to gamblers, so Harry loaned him a lot of money and told him to take three months off. In Marie's opinion Harry Holt was a genuinely great man. But it was getting too frantic at the shop, with everyone trying to do his or her own job and Jessie's. The work load was becoming too much for her, and she couldn't stand it any more.

Sometimes I would advise her to stay with it; other times I would take the other position.

"Why don't you quit?"

"I can't let Harold down," said Marie. "Especially now when he's shorthanded with Jessie gone."

"But you're becoming a nervous wreck."

"No I'm not." She shook the suggestion off. "Besides, I need to work. The way you do."

There was no question of our going out much any more in the evenings, or of Marie paying much attention to my needs. Sometimes I could not tell whether she was glad or sorry to see me. She said she was through with men; she wanted to try being alone. She would suddenly get irritable. One morning I woke up with her and was looking forward to spending a few hours there just reading and relaxing, and Marie threw a fit. "I don't want you staying here! I want to be alone, don't you understand? I don't want a man in my house," she screamed, "to-to-to think he can hang around and use this as his second home! I purposely broke up with Jack because I wanted to be alone. Now get out! I don't want anyone around my house in the morning!"

That night she called to apologize. I stayed away from Marie for a week; then we started seeing each other again. I contented myself with the thought that the recognition I was getting from other sources allowed me to be less needy with Marie, and to make do with the little I was receiving from her. Paradoxically, it was a very good time in my career. My book had just come out, it was getting fine reviews, I was giving talks and going on television. I don't think Marie was particularly competitive about any of this. She always wished me well. She had a great, abstract faith in my abilities: it was only that she didn't have the energy to cheer me on. Oh, it would have been nice, very nice, to have my girl friend in the audience to smile at me and tell me afterwards I had sounded fine. But Marie had no inclination to play this role. If it had been Jack, I thought bitterly, she would have pulled herself out of a deathbed and gotten into a taxi to watch him speak in front of all those people. But then, aside from the fact that she loved Jack so much more than me, it would have been extraordinary for someone as nervous as Jack to give a public speech and it was not extraordinary for me. "You'll do fine, you don't need me there," she patted my cheek confidently and wearily.

But there was one event to which I really wanted her to come. I was asked to give a speech at the American Humanist Society. I begged her to try to make it—she said she would, if she felt at all up to it after work. Maybe she wouldn't be able to stay for the whole speech, but she would do her best to come for part of it.

The night I was to give the speech, I searched the incoming audience from the dais. It was an old wood-paneled room with good acoustics, and portraits of the founders on the walls. I was nervous but looking forward to giving the talk. I winked at Bruno, who waved and took a seat with Dawn in the second row. The Kroegels were there too: Charlie came up to the rostrum to wish me good luck. Even some people from the old Harlem agency had shown up. Natalie was there to hear me. And my whole family. It was a decent-sized crowd, not packed, but respectable. The announcer asked me if I was ready to start. Marie still had not come in, as I could tell from watching the back, but I realized I had better not depend on her being on time. If she missed the first ten minutes, that was all right too.

The speech seemed to go over well. People responded and laughed, I became more and more relaxed. The whole time I was up there, though, I was conscious of Marie's absence. I kept staring toward the back, where the clock was, hoping she would prance through the iron-studded leather doors.

Afterwards, instead of going out with everyone for a drink, I excused myself and hailed a taxi to Marie's. I was pleased with the success of the evening, but now I wanted to be with a lover and unwind.

"How did it go?" she asked me when she let me in.

"Fine." I left it at that, to see what else she would ask.

She had already turned to go back to the television set in her bedroom. "Why don't you come in and watch the rest of the Academy Awards with me?" Marie said. She sat with crossed legs, in her white nightgown, on the edge of the bed. "Marlon Brando won an Oscar and he turned it down and some Indian girl with braids made a speech in his place."

I lay back on the deep four-poster mattress, watching Marie's Sony Trinitron TV, wondering if she would ask me any more about my evening. But her eyes were on the television screen, the parade of introductions and opened envelopes. "Who else won?" I asked. She rattled off the rest of the winners, what each had said in his or her acceptance speech, what they had worn. . . . Talking excitedly in shorthand, trying to say everything at once, she sounded spaced-out. I had seen her be this way too many times.

All energy and pride were seeping out of me, replaced by a deep burning anger.

During a commercial I went into the living room, and sat in the dark in her wheelchair.

"Aren't you going to come in and watch the rest?" she asked timidly.

"I don't think so. I think I'll stay out here and brood."

"Please?" Marie said piercingly. Much as I didn't like compromising, I felt like a fool sulking in the dark, so I followed her back into the bedroom. I had already decided not to say anything about my grievance against her. What was the use? I decided to get through the rest of the evening without straining matters more. I sat up against her pillows. As always happens, as soon as I decide to let things pass, like an adult, I become peevish. "There's nothing to watch, it's all over anyway," I snapped. "All that's left is the singing of 'God Bless America.'"

She shut off the TV. "Boy, are you in a bad mood."

"I was in a great mood before I came here."

She started to answer that, but changed her mind. "How did it go?"

"Fine. What do you care? You didn't think it was important enough to come, why do you want to hear about it? You didn't think enough of me to show up."

"I was so tired when I got home from work that all I wanted to do was curl up in bed and watch the Academy Awards," she explained, as though *anyone* would sympathize with that.

"You don't give a damn about me. You told me you'd do everything in your power to be there, right? You never had any intention of coming! You knew it was important to me."

"Don't yell."

"I'll yell if I feel like it! You know how important it was to me. But you couldn't pass up your frigging Oscar show."

"I always watch the Academy Awards," she said, with tears in her eyes.

"I can't believe you! You sound like some programmed nitwit. It wouldn't have killed you to miss them once. It's all in the newspapers the next day."

"It's *true,* I always watch them," she cried. "Always. I've never missed them. And nobody ever asked me to miss them!"

Ordinarily, her tears would have had the effect of chastening me. But this time it did the opposite. "I don't care if you cry or not, I'm furious at you! You've shown your true colors this time. You couldn't care less that this evening was important to me. You know why? Because I matter nothing to you. I'm like the milk-man. I'm less than the milkman! You would be nicer to the milk-man, you would go out of your way to charm him. With me, you can't be bothered, I'm only your lover, that's all. Is something cru-cial happening to me? Where I might need *your* support? 'We'll check the *TV Guide* pages and see if we can make it. No, sorry, the Miss America pageant is on tonight! I don't want to miss Lawrence Welk.' Did I assure you once you were capable of mak-ing sacrifices for others? Well, forget it, Marie. I take it back. I've had it up to *here* with your selfishness."

"Well, so have I!" she responded.

"Well, good. Shut up and let me finish. I've been telling myself for weeks, Be patient, she'll come around. She's—self-absorbed. She'll snap out of it; she'll pay attention to you soon. But you know what? It's insulting. That I have to hang around here while you grieve for Jack. And you know what else is insulting? That picture, that *shrine* to the two of you. Why do I have to see that every time I come over and sleep with you? Why do I have to wake up to it in the morning? Why don't you have any sensitivity for *my* feelings and put it away or turn it to the wall or just GET RID OF IT while I'm here?"

"You're right," she said. "I should get rid of it. It has no right being here any more." She walked over to the dresser and picked up the photograph and smashed it against the wall. It was over be-fore I could stop her. I had never expected that! Glass shards had splattered, centrifugally, flying from the wall, onto the bed, the carpet, a shower of broken glass everywhere, and the room still rang with the echo of the crash.

Her lip twitched a little in a smile. The Mad Scene, Ophelia. Her white nightgown. Marie was shaking. From self-righteous anger I'd gone in a second to horrified remorse. What had I done? Who had smashed the picture, she or I? She had merely followed my unspoken demand. But it was as though I had killed a human being. I had been jealous of Jack, wanted him smashed, and now the truth was handed back to me in a gesture that went much further than I had imagined.

I keep seeing her slamming it against the wall with the back of her hand. Shattering the image of their love: and in that moment of its destruction I understood how strongly she must have loved him. It was a kind of love I knew nothing about. And I had acted the spoiler.

Marie had started to leave the room.

"Where are you going?" I snapped out of my trance.

"I'm going to take my medicine."

"You've had enough of that already, haven't you?" I said, reaching to detain her as she swept past me. The nightgown stuff slipped out of my hands. I waited a second, then crept past the doorway to try to spy on her, in case she decided to swallow the bottle. Unfortunately I couldn't see what she was doing. I was afraid she would make a run for the window. Death was in the air, I could feel it.

"What are you taking so long for?" I called.

"I'm finished." She came back into the bedroom and gave me a bold look, and started to undo her hair. "There's glass all over," she said surprised, as if noticing it for the first time.

"I'll pick it up!" I volunteered.

"No I will." She knelt down in her nightgown on the carpet. I kept an eye on her while trying not to be too obvious. "You can pick up the pieces on the bed," she told me, looking up astonished to see me staring down at her.

"Why don't I pick up the pieces on the floor, and you do the ones on the bed?" I suggested, my voice a little like a kindergarten teacher's. I was worried, each time she dropped below my sight lines, that she would slit her wrists. Marie made no answer. I gathered the splints from the quilt top in my hand. "Be very careful of the small pieces. They're sharp on the edges," I said. "Don't pick them up by the edges, all right? Just lift one end and lie it on a stack. Marie? Are you listening?"

"I'm listening," she said, sounding far away.

"Why don't you let me do that? Let me see your pile so far. I'm going to go into the kitchen and dump mine, so I'll take yours with me." I crouched down beside her and she opened her hand.

"Here," she said helplessly.

"I'll take them." I picked each piece out of her palm, separately. "Don't close your hand on them when you pick them up. Okay? Just hold them flat. Or put them right in the wastebasket. That's the best idea. I'm going to go into the kitchen now and bring back the dustpan. I'll be right back." I ran into the kitchen, dropped my pile in the waste bin and grabbed the dustpan and broom. "Okay, here's the dust pan! Marie. Just . . . just put them in the wastebasket. Just the big pieces, I'll take the small pieces." I got down beside her on my hands and knees.

"I'm goin' to bed," she said in a baby talk voice. She seemed to be regressing a few years each minute.

"That's a good idea. Let's go to bed. We'll do this in the morning." I took off my clothes ostentatiously to show her what a good idea it was. She stood there transfixed. I threw open the covers. "Okay I'm in bed, Marie. You come too now."

She slid into bed uncertainly, with her nightgown still on. I reached over and turned off the light. I heard her breathing staccato in the darkness. Then the pressure of her body was no longer next to me, she had dropped over the side.

"Marie, what are you doing?"

"I'm p . . . g . . . as. . . . "

"I can't hear you."

"I'm picking glash. . . ."

"In the dark?" Silence.

"Huh?"

"It's dangerous to pick up glass in the dark. You could cut yourself." I turned on the bed lamp.

"Turn off the light!" she shrieked.

"All right, I'll turn it off—if you stop picking up the glass." No answer. I turned off the light. "Marie, where are you?" I looked over the side and she wasn't there. She must have crept to the other side. Maybe she was under the bed. "Can't this wait till morning?"

"Shin . . ."

"What?"

"Shinn . . . Jess . . . doe . . . to ki . . ."

"I don't understand you when you talk like that. You're talking slurred."

"Jes . . ."

"Jesse? What about Jesse? Something happened at work? . . . Where *are* you?" I felt around on all four sides, until my hand finally landed on her hair. She giggled. "What are you doing all the way over there?" I asked, trying to make it sound like a joke.

Marie mumbled something which I deciphered as: "I'm putting together the glass for the picture."

"The glass is broken. There's no way you can put it together. Tomorrow we'll get a new glass frame. There's nothing wrong with the picture. The picture's fine, it's perfect. I saw the picture, it's in good shape. It's only the glass that's ruined. We can get a new frame for it tomorrow. *Marie,* can't we do this tomorrow? You'll cut yourself. I'm worried!"

"I won't cut myself," she said coherently.

"Will you please come back to bed? For me? Okay? Do it for me: I'm the one who's worried, so do it as a favor to me."

Marie crawled into the bed. I waited to see what she would do next. She hugged me, then she took off her nightgown and I felt her hot, naked body and her underpants. She must have been running a fever. When she had settled in, I reached over her and turned on the lamp for a moment. I wanted to check her wrists.

"Hm?" she asked.

"Let me just see something. I just want to look at your hand." Her fingers were crossed with blood. "See, you *are* bleeding. I told you you would cut yourself."

She smiled helplessly, as if to say, it was an accident.

"We can fix that up. We'll wash it off with some iodine and a bandage."

"Mm!" She shook her head *no* from side to side.

"Why? We'll go in the bathroom and take care of it."

Suddenly she got very frightened. Marie held on to me tightly.

"What are you afraid of?" I asked, bending over her. She wouldn't answer, but kept shaking her head and grimacing as though a gag were tied to her mouth. I wondered for a moment if she was play-acting. "What is it? I'll go with you. Tell me. Come on, you can tell me, honey. I won't get angry."

"Some's hi . . . !" she said softly.

"I didn't hear you. Could you say it again, slower?"

"Sum ba zee hi n."

"I can't understand you when you talk like that. Could you . . . could you enunciate a little clearer? Try." I put my ear up against her mouth.

"Somebody's-h-h-hiding-in-the-bathroom!" she whispered.

Oh no, I sighed to myself. I was beginning to feel out of my professional depth. "I don't think anyone is in there, Marie."

"I heard!"

"Maybe you heard Janie."

"She's not home tonight," she whispered, begging me to whisper too.

"She could have come home while we weren't paying attention, and gone into the bathroom. Janie?" I called out, to Marie's distress.

No answer. "See, it's quiet. I don't hear anything."

"He's hiding in there."

"Who? Who's hiding?"

She shook her head mutely, as if she didn't have permission to tell.

"Is it Jesse?" I guessed wildly.

She shook her head no.

"I'm sure it's nothing."

"Would you go check?" asked Marie in a high breaking voice.

"Of course I'll check. You wait here. I'll be back in a second." I tiptoed into the bathroom, she had almost gotten me worried that a quiet intruder was concealed somewhere. I switched on the bathroom light. There was no one. I wet a washcloth with cold water. Then I opened the medicine cabinet and found some Band-aids and mercurochrome.

"There was no one there," I said. "Here, I brought you some bandages for your cuts." I wiped off the blood with the washcloth. Then I unpeeled the Band-aids and put them over Marie's fingers. "Would you like a glass of water?"

"I gotta take my me'cine."

"You already took enough medicine for tonight. How much did you take. How much did you take before?" I poked her for an answer.

"Just two . . . of each."

"Is that too much?" Silence. "Marie, is that too much? What's the normal dosage?"

"Two." She yawned; suddenly she was very sleepy. "I want to go to sleep."

I was afraid of that yawn, knowing that if she had swallowed sleeping pills I should keep her up. Maybe walk her back and forth all night. At the same time I thought it could be nothing but my projection, because I was a suicidal type and because I felt so guilty. "Marie—just answer me this. Did you take an overdose to kill yourself or not?"

"No."

"I'll turn the light off."

"I don't feel like making love. Is that all right?" she begged.

"Yes, it's all right. We don't have to make love." I hugged her. "Just go to sleep."

Embarrassing to admit, I was aroused by her. All that had gone on, the pathos, the release of angry feelings and her own frailty had turned me on; and my erect state could not have escaped her attention, since I was pressing against her as she faced away from me.

"Can you go to sleep?" she asked.

"I'll try."

Marie turned around and snuggled close in my arms. "I'm sorry I can't make love, but it's just too much."

"I understand."

I tried to will the swelling to go down; it was no use. It would be a long night.

I stayed very still while she squeezed her leg through mine. She started breathing faster and faster. I felt her grip tighten as she rubbed herself against me; harder and harder using my leg for friction; then she sighed once, and unloosened her hold. She rolled together in a ball.

I lay awake in the dark. It was past three o'clock. I thought to myself that this would be the last night I would ever spend with her. I had no business here; I felt like an interloper. She didn't need a lover, she needed a nurse or else constant psychiatric attention. A word came into my mind: *schizophrenic*.

She frightened me. A good scare had accomplished what all the other disappointments and wounds had never managed to do: it had set me free of Marie.

VIII

I live alone. And with good reason. I don't understand
other people, I can't figure out what goes on inside them. It isn't
that I am solipsistic. I believe completely that there are other people besides me. I know there is a real world out there, because
I've come up against it too often to doubt. If you were to tell me
that we were all inside a dream, or that there is no such thing as
cause and effect, I would think you were just trying to be clever.
So first things first: the world exists, and I exist along with two
billion other people, and I'm no more important than any of those
two billion, and the only difference between them and me is that
I'm quite familiar with my thoughts but I feel estranged from
theirs.

Do you know that moment when someone is talking to you and
out comes a fury that has nothing to do with the subject, or seems
completely disproportionate, and makes you wonder if maybe this
person is much more neurotic than you had thought, and you listen holding your breath and hope that the harangue will end soon
and the room gets darker and a bit queasy?

They all seem so crazy. How can I imagine what goes on in
another person? At best I can report what he or she said, and train
myself to be an accurate observer of clothes and gestures; but, in a
sense, I remain just as distant from them that way as if I never
tried. Do what I may, I remain naïve. And this naïveté is something I can never seem to get rid of, because it is not a question of
innocence but of blocked viewpoint. Oh, I make little stabs at empathy, occasional swoops in the direction of generosity or compassion or whatever mature wisdom is supposed to be these days. But

it's still as if I were looking through barely separated fingers at a world which starts and ends with me.

Perhaps if I were a little less confident of my snap judgments and intuitions, I would be forced into the world of others. But I'm too used to judging people on my own terms, from a certain trick perspective. The trick of this perspective, its advantage and its enslavement to naïveté, is that it is designed to make me look superior. So I listen to people, not hearing everything, but listening to the part that will show me how they are neurotic, tautological, self-deceptive. It makes an interesting if limited music. And yet I end up attending to their hysteria with an envious fascination that has at the bottom of it the suspicion that they are really closer to life, in their confusions, than I in my self-controlled path. Their hysteria becomes a wet loam whose moisture I need, to feel myself human.

Of course it could be that I am crazier in my own way than anyone. But I don't think so. I think only that my viewpoint, or my *humanity,* is limited. If Marie had written her side of the story, and if Jack had written his side, you would have the truth. If I could have gotten into their skins more—but that's another writer. Sometimes we are brought in our understanding just outside the door and left there.

I had come to the conclusion that night that Marie was schizophrenic. But I knew very well that she wasn't; I had only used that as a handy label when I needed to run. It was cowardly of me, but it worked. How often have I said about a lover since, "This woman is crazy," and with that diagnosis absolved myself of final responsibility for her? I have mentally handed each and every one over to the practitioners, who, everyone knows, get paid to handle the incurable neurotics of this world. And so I have remained a bachelor.

Jack? I have run into him several times: once at a benefit party for Chilean prisoners, then a few years later at an art opening. He always leaps away like a rabbit as soon as he sees me, as though he had come across the Antichrist. At first I felt superior to his panic: you would think he would have more social grace. But the truth of the matter is that there is something very moving about Jack's quirky flight at my approach. I have never found him so dignified or full of integrity as in his rejection of me. Not because I think of myself as an ogre who should be rebuffed, but because the seriousness of what has passed between us deserves to be honored in this way. Hawthorne says it in *The Blithedale Romance:* "When a real and strong affection has come to an end, it is not well to mock the sacred with any show of those commonplace civilities that belong to ordinary intercourse." Jack understood this instinctively, with his fine training in privacy, and was able to practice it. Whereas, I, I never knew when to leave off: I keep approaching him in social gatherings, inviting him to talk things out, to go and have a drink with me,—even writing him letters, which he has never answered.

I miss his energy. His eyes are black crows, magpies that tear into things. I'm always coming across his name in magazines; he seems to have won a following among readers who appreciate a wider culture than is usually encountered in the periodicals. But strangely enough, I never agree with the critical opinions he expresses now, although when we were younger we had almost identical tastes. I even wonder if we *could* be friends again. Perhaps we would have grown away from each other, even without Marie.

But I don't want to make excuses. What I did was wrong; I see that clearly now. The moment I went after Marie I forfeited our friendship. It was one of the biggest mistakes I ever made in my life, to sleep with my best friend's girl. Such violations carry a horror, and a hurt, which is far in excess of the ostensible affront; it does no good to try to minimize the outrage by saying that it is, after all, "merely" a screw. When I was younger I fell briefly under the influence of certain ideas that were in the air, that we were living in a pleasure-seeking universe and that what feels good is the only index of action, especially when it comes to sex. But now I see that taboos make sense: pragmatically as well as ethically. You don't kill, you don't betray, you probably don't break the incest laws, or covet your neighbor's wife, and you don't make love to your friend's girl.

I don't know if I entirely regret having made that mistake. How else could I have learned that you can't get away with following your instincts, and that some rules make sense because they allude to the accumulated experience of the inelasticity of people in adjusting to certain difficult situations? I watch myself more closely now. My morality has grown narrower.

I think so often of Marie. I think of how she'd said, one time when I'd proposed that we get married: "You shouldn't joke about a thing like that with a girl." If only she had taken my words seriously we might be married now, and living together in a nice apartment (she always had such nice apartments)—unhappily, probably—but maybe not. We might have adjusted. I imagine us entertaining a lot: Marie's bright greeting of company at the door. It would have been a different life. I'm always thinking I'll see her. For a while—oh, months after we broke up—it bothered me that I never did run into her. We lived in the same area, it seemed strange I never caught a glimpse of her. I knew she liked a cheese store on Lexington Avenue, and I would look into it each time I passed. But I never saw her. Then I thought she might have died. I suffered through her death in my mind a number of times: her fragile lung condition, and the guilt I felt at leaving her in a time of sickness, made her death seem real. I kept expecting to learn of it, and pictured how I would attend the funeral. . . .

Then I imagined her recuperating in Arizona, where she had been sent to a mountainous dry climate for her chest. Not only had she *not* died, but on the contrary, I saw her rebounding with a zest that made her stronger than an ordinary person, like athletes who had had polio in their youth.

Sometimes, in movies, I'm reminded of her. A brittle, funny comeback line the heroine makes, a gesture of uncovered vulnerability. Or a young woman's death scene. I saw an old movie recently, *Three Comrades,* by the great romantic director Frank Borzage (with a script by F. Scott Fitzgerald). A wonderful film. The three friends were played by Robert Young, Robert Taylor, and Franchot Tone, but the one who stole the film was the heroine, Margaret Sullavan. And suddenly I understood the genre Marie was aiming for. I even sympathized with the way she dreamed she might pull it off, by swimming into the middle of all that masculine camaraderie, and winning each man's affection, while threatening no one's friendship. Margaret Sullavan had done it, with an exquisite intelligence which took in all, tempered by the highest tact to use the information well, and not to wound with it. There was even a physical resemblance between Marie and that odd, indescribable face of Sullavan's, so mobile, looking quickly at you and then to the side, a sense of freckles that have recently disappeared; her character's brave spirit, gallantry and pluck, sheathed in a body which is always breaking down through weakness and fainting spells (all imperfections finally excused by terminal illness); light delicate hair, a willowy body, not voluptuous but given to girlish raptures in which every limb is animated by inner fire.

Such creatures belong to the movies, up on the screen. It doesn't work in real life. I have forgiven Marie her fickleness, her faults, because I see now she stepped out of another universe, where fatalism is the key to character, and forgiveness the price the audience pays for being entertained by moral error. She belonged up there in the shadows where Margaret Sullavan carried on with Katharine Hepburn, Gene Tierney, Constance Bennet and her sister Joan. I was thankful to get a glimpse of how that exquisite sensibility might look in real life, if it ever did or should come down to real life.

What a jolt I got when I turned on the TV one day and saw her in a hair-spray commercial! There were five beauties, and each had a second to twirl her hair. Marie was the brunette. She had grown hers back to the shoulder length it was when I first met her. She twirled it springily, with what you would call a "personality smile": lips compressed, but strong mirth lines from the dimples in her cheeks down the edges of her mouth. Why had I never noticed that? The trick was in keeping her lips just barely parted.

What is left of all that? I don't know. I've no desire to become her lover again; I merely want to see her. A simple itch—I'm curious. I want so much to see Marie, I begin collaging pieces of her face from women that I pass, taking dark red lips from this one, a raised eyebrow from that. Each time I wander by a glassed-in café or bistro, the kind that are popping up all over New York now, where smartly-dressed layabouts nurse a glass of white wine, a pitcher of sangria, I expect to see Marie. And once I thought I did see her. It was just a flash of cheekbones, and a big cheery laugh that was brighter than her companions'. But there was also something tired around the eyes, and I knew it couldn't have been Marie. And I didn't go back for a second look.

Of course the stupid part is that we live so close to each other. Instead of waiting for coincidence to throw us together, I could simply phone her. But what would I say. "I miss you? Let's meet for lunch?" We'd done that before. We had already said everything we had to say to each other.

I still have that denim shirt of hers. Sometimes I come across it in my dresser drawer. I've thought of throwing it out, but I'm superstitious. Besides, it was a gift. We had been caught in a thunderstorm. My white shirt hadn't dried overnight; I hated to wear the same wilted clothes two days in a row to the office.

"I think my shirt has had it," I murmured half-aloud.

"Here," Marie said, leaning undressed over the bed to look in her bottom bureau drawer. "Take this one." (Maybe, a little bit, she did love me.) It was a dungaree workman's shirt. I tried it on, naturally finding it tight around the shoulders; but if I rolled up the sleeves it would do fine. I loved the way it felt against my skin: the denim was wrinkled and puckered, fresh from the washing machine.

"That looks great on you," she commented. "Really sexy."

"It's such a nice shirt—are you sure you want to loan it to me?" I asked, for the sake of form, already possessing it.

"Take it," she said in a husky German accent, Marlene Dietrich saying good-bye to her soldier-lover. "A *souvenir*."

"Okay, but you keep my shirt in return," I said.

Marie slipped out of bed and threw my white shirt mockingly around her shoulders; the sleeves dropped past her hands and she laughed, and looked dubiously at me. Then she took it off. I was so fond of her body that morning: the back with its eloquent cleft.

Coming up from behind to reap the surprise of her full breasts, I put my arms around her.

I put my arms around her.